"The Pardone..."
Earth controlled by alien-implanted biocomputerchips can a single hacker program the way back to freedom?

"Forever Yours, Anna" by Kate Wilhelm—Hired to track a mystery woman through the use of graphology, would he discover the trail to a revolutionary scientific breakthrough?

"Second Going" by James Tiptree, Jr.—It was a first contact that would never be forgotten, one that would forever change the relationship of mortals and gods!

"All Fall Down" by Don Sakers—When plague threatens to destroy the human race, can one man convince the alien Hlutr that humanity is worth saving?

These are just a few of the possible futures you'll discover in—

THE 1988 ANNUAL WORLD'S BEST SF

Anthologies from DAW include

ISAAC ASIMOV PRESENTS THE GREAT
  SF STORIES
  The best stories of the last four decades.
Edited by Isaac Asimov and Martin H. Greenberg.

THE ANNUAL WORLD'S BEST SF
  The best of the current year.
Edited by Donald A. Wollheim with Arthur W. Saha.

THE YEAR'S BEST HORROR STORIES
  An annual of terrifying tales.
Edited by Karl Edward Wagner.

THE YEAR'S BEST FANTASY STORIES
  An annual of high imagination.
Edited by Arthur W. Saha.

SWORD AND SORCERESS
  Original stories of magical and heroic women.
Edited by Marion Zimmer Bradley.

DONALD A. WOLLHEIM

PRESENTS

THE

1988

ANNUAL

WORLD'S BEST

SF

DAW BOOKS, INC.

DONALD A. WOLLHEIM, PUBLISHER

1633 Broadway, New York, NY 10019

This is for the latest addition to
the DAW family:

Zoë Alexandra Wollheim Stampfel
Third generation of a Futurian dynasty.

CONTENTS

INTRODUCTION

Coming events cast their shadows before them. Is this true in the case of science fiction? Does this prophetic branch of imaginative literature really predict the events of a coming century?

I write this in 1988, when the big coming event, the dawn of the Twenty-first Century is only twelve years away (if you regard the awesome date 2000 which in the popular mind would end this Twentieth Century) or thirteen (since technically the year 2001 is the first year of that coming hundred). With little more than a decade to go, can we then with any hope of accuracy predict the nature of life in the coming epoch?

The only guide we have is the history of the past centuries as reflected in the writings of the imaginative writers of a hundred years ago—or two hundred. The result is curiously the same for both periods—the discoveries, inventions and social changes which were to dominate and alter the years that were ahead failed to predict the real factors of change which were about to come. Oddly enough, these unpredictables emerged in the final decade of each century. Is this also to be true of the final decade of this century—the fateful Nineties that are on their way?

Consider the Nineteenth Century. In 1788, no one foresaw the impact of the steam engine. Although the theory and a laboratory example or two had already been announced, it was to be the steam engine which primarily dominated and altered every life on the planet during the 1800s. The Industrial Revolution could not have occurred without steam power. Yet a steam-driven boat was not made practical until 1803, and the

9

steam-driven railroad engine did not come into practical use until a little bit later. And the railroads and the power-driven vessels were to totally change the world.

The overthrow of "divine" aristocratic rule, fundamentally implied by the American Colonial Revolution of 1776, did not come into full blossom until 1792 with the French Revolution—and the consequent social upheavals that inevitably followed. Who could have predicted the rise of Napoleon Bonaparte, an upstart officer of common birth, in 1788? Yet it was only seven years before he seized the minds of men, established the rule of the middle class, and set an example by crowning himself—an example followed economically by the self-made barons of industry, of common-stock birth, who ultimately called the tune of that century. The 1800s saw the dawning of electrical power, the telegraph, the submarine—and hinted at atomic power (though never named as such).

Consider now the year 1888. Did any science fiction fantasist foresee the startling innovation of the transistor—which has turned the last half of the Twentieth Century into a vastly different world? No. None did. None could have. The airplane was an old idea but in 1888 still lacked the type of engine which could overcome its own weight and still fly. The internal combustion engine, which had been invented in theory, did not come into practical construction until 1895 and the years following. Yet the automobile and the airplane certainly altered the entire world of the 1900s. Bear in mind that it was in 1903 that the first powered airplane made its initial flight. Yet in two decades, airplanes and automobiles were rapidly changing the face of the world.

The idea of atomic power was indeed hinted at by Jules Verne and others, but it was to be several more decades before this became a reality. The consequences turned out to be less Utopian than Wells and his contemporaries would have dared predict. Social changes, started by the radical concept of "Liberty, Equality, Fraternity" of 1792, became more crystallized and now, in 1988, we find the Earth divided between two contesting views of what human social organization should be. The Twenty-first Century will see this dispute continue—and possibly be resolved.

But do we have any evidence of coming events and discoveries which could change the Twenty-first Century world as radically as those of the 1790s and 1890s changed their following epochs? The answer is probably yes. In laboratories there is evidence that superconductors can be made that will be practical at normal temperatures. If so, that alone would alter the living conditions of every person on the globe. In theory, there is now a hint of a fifth force which may be counter to gravity. Consider the possibilities of that, if it can be proven and technologically made use of. Evidence is also accumulating that things atomically happen that exceed the speed of light—that are immediate and simultaneous regardless of the distances involved. The artificial satellite was predicted back in the Nineteenth Century but did not come about until the middle of this one because it required the transistor to make it worthwhile.

So watch the next decade. Something may be discovered which will alter every vision of the coming century—even as happened during the last ten years of each preceding century. We are on the verge of astonishing events.

Now we come to this anthology which represents some of the best science fiction of this year. We note in surveying the contents that stress seems to be mainly on the human element—on the question of what makes a human being and what would change a human being? Scientific conjecture is minimal in most of these stories. We have here a period of reflection. What is the future of humanity itself? How can people cope with the ever expanding universe of knowledge and access to power? Read and think—and enjoy. Science fiction is the food of the mind. It is not always prophecy and prediction.

—DONALD A. WOLLHEIM

THE PARDONER'S TALE
By Robert Silverberg

*What is to come of this age of computers
and credit cards and the electronic mechani-
zation of social life? Here we have a tale of
a new and strange profession developing on
the margin of the days to come—that of the
pardoner. What exactly is a pardoner? Read
on. Some of your descendants may have
need for one.*

"Key sixteen, Housing Omicron Kappa, aleph sub-one,"
I said to the software on duty at the Alhambra gate
of the Los Angeles Wall.

Software isn't generally suspicious. This wasn't even
very smart software. It was working off some great
biochips—I could feel them jigging and pulsing as the
electron stream flowed through them—but the software itself was just a kludge. Typical gatekeeper stuff.

I stood waiting as the picoseconds went ticking away
by the millions.

"Name, please," the gatekeeper said finally.

"John Doe. Beta Pi Upsilon, ten-four-three-two-
four-X."

The gate opened. I walked into Los Angeles.

As easy as Beta Pi.

The wall that encircles L.A. is 100, 150 feet thick.
Its gates are more like tunnels. When you consider
that the wall runs completely around the L.A. basin,
from the San Gabriel Valley to the San Fernando
Valley and then over the mountains and down the

coast and back the far side past Long Beach, and that it's at least 60 feet high and all that distance deep, you can begin to appreciate the mass of it. Think of the phenomenal expenditure of human energy that went into building it—muscle and sweat, sweat and muscle. I think about that a lot.

I suppose the walls around our cities were put there mostly as symbols. They highlight the distinction between city and countryside, between citizen and uncitizen, between control and chaos, just as city walls did 5000 years ago. But mainly they serve to remind us that we are all slaves nowadays. You can't ignore the walls. You can't pretend they aren't there. *We made you build us,* is what they say, *and don't you ever forget that.* All the same, Chicago doesn't have a wall 60 feet high and 150 feet thick. Houston doesn't. Phoenix doesn't. They make do with less. But L.A. is the main city. I suppose the Los Angeles Wall is a statement: *I am the Big Cheese. I am the Ham What Am.*

The walls aren't there because the Entities are afraid of attack. They know how invulnerable they are. We know it, too. They just want to decorate their capital with something a little special. What the hell; it isn't *their* sweat that goes into building the walls. It's ours. Not mine personally, of course. But ours.

I saw a few Entities walking around just inside the wall, preoccupied, as usual, with God knows what and paying no attention to the humans in the vicinity. These were low-caste ones, the kind with the luminous orange spots along their sides. I gave them plenty of room. They have a way sometimes of picking a human up with those long elastic tongues, like a frog snapping up a fly, and letting him dangle in mid-air while they study him with those saucer-sized yellow eyes. I don't care for that. You don't get hurt, but it isn't agreeable to be dangled in mid-air by something that looks like a 15-foot-high purple squid standing on the tips of its tentacles. Happened to me once in St. Louis, long ago, and I'm in no hurry to have it happen again.

The first thing I did when I was inside L.A. was find a car. On Valley Boulevard about two blocks in from

the wall I saw a '31 Toshiba El Dorado that looked
good to me, and I matched frequencies with its lock
and slipped inside and took about 90 seconds to reprogram its drive control to my personal metabolic cues.
The previous owner must have been fat as a hippo and
probably diabetic: Her glycogen index was absurd and
her phosphines were wild.

Not a bad car—a little slow in the shift, but what
can you expect, considering the last time any cars were
manufactured on this planet was the year 2034?

"Pershing Square," I told it.

It had nice capacity, maybe 60 megabytes. It turned
south right away and found the old freeway and drove
off toward downtown. I figured I'd set up shop in the
middle of things, work two or three pardons to keep
my edge sharp, get myself a hotel room, a meal,
maybe hire some companionship. And then think about
the next move. It was winter, a nice time to be in L.A.
That golden sun, those warm breezes coming down
the canyons.

I hadn't been out on the Coast in years. Working
Florida mainly, Texas, sometimes Arizona. I hate the
cold. I hadn't been in L.A. since '36. A long time to
stay away, but maybe I'd been staying away deliberately. I wasn't sure. That last L.A. trip had left bad-
tasting memories. There had been a woman who wanted
a pardon and I sold her a stiff. You have to stiff the
customers now and then or else you start looking too
good, which can be dangerous; but she was young and
pretty and full of hope, and I could have stiffed the
next one instead of her, only I didn't. Sometimes I've
felt bad, thinking back over that. Maybe that's what
had kept me away from L.A. all this time.

A couple of miles east of the big downtown interchange, traffic began backing up. Maybe an accident
ahead, maybe a roadblock. I told the Toshiba to get
off the freeway.

Slipping through roadblocks is scary and calls for a
lot of hard work. I knew that I probably could fool
any kind of software at a roadblock and certainly any
human cop, but why bother if you don't have to?

I asked the car where I was.

The screen lit up. ALAMEDA NEAR BANNING, it said. A long walk to Pershing Square. I had the car drop me at Spring Street. "Pick me up at eighteen-thirty hours," I told it. "Corner of—umm—Sixth and Hill." It went away to park itself and I headed for the square to peddle some pardons.

It isn't hard for a good pardoner to find buyers. You can see it in their eyes: the tightly controlled anger, the smoldering resentment. And something else, something intangible, a certain sense of having a shred or two of inner integrity left that tells you right away. Here's somebody willing to risk a lot to regain some measure of freedom. I was in business within 15 minutes.

The first one was an aging-surfer sort, barrel chest and that sun-bleached look. The Entities haven't allowed surfing for ten, 15 years—they've got their plankton seines just offshore from Santa Barbara to San Diego, gulping in the marine nutrients they have to have, and any beach boy who tried to take a whack at the waves out there would be chewed right up. But this guy must have been one hell of a performer in his day. The way he moved through the park, making little balancing moves as if he needed to compensate for the irregularities of the earth's rotation, you could see how he would have been in the water. Sat down next to me, began working on his lunch. Thick forearms, gnarled hands. A wall laborer. Muscles knotting in his cheeks: the anger forever simmering just below boil.

I got him talking after a while. A surfer, yes. Lost in the faraway and gone. He began sighing to me about legendary beaches where the waves were tubes and they came pumping end to end. "Trestle Beach," he murmured. "That's north of San Onofre. You used to sneak through Camp Pendleton. Sometimes the Marines would open fire, just warning shots. Or Hollister Ranch, up by Santa Barbara." His blue eyes got misty. "Huntington Beach. Oxnard. I got everywhere, man."

He flexed his huge fingers. "Now these fucking Entity hodads own the shore. Can you believe it? They *own* it. And I'm pulling wall, my second time around, seven days a week next ten years."

"Ten?" I said. "That's a shitty deal."

"You know anyone who doesn't have a shitty deal?"

"Some," I said. "They buy out."

"Yeah."

"It can be done."

A careful look. You never know who might be a borgmann. Those stinking collaborators are everywhere.

"Can it?"

"All it takes is money," I said.

"And a pardoner."

"That's right."

"One you can trust."

I shrugged. "You've got to go on faith, man."

"Yeah," he said. Then, after a while: "I heard of a guy, he bought a three-year pardon and wall passage thrown in. Went up north, caught a krill trawler, wound up in Australia, on the Reef. Nobody's ever going to find him there. He's out of the system. Right out of the fucking system. What do you think that cost?"

"About twenty grand," I said.

"Hey, that's a sharp guess!"

"No guess."

"Oh?" Another careful look. "You don't sound local."

"I'm not. Just visiting."

"That's still the price? Twenty grand?"

"I can't do anything about supplying krill trawlers. You'd be on your own once you were outside the wall."

"Twenty grand just to get through the wall?"

"And a seven-year labor exemption."

"I pulled ten," he said.

"I can't get you ten. It's not in the configuration, you follow? But seven would work. You could get so far, in seven, that they'd lose you. You could god-damn *swim* to Australia. Come in low, below Sydney, no seines there."

"You know a hell of a lot."

"My business to know." I said. "You want me to run an asset check on you?"

"I'm worth seventeen five. Fifteen hundred real, the rest collat. What can I get for seventeen five?"

"Just what I said. Through the wall and seven years' exemption."

"A bargain rate, hey?"

"I take what I can get," I said. "Give me your wrist. And don't worry. This part is read only."

I keyed his data implant and patched mine in. He had $1500 in the bank and a collateral rating of 16 thou, exactly as he had claimed. We eyed each other very carefully now. As I said, you never know who the borgmanns are.

"You can do it right here in the park?" he asked.

"You bet. Lean back, close your eyes, make like you're snoozing in the sun. The deal is that I take a thousand of the cash now and you transfer five thou of the collateral bucks to me, straight labor-debenture deal. When you get through the wall, I get the other five hundred cash and five thou more on sweat security. The rest you pay off at three thou a year, plus interest, wherever you are, quarterly key-ins. I'll program the whole thing, including beep reminders on payment dates. It's up to you to make your travel arrangements, remember I can do pardons and wall transits, but I'm not a goddamn travel agent. Are we on?"

He put his head back and closed his eyes.

"Go ahead," he said.

It was finger-tip stuff, straight circuit emulation, my standard hack. I picked up all his identification codes, carried them into central, found his records. He seemed real, nothing more or less than he had claimed. Sure enough, he had drawn a lulu of a labor tax, ten years on the wall. I wrote him a pardon good for the first seven of that. Had to leave the final three on the books, for purely technical reasons, but the computers weren't going to be able to find him by then. I gave him a wall-transit pass, too, which meant writing in a new skills class for him, programmer third grade. He didn't think like a programmer and he didn't look like a programmer, but the wall software wasn't going to figure that out. Now I had made him a member of the human elite, the relative handful of us who are free to go in and out of the walled cities as we wished. In return for these little favors, I signed over his entire life's savings to various accounts of mine, payable as arranged, part now, part later. He wasn't worth a nickel anymore, but he was a free man. That's not such a terrible trade-off.

Oh, and the pardon was a valid one. I had decided not to write any stiffs while I was in Los Angeles. A kind of sentimental atonement, you might say, for the job I had done on that woman all those years back.

You absolutely have to write stiffs once in a while, you understand. So that you don't look too good, so that you don't give the Entities reason to hunt you down. Just as you have to ration the number of pardons you do. I didn't have to be writing pardons at all, of course. I could have just authorized the system to pay me so much a year, 50 thou, 100 thou, and taken it easy forever. But where's the challenge in that?

So I write pardons, but no more than I need to cover my expenses, and I deliberately fudge some of them, making myself look as incompetent as the rest, so the Entities don't have a reason to begin trying to track the identifying marks of my work. My conscience hasn't been too sore about that. It's a matter of survival, after all. And most other pardoners are out-and-out frauds, you know. At least with me, you stand a better-than-ever chance of getting what you're paying for.

The next one was a tiny Japanese woman, the classic style, sleek, fragile, doll-like. Crying in big wild gulps that I thought might break her in half, while a gray-haired older man in a shabby business suit—her grandfather, you'd guess—was trying to comfort her. Public crying is a good indicator of Entity trouble.

"Maybe I can help," I said, and they were both so distraught that they didn't even bother to be suspicious.

He was her father-in-law, not her grandfather. The husband was dead, killed by burglars the year before. There were two small kids. Now she had received her new labor-tax ticket. She had been afraid they were going to send her out to work on the wall, which, of course, wasn't likely to happen: The assignments are pretty random, but they usually aren't crazy, and what use would a 90-pound woman be in hauling stone blocks around? The father-in-law had some friends who were in the know, and they managed to bring up the hidden encoding on her ticket. The computers hadn't sent her to the wall, no. They had sent her to Area Five. And they had classified her T.T.D. classification.

"The wall would have been better," the old man said. "They'd see right away she wasn't strong enough for heavy work, and they'd find something else, something she could do. But Area Five? Who ever comes back from that?"

"You know what Area Five is?" I said.

"The medical-experiment place. And this mark here, T.T.D. I know what that stands for, too."

She began to moan again. I couldn't blame her. T.T.D. means Test to Destruction. The Entities want to find out how much work we can really do, and they feel that the only reliable way to discover that is to put us through tests that show where the physical limits are.

"I will die," she wailed. "My babies! My babies!"

"Do you know what a pardoner is?" I asked the father-in-law.

A quick, excited response: sharp intake of breath, eyes going bright, head nodding vehemently. Just as quickly, the excitement faded, giving way to bleakness, helplessness, despair.

"They all cheat you," he said.

"Not all."

"Who can say? They take your money, they give you nothing."

"You know that isn't true. Everybody can tell you stories of pardons that came through."

"Maybe. Maybe," the old man said. The woman sobbed quietly. "You know of such a person?"

"For three thousand dollars," I said, "I can take the T.T.D. off her ticket. For five more, I can write an exemption from service good until her children are in high school."

Sentimental me. A 50 percent discount, and I hadn't even run an asset check. For all I knew, the father-in-law was a millionaire. But no; he'd have been off cutting a pardon for her, then, and not sitting around like this in Pershing Square.

He gave me a long, deep, appraising look—peasant shrewdness coming to the surface.

"How can we be sure of that?" he asked.

I might have told him that I was the king of my profession, the best of all pardoners, a genius hacker with the truly magic touch who could slip into any computer ever designed and make it dance to my tune. Which would have been nothing more than the truth. But all I said was that he'd have to make up his own mind, that I couldn't offer any affidavits or guarantees, that I was available if he wanted me and otherwise it was all the same to me if she preferred to stick with her T.T.D. ticket. They went off and conferred for a couple of minutes. When they came back, he silently rolled up his sleeve and presented his implant to me. I keyed his credit balance: 30 thou or so, not bad. I transferred eight of it to my accounts, half to Seattle, the rest to Los Angeles. Then I took her wrist, which was about two of my fingers thick, and got into her implant and wrote her the pardon that would save her life. Just to be certain, I ran a double validation check on it. It's always possible to stiff a customer unintentionally, though I've never done it. But I didn't want this particular one to be my first.

"Go on," I said. "Home. Your kids are waiting for their lunch."

Her eyes glowed. "If I could only thank you somehow—"

"I've already banked my fee. Go. If you ever see me again, don't say hello."

"This will work?" the old man asked.

"You say you have friends who know things. Wait seven days, then tell the data bank that she's lost her ticket. When you get the new one, ask your pals to decode it for you. You'll see. It'll be all right."

I don't think he believed me. I think he was more than half sure I had swindled him out of one fourth of his life's savings, and I could see the hatred in his eyes. But that was his problem. In a week he'd find out that I really had saved his daughter-in-law's life, and then he'd rush down to the square to tell me how sorry he was that he had had such terrible feelings toward me. Only by then I'd be somewhere else, far away.

They shuffled out the east side of the park, pausing a couple of times to peer over their shoulders at me as if they thought I was going to transform them into pillars of salt the moment their backs were turned. Then they were gone.

I'd earned enough now to get me through the week I planned to spend in L.A. But I stuck around anyway, hoping for a little more. My mistake.

This one was Mr. Invisible, the sort of man you'd never notice in a crowd, gray on gray, thinning hair, mild, bland, apologetic smile. But his eyes had a shine. I forget whether he started talking first to me, or me to him, but pretty soon we were jockeying around trying to find out things about each other. He told me he was from Silver Lake. I gave him a blank look. How in hell am I supposed to know all the zillion L.A. neighborhoods? Said that he had come down here to see someone at the big government H.Q. on Figueroa Street. All right: probably an appeals case. I sensed a customer.

Then he wanted to know where I was from. Santa Monica? West L.A.? Something in my accent, I guess. "I'm a traveling man," I said. "Hate to stay in one place." True enough. I need to hack or I go crazy; if I did all my hacking in just one city, I'd be virtually begging them to slap a trace on me sooner or later, and that would be the end. I didn't tell him any of that. "Came in from Utah last night. Wyoming before that." Not true, either one. "Maybe New York next." He looked at me as if I'd said I was planning a voyage to the moon. People out here, they don't go East a lot. These days, most people don't go anywhere.

Now he knew that I had wall-transit clearance, or else that I had some way of getting it when I wanted it. That was what he was looking to find out. In no time at all, we were down to basics.

He said he had drawn a new ticket, six years at the salt-field-reclamation site out back of Mono Lake. People die like May flies out there. What he wanted was a transfer to something softer, like Operations and Maintenance, and it had to be within the walls, preferably in one of the districts out by the ocean, where the air is cool and clear. I quoted him a price and he accepted without a quiver.

"Let's have your wrist," I said.

He held out his right hand, palm upward. His implant access was a pale-yellow plaque, mounted in the usual place but rounder than the standard kind and of a slightly smoother texture. I didn't see any great significance in that. As I had done maybe 1000 times before, I put my own arm over his, wrist to wrist, access to access. Our biocomputers made contact, and instantly I knew I was in trouble.

Human beings have been carrying biochip-based computers in their bodies for the past 40 years or so—long before the Entity invasion, anyway—but for most people it's just something they take for granted, like their vaccination mark. They use them for the things they're meant to be used for and don't give them a thought beyond that. The biocomputer's just a commonplace tool for them, like a fork, like a shovel. You have to have the hacker sort of mentality to be willing to turn your biocomputer into something more. That's why, when the Entities came and took us over and made us build walls around our cities, most people reacted just like sheep, letting themselves be herded inside and politely staying there. The only ones who can move around freely now—because we know how to manipulate the mainframes through which the Entities rule us—are the hackers. And there aren't many of us. I could tell right away that I had hooked myself on to one now.

The moment we were in contact, he came at me like a storm.

The strength of his signal let me know I was up against something special and that I'd been hustled. He hadn't been trying to buy a pardon at all. What he was looking for was a duel—Mr. Macho behind the bland smile, out to show the new boy in town a few of his tricks.

No hacker had ever mastered me in a one-on-one anywhere. Not ever. I felt sorry for him but not much.

He shot me a bunch of stuff, cryptic but easy, just by way of finding out my parameters. I caught it and stored it and laid an interrupt on him and took over the dialog. My turn to test him. I wanted him to begin to see who he was fooling around with. But just as I began to execute, he put an interrupt on *me*. That was a new experience. I stared at him with some respect.

Usually, any hacker anywhere will recognize my signal in the first 30 seconds, and that'll be enough to finish their interchange. He'll know that there's no point in continuing. But this guy either wasn't able to identify me or just didn't care, and he came right back with his interrupt. Amazing. So was the stuff he began laying on me next.

He went right to work, really trying to scramble my architecture. Reams of stuff came flying at me up in the heavy-megabyte zone.

JSPIKE ABLTAG. NSLICE DZCNT.

I gave it right back to him, twice as hard.

MAXFRG. MINPAU SPKTOT JSPIKE.

He didn't mind at all.

MAXDZ EBURST

IBURST.

PREBST.

NOBRST.

Mexican standoff. He was still smiling. Not even a trace of sweat on his forehead. Something eerie about him, something new and strange. This is some kind of borgmann hacker, I realized suddenly. He must be working for the Entities, roving the city, looking to make trouble for freelancers like me. Good as he was, and he was plenty good, I despised him. A hacker who had become a borgmann—now, that was truly disgusting. I wanted to short him. I wanted to burn him out. I had never hated anyone so much in my life.

I couldn't do a thing with him.

I was baffled. I was the Data King, the Megabyte Monster. All my life, I had floated back and forth across a world in chains, picking every lock I came across. And now this nobody was tying me in knots. Whatever I gave him, he parried; and what came back from him was getting increasingly bizarre. He was working with an algorithm I had never seen before and was having serious trouble solving. After a little while, I couldn't even figure out what he was doing to me, let alone what I was going to do to cancel it. It was getting so I could barely execute. He was forcing me inexorably toward a wetware crash.

"Who are you?" I yelled.

He laughed in my face.

And kept pouring it on. He was threatening the integrity of my implant, going at me down on the microcosmic level, attacking the molecules themselves. Fiddling around with electron shells, reversing charges and mucking up valences, clogging my gates, turning my circuits to soup. The computer that is implanted in my brain is nothing but a lot of organic chemistry, after all. So is my brain. If he kept this up, the computer would go and the brain would follow, and I'd spend the rest of my life in the bibble-babble academy.

This wasn't a sporting contest. This was murder.

I reached for the reserves, throwing up all the defensive blockages I could invent. Things I had never had to use in my life, but they were there when I needed them, and they did slow him down. For a moment, I was able to halt his ball-breaking onslaught and even push him back—and give myself the breathing space to set up a few offensive combinations of my own. But before I could get them running, he shut me down once more and started to drive me toward Crashville all over again. He was unbelievable.

I blocked him. He came back again. I hit him hard and he threw the punch into some other neutral channel altogether and it went fizzling away.

I hit him again. Again he blocked it.

Then he hit me, and I went reeling and staggering and managed to get myself together when I was about three nanoseconds from the edge of the abyss.

I began to set up a new combination. But even as I did it, I was reading the tone of his data, and what I was getting was absolute cool confidence. He was waiting for me. He was ready for anything I could throw. He was in that realm beyond mere self-confidence into utter certainty.

What it was coming down to was this: I was able to keep him from ruining me, but only just barely, and I wasn't able to lay a glove on him at all. And he seemed to have infinite resources behind him. I didn't worry him. He was tireless. He didn't appear to degrade at all. He just took all I could give and kept throwing new stuff at me, coming at me from six sides at once.

Now I understood for the first time what it must have felt like for all the hackers I had beaten. Some of them must have felt pretty cocky, I suppose, until they ran into me. It costs more to lose when you think you're good. When you *know* you're good. People like that, when they lose, they have to reprogram their whole sense of their relation to the universe.

I had two choices. I could go on fighting until he wore me down and crashed me. Or I could give up right now. In the end, everything comes down to yes or no, on or off, one or zero, doesn't it?

I took a deep breath. I was staring straight into chaos.

"All right," I said. "I'm beaten. I quit."

I wrenched my wrist free of his, trembled, swayed, went toppling down onto the ground.

A minute later, five cops jumped me and trussed me up like a turkey and hauled me away, with my implant arm sticking out of the package and a security lock wrapped around my wrist, as if they were afraid I was going to start pulling data right out of the air.

Where they took me was Figueroa Street, the big black-marble 90-story job that is the home of the puppet city government. I didn't give a damn. I was numb. They could have put me in the sewer and I wouldn't have cared. I wasn't damaged—the automatic circuit check was still running, and it came up green—but the humiliation was so intense that I felt crushed. I felt destroyed. The only thing I wanted to know was the name of the hacker who had done it to me.

The Figueroa Street building has ceilings about 20 feet high everywhere, so that there is room for Entities to move around. Voices reverberate in those vast open spaces like echoes in a cavern. The cops sat me down in a hallway, still all wrapped up, and kept me there for a long time. Blurred sounds went lolloping up and down the passage. I wanted to hide from them. My brain felt raw. I had taken one hell of a pounding.

Now and then, a couple of towering Entities would come rumbling through the hall, tiptoeing on their tentacles in that weirdly dainty way of theirs. With them came a little entourage of humans whom they ignored entirely, as they always do. They know that we're intelligent, but they just don't care to talk to us. They let their computers do that, via the borgmann interface, and may his signal degrade forever for having sold us out. Not that they wouldn't have conquered us anyway, but Borgmann made it ever so much easier for them to push us around by showing them how to connect our little biocomputers to their huge mainframes. I bet he was very proud of himself, too: just wanted to see if his gadget would work, and to hell with the fact that he was selling us into eternal bondage.

Nobody has ever figured out why the Entities are here or what they want from us. They simply came, that's all. Saw. Conquered. Rearranged us. Put us to work doing god-awful unfathomable tasks. Like a bad dream.

And there wasn't any way we could defend ourselves against them. Didn't seem that way to us at first—we were cocky; we were going to wage guerrilla war and wipe them out—but we learned fast how wrong we were, and we are theirs for keeps. There's nobody left with anything close to freedom except the handful of hackers like me; and, as I've explained, we're not dopey enough to try any serious sort of counterattack. It's a big enough triumph for us just to be able to dodge around from one city to another without having to get authorization.

Looked like all that was finished for me now. Right then, I didn't give a damn. I was still trying to integrate the notion that I had been beaten; I didn't have capacity left over to work on a program for the new life I would be leading now.

"Is this the pardoner over here?" someone said.

"That one, yeah."

"She wants to see him now."

"You think we should fix him up a little first?"

"She said now."

A hand at my shoulder, rocking me gently. "Up, fellow. It's interview time. Don't make a mess or you'll get hurt."

I let them shuffle me down the hall and through a gigantic doorway and into an immense office with a ceiling high enough to give an Entity all the room it would want. I didn't say a word. There weren't any Entities in the office, just a woman in a black robe, sitting behind a wide desk at the far end. It looked like a toy desk in that colossal room. She looked like a toy woman. The cops left me alone with her. Trussed up like that, I wasn't any risk.

"Are you John Doe?" she asked.

I was halfway across the room, studying my shoes. "What do you think?" I said.

"That's the name you gave upon entry to the city."

"I give lots of names. John Smith, Richard Roe. Joe Blow. It doesn't matter much to the gate software what name I give."

"Because you've gimmicked the gate?" She paused. "I should tell you, this is a court of inquiry."

"You already know everything I could tell you. Your borgmann hacker's been swimming around in my brain."

"Please," she said. "This'll be easier if you cooperate. The accusation is illegal entry, illegal seizure of a vehicle and illegal interfacing activity, specifically, selling pardons. Do you have a statement?"

"No."

"You deny that you're a pardoner?"

"I don't deny, I don't affirm. What's the goddamned use?"

"Look up at me," she said.

"That's a lot of effort."

"Look up," she said. There was an odd edge to her voice. "Whether you're a pardoner or not isn't the issue. We know you're a pardoner. *I* know you're a pardoner." And she called me by a name I hadn't used in a very long time. Not since '36, as a matter of fact.

I looked at her. Stared. Had trouble believing I was seeing what I saw. Felt a rush of memories come flooding up. Did some mental editing work on her face, taking out some lines here, subtracting a little flesh in a few places, adding some in others. Stripping away the years.

"Yes," she said. "I'm who you think I am."

I gaped. This was worse than what the hacker had done to me. But there was no way to run from it.

"You work for them?" I asked.

"The pardon you sold me wasn't any good. You knew that, didn't you? I had someone waiting for me in San Diego, but when I tried to get through the wall, they stopped me just like that and dragged me away screaming. I could have killed you. I would have gone to San Diego and then we would have tried to make it to Hawaii in his boat."

"I didn't know about the guy in San Diego," I said.

"Why should you? It wasn't your business. You took my money, you were supposed to get my pardon. That was the deal."

Her eyes were gray with golden sparkles in them. I had trouble looking into them.

"You still want to kill me?" I asked. "Are you planning to kill me now?"

"No and no." She used my old name again. "I can't tell you how astounded I was when they brought you in here. A pardoner, they said. John Doe. Pardoners, that's my department. They bring all of them to me. I used to wonder years ago if they'd ever bring *you* in, but after a while I figured, No, not a chance; he's probably a million miles away, he'll never come back this way again. And then they brought in this John Doe, and I saw your face."

"Do you think you could manage to believe," I said, "that I've felt guilty for what I did to you ever since? You don't have to believe it. But it's the truth."

"I'm sure it's been unending agony for you."

"I mean it, Please. I've stiffed a lot of people, yes, and sometimes I've regretted it and sometimes I haven't, but you were one that I regretted. You're the one I've regretted most. This is the absolute truth."

She considered that. I couldn't tell whether she believed it even for a fraction of a second, but I could see that she was considering it.

"Why did you do it?" she asked after a bit.

"I stiff people because I don't want to seem perfect." I told her. "You deliver a pardon every single time, word gets around, people start talking, you start to become legendary. And then you're known everywhere, and sooner or later the Entities get hold of you, and that's that. So I always make sure to write a lot of stiffs. I tell people I'll do my best, but there aren't any guarantees, and sometimes it doesn't work."

"You deliberately cheated me."

"Yes."

"I thought you did. you seemed so cool, so professional. So perfect. I was sure the pardon would be valid. I couldn't see how it would miss. And then I got to the wall and they grabbed me. So I thought, That bastard sold me out. He was too good just to have flubbed it up." Her tone was calm, but the anger was still in her eyes. "Couldn't you have stiffed the next one? Why did it have to be me?"

I looked at her for a long time.

"Because I loved you," I said.

"Shit," she said. "You didn't even know me. I was just some stranger who had hired you."

"That's just it. There I was full of all kinds of crazy instant lunatic fantasies about you, all of a sudden ready to turn my nice, orderly life upside down for you, and all you could see was somebody you had hired to do a job. I didn't know about the guy in San Diego. All I knew was I saw you and I wanted you. You don't think that's love? Well, call it something else, then, whatever you want. I never let myself feel it before. It isn't smart, I thought; it ties you down, the risks are too big. And then I saw you and I talked to you a little and I thought something could be happening between us and things started to change inside me, and I thought, Yeah, yeah, go with it this time, let it happen, this may make everything different. And you stood there not seeing it, not even beginning to notice, just jabbering on and on about how important the pardon was for you. So I stiffed you. And afterward I thought, Jesus, I ruined that girl's life and it was just because I got myself into a snit, and that was a fucking petty thing to have done. So I've been sorry ever since. You don't have to believe that. I didn't know about San Diego. That makes it even worse for me." She didn't say anything all this time, and the silence felt enormous. So after a moment I said, "Tell me one thing, at least. That guy who wrecked me in Pershing Square: Who was he?"

"He wasn't anybody," she said.

"What does that mean?"

"He isn't a who. He's a *what*. It's an android, a mobile antipardoner unit, plugged right into the big Entity mainframe in Culver City. Something new that we have going around town."

"Oh," I said. "Oh."

"The report is that you gave it one hell of a workout."

"It gave me one, too. Turned my brain half to mush."

"You were trying to drink the sea through a straw. For a while, it looked like you were really going to do it, too. You're one goddamned hacker, you know that?"

"Why did you go to work for them?" I said.

She shrugged. "Everybody works for them. Except people like you. You took everything I had and didn't give me my pardon. So what was I supposed to do?"

"I see."

"It's not such a bad job. At least I'm not out there on the wall. Or being sent off for T.T.D."

"No," I said. "It's probably not so bad. If you don't mind working in a room with such a high ceiling. Is that what's going to happen to me? Sent off for T.T.D.?"

"Don't be stupid. You're too valuable."

"To whom?"

"The system always needs upgrading. You know it better than anyone alive. You'll work for us."

"You think I'm going to turn borgmann?" I said, amazed.

"It beats T.T.D.," she said.

I fell silent again. I was thinking that she couldn't possibly be serious, that they'd be fools to trust me in any kind of responsible position. And ever bigger fools to let me near their computer.

"All right," I said. "I'll do it. On one condition."

"You really have balls, don't you?"

"Let me have a rematch with that android of yours. I need to check something out. And afterward we can discuss what kind of work I'd be best suited for here. OK?"

"You know you aren't in any position to lay down conditions."

"Sure I am. What I do with computers is a unique art. You can't make me do it against my will. You can't make me do anything against my will."

She thought about that. "What good is a rematch?"

"Nobody ever beat me before. I want a second try."

"You know it'll be worse for you than before."

"Let me find that out."

"But what's the point?"

"Get me your android and I'll show you the point," I said.

She went along with it. Maybe it was curiosity, maybe it was something else, but she patched herself into the computer net and pretty soon they brought in the android I had encountered in the park, or maybe another one with the same face. It looked me over pleasantly, without the slightest sign of interest.

Someone came in and took the security lock off my wrist and left again. She gave the android its instructions and it held out its wrist to me and we made contact. And I jumped right in.

I was raw and wobbly and pretty damned battered, still, but I knew what I needed to do and I knew I had to do it fast. The thing was to ignore the android completely—it was just a terminal, it was just a unit— and go for what lay behind it. So I bypassed the android's own identity program, which was clever but shallow. I went right around it while the android was still setting up its combinations, dived underneath, got myself instantly from the unit level to the mainframe level and gave the master Culver City computer a hearty handshake.

Jesus, that felt good!

All that power, all those millions of megabytes squatting there, and I was plugged right into it. Of course, I felt like a mouse hitchhiking on the back of an elephant. That was all right. I might be a mouse, but that mouse was getting a tremendous ride. I hung on tight and went soaring along on the hurricane winds of that colossal machine.

And as I soared, I ripped out chunks of it by the double handful and tossed them to the breeze.

It didn't even notice for a good tenth of a second. That's how big it was. There I was, tearing great blocks of data out of its gut, joyously ripping and rending. And it didn't know it, because even the most magnificent computer ever assembled is still stuck with operating at the speed of light, and when the best you can do is 186,000 miles a second, it can take quite a while for the alarm to travel the full distance down all your neural channels. That thing was *huge*. Mouse riding on elephant, did I say? Amoeba piggybacking on Brontosaurus was more like it.

God knows how much damage I was able to do. But, of course, the alarm circuitry did cut in eventually. Internal gates came clanging down and all sensitive areas were sealed away and I was shrugged off with the greatest of ease. There was no sense in staying around, waiting to get trapped, so I pulled myself free.

I had found out what I needed to know. Where the defenses were, how they worked. This time the computer had kicked me out, but it wouldn't be able to the next. Whenever I wanted, I could go in there and smash whatever I felt like.

The android crumpled to the carpet. It was nothing but an empty husk now.

Lights were flashing on the office wall.

She looked at me, appalled. "What did you *do*?"

"I beat your android," I said. "It wasn't all that hard, once I knew the scoop."

"You damaged the main computer."

"Not really. Not much. I just gave it a little tickle. It was surprised seeing me get access in there, that's all."

"I think you really damaged it."

"Why would I want to do that?"

"The question ought to be why you haven't done it already. Why you haven't gone in there and crashed the hell out of their programs."

"You think I could do something like that?"

She studied me. "I think maybe you could, yes."

"Well, maybe so. Or maybe not. But I'm not a

crusader, you know. I like my life the way it is. I move around; I do as I please. It's a quiet life. I don't start revolutions. When I need to gimmick things, I gimmick them just enough and no more. And the Entities don't even know I exist. If I stick my finger in their eye, they'll cut my finger off. So I haven't done it."

"But now you might," she said.

I began to get uncomfortable. "I don't follow you," I said, though I was beginning to think that I did.

"You don't like risk. You don't like being conspicuous. But if we take your freedom away, if we tie you down in L.A. and put you to work, what the hell would you have to lose? You'd go right in there. You'd gimmick things but good." She was silent for a time. "Yes," she said. "You really would. I see it now, that you have the capability and that you could be put in a position where you'd be willing to use it. And then you'd screw everything up for all of us, wouldn't you?"

"What?"

"You'd fix the Entities, sure. You'd do such a job on their computer that they'd have to scrap it and start all over again. Isn't that so?"

She was on to me, all right.

"But I'm not going to give you the chance. I'm not crazy. There isn't going to be any revolution and I'm not going to be its heroine and you aren't the type to be a hero. I understand you now. It isn't safe to fool around with you. Because if anybody did, you'd take your little revenge, and you wouldn't care what you brought down on everybody else's head. You could ruin their computer, but then they'd come down on us and they'd make things twice as hard for us as they already are, and you wouldn't care. We'd all suffer, but you wouldn't care. No. My life isn't so terrible that I need you to turn it upside down for me. You've already done it to me once. I don't need it again."

She looked at me steadily, and all the anger seemed to be gone from her and there was only contempt left.

"After a little while, she said, "Can you go in there

again and gimmick things so that there's no record of your arrest today?"

"Yeah. Yeah, I could do that."

"Do it, then. And then get going. Get the hell out of here, fast."

"Are you serious?"

"You think I'm not?"

I shook my head. I understood. And I knew that I had won and I had lost at the same time.

She made an impatient gesture, a shoo-fly gesture.

I nodded. I felt very, very small.

"I just want to say, all that stuff about how much I regretted the thing I did to you back then—it was true. Every word of it."

"It probably was," she said. "Look, do your gimmicking and edit yourself out, and then I want you to start moving. Out of the building. Out of the city. OK? Do it real fast."

I hunted around for something else to say and couldn't find it. Quit while you're ahead, I thought. She gave me her wrist and I did the interface with her. As my implant access touched hers, she shuddered a little. It wasn't much of a shudder, but I noticed it. I felt it, all right. I think I'm going to feel it every time I stiff anyone, ever again. Any time I even think of stiffing anyone.

I went in and found the John Doe arrest entry and got rid of it, and then I searched out her civil-service file and promoted her up two grades and doubled her pay. Not much of an atonement. But what the hell, there wasn't much I could do. Then I cleaned up my traces behind me and exited the program.

"All right," I said. "It's done."

"Fine," she said and rang for her cops.

They apologized for the case of mistaken identity and let me out of the building and turned me loose on Figueroa Street. It was late afternoon, and the street was getting dark and the air was cool. Even in Los Angeles, winter is winter, of a sort. I went to a street access and summoned the Toshiba from wherever it had parked itself, and it came driving up five or ten

minutes later, and I told it to take me north. The
going was slow, rush-hour stuff, but that was OK. I
went to the wall at the Sylmar gate, 50 miles or so out
of town. The gatekeeper asked me my name. "Richard Roe," I said. "Beta Pi Upsilon, ten-four-three-
two-four-X Destination San Francisco."

It rains a lot in San Francisco in the winter. Still, it's
a pretty town. I would have preferred Los Angeles at
that time of year, but what the hell. Nobody gets all
his first choices all the time. The gate opened and the
Toshiba went through. Easy as Beta Pi.

RACHEL IN LOVE
By Pat Murphy

*Animals have minds and self-identities, but
they are strictly limited by the necessities of
their struggle to eat, survive and reproduce.
What need then does an animal of the wild
have for the heavy and contemplative brain
of a human who must live in a highly complex and devious society? This is the story of
an experiment in that direction—and a vivid
exposition of the conflict between natural
emotion and unnatural intelligence.*

It is a Sunday morning in summer and a small brown
chimpanzee named Rachel sits on the living room
floor of a remote ranch house on the edge of the
Painted Desert. She is watching a Tarzan movie on
television. Her hairy arms are wrapped around her
knees and she rocks back and forth with suppressed
excitement. She knows that her father would say that
she's too old for such childish amusements—but since
Aaron is still sleeping, he can't chastise her.

On the television, Tarzan has been trapped in a
bamboo cage by a band of wicked Pygmies. Rachel is
afraid that he won't escape in time to save Jane from
the ivory smugglers who hold her captive. The movie
cuts to Jane, who is tied up in the back of a jeep, and
Rachel whimpers softly to herself. She knows better
than to howl: she peeked into her father's bedroom
earlier, and he was still in bed. Aaron doesn't like her
to howl when he is sleeping.

When the movie breaks for a commercial, Rachel

goes to her father's room. She is ready for breakfast and she wants him to get up. She tiptoes to the bed to see if he is awake.

His eyes are open and he is staring at nothing. His face is pale and his lips are a purplish color. Dr. Aaron Jacobs, the man Rachel calls father, is not asleep. He is dead, having died in the night of a heart attack.

When Rachel shakes him, his head rocks back and forth in time with her shaking, but his eyes do not blink and he does not breathe. She places his hand on her head, nudging him so that he will waken and stroke her. He does not move. When she leans toward him, his hand falls limply to dangle over the edge of the bed.

In the breeze from the open bedroom window, the fine wisps of gray hair that he had carefully combed over his bald spot each morning shift and flutter, exposing the naked scalp. In the other room, elephants trumpet as they stampede across the jungle to rescue Tarzan. Rachel whimpers softly, but her father does not move.

Rachel backs away from her father's body. In the living room, Tarzan is swinging across the jungle on vines, going to save Jane. Rachel ignores the television. She prowls through the house as if searching for comfort—stepping into her own small bedroom, wandering through her father's laboratory. From the cages that line the walls, white rats stare at her with hot red eyes. A rabbit hops across its cage, making a series of slow dull thumps, like a feather pillow tumbling down a flight of stairs.

She thinks that perhaps she made a mistake. Perhaps her father is just sleeping. She returns to the bedroom, but nothing has changed. Her father lies open-eyed on the bed. For a long time, she huddles beside his body, clinging to his hand.

He is the only person she has ever known. He is her father, her teacher, her friend. She cannot leave him alone.

The afternoon sun blazes through the window, and

still Aaron does not move. The room grows dark, but Rachel does not turn on the lights. She is waiting for Aaron to wake up. When the moon rises, its silver light shines through the window to cast a bright rectangle on the far wall.

Outside, somewhere in the barren rocky land surrounding the ranch house, a coyote lifts its head to the rising moon and wails, a thin sound that is as lonely as a train whistling through an abandoned station. Rachel joins in with a desolate howl of loneliness and grief. Aaron lies still and Rachel knows that he is dead.

When Rachel was younger, she had a favorite bedtime story. —Where did I come from? she would ask Aaron, using the abbreviated gestures of ASL, American Sign language.—Tell me again.

"You're too old for bedtime stories," Aaron would say.

—Please, she'd sign. —Tell me the story.

In the end, he always relented and told her. "Once upon a time, there was a good little girl named Rachel," he said. "She was a pretty girl, with long golden hair like a princess in a fairy tale. She lived with her father and her mother and they were all very happy."

Rachel would snuggle contentedly beneath her blankets. The story, like any good fairy tale, had elements of tragedy. In the story, Rachel's father worked at a university, studying the workings of the brain and charting the electric fields that the nervous impulses of an active brain produced. But the other researchers at the university didn't understand Rachel's father; they distrusted his research and cut off his funding. (During this portion of the story, Aaron's voice took on a bitter edge.) So he left the university and took his wife and daughter to the desert, where he could work in peace.

He continued his research and determined that each individual brain produced its own unique pattern of fields, as characteristic as a fingerprint. (Rachel found this part of the story quite dull, but Aaron insisted on including it.) The shape of this "Electric Mind," as he called it, was determined by habitual patterns of thoughts and emotions. Record the Electric Mind, he postulated, and you could capture an individual's personality.

Then one sunny day, the doctor's wife and beautiful daughter went for a drive. A truck barreling down a winding cliffside road lost its brakes and met the car head-on, killing both the girl and her mother. (Rachel clung to Aaron's hand during this part of the story, frightened by the sudden evil twist of fortune.)

But though Rachel's body had died, all was not lost. In his desert lab, the doctor had recorded the electrical patterns produced by his daughter's brain. The doctor had been experimenting with the use of external magnetic fields to impose the patterns from one animal onto the brain of another. From an animal supply house, he obtained a young chimpanzee. He used a mixture of norepinephrin-based transmitter substances to boost the speed of neural processing in the chimp's brain, and then he imposed the pattern of his daughter's mind upon the brain of this young chimp, combining the two after his own fashion, saving his daughter in his own way. In the chimp's brain was all that remained of Rachel Jacobs.

The doctor named the chimp Rachel and raised her as his own daughter. Since the limitations of the chimpanzee larynx made speech very difficult, he instructed her in ASL. He taught her to read and to write. They were good friends, the best of companions.

By this point in the story, Rachel was usually asleep. But it didn't matter—she knew the ending. The doctor, whose name was Aaron Jacobs, and the chimp named Rachel lived happily ever after.

Rachel likes fairy tales and she likes happy endings. She has the mind of a teenage girl, but the innocent heart of a young chimp.

Sometimes, when Rachel looks at her gnarled brown fingers, they seem alien, wrong, out of place. She remembers having small, pale, delicate hands. Memories lie upon memories, layers upon layers, like the sedimentary rocks of the desert buttes.

Rachel remembers a blonde-haired fair-skinned woman who smelled sweetly of perfume. On a Halloween long ago, this woman (who was, in these memories, Rachel's mother) painted Rachel's fingernails bright red because Rachel was dressed as a gypsy and gypsies like red. Rachel remembers the woman's hands: white hands with faintly blue veins hidden just beneath the skin, neatly clipped nails painted rose pink.

But Rachel also remembers another mother and another time. Her mother was dark and hairy and smelled sweetly of overripe fruit. She and Rachel lived in a wire cage in a room filled with chimps and she hugged Rachel to her hairy breast whenever any people came into the room. Rachel's mother groomed Rachel constantly, picking delicately through her fur in search of lice that she never found.

Memories upon memories: jumbled and confused, like random pictures clipped from magazines, a bright collage that makes no sense. Rachel remembers cages: cold wire mesh beneath her feet, the smell of fear around her. A man in a white lab coat took her from the arms of her hairy mother and pricked her with needles. She could hear her mother howling, but she could not escape from the man.

Rachel remembers a junior high school dance where she wore a new dress: she stood in a dark corner of the gym for hours, pretending to admire the crepe paper decorations because she felt too shy to search among the crowd for her friends.

She remembers when she was a young chimp: she huddled with five other adolescent chimps in the stuffy freight compartment of a train, frightened by the alien smells and sounds.

She remembers gym class: gray lockers and ugly gym suits that revealed her skinny legs. The teacher made everyone play softball, even Rachel who was unathletic and painfully shy. Rachel at bat, standing at the plate, was terrified to be the center of attention. "Easy out," said the catcher, a hard-edged girl who

ran with the wrong crowd and always smelled of cigarette smoke. When Rachel swung at the ball and missed,
the outfielders filled the air with malicious laughter.

Rachel's memories are as delicate and elusive as the
dusty moths and butterflies that dance among the rabbit brush and sage. Memories of her girlhood never
linger; they land for an instant, then take flight, leaving Rachel feeling abandoned and alone.

Rachel leaves Aaron's body where it is, but closes
his eyes and pulls the sheet up over his head. She does
not know what else to do. Each day she waters the
garden and picks some greens for the rabbits. Each
day, she cares for the animals in the lab, bringing
them food and refilling their water bottles. The weather
is cool, and Aaron's body does not smell too bad,
though by the end of the week, a wide line of ants
runs from the bed to the open window.

At the end of the first week, on a moonlit evening,
Rachel decides to let the animals go free. She releases
the rabbits one by one, climbing on a stepladder to
reach down into the cage and lift each placid bunny
out. She carries each one to the back door, holding it
for a moment and stroking the soft warm fur. Then
she sets the animal down and nudges it in the direction
of the green grass that grows around the perimeter of
the fenced garden.

The rats are more difficult to deal with. She manages to wrestle the large rat cage off the shelf, but it is
heavier than she thought it would be. Though she
slows its fall, it lands on the floor with a crash and the
rats scurry to and fro within. She shoves the cage
across the linoleum floor, sliding it down the hall, over
the doorsill, and onto the back patio. When she opens
the cage door, rats burst out like popcorn from a
popper, white in the moonlight and dashing in all
directions.

Once, while Aaron was taking a nap, Rachel walked
along the dirt track that led to the main highway. She
hadn't planned on going far. She just wanted to see

what the highway looked like, maybe hide near the mailbox and watch a car drive past. She was curious about the outside world and her fleeting fragmentary memories did not satisfy that curiosity.

She was halfway to the mailbox when Aaron came roaring up in his old jeep. "Get in the car," he shouted at her. "Right now!" Rachel had never seen him so angry. She cowered in the jeep's passenger seat, covered with dust from the road, unhappy that Aaron was so upset. He didn't speak until they got back to the ranch house, and then he spoke in a low voice, filled with bitterness and suppressed rage.

"You don't want to go out there," he said. "You wouldn't like it out there. The world is filled with petty, narrow-minded, stupid people. They wouldn't understand you. And anyone they don't understand, they want to hurt. They hurt anyone who's different. If they know that you're different, they punish you, hurt you. They'd lock you up and never let you go."

He looked straight ahead, staring through the dirty windshield. "It's not like the shows on TV, Rachel," he said in a softer tone. "It's not like the stories in books."

He looked at her then and she gestured frantically.
—I'm sorry. I'm sorry.

"I can't protect you out there," he said. "I can't keep you safe."

Rachel took his hand in both of hers. He relented then, stroking her head. "Never do that again," he said. "Never."

Aaron's fear was contagious. Rachel never again walked along the dirt track and sometimes she had dreams about bad people who wanted to lock her in a cage.

Two weeks after Aaron's death, a black-and-white police car drives slowly up to the house. When the policemen knock on the door, Rachel hides behind the couch in the living room. They knock again, try the knob, then open the door, which she had left unlocked.

Suddenly frightened, Rachel bolts from behind the

couch, bounding toward the back door. Behind her, she hears one man yell, "My God! It's a gorilla!"

By the time he pulls his gun, Rachel has run out the back door and away into the hills. from the hills she watches as an ambulance drives up and two men in white take Aaron's body away. Even after the ambulance and the police car drive away, Rachel is afraid to go back to the house. Only after sunset does she return.

Just before dawn the next morning, she wakens to the sound of a truck jouncing down the dirt road. She peers out the window to see a pale green pickup. Sloppily stenciled in white on the door are the words: PRIMATE RESEARCH CENTER. Rachel hesitates as the truck pulls up in front of the house. By the time she has decided to flee, two men are getting out of the truck. One of them carries a rifle.

She runs out the back door and heads for the hills, but she is only halfway to hiding when she heard a sound like a sharp intake of breath and feels a painful jolt in her shoulder. Suddenly, her legs give way and she is tumbling backward down the sandy slope, dust coating her red-brown fur, her howl becoming a whimper, then fading to nothing at all. She falls into the blackness of sleep.

The sun is up. Rachel lies in a cage in the back of the pickup truck. She is partially conscious and she feels a tingling in her hands and feet. Nausea grips her stomach and bowels. Her body aches.

Rachel can blink, but otherwise she can't move. From where she lies, she can see only the wire mesh of the cage and the side of the truck. When she tries to turn her head, the burning in her skin intensifies. She lies still, wanting to cry out, but unable to make a sound. She can only blink slowly, trying to close out the pain. But the burning and nausea stay.

The truck jounces down a dirt road, then stops. It rocks as the men get out. The doors slam. Rachel hears the tailgate open.

A woman's voice: "Is that the animal the County

Sheriff wanted us to pick up?" A woman peers into the cage. She wears a white lab coat and her brown hair is tied back in a single braid. Around her eyes, Rachel can see small wrinkles, etched by years of living in the desert. The woman doesn't look evil. Rachel hopes that the woman will save her from the men in the truck.

"Yeah. It should be knocked out for at least another half hour. Where do you want it?"

"Bring it into the lab where we had the rhesus monkeys. I'll keep it there until I have an empty cage in the breeding area."

Rachel's cage scrapes across the bed of the pickup. She feels each bump and jar as a new pain. The man swings the cage onto a cart and the woman pushes the cart down a concrete corridor. Rachel watches the walls pass just a few inches from her nose.

The lab contains rows of cages in which small animals sleepily move. In the sudden stark light of the overhead fluorescent bulbs, the eyes of white rats gleam red.

With the help of one of the men from the truck, the woman manhandles Rachel onto a lab table. The metal surface is cold and hard, painful against Rachel's skin. Rachel's body is not under her control; her limbs will not respond. She is still frozen by the tranquilizer, able to watch, but that is all. She cannot protest or plead for mercy.

Rachel watches with growing terror as the woman pulls on rubber gloves and fills a hypodermic needle with a clear solution. "Mark down that I'm giving her the standard test for tuberculosis; this eyelid should be checked before she's moved in with the others. I'll add thiabendazole to her feed for the next few days to clean out any intestinal worms. And I suppose we might as well de-flea her as well," the woman says. The man grunts in response.

Expertly, the woman closes one of Rachel's eyes. With her open eye, Rachel watches the hypodermic needle approach. She feels a sharp pain in her eyelid.

In her mind, she is howling, but the only sound she can manage is a breathy sigh.

The woman sets the hypodermic aside and begins methodically spraying Rachel's fur with a cold, foul-smelling liquid. A drop strikes Rachel's eye and burns. Rachel blinks, but she cannot lift a hand to rub her eye. The woman treats Rachel with casual indifference, chatting with the man as she spreads Rachel's legs and sprays her genitals. "Looks healthy enough. Good breeding stock."

Rachel moans, but neither person notices. At last, they finish their torture, put her in a cage, and leave the room. She closes her eyes, and the darkness returns.

Rachel dreams. She is back at home in the ranch house. It is night and she is alone. Outside, coyotes yip and howl. The coyote is the voice of the desert, wailing as the wind wails when it stretches itself thin to squeeze through a crack between two boulders. The people native to this land tell tales of Coyote, a god who was a trickster, unreliable, changeable, mercurial.

Rachel is restless, anxious, unnerved by the howling of the coyotes. She is looking for Aaron. In the dream, she knows he is not dead, and she searches the house for him, wandering from his cluttered bedroom to her small room to the linoleum-tiled lab.

She is in the lab when she hears something tapping: a small dry scratching, like a wind-blown branch against the window, though no tree grows near the house and the night is still. Cautiously, she lifts the curtain to look out.

She looks into her own reflection: a pale oval face, long blonde hair. The hand that holds the curtain aside is smooth and white with carefully clipped fingernails. But something is wrong. Superimposed on the reflection is another face peering through the glass: a pair of dark brown eyes, a chimp face with red-brown hair and jug-handle ears. She sees her own reflection and she sees the outsider; the two images merge and blur. She is afraid, but she can't drop the curtain and shut the ape face out.

She is a chimp looking in through the cold, bright windowpane; she is a girl looking out; she is a girl looking in; she is an ape looking out. She is afraid and the coyotes are howling all around.

Rachel opens her eyes and blinks until the world comes into focus. The pain and tingling have retreated, but she still feels a little sick. Her left eye aches. When she rubs it, she feels a raised lump on the eyelid where the woman pricked her. She lies on the floor of a wire mesh cage. The room is hot and the air is thick with the smell of animals.

In the cage beside her is another chimp, an older animal with scruffy dark brown fur. He sits with his arms wrapped around his knees, rocking back and forth, back and forth. His head is down. As he rocks, he murmurs to himself, a meaningless cooing that goes on and on. On his scalp, Rachel can see a gleam of metal: a permanently implanted electrode protrudes from a shaven patch. Rachel makes a soft questioning sound, but the other chimp will not look up.

Rachel's own cage is just a few feet square. In one corner is a bowl of monkey pellets. A water bottle hangs on the side of the cage. Rachel ignores the food, but drinks thirstily.

Sunlight streams through the windows, sliced into small sections by the wire mesh that covers the glass. She tests her cage door, rattling it gently at first, then harder. It is securely latched. The gaps in the mesh are too small to admit her hand. She can't reach out to work the latch.

The other chimp continues to rock back and forth. When Rachel rattles the mesh of her cage and howls, he lifts his head wearily and looks at her. His red-rimmed eyes are unfocused; she can't be sure he sees her.

—Hello, she gestures tentatively. —What's wrong?

He blinks at her in the dim light. —Hurt, he signs in ASL. He reaches up to touch the electrode, fingering the skin that is already raw from repeated rubbing.

—Who hurt you? she asks. He stares at her blankly and she repeats the question. —Who?

—Men, he signs.

As if on cue, there is the click of a latch and the door to the lab opens. A bearded man in a white coat steps in, followed by a clean-shaven man in a suit. The bearded man seems to be showing the other man around the lab. ". . . only preliminary testing so far," the bearded man is saying. "We've been hampered by a shortage of chimps trained in ASL." The two men stop in front of the old chimp's cage. "This old fellow is from the Oregon Center. Funding for the language program was cut back and some of the animals were dispersed to other programs." The old chimp huddles at the back of the cage, eyeing the bearded man with suspicion.

—Hungry? the bearded man signs to the old chimp. He holds up an orange where the old chimp can see it.

—Give orange, the old chimp gestures. He holds out his hand, but comes no nearer to the wire mesh than he must to reach the orange. With the fruit in hand, he retreats to the back of his cage.

The bearded man continues, "This project will provide us with the first solid data on neural activity during use of sign language. But we really need greater access to chimps with advanced language skills. People are so damn protective of their animals."

"Is this one of yours?" the clean-shaven man asks, pointing to Rachel. She cowers in the back of the cage, as far from the wire mesh as she can get.

"No, not mine. She was someone's household pet, apparently. The county sheriff had us pick her up." The bearded man peers into her cage. Rachel does not move; she is terrified that he will somehow guess that she knows ASL. She stares at his hands and thinks about those hands putting an electrode through her skull. "I think she'll be put in breeding stock," the man says as he turns away.

Rachel watches them go, wondering at what terrible people these are. Aaron was right: they want to punish her, put an electrode in her head.

After the men are gone, she tries to draw the old chimp into conversation, but he will not reply. He ignores her as he eats his orange. Then he returns to his former posture, hiding his head and rocking himself back and forth.

Rachel, hungry despite herself, samples one of the food pellets. It has a strange medicinal taste, and she puts it back in the bowl. She needs to pee, but there is no toilet and she cannot escape the cage. At last, unable to hold it, she pees in one corner of the cage. The urine flows through the wire mesh to soak the litter below, and the smell of warm piss fills her cage. Humiliated, frightened, her head aching, her skin itchy from the flea spray, Rachel watches as the sunlight creeps across the room.

The day wears on. Rachel samples her food again, but rejects it, preferring hunger to the strange taste. A black man comes and cleans the cages of the rabbits and rats. Rachel cowers in her cage and watches him warily, afraid that he will hurt her, too.

When night comes, she is not tired. Outside, coyotes howl. Moonlight filters in through the high windows. She draws her legs up toward her body, then rests with her arms wrapped around her knees. Her father is dead, and she is a captive in a strange place. For a time, she whimpers softly, hoping to awaken from this nightmare and find herself at home in bed. When she hears the click of a key in the door to the room, she hugs herself more tightly.

A man in green coveralls pushes a cart filled with cleaning supplies into the room. He takes a broom from the cart, and begins sweeping the concrete floor. Over the rows of cages, she can see the top of his head bobbing in time with his sweeping. He works slowly and methodically, bending down to sweep carefully under each row of cages, making a neat pile of dust, dung, and food scraps in the center of the aisle.

The janitor's name is Jake. He is a middle-aged deaf man who has been employed by the Primate Research Center for the past seven years. He works night shift.

The personnel director at the Primate Research Center likes Jake because he fills the federal quota for handicapped employees, and because he has not asked for a raise in five years. There have been some complaints about Jake—his work is often sloppy—but never enough to merit firing the man.

Jake is an unambitious, somewhat slow-witted man. He likes the Primate Research Center because he works alone, which allows him to drink on the job. He is an easy-going man, and he likes the animals. Sometimes, he brings treats for them. Once, a lab assistant caught him feeding an apple to a pregnant rhesus monkey. The monkey was part of an experiment on the effect of dietary restrictions on fetal brain development, and the lab assistant warned Jake that he would be fired if he was ever caught interfering with the animals again. Jake still feeds the animals, but he is more careful about when he does it, and he has never been caught again.

As Rachel watches, the old chimp gestures to Jake. —Give banana, the chimp signs. —Please banana. Jake stops sweeping for a minute and reaches down to the bottom shelf of his cleaning cart. He returns with a banana and offers it to the old chimp. The chimp accepts the banana and leans against the mesh while Jake scratches his fur.

When Jake turns back to his sweeping, he catches sight of Rachel and sees that she is watching him. Emboldened by his kindness to the old chimp, Rachel timidly gestures to him. —Help me.

Jake hesitates, then peers at her more closely. Both his eyes are shot with a fine lacework of red. His nose displays the broken blood vessels of someone who has been friends with the bottle for too many years. He needs a shave. But when he leans close, Rachel catches the scent of whiskey and tobacco. The smells remind her of Aaron and give her courage.

—Please help me, Rachel signs. —I don't belong here.

For the last hour, Jake has been drinking steadily.

His view of the world is somewhat fuzzy. He stares at her blearily.

Rachel's fear that he will hurt her is replaced by the fear that he will leave her locked up and alone. Desperately she signs again. —Please please please. Help me. I don't belong here. Please help me go home.

He watches her, considering the situation. Rachel does not move. She is afraid that any movement will make him leave. With a majestic speed dictated by his inebriation, Jake leans his broom on the row of cages behind him and steps toward Rachel's cage again. —You talk? he signs.

—I talk, she signs.

—Where did you come from

—From my father's house, she signs. —Two men came and shot me and put me here. I don't know why. I don't know why they locked me in jail.

Jake looks around, willing to be sympathetic, but puzzled by her talk of jail. —This isn't jail, he signs. —This is a place where scientists raise monkeys.

Rachel is indignant. —I am not a monkey, she signs. —I am a girl.

Jake studies her hairy body and her jug-handle ears. —You look like a monkey.

Rachel shakes her head. —No. I am a girl.

Rachel runs her hands back over her head, a very human gesture of annoyance and unhappiness. She signs sadly, —I don't belong here. Please let me out.

Jake shifts his weight from foot to foot, wondering what to do. —I can't let you out. I'll get in big trouble.

—Just for a little while? Please?

Jake glances at his cart of supplies. He has to finish off this room and two corridors of offices before he can relax for the night.

—Don't go, Rachel signs, guessing his thoughts.

—I have work to do.

She looks at the cart, then suggests eagerly, —Let me out and I'll help you work.

Jake frowns. —If I let you out, you will run away.

—No, I won't run. I will help. Please let me out.

—You promise to go back?

Rachel nods.

Warily he unlatches the cage. Rachel bounds out, grabs a whisk broom from the cart, and begins industriously sweeping bits of food and droppings from beneath the row of cages. —Come on, she signs to Jake from the end of the aisle. —I will help.

When Jake pushes the cart from the room filled with cages, Rachel follows him closely. The rubber wheels of the cleaning cart rumble softly on the linoleum floor. They pass through a metal door into a corridor where the floor is carpeted and the air smells of chalk dust and paper.

Offices let off the corridor, each one a small room furnished with a desk, bookshelves, and a blackboard. Jake shows Rachel how to empty the wastebaskets into a garbage bag. While he cleans the blackboards, she wanders from office to office, trailing the trash-filled garbage bag.

At first, Jake keeps a close eye on Rachel. But after cleaning each blackboard, he pauses to refill a cup from the whiskey bottle that he keeps wedged between the Saniflush and the window cleaner. By the time he is halfway through the second cup; he is treating her like an old friend, telling her to hurry up so that they can eat dinner.

Rachel works quickly, but she stops sometimes to gaze out the office windows. Outside, moonlight shines on a sandy plain, dotted here and there with scrubby clumps of rabbit brush.

At the end of the corridor is a larger room in which there are several desks and typewriters. In one of the wastebaskets, buried beneath memos and candybar wrappers, she finds a magazine. The title is *Love Confessions* and the cover has a picture of a man and woman kissing. Rachel studies the cover, then takes the magazine, tucking it on the bottom shelf of the cart.

Jake pours himself another cup of whiskey and pushes the cart to another hallway. Jake is working slower now, and as he works he makes humming noises, tuneless sounds that he feels only as pleasant vibrations. The last few blackboards are sloppily done, and Rachel, finished with the wastebaskets, cleans the places that Jake missed.

They eat dinner in the janitor's storeroom, a stuffy windowless room furnished with an ancient grease-stained couch, a battered black-and-white television, and shelves of cleaning supplies. From a shelf, Jake takes the paper bag that holds his lunch: a baloney sandwich, a bag of barbecued potato chips, and a box of vanilla wafers. From behind the gallon jugs of liquid cleanser, he takes a magazine. He lights a cigarette, pours himself another cup of whiskey, and settles down on the couch. After a moment's hesitation, he offers Rachel a drink, pouring a shot of whiskey into a chipped ceramic cup.

Aaron never let Rachel drink whiskey, and she samples it carefully. At first the smell makes her sneeze, but she is fascinated by the way that the drink warms her throat, and she sips some more.

As they drink, Rachel tells Jake about the men who shot her and the woman who pricked her with a needle, and he nods. —The people here are crazy, he signs.

—I know, she says, thinking of the old chimp with the electrode in his head. —You won't tell them I can talk, will you?

Jake nods. —I won't tell them anything.

—They treat me like I'm not real, Rachel signs sadly. Then she hugs her knees, frightened at the thought of being held captive by crazy people. She considers planning her escape: she is out of the cage and she is sure she could outrun Jake. As she wonders about it, she finishes her cup of whiskey. The alcohol takes the edge off her fear. She sits close beside Jake on the couch, and the smell of his cigarette smoke reminds her of Aaron. For the first time since Aaron's death she feels warm and happy.

She shares Jake's cookies and potato chips and looks at the *Love Confessions* magazine that she took from the trash. the first story that she reads is about a woman named Alice. The headline reads: "I became a

Go-go dancer to pay off my husband's gambling debts, and now he wants me to sell my body."

Rachel sympathizes with Alice's loneliness and suffering. Alice, like Rachel, is alone and misunderstood. As Rachel slowly reads, she sips her second cup of whiskey. The story reminds her of a fairy tale: the nice man who rescues Alice from her terrible husband replaces the handsome prince who rescues the princess. Rachel glances at Jake and wonders if he will rescue her from the wicked people who locked her in the cage.

She has finished the second cup of whiskey and eaten half Jake's cookies when Jake says that she must go back to her cage. She goes reluctantly, taking the magazine with her. He promises that he will come for her again the next night, and with that she must be content. She puts the magazine in one corner of the cage and curls up to sleep.

She wakes early in the afternoon. A man in a white coat is wheeling a low cart into the lab.

Rachel's head aches with hangover and she feels sick. As she crouches in one corner of her cage, he stops the cart beside her cage and then locks the wheels. "Hold on there," he mutters to her, then slides her cage onto the cart.

The man wheels her through long corridors, where the walls are cement blocks, painted institutional green. Rachel huddles unhappily in the cage, wondering where she is going and whether Jake will ever be able to find her.

At the end of a long corridor, the man opens a thick metal door and a wave of warm air strikes Rachel. It stinks of chimpanzees, excrement, and rotting food. On either side of the corridor are metal bars and wire mesh. Behind the mesh, Rachel can see dark hairy shadows. In one cage, five adolescent chimps swing and play. In another, two females huddle together, grooming each other. The man slows as he passes a cage in which a big male is banging on the wire with his fist, making the mesh rattle and ring.

"Now, Johnson," says the man. "Cool it. Be nice. I'm bringing you a new little girlfriend."

With a series of hooks, the man links Rachel's cage with the cage next to Johnson's and opens the doors. "Go on, girl," he says. "See the nice fruit." In the cage is a bowl of sliced apples with an attendant swarm of fruit flies.

At first, Rachel will not move into the new cage. She crouches in the cage on the cart, hoping that the man will decide to take her back to the lab. She watches him get a hose and attach it to a water faucet. But she does not understand his intention until he turns the stream of water on her. A cold blast strikes her on the back and she howls, fleeing into the new cage to avoid the cold water. Then the man closes the doors, unhooks the cage, and hurries away.

The floor is bare cement. Her cage is at one end of the corridor and two walls are cement block. A door in one of the cement block walls leads to an outside run. The other two walls are wire mesh: one facing the corridor; the other, Johnson's cage.

Johnson, quiet now that the man has left, is sniffing around the door in the wire mesh wall that joins their cages. Rachel watches him anxiously. Her memories of other chimps are distant, softened by time. She remembers her mother; she vaguely remembers playing with other chimps her age. But she does not know how to react to Johnson when he stares at her with great intensity and makes a loud huffing sound. She gestures to him in ASL, but he only stares harder and huffs again. Beyond Johnson, she can see other cages and other chimps, so many that the wire mesh blurs her vision and she cannot see the other end of the corridor.

To escape Johnson's scrutiny, she ducks through the door into the outside run, a wire mesh cage on a white concrete foundation. Outside there is barren ground and rabbit brush. The afternoon sun is hot and all the other runs are deserted until Johnson appears in the run beside hers. His attention disturbs her and she goes back inside.

She retreats to the side of the cage farthest from
Johnson. A crudely built wooden platform provides
her with a place to sit. Wrapping her arms around her
knees, she tries to relax and ignore Johnson. She
dozes off for a while, but wakes to a commotion across
the corridor.

In the cage across the way is a female chimp in heat.
Rachel recognizes the smell from her own times in
heat. Two keepers are opening the door that separates
the female's cage from the adjoining cage, where a
male stands, watching with great interest. Johnson is
shaking the wire mesh and howling as he watches.

"Mike here is a virgin, but Susie knows what she's
doing," one keeper was saying to the other. "So it
should go smoothly. But keep the hose ready."

"Yeah?"

"Sometimes they fight. We only use the hose to
break it up if it gets real bad. Generally, they do
okay."

Mike stalks into Susie's cage. The keepers lower the
cage door, trapping both chimps in the same cage.
Susie seems unalarmed. She continues eating a slice of
orange while Mike sniffs at her genitals with every
indication of great interest. She bends over to let Mike
finger her pink bottom, the sign of estrus.

Rachel finds herself standing at the wire mesh, making low moaning noises. She can see Mike's erection,
hear his grunting cries. He squats on the floor of
Susie's cage, gesturing to the female. Rachel's feelings
are mixed: she is fascinated, fearful, confused. She
keeps thinking of the description of sex in the *Love
Confessions* story: When Alice feels Danny's lips on
hers, she is swept away by the passion of the moment.
He takes her in his arms and her skin tingles as if she
were consumed by an inner fire.

Susie bends down and Mike penetrates her with a
loud grunt, thrusting violently with his hips. Susie cries
out shrilly and suddenly leaps up, knocking Mike away.
Rachel watches, overcome with fascination. Mike, his
penis now limp, follows Susie slowly to the corner of
the cage, where he begins grooming her carefully.

Rachel finds that the wire mesh has cut her hands where she gripped it too tightly.

It is night, and the door at the end of the corridor creaks open. Rachel is immediately alert, peering through the wire mesh and trying to see down to the end of the corridor. She bangs on the wire mesh. As Jake comes closer, she waves a greeting.

When Jake reaches for the lever that will raise the door to Rachel's cage, Johnson charges toward him, howling and waving his arms above his head. He hammers on the wire mesh with his fists, howling and grimacing at Jake. Rachel ignores Johnson and hurries after Jake.

Again Rachel helps Jake clean. In the laboratory, she greets the old chimp, but the animal is more interested in the banana that Jake has brought than in conversation. The chimp will not reply to her questions, and after several tries, she gives up.

While Jake vacuums the carpeted corridors, Rachel empties the trash, finding a magazine called *Modern Romance* in the same wastebasket that had provided *Love Confessions*.

Later, in the Janitor's lounge, Jake smokes a cigarette, sips whiskey, and flips through one of his own magazines. Rachel reads love stories in *Modern Romance*.

Every once in a while, she looks over Jake's shoulder at grainy pictures of naked women with their legs spread wide apart. Jake looks for a long time at a picture of a blonde woman with big breasts, red fingernails, and purple-painted eyelids. The woman lies on her back and smiles as she strokes the pinkness between her legs. The picture on the next page shows her caressing her own breasts, pinching the dark nipples. The final picture shows her looking back over her shoulder. She is in the position that Susie took when she was ready to be mounted.

Rachel looks over Jake's shoulder at the magazine, but she does not ask questions. Jake's smell began to change as soon as he opened the magazine; the scent of nervous sweat mingles with the aromas of tobacco and whiskey. Rachel suspects that questions would not be welcome just now.

At Jake's insistence, she goes back to her cage before dawn.

Over the next week, she listens to the conversations of the men who come and go, bringing food and hosing out the cages. From the men's conversation, she learns that the Primate Research Center is primarily a breeding facility that supplies researchers with domestically bred apes and monkeys of several species. It also maintains its own research staff. In indifferent tones, the men talk of horrible things. The adolescent chimps at the end of the corridor are being fed a diet high in cholesterol to determine cholesterol's effects on the circulatory system. A group of pregnant females are being injected with male hormones to determine how that will affect the female offspring. A group of infants is being fed a low protein diet to determine adverse effects on their brain development.

The men look through her as if she were not real, as if she were a part of the wall, as if she were no one at all. She cannot speak to them; she cannot trust them.

Each night, Jake lets her out of her cage and she helps him clean. He brings treats: barbequed potato chips, fresh fruit, chocolate bars, and cookies. He treats her fondly, as one would treat a precocious child. And he talks to her.

At night, when she is with Jake, Rachel can almost forget the terror of the cage, the anxiety of watching Johnson pace to and fro, the sense of unreality that accompanies the simplest act. She would be content to stay with Jake forever, eating snack food and reading confessions magazines. He seems to like her company. But each morning, Jake insists that she must go back to the cage and the terror. By the end of the first week, she has begun plotting her escape.

Whenever Jake falls asleep over his whiskey, something that happens three nights out of five, Rachel prowls the center alone, surreptitiously gathering things that she will need to survive in the desert: a plastic jug filled with water, a plastic bag of food pellets, a large beach towel that will serve as a blanket on the cool desert nights, a discarded plastic shopping bag in which she can carry the other things. Her best find is a road map on which the Primate Center is marked in red. She knows the address of Aaron's ranch and finds it on the map. She studies the roads and plots a route home. Cross country, assuming that she does not get lost, she will have to travel about fifty miles to reach the ranch. She hides these things behind one of the shelves in the janitor's storeroom.

Her plans to run away and go home are disrupted by the idea that she is in love with Jake, a notion that comes to her slowly, fed by the stories in the confessions magazines. When Jake absent-mindedly strokes her, she is filled with a strange excitement. She longs for his company and misses him on the weekends when he is away. She is happy only when she is with him, following him through the halls of the center, sniffing the aroma of tobacco and whiskey that is his own perfume. She steals a cigarette from his pack and hides it in her cage, where she can savor the smell of it at her leisure.

She loves him, but she does not know how to make him love her back. Rachel knows little about love: she remembers a high school crush where she mooned after a boy with a locker near hers, but that came to nothing. She reads the confessions magazines and Ann Landers' column in the newspaper that Jake brings with him each night, and from these sources, she learns about romance. One night, after Jake falls asleep, she types a badly punctuated, ungrammatical letter to Ann. In the letter, she explains her situation and asks for advice on how to make Jake love her. She slips the letter into a sack labeled "Outgoing Mail," and for the next week she reads Ann's column with increased interest. But her letter never appears.

Rachel searches for answers in the magazine pictures that seem to fascinate Jake. She studies the naked women, especially the big-breasted woman with the purple smudges around her eyes.

One night, in a secretary's desk, she finds a plastic case of eyeshadow. She steals it and takes it back to her cage. The next evening, as soon as the Center is quiet, she upturns her metal food dish and regards her reflection in the shiny bottom. Squatting, she balances the eye shadow case on one knee and examines its contents: a tiny makeup brush and three shades of eye shadow—INDIAN BLUE, FOREST GREEN, and WILDLY VIOLET. Rachel chooses the shade labeled WILDLY VIOLET.

Using one finger to hold her right eye closed, she dabs her eyelid carefully with the makeup brush, leaving a gaudy orchid-colored smudge on her brown skin. She studies the smudge critically, then adds to it, smearing the color beyond the corner of her eyelid until it disappears in her brown fur. The color gives her a eye a carnival brightness, a lunatic gaiety. Working with great care, she matches the effect on the other side, then smiles at herself in the glass, blinking coquettishly.

In the other cage, Johnson bares his teeth and shakes the wire mesh. She ignores him.

When Jake comes to let her out, he frowns at her eyes. —Did you hurt yourself? he asks.

—No, she says. Then, after a pause. —Don't you like it?"

Jake squats beside her and stares at her eyes. Rachel puts a hand on his knee and her heart pounds at her own boldness. —You are a very strange monkey, he signs.

Rachel is afraid to move. Her hand on his knee closes into a fist; her face folds in on itself, puckering around the eyes.

Then, straightening up, he signs, —I liked your eyes better before.

He likes her eyes. She nods without taking her eyes from his face. Later, she washes her face in the women's restroom, leaving dark smudges the color of bruises on a series of paper towels.

*   *   *

Rachel is dreaming. She is walking through the Painted Desert with her hairy brown mother, following a red rock canyon that Rachel somehow knows will lead her to the Primate Research Center. Her mother is lagging behind: she does not want to go to the center; she is afraid. In the shadow of a rock outcropping. Rachel stops to explain to her mother that they must go to the center because Jake is at the center.

Rachel's mother does not understand sign language. She watches Rachel with mournful eyes, then scrambles up the canyon wall, leaving Rachel behind. Rachel climbs after her mother, pulling herself over the edge in time to see the other chimp loping away across the wind-blown red cinder-rock and sand.

Rachel bounds after her mother, and as she runs she howls like an abandoned infant chimp, wailing her distress. The figure of her mother wavers in the distance, shimmering in the heat that rises from the sand. The figure changes. Running away across the red sands is a pale blonde woman wearing a purple sweatsuit and jogging shoes, the sweet-smelling mother that Rachel remembers. The woman looks back and smiles at Rachel. "Don't howl like an ape, daughter," she calls. "Say Mama."

Rachel runs silently, dream running that takes her nowhere. The sand burns her feet and the sun beats down on her head. The blonde woman vanishes in the distance, and Rachel is alone. She collapses on the sand, whimpering because she is alone and afraid.

She feels the gentle touch of fingers grooming her fur, and for a moment, still half asleep, she believes that her hairy mother has returned to her. She opens her eyes and looks into a pair of dark brown eyes, separated from her by wire mesh. Johnson. He has reached through a gap in the fence to groom her. As he sorts through her fur, he makes soft cooing sounds, gentle comforting noises.

Still half asleep, she gazes at him and wonders why she was so fearful. He does not seem so bad. He grooms her for a time, and then sits nearby, watching her through the mesh. She brings a slice of apple from her dish of food and offers it to him. With her free hand, she makes the sign for apple. When he takes it, she signs again: apple. He is not a particularly quick student, but she has time and many slices of apple.

All Rachel's preparations are done, but she cannot bring herself to leave the center. Leaving the center means leaving Jake, leaving potato chips and whiskey, leaving security. To Rachel, the thought of love is always accompanied by the warm taste of whiskey and potato chips.

Some nights, after Jake is asleep, she goes to the big glass doors that lead to the outside. She opens the doors and stands on the steps, looking down into the desert. Sometimes a jackrabbit sits on its haunches in the rectangles of light that shine through the glass doors. Sometimes she sees kangaroo rats, hopping through the moonlight like rubber balls bouncing on hard pavement. Once, a coyote trots by, casting a contemptuous glance in her direction.

The desert is a lonely place. Empty. Cold. She thinks of Jake snoring softly in the janitor's lounge. And always she closes the door and returns to him.

Rachel leads a double life: janitor's assistant by night, prisoner and teacher by day. She spends her afternoons drowsing in the sun and teaching Johnson new signs.

On a warm afternoon, Rachel sits in the outside run, basking in the sunlight. Johnson is inside, and the other chimps are quiet. She can almost imagine she is back at her father's ranch, sitting in her own yard. She naps and dreams of Jake.

She dreams that she is sitting in his lap on the battered old couch. Her hand is on his chest: a smooth pale hand with red-painted fingernails. When she looks at the dark screen of the television set, she can see her reflection. She is a thin teenager with blonde hair and blue eyes. She is naked.

Jake is looking at her and smiling. He runs a hand down her back and she closes her eyes in ecstasy.

But something changes when she closes her eyes. Jake is grooming her as her mother used to groom her, sorting through her hair in search of fleas. She opens her eyes and sees Johnson, his diligent fingers searching through her fur, his intent brown eyes watching her. The reflection on the television screen shows two chimps, tangled in each others' arms.

Rachel wakes to find she is in heat for the first time since she came to the center. The skin surrounding her genitals is swollen and pink.

For the rest of the day, she is restless, pacing to and fro in her cage. On his side of the wire mesh wall, Johnson is equally restless, following her when she goes outside, sniffing long and hard at the edge of the barrier that separates him from her.

That night, Rachel goes eagerly to help Jake clean. She follows him closely, never letting him get far from her. When he is sweeping, she trots after him with the dustpan and he almost trips over her twice. She keeps waiting for him to notice her condition, but he seems oblivious.

As she works, she sips from a cup of whiskey. Excited, she drinks more than usual, finishing two full cups. The liquor leaves her a little disoriented, and she sways as she follows Jake to the janitor's lounge. She curls up close behind him on the couch. He relaxes with his arms resting on the back of the couch, his legs stretching out before him. She moves so that she presses against him.

He stretches, yawns, and rubs the back of his neck as if trying to rub away stiffness. Rachel reaches around behind him and begins to gently rub his neck, reveling in the feel of his skin, his hair against the backs of her hands. The thoughts that hop and skip through her mind are confusing. Sometimes it seems that the hair that tickles her hands is Johnson's; sometimes, she knows it is Jake's. And sometimes it doesn't seem to matter. Are they really so different? They are not so different.

She rubs his neck, not knowing what to do next. In the confessions magazines, this is where the man crushes

the woman in his arms. Rachel climbs into Jake's lap
and hugs him, waiting for him to crush her in his arms.
He blinks at her sleepily. Half asleep, he strokes her,
and his moving hand brushes near her genitals. She
presses herself against him, making a soft sound in her
throat. She rubs her hip against his crotch, aware now
of a slight change in his smell, in the tempo of his
breathing. He blinks at her again, a little more awake
now. She bares her teeth in a smile and tilts her head
back to lick his neck. She can feel his hands on her
shoulders, pushing her away, and she knows what he
wants. She slides from his lap and turns, presenting
him with her pink genitals, ready to be mounted,
ready to have him penetrate her. She moans in antici-
pation, a low inviting sound.

He does not come to her. She looks over her shoulder and he is still sitting on the couch, watching her
through half-closed eyes. He reaches over and picks
up a magazine filled with pictures of naked women.
His other hand drops to his crotch and he is lost in his
own world.

Rachel howls like an infant who has lost its mother,
but he does not look up. He is staring at the picture of
the blonde woman.

Rachel runs down dark corridors to her cage, the
only home she has. When she reaches her corridor,
she is breathing hard and making small lonely whimpering noises. In the dimly lit corridor, she hesitates
for a moment, staring into Johnson's cage. The male
chimp is asleep. She remembers the touch of his hands
when he groomed her.

From the corridor, she lifts the gate that leads into
Johnson's cage and enters. He wakes at the sound of
the door and sniffs the air. When he sees Rachel, he
stalks toward her, sniffing eagerly. She let him finger
her genitals, sniff deeply of her scent. His penis is
erect and he grunts in excitement. She turns and presents herself to him and he mounts her, thrusting deep
inside. As he penetrates, she thinks, for a moment, of
Jake and of the thin blonde teenage girl named Rachel, but then the moment passes. Almost against her

will she cries out, a shrill exclamation of welcoming and loss.

After he withdraws his penis, Johnson grooms her gently, sniffing her genitals and softly stroking her fur. She is sleepy and content, but she knows she cannot delay.

Johnson is reluctant to leave his cage, but Rachel takes him by the hand and leads him to the janitor's lounge. His presence gives her courage. She listens at the door and hears Jake's soft breathing. Leaving Johnson in the hall, she slips into the room. Jake is lying on the couch, the magazine draped over his legs. Rachel takes the equipment that she has gathered and stands for a moment, staring at the sleeping man. His baseball cap hangs on the arm of a broken chair, and she takes that to remember him by.

Rachel leads Johnson through the empty halls. A kangaroo rat, collecting seeds in the dried grass near the glass doors, looks up curiously as Rachel leads Johnson down the steps. Rachel carries the plastic shopping bag slung over her shoulder. Somewhere in the distance, a coyote howls, a long yapping wail. His cry is joined by others, a chorus in the moonlight.

Rachel takes Johnson by the hand and leads him into the desert.

A cocktail waitress, driving from her job in Flagstaff to her home in Winslow, sees two apes dart across the road, hurrying away from the bright beams of her headlights. After wrestling with her conscience (she does not want to be accused of drinking on the job), she notifies the county sheriff.

A local newspaper reporter, an eager young man fresh out of journalism school, picks up the story from the police report and interviews the waitress. Flattered by his enthusiasm for her story and delighted to find a receptive ear, she tells him the details that she failed to mention to the police: one of the apes was wearing a baseball cap and carrying what looked like a shopping bag.

The reporter writes up a quick humorous story for

the morning edition, and begins researching a feature article to be run later in the week. He knows that the newspaper, eager for news in a slow season, will play a human-interest story up big—kind of *Lassie, Come Home* with chimps.

Just before dawn, a light rain begins to fall, the first rain of spring. Rachel searches for shelter and finds a small cave formed by three tumbled boulders. It will keep off the rain and hide them from casual observers. She shares her food and water with Johnson. He has followed her closely all night, seemingly intimidated by the darkness and the howling of distant coyotes. She feels protective toward him. At the same time, having him with her gives her courage. He knows only a few gestures in ASL, but he does not need to speak. His presence is comfort enough.

Johnson curls up in the back of the cave and falls asleep quickly. Rachel sits in the opening and watches dawnlight wash the stars from the sky. The rain rattles against the sand, a comforting sound. She thinks about Jake. The baseball cap on her head still smells of his cigarettes, but she does not miss him. Not really. She fingers the cap and wonders why she thought she loved Jake.

The rain lets up. The clouds rise like fairy castles in the distance and the rising sun tints them pink and gold and gives them flaming red banners. Rachel remembers when she was young and Aaron read her the story of Pinnochio, the little puppet who wanted to be a real boy. At the end of his adventures, Pinnochio, who has been brave and kind, gets his wish. He becomes a real boy.

Rachel had cried at the end of the story and when Aaron asked why, she had rubbed her eyes on the backs of her hairy hands. —I want to be a real girl, she signed to him. —A real girl.

"You are a real girl," Aaron had told her, but somehow she had never believed him.

The sun rises higher and illuminates the broken rock turrets of the desert. There is a magic in this barren land of unassuming grandeur. Some cultures send their young people to the desert to seek visions and guidance, searching for true thinking spawned by the openness of the place, the loneliness, the beauty of emptiness.

Rachel drowses in the warm sun and dreams a vision that has the clarity of truth. In the dream, her father comes to her. "Rachel," he says to her, "it doesn't matter what anyone thinks of you. You're my daughter."

—I want to be a real girl, she signs.

"You *are* real," her father says. "And you don't need some two-bit drunken janitor to prove it to you." She knows she is dreaming, but she also knows that her father speaks the truth. She is warm and happy and she doesn't need Jake at all. The sunlight warms her and a lizard watches her from a rock, scurrying for cover when she moves. She picks up a bit of loose rock that lies on the floor of the cave. Idly, she scratches on the dark red sandstone wall of the cave. A lopsided heart shape. Within it, awkwardly printed: Rachel and Johnson. Between them, a plus sign. She goes over the letters again and again, leaving scores of fine lines on the smooth rock surface. Then, late in the morning, soothed by the warmth of the day, she sleeps.

Shortly after dark, an elderly rancher in a pickup truck spots two apes in a remote corner of his ranch. They run away and lose him in the rocks, but not until he has a good look at them. He calls the police, the newspaper, and the Primate Center.

The reporter arrives first thing the next morning, interviews the rancher, and follows the men from the Primate Center as they search for evidence of the chimps. They find monkey shit near the cave, confirming that the runaways were indeed nearby. The news reporter, an eager and curious young man, squirms on his belly into the cave and finds the names scratched on the cave wall. He peers at it. He might have dismissed them as the idle scratchings of kids, except that the names match the names of the missing chimps.

"Hey," he called to his photographer. "Take a look at this."

The next morning's newspaper displays Rachel's crudely scratched letters. In a brief interview, the rancher mentioned that the chimps were carrying bags. "Looked like supplies," he said. "They looked like they were in for a long haul."

On the third day, Rachel's water runs out. She heads toward a small town, marked on the map. They reach it in the early morning—thirst forces them to travel by day. Beside an isolated ranch house, she finds a faucet. She is filling her bottle when Johnson grunts in alarm.

A dark-haired woman watches from the porch of the house. She does not move toward the apes, and Rachel continues filling the bottle. "It's all right, Rachel," the woman, who has been following the story in the papers, calls out. "Drink all you want."

Startled, but still suspicious, Rachel caps the bottle and, keeping her eyes on the woman, drinks from the faucet. The woman steps back into the house. Rachel motions Johnson to do the same, signaling for him to hurry and drink. She turns off the faucet when he is done.

They are turning to go when the woman emerges from the house carrying a plate of tortillas and a bowl of apples. She sets them on the edge of the porch and says, "These are for you."

The woman watches through the window as Rachel packs the food into her bag. Rachel puts away the last apple and gestures her thanks to the woman. When the woman fails to respond to the sign language, Rachel picks up a stick and writes in the sand of the yard. "THANK YOU," Rachel scratches, then waves goodbye and sets out across the desert. She is puzzled, but happy.

The next morning's newspaper includes an interview with the dark-haired woman. She describes how Rachel turned on the faucet and turned it off when she was through, how the chimp packed the apples neatly in her bag and wrote in the dirt with a stick.

The reporter also interviews the director of the Primate Research Center. "These are animals," the director explains angrily. "But people want to treat them like they're small hairy people." He describes the Center as "primarily a breeding center with some facilities for medical research." The reporter asks some pointed questions about their acquisition of Rachel.

But the biggest story is an investigative piece. The reporter reveals that he has tracked down Aaron Jacobs' lawyer and learned that Jacobs left a will. In this will, he bequeathed all his possessions—including his house and surrounding land—to "Rachel, the chimp I acknowledge as my daughter."

The reporter makes friends with one of the young women in the typing pool at the research center, and she tells him the office scuttlebutt: people suspect that the chimps may have been released by a deaf and drunken janitor, who was subsequently fired for negligence. The reporter, accompanied by a friend who can communicate in sign language, finds Jake in his apartment in downtown Flagstaff.

Jake, who has been drinking steadily since he was fired, feels betrayed by Rachel, by the Primate Center, by the world. He complains at length about Rachel: They had been friends, and then she took his baseball cap and ran away. He just didn't understand why she had run away like that.

"You mean she could talk?" the reporter asks through his interpreter.

—Of course she can talk, Jake signs impatiently. — She is a smart monkey.

The headlines read: "Intelligent chimp inherits fortune!" Of course, Aaron's bequest isn't really a fortune and she isn't just a chimp, but close enough. Animal rights activists rise up in Rachel's defense. The case is discussed on the national news. Ann Landers reports receiving a letter from a chimp named Rachel; she had thought it was a hoax perpetrated by the boys at Yale. The American Civil Liberties Union assigns a lawyer to the case.

By day, Rachel and Johnson sleep in whatever hiding places they can find: a cave; a shelter built for range cattle; the shell of an abandoned car, rusted from long years in a desert gully. Sometimes Rachel dreams of jungle darkness, and the coyotes in the distance become a part of her dreams, their howling becomes the cries of her fellow apes.

The desert and the journey have changed her. She is wiser, having passed through the white-hot love of adolescence and emerged on the other side. She dreams, one day, of the ranch house. In the dream, she has long blonde hair and pale white skin. Her eyes are red from crying and she wanders the house restlessly, searching for something that she has lost. When she hears coyotes howling, she looks through a window at the darkness outside. The face that looks in at her has jug-handle ears and shaggy hair. When she sees the face, she cries out in recognition and opens the window to let herself in.

By night, they travel. The rocks and sands are cool beneath Rachel's feet as she walks toward her ranch. On television, scientists and politicians discuss the ramifications of her case, describe the technology uncovered by investigation of Aaron Jacobs' files. Their debates do not affect her steady progress toward her ranch or the stars that sprinkle the sky above her.

It is night when Rachel and Johnson approach the ranchhouse. Rachel sniffs the wind and smells automobile exhaust and strange humans. From the hills, she can see a small camp beside a white van marked with the name of a local television station. She hesitates, considering returning to the safety of the desert. Then she takes Johnson by the hand and starts down the hill. Rachel is going home.

AMERICA
By Orson Scott Card

*The difference between Latin America and
North America's United States has always
been vast; the first being in virtual colonial
aspect to the Empire of the Dollar. Now
beyond the border between Mexico and the
U.S.A. there lives another race, that of the
native Americans miscalled Indians. The majority of the inhabitants of those countries
are among the dispossessed of the world.
This may change; indeed, as history always
calls the tune, no matter how long or in
what fashion it takes, it will change.*

Sam Monson and Anamari Boagente had two encounters in their lives, forty years apart. The first encounter lasted for several weeks in the high Amazon jungle,
the village of Agualinda. The second was for only an
hour near the ruins of the Glen Canyon Dam, on the
border between Navaho country and the State of
Deseret.

When they met the first time, Sam was a scrawny
teenager from Utah and Anamari was a middle-aged
spinster Indian from Brazil. When they met the second time, he was governor of Deseret, the last European state in America, and she was, to some people's
way of thinking, the mother of God. It never occurred
to anyone that they had ever met before, except me. I
saw it plain as day, and pestered Sam until he told me
the whole story. Now Sam is dead and she's long
gone, and I'm the only one who knows the truth. I
thought for a long time that I'd take this story untold

71

to my grave, but I see now that I can't do that. The
way I see it, I won't be allowed to die until I write this
down. All my real work was done long since, so why
else am I alive? I figure the land has kept me breathing so I can tell the story of its victory, and it has kept
you alive so you can hear it. Gods are like that. It isn't
enough for them to run everything. They want to be
famous, too.

Agualinda, Amazonas

Passengers were nothing to her. Anamari only cared
about helicopters when they brought medical supplies.
This chopper carried a precious packet of benaxidene;
Anamari barely noticed the skinny, awkward boy who
sat by the crates, looking hostile. Another Yanqui
who doesn't want to be stuck out in the jungle. Nothing new about that. Norteamericanos were almost invisible to Anamari by now. They came and went.

It was the Brazilian government people she had to
worry about, the petty bureaucrats suffering through
years of virtual exile in Mannaus, working out their
frustration by being petty tyrants over the helpless
Indians. No I'm sorry we don't have any more penicil-
lin, no more syringes, what did you do with the AIDS
vaccine we gave you three years ago? Do you think
we're made of money here? Let them come to town if
they want to get well. There's a hospital in São Paulo
de Olivença, send them there, we're not going to turn
you into a second hospital out there in the middle of
nowhere, not for a village of a hundred filthy Baniwas,
it's not as if yóu're a doctor, you're just an old with-
ered up Indian woman yourself, you never graduated
from the medical schools, we can't spare medicines for
you. It made them feel so important, to decide whether
or not an Indian child would live or die. As often as
not they passed sentence of death by refusing to send
supplies. It made them feel powerful as God.

Anamari knew better than to protest or argue—it
would only make that bureaucrat likelier to kill again
in the future. But sometimes, when the need was great
and the medicine was common, Anamari would go to

the Yanqui geologists and ask if they had this or that. Sometimes they would share, but if they didn't, they wouldn't lift a finger to get any. They were not tyrants like the Brazilian bureaucrats. They just didn't give a damn. They were there to make money.

That was what Anamari saw when she looked at the sullen light-haired boy in the helicopter—another Norteamericano, just like all the other Norteamericanos, only younger.

She had the benaxidene, and so she immediately began spreading word that all the Baniwas should come for injections. It was a disease that had been introduced during the war between Guyana and Venezuela two years ago; as usual, most of the victims were not citizens of either country, just the Indios of the jungle, waking up one morning with their joints stiffening, hardening until no movement was possible. Benaxidene was the antidote, but you had to have it every few months or your joints would stiffen up again. As usual, the bureaucrats had diverted a shipment and there were a dozen Baniwas bedridden in the village. As usual, one or two of the Indians would be too far gone for the cure; one or two of their joints would be stiff for the rest of their lives. As usual, Anamari said little as she gave the injections, and the Baniwas said less to her.

It was not until the next day that Anamari had time to notice the young Yanqui boy wandering around the village. He was wearing rumpled white clothing, already somewhat soiled with the greens and browns of life along the rivers of the Amazon jungle. He showed no sign of being interested in anything, but an hour into her rounds, checking on the results of yesterday's benaxidene treatments, she became aware that he was following her.

She turned around in the doorway of the government-built hovel and faced him. "O que e'?" she demanded. What do you want?

To her surprise, he answered in halting Portuguese. Most of these Yanquis never bothered to learn the language at all, excepting her and everybody else to speak English. "Posso ajudar?" he asked. Can I help?

"Não," she said. "Mas pode olhar." You can watch.

He looked at her in bafflement.

She repeated her sentence slowly, enunciating clearly. "Pode olhar."

"Eu?" Me?

"Você, sim. And I can speak English."

"I don't want to speak English."

"Tanto faz," she said. Makes no difference.

He followed her into the hut. It was a little girl, lying naked in her own feces. She had palsy from a bout with meningitis years ago, when she was an infant, and Anamari figured that the girl would probably be one of the ones for whom the benaxidene came too late. That's how things usually worked—the weak suffer most. But no, her joints were flexing again, and the girl smiled at them, that heartbreakingly happy smile that made palsy victims so beautiful at times.

So. Some luck after all, the benaxidene had been in time for her. Anamari took the lid off the clay waterjar that stood on the one table in the room, and dipped one of her clean rags in it. She used it to wipe the girl, then lifted her frail, atrophied body and pulled the soiled sheet out from under her. On impulse, she handed the sheet to the boy.

"Leva fora," she said. And, when he didn't understand, "Take it outside."

He did not hesitate to take it, which surprised her. "Do you want me to wash it?"

"You could shake off the worst of it," she said. "Out over the garden in back. I'll wash it later."

He came back in, carrying the wadded-up sheet, just as she was leaving. "All done here," she said. "We'll stop by my house to start that soaking. I'll carry it now."

He didn't hand it to her. "I've got it," he said. "Aren't you going to give her a clean sheet?"

"There are only four sheets in the village," she said. "Two of them are on my bed. She won't mind lying on the mat. I'm the only one in the village who cares about linens. I'm also the only one who cares about this girl."

"She likes you," he said.

"She smiles like that at everybody.

"So maybe she likes everybody."

Anamari grunted and led the way to her house. It was two government hovels pushed together. The one served as her clinic, the other as her home. Out back she had two metal washtubs. She handed one of them to the Yanqui boy, pointed at the rainwater tank, and told him to fill it. He did. It made her furious.

"What do you want!" she demanded.

"Nothing," he said.

"Why do you keep hanging around!"

"I thought I was helping." His voice was full of injured pride.

"I don't need your help." She forgot that she had meant to leave the sheet to soak. She began rubbing it on the washboard.

"Then why did you ask me to . . ."

She did not answer him, and he did not complete the question.

After a long time he said, "You were trying to get rid of me, weren't you?"

"What do you want here?" she said. "Don't I have enough to do, without a Norteamericano *boy* to look after?"

Anger flashed in his eyes, but he did not answer until the anger was gone. "If you're tired of scrubbing, I can take over."

She reached out and took his hand, examined it for a moment. "Soft hands," she said. "Lady hands. You'd scrape your knuckles on the washboard and bleed all over the sheet."

Ashamed, he put his hands in his pockets. A parrot flew past him, dazzling green and red; he turned in surprise to look at it. It landed on the rainwater tank. "Those sell for a thousand dollars in the States," he said.

Of course the Yanqui boy evaluates everything by

price. "Here they're free," she said. "The Baniwas eat them. And wear the feathers."

He looked around at the other huts, the scraggly gardens. "The people are very poor here," he said. "The jungle life must be hard."

"Do you think so?" she snapped. "The jungle is very kind to these people. It has plenty for them to eat, all year. The Indians of the Amazon did not know they were poor until Europeans came and made them buy pants, which they couldn't afford, and built houses, which they couldn't keep up, and plant gardens. Plant gardens! In the midst of this magnificent Eden. The jungle life was good. The Europeans made them poor."

"Europeans?" asked the boy.

"Brazilians. They're all Europeans. Even the black ones have turned European. Brazil is just another European country, speaking a European language. Just like you Norteamericanos. You're Europeans too."

"I was born in America," he said. "So were my parents and grandparents and great-grandparents."

"But your bis-bis-avós, they came on a boat."

"That was a long time ago," he said.

"A long time!" She laughed. "I am a pure Indian. For ten thousand generations I belong to this land. You are a stranger here. A fourth-generation stranger."

"But I'm a stranger who isn't afraid to touch a dirty sheet," he said. He was grinning defiantly.

That was when she started to like him. "How old are you?" she asked.

"Fifteen," he said.

"Your father's a geologist?"

"No. He heads up the drilling team. They're going to sink a test well here. He doesn't think they'll find anything, though."

"They will find plenty of oil," she said.

"How do you know?"

"Because I dreamed it," she said. "Bulldozers cutting down the trees, making an airstrip, and planes coming and going. They'd never do that, unless they found oil. Lots of oil."

She waited for him to make fun of the idea of

dreaming true dreams. But he didn't. He just looked at her.

So she was the one who broke the silence. "You came to this village to kill time while your father is away from you, on the job, right?"

"No," he said. "I came here because he hasn't started to work yet. The choppers start bringing in equipment tomorrow."

"You would rather be away from your father?"

He looked away. "I'd rather see him in hell."

"This *is* hell," she said, and the boy laughed. "Why did you come here with him?"

"Because I'm only fifteen years old, and he has custody of me this summer."

"Custody," she said. "Like a criminal."

"He's the criminal," he said bitterly.

"And his crime?"

He waited a moment, as if deciding whether to answer. When he spoke, he spoke quietly and looked away. Ashamed. Of his father's crime. "Adultery," he said. The word hung in the air. The boy turned back and looked her in the face again. His face was tinged with red.

Europeans have such transparent skin, she thought. All their emotions show through. She guessed a whole story from his word—a beloved mother betrayed, and now he had to spend the summer with her betrayer. "Is that a *crime*?"

He shrugged. "Maybe not to Catholics."

"You're Protestant?"

He shook his head. "Mormon. But I'm a heretic."

She laughed. "You're a heretic, and your father is an adulterer."

He didn't like her laughter. "And you're a virgin," he said. His words seemed calculated to hurt her.

She stopped scrubbing, stood there looking at her hands. "Also a crime?" she murmured.

"I had a dream last night," he said. "In my dream your name was Anna Marie, but when I tried to call you that, I couldn't. I could only call you by another name."

"What name?" she asked.

"What does it matter? It was only a dream." He was taunting her. He knew she trusted in dreams.

"You dreamed of me, and in the dream my name was Anamari?"

"It's true, isn't it? That *is* your name, isn't it?" He didn't have to add the other half of the question: You *are* a virgin, aren't you?

She lifted the sheet from the water, wrung it out and tossed it to him. He caught it, vile water spattering his face. He grimaced. She poured the washwater onto the dirt. It spattered mud all over his trousers. He did not step back. Then she carried the tub to the water tank and began to fill it with clean water. "Time to rinse," she said.

"You dreamed about an airstrip," he said. "And I dreamed about you."

"In your dreams you better start to mind your own business," she said.

"I didn't ask for it, you know," he said. "But I followed the dream out to this village, and you turned out to be a dreamer, too."

"That doesn't mean you're going to end up with your pinto between my legs, so you can forget it," she said.

He looked genuinely horrified. "Geez, what are you talking about! That would be fornication! Plus you've got to be old enough to be my mother!"

"I'm forty-two," she said. "If it's any of your business."

"You're *older* than my mother," he said. "I couldn't possibly think of you sexually. I'm sorry if I gave that impression."

She giggled. "You are a very funny boy, Yanqui. First you say I'm a virgin—"

"That was in the dream," he said.

"And then you tell me I'm older than your mother and too ugly to think of me sexually."

He looked at her ashen with shame. "I'm sorry, I was just trying to make sure you knew that I would never—"

"You're trying to tell me that you're a good boy."
"Yes," he said.

She giggled again. "You probably don't even play with yourself," she said.

His face went red. He struggled to find something to say. Then he threw the wet sheet back at her and walked furiously away. She laughed and laughed. She liked this boy very much.

The next morning he came back and helped her in the clinic all day. His name was Sam Monson, and he was the first European she ever knew who dreamed true dreams. She had thought only Indios could do that. Whatever god it was that gave her dreams to her, perhaps it was the same god giving dreams to Sam. Perhaps that god brought them together here in the jungle. Perhaps it was that god who would lead the drill to oil, so that Sam's father would have to keep him here long enough to accomplish whatever the god had in mind.

It annoyed her that the god had mentioned she was a virgin. That was nobody's business but her own.

Life in the jungle was better than Sam ever expected. Back in Utah, when Mother first told him that he had to go to the Amazon with the old bastard, he had feared the worst. Hacking through thick viney jungles with a machete, crossing rivers of piranha in tick-infested dugouts, and always sweat and mosquitos and thick, heavy air. Instead the American oilmen lived in a pretty decent camp, with a generator for electric light. Even though it rained all the time and when it didn't it was so hot you wished it would, it wasn't constant danger as he had feared, and he never had to hack through jungle at all. There were paths, sometimes almost roads, and the thick, vivid green of the jungle was more beautiful than he had ever imagined. He had not realized that the American West was such a desert. Even California, where the old bastard lived when he wasn't traveling to drill wells, even those wooded hills and mountains were gray compared to the jungle green.

The Indians were quiet little people, not headhunters. Instead of avoiding them, like the adult Americans did, Sam found that he could be with them, come to know them, even help them by working with Anamari. The old bastard could sit around and drink his beer with the guys—adultery *and* beer, as if one contemptible sin of the flesh weren't enough—but Sam was actually doing some good here. If there was anything Sam could do to prove he was the opposite of his father, he would do it; and because his father was a weak, carnal, earthy man with no self-control, then Sam had to be a strong, spiritual, intellectual man who did not let any passions of the body rule him. Watching his father succumb to alcohol, remembering how his father could not even last a month away from Mother without having to get some whore into his bed, Sam was proud of his self-discipline. He ruled his body; his body did not rule him.

He was also proud to have passed Anamari's test on the first day. What did he care if human excrement touched his body? He was not afraid to breathe the hot stink of suffering, he was not afraid of the innocent dirt of a crippled child. Didn't Jesus touch lepers? Dirt of the body did not disgust him. Only dirt of the soul.

Which was why his dreams of Anamari troubled him. During the day they were friends. They talked about important ideas, and she told him stories of the Indians of the Amazon, and about her education as a teacher in São Paulo. She listened when he talked about history and religion and evolution and all the theories and ideas that danced in his head. Even Mother never had time for that, always taking care of the younger kids or doing her endless jobs for the church. Anamari treated him like his ideas mattered.

But at night, when he dreamed, it was something else entirely. In those dreams he kept seeing her naked, and the voice kept calling her "Virgem America." What her virginity had to do with America he had no idea—even true dreams didn't always make sense—but he knew this much: when he dreamed of

Anamari naked, she was always reaching out to him, and he was filled with such strong passions that more than once he awoke from the dream to find himself throbbing with imaginary pleasure, like Onan in the Bible, Judah's son, who spilled his seed upon the ground and was struck dead for it.

Sam lay awake for a long time each time this happened, trembling, fearful. Not because he thought God would strike him down—he knew that if God hadn't struck his father dead for adultery, Sam was certainly in no danger because of an erotic dream. He was afraid because he knew that in these dreams he revealed himself to be exactly as lustful and evil as his father. He did not want to feel any sexual desire for Anamari. She was old and lean and tough, and he was afraid of her, but most of all Sam didn't want to desire her because he was not like his father, he would never have sexual intercourse with a woman who was not his wife.

Yet when he walked into the village of Agualinda, he felt eager to see her again, and when he found her—the village was small, it never took long—he could not erase from his mind the vivid memory of how she looked in the dreams, reaching out to him, her breasts loose and jostling, her slim hips rolling toward him—and he would bite his cheek for the pain of it, to distract him from desire.

It was because he was living with Father; the old bastard's goatishness was rubbing off on him, that's all. So he spent as little time with his father as possible, going home only to sleep at night.

The harder he worked at the jobs Anamari gave him to do, the easier it was to keep himself from remembering his dream of her kneeling over him, touching him, sliding along his body. Hoe the weeds out of the corn until your back is on fire with pain! Wash the Baniwa hunter's wound and replace the bandage! Sterilize the instruments in the alcohol! Above all, do not, even accidentally, let any part of your body brush against hers; pull away when she is near you, turn away so you don't feel her warm breath as she leans over your shoulder, start a bright conversation whenever there is a silence filled only with the sound of insects and the sight of a bead of sweat slowly etching its way from her neck down her chest to disappear between her breasts where she only tied her shirt instead of buttoning it.

How could she possibly be a virgin, after the way she acted in his dreams?

"Where do you think the dreams come from?" she asked.

He blushed, even though she could not have guessed what he was thinking. Could she?

"The dreams," she said. "Why do you think we have dreams that come true?"

It was nearly dark. "I have to get home," he said. She was holding his hand. When had she taken his hand like that, and why?

"I have the strangest dream," she said. "I dream of a huge snake, covered with bright green and red feathers."

"Not all the dreams come true," he said.

"I hope not," she answered. "Because this snake comes out of—I give birth to this snake."

"Quetzal," he said.

"What does that mean?"

"The gathered serpent god of the Aztecs. Or maybe the Mayas. Mexican, anyway. I have to go home."

"But what does it mean?"

"It's almost dark," he said.

"Stay and talk to me!" she demanded. "I have room, you can stay the night."

But Sam had to get back. Much as he hated staying with his father, he dared not spend a night in this place. Even her invitation aroused him. He would never last a night in the same house with her. The dream would be too strong for him. So he left her and headed back along the path through the jungle. All during the walk he couldn't get Anamari out of his mind. It was as if the plants were sending him the vision of her, so his desire was even stronger than when he was with her.

The leaves gradually turned from green to black in the seeping dark. the hot darkness did not frighten him; it seemed to invite him to step away from the path into the shadows, where he would find the moist relief, the cool release of all his tension. He stayed on the path, and hurried faster.

He came at last to the oilmen's town. The generator was loud, but the insects were louder, swarming around the huge area light, casting shadows of their demonic dance. He and his father shared a large one-room house on the far edge of the compound. The oil company provided much nicer hovels than the Brazilian government.

A few men called out to greet him. He waved, even answered once or twice, but hurried on. His groin felt so hot and tight with desire that he was sure that only the shadows and his quick stride kept everyone from seeing. It was maddening: the more he thought of trying to calm himself, the more visions of Anamari slipped in and out of his waking mind, almost to the point of hallucination. His body would not relax. He was almost running when he burst into the house.

Inside, Father was washing his dinner plate. He glanced up, but Sam was already past him. "I'll heat up your dinner."

Sam flopped down on his bed. "Not hungry."

"Why are you so late?" asked his father.

"We got to talking."

"It's dangerous in the jungle at night. You think it's safe because nothing bad ever happens to you in the daytime, but it's dangerous."

"Sure, Dad. I know." Sam got up, turned his back to take off his pants. Maddeningly, he was still aroused; he didn't want his father to see.

But with the unerring instinct of prying parents, the old bastard must have sensed that Sam was hiding something. When Sam was buck naked, Father walked around, and *looked,* just as if he never heard of privacy. Sam blushed in spite of himself. His father's eyes went small and hard. I hope I don't ever look like that, thought Sam. I hope my face doesn't get that ugly suspicious expression on it. I'd rather die than look like that.

"Well, put on your pajamas," Father said. "I don't want to look at that forever."

Sam pulled on his sleeping shorts.

"What's going on over there?" asked Father.

"Nothing," said Sam.

"You must do *something* all day."

"I told you, I help her. She runs a clinic, and she also tends a garden. She's got no electricity, so it takes a lot of work."

"I've done a lot of work in my time, Sam, but I don't come home like *that*."

"No, you always stopped and got it off with some whore along the way."

The old bastard whipped out his hand and slapped Sam across the face. It stung, and the surprise of it wrung tears from Sam before he had time to decide not to cry.

"I never slept with a whore in my life," said the old bastard.

"You only slept with one woman who wasn't," said Sam.

Father slapped him again, only this time Sam was ready, and he bore the slap stoically, almost without flinching.

"I had one affair," said Father.

"You got caught once," said Sam. "There were dozens of women."

Father laughed derisively. "What did you do, hire a detective? There was only the one."

But Sam knew better. He had dreamed these women for years. Laughing, lascivious women. It wasn't until he was twelve years old that he found out enough about sex to know what it all meant. By then he had long since learned that any dream he had more than once was true. So when he had a dream of Father with one of the laughing women, he woke up, holding the dream in his memory. He thought through it from beginning to end, remembering all the details he could. The name of the motel. The room number. It was midnight, but Father was in California, so it was an hour earlier. Sam got out of bed and walked quietly into the kitchen and dialed directory assistance. There was such a motel. He wrote down the number. Then Mother was there, asking him what he was doing.

"This is the number of the Seaview Motor Inn," he said. "Call this number and ask for room twenty-one-twelve and then ask for Dad."

Mother looked at him strangely, like she was about to scream or cry or hit him or throw up. "Your father is at the Hilton," she said.

But he just looked right back at her and said, "No matter who answers the phone, ask for Dad."

So she did. A woman answered, and Mom asked for Dad by name, and he was there. "I wonder how we can afford to pay for two motel rooms on the same night," Mom said coldly. "Or are you splitting the cost with your friend?" Then she hung up the phone and burst into tears.

She cried all night as she packed up everything the old bastard owned. By the time Dad got home two days later, all his things were in storage. Mom moved fast when she made up her mind. Dad found himself divorced and excommunicated all in the same week, not two months later.

Mother never asked Sam how he knew where Dad was that night. Never even hinted at wanting to know. Dad never asked him how Mom knew to call that number, either. An amazing lack of curiosity, Sam thought sometimes. Perhaps they just took it as fate. For a while it was secret, then it stopped being secret, and it didn't matter how the change happened. But one thing Sam knew for sure—the woman at the Seaview Motor Inn was not the first woman, and the Seaview was not the first motel. Dad had been an adulterer for years, and it was ridiculous for him to lie about it now.

But there was no point in arguing with him, especially when he was in the mood to slap Sam around.

"I don't like the idea of you spending so much time with an older woman," said Father.

"She's the closest thing to a doctor these people have. She needs my help and I'm going to keep helping her," said Sam.

"Don't talk to me like that, little boy."

"You don't know anything about this, so just mind your own business."

Another slap. "You're going to get tired of this before I do, Sammy."

"I love it when you slap me, Dad. It confirms my moral superiority."

Another slap, this time so hard that Sam stumbled under the blow, and he tasted blood inside his mouth. "How hard next time, Dad?" he said. "You going to knock me down? Kick me around a little? Show me who's boss?"

"You've been asking for a beating ever since we got here."

"I've been asking to be left alone."

"I know women, Sam. You have no business getting involved with an older woman like that."

"I help her wash a little girl who has bowel movements in bed, Father. I empty pails of vomit. I wash clothes and help patch leaking roofs and while I'm doing all these things we talk. Just talk. I don't imagine you have much experience with that, Dad. You probably never talk at all with the women *you* know, at least not after the price is set."

It was going to be the biggest slap of all, enough to knock him down, enough to bruise his face and black his eye. But the old bastard held it in. Didn't hit him. Just stood there, breathing hard, his face red, his eyes tight and piggish.

"You're not as pure as you think," the old bastard finally whispered. "You've got every desire you despise in me."

"I don't despise you for *desire*," said Sam.

"The guys on the crew have been talking about you and this Indian bitch, Sammy. You may not like it, but I'm your father and it's my job to warn you. These Indian women are easy, and they'll give you a disease."

"The guys on the crew," said Sam. "What do they know about Indian women? They're all fags or jerk-offs."

"I hope someday you say that where they can hear you, Sam. And I hope when it happens I'm not there to stop what they do to you."

"I would never *be* around men like that, Daddy, if the court hadn't given you shared custody. A no-fault divorce. What a joke."

More than anything else, those words stung the old bastard. Hurt him enough to shut him up. He walked out of the house and didn't come back until Sam was long since asleep.

Asleep and dreaming.

Anamari knew what was on Sam's mind, and to her surprise she found it vaguely flattering. She had never known the shy affection of a boy. When she was a teenager, she was the one Indian girl in the schools in Sâo Paulo. Indians were so rare in the Europeanized parts of Brazil that she might have seemed exotic, but in those days she was still so frightened. The city was sterile, all concrete and harsh light, not at all like the deep soft meadows and woods of Xingu Park. Her tribe, the Kuikuru, were much more Europeanized than the jungle Indians—she had seen cars all her life, and spoke Portuguese before she went to school. But the city made her hungry for the land, the cobble-stones hurt her feet, and these intense, competitive children made her afraid. Worst of all, true dreams stopped in the city. She hardly knew who she was, if she was not a true dreamer. So if any boy desired her then, she would not have known it. She would have rebuffed him inadvertently. And then the time for such things had passed. Until now.

"Last night I dreamed of a great bird, flying west, away from land. Only its right wing was twice as large as its left wing. It had great bleeding wounds along the edges of its wings, and the right wing was the sickest of all, rotting in the air, the feathers dropping off."

"Very pretty dream," said Sam. Then he translated, to keep in practice. "Que sonho lindo."

"Ah, but what does it mean?"

"What happened next?"

"I was riding on the bird. I was very small, and I held a small snake in my hands—"

"The feathered snake."

"Yes. And I turned it loose, and it went and ate up all the corruption, and the bird was clean. And that's all. You've got a bubble in that syringe. The idea is to inject medicine, not air. What does the dream mean?"

"What, you think I'm a Joseph? A Daniel?"

"How about a Sam?"

"Actually, your dream is easy. Piece of cake."

"What?"

"Piece of cake. Easy as pie. That's how the cookie crumbles. Man shall not live by bread alone. All I can think of are bakery sayings. I must be hungry."

"Tell me the dream or I'll poke this needle into your eye."

"That's what I like about you Indians. Always you have torture on your mind."

She planted her foot against him and knocked him off his stool onto the packed dirt floor. A beetle skittered away. Sam held up the syringe he had been working with; it was undamaged. He got up, set it aside. "The bird," he said, "is North and South America. Like wings, flying west. Only the right wing is bigger." He sketched out a rough map with his toe on the floor.

"That's the shape, maybe," she said. "I could be."

"And the corruption—show me where it was."

With her toe, she smeared the map here, there.

"It's obvious," said Sam.

"Yes," she said. "Once you think of it as a map. The corruption is all the Europeanized land. And the only healthy places are where the Indians still live."

"Indians or half-Indians," said Sam. "All your dreams are about the same thing, Anamari. Removing the Europeans from North and South America. Let's face it. You're an Indian chauvinist. You give birth to the resurrection god of the Aztecs, and then you send it out to destroy the Europeans."

"But why do I dream this?"

"Because you hate Europeans."

"No," she said. "That isn't true."

'Sure it is."

"I don't hate *you*."

"Because you know me. I'm not a European anymore, I'm a person. Obviously you've got to keep that from happening anymore, so you can keep your bigotry alive."

"You're making fun of me, San."

He shook his head. "No, I'm not. These are true dreams, Anamari. They tell you your destiny."

She giggled. "If I give birth to a feathered snake, I'll know the dream was true."

"To drive the Europeans out of America."

"No," she said. "I don't care what the dream says. I won't do that. Besides, what about the dream of the flowering weed?"

"Little weed in the garden, almost dead, and then you water it and it grows larger and larger and more beautiful—"

"And something else," she said. "At the very end of the dream, all the other flowers in the garden have changed. To be just like the flowering weed." She reached out and rested her hand on his arm. "Tell me *that* dream."

His arm became still, lifeless under her hand. "Black is beautiful," he said.

"What does *that* mean?"

"In America. The U.S., I mean. For the longest time, the blacks, the former slaves, they were ashamed to be black. The whiter you were, the more status you had—the more honor. But when they had their revolution in the sixties—"

"You don't remember the sixties, little boy."

"Heck, I barely remember the seventies. But I read books. One of the big changes, and it made a huge difference, was that slogan. Black is beautiful. The blacker the better. They said it over and over. Be proud of blackness, not ashamed of it. And in just a few years, they turned the whole status system upside down."

She nodded. "The weed came into flower."

"So. All through Latin America, Indians are very low status. If you want a Bolivian to pull a knife on you, just call him an Indian. Everybody who possibly can, pretends to be of pure Spanish blood. Pure-blooded Indians are slaughtered wherever there's the slightest excuse. Only in Mexico is it a little bit different."

"What you tell me from my dreams, Sam, this is no small job to do. I'm one middle-aged Indian woman, living in the jungle. I'm supposed to tell all the Indians of America to be proud? When they're the poorest of the poor and the lowest of the low?"

"When you give them a name, you create them. Benjamin Franklin did it, when he coined the name *American* for the people of the English colonies. They weren't New Yorkers or Virginians, they were Americans. Same thing for you. It isn't Latin Americans against Norteamericanos. It's Indians and Europeans. Somos todos indios. We're all Indians. Think that would work as a slogan?"

"Me. A revolutionary."

"Nós somos os americanos. Vai fora, Europa! America p'ra americanos! All kinds of slogans."

"I'd have to translate them into Spanish."

"Indios moram na India. Americanos moram na America. America nossa! No, better still: Nossa America! Nuestra America! It translates. Our America."

"You're a very fine slogan maker."

He shivered as she traced her finger along his shoulder and down the sensitive skin of his chest. She made a circle on his nipple and it shriveled and hardened, as if he were cold.

"Why are you silent now?" She laid her hand flat on his abdomen, just above his shorts, just below his navel. "You never tell me your own dreams," she said. "But I know what they are."

He blushed.

"See? Your skin tells me, even when your mouth

says nothing. I have dreamed these dreams all my life, and they troubled me, all the time, but now you tell me what they mean, a white-skinned dream-teller, you tell me that I must go among the Indians and make them proud, make them strong, so that everyone with a drop of Indian blood will call himself an Indian, and Europeans will lie and claim native ancestors, until America is all Indian. You tell me that I will give birth to the new Quetzalcoatl, and he will unify and heal the land of its sickness. But what you never tell me is this: Who will be the father of my feathered snake?"

Abruptly he got up and walked stiffly away. To the door, keeping his back to her, so she couldn't see how alert his body was. But she knew.

"I'm fifteen," said Sam, finally.

"And I'm very old. The land is older. Twenty million years. What does it care of the quarter-century between us?"

"I should never have come to this place."

"You never had a choice," she said. "My people have always known the god of the land. Once there was a perfect balance in this place. All the people loved the land and tended it. Like the garden of Eden. And the land fed them. It gave them maize and bananas. They took only what they needed to eat, and they did not kill animals for sport or humans for hate. But then the Incas turned away from the land and worshiped gold and the bright golden sun. The Aztecs soaked the ground in the blood of their human sacrifices. The Pueblos cut down the forests of Utah and Arizona and turned them into red-rock deserts. The Iroquois tortured their enemies and filled the forest with their screams of agony. We found tobacco and coca and peyote and coffee and forgot the dreams the land gave us in our sleep. And so the land rejected us. The land called to Columbus and told him lies and seduced him and he never had a chance, did he? Never had a choice. The land brought the Europeans to punish us. Disease and slavery and warfare killed most of us, and the rest of us tried to pretend we were Europeans rather than endure any more of the punish-

ment. The land was our jealous lover, and it hated us
for a while.

"Some Catholic you are," said Sam. "I don't believe in your Indian gods."

"Say *Deus* or *Cristo* instead of *the land* and the story
is the same," she said. "But now the Europeans are
worse than we Indians ever were. The land is suffering
from a thousand different poisons, and you threaten to
kill all of life with your weapons of war. We Indians
have been punished enough, and now it's our turn to
have the land again. The land chose Columbus exactly
five centuries ago. Now you and I dream our dreams,
the way he dreamed."

"That's a good story," Sam said, still looking out
the door. It sounded so close to what the old prophets
in the Book of Mormon said would happen to America; close, but dangerously different. As if there were
no hope for the Europeans anymore. As if their chance
had already been lost, as if no repentance would be
allowed. They would not be able to pass the land on to
the next generation. Someone else would inherit. It
made him sick at heart, to realize what the white man
had lost, had thrown away, had torn up and destroyed.

"But what should I do with my story?" she asked.
He could hear her coming closer, walking up behind
him. He could almost feel her breath on his shoulder.
"How can I fulfill it?"

By yourself. Or at least without me. "Tell it to the
Indians. You can cross all these borders in a thousand
different places, and you speak Portuguese and Spanish and Arawak and Carib, and you'll be able to tell
your story in Quechua, too, no doubt, crossing back
and forth between Brazil and Colombia and Bolivia
and Peru and Venezuela, all close together here, until
every Indian knows about you and calls you by the
name you were given in my dream."

"Tell me my name."

"Virgem America. See? The land or god or whatever it is wants you to be a virgin."

She giggled. "Nossa senhora," she said. "Don't you
see? I'm the new Virgin *Mother*. It wants me to be a

mother, all the old legends of the Holy Mother will transfer to me; they'll call me virgin no matter what the truth is. How the priests will hate me. How they'll try to kill my son. But he will live and become Quetzalcoatl, and he will restore America to the true Americans. That is the meaning of my dreams. My dreams and yours."

"Not me," he said. "Not for any dream or any god." He turned to face her. His fist was pressed against his groin, as if to crush out all rebellion there. "My body doesn't rule me," he said. "Nobody controls me but myself."

"That's very sick," she said cheerfully. "All because you hate your father. Forget that hate, and love me instead."

His face became a mask of anguish, and then he turned and fled.

He even thought of castrating himself, that's the kind of madness that drove him through the jungle. He could hear the bulldozers carving out the airstrip, the screams of falling timbers, the calls of birds and cries of animals displaced. It was the terror of the tortured land, and it maddened him even more as he ran between thick walls of green. The rig was sucking oil like heartblood from the forest floor. The ground was wan and trembling under his feet. And when he got home he was grateful to lift his feet off the ground and lie on his mattress, clutching his pillow, panting or perhaps sobbing from the exertion of his run.

He slept, soaking his pillow in afternoon sweat, and in his sleep the voice of the land came to him like whispered lullabies. I did not choose you, said the land. I cannot speak except to those who hear me, and because it is in your nature to hear and listen, I spoke to you and led you here to save me, save me, save me. Do you know the desert they will make of me? Encased in burning dust or layers of ice, either way I'll be dead. My whole purpose is to thrust life upward out of my soils, and feel the press of living feet, and hear the songs of birds and the low music of the animals, growl-

ing, lowing, chittering, whatever voice they choose.
That's what I ask of you, the dance of life, just once to
make the man whose mother will teach him to be
Quetzalcoatl and save me, save me, save me.

He heard that whisper and he dreamed a dream. In
his dream he got up and walked back to Agualinda,
not along the path, but through the deep jungle itself.
A longer way, but the leaves touched his face, the
spiders climbed on him, the tree lizards tangled in his
hair, the monkeys dunged him and pinched him and
jabbered in his ear, the snakes entwined around his
feet; he waded streams and fish caressed his naked
ankles, and all the way they sang to him, songs that
celebrants might sing at the wedding of a king. Somehow, in the way of dreams, he lost his clothing without
removing it, so that he emerged from the jungle naked, and walked through Agualinda as the sun was
setting, all the Baniwas peering at him from their
doorways, making clicking noises with their teeth.

He awoke in darkness. He heard his father breathing. He must have slept through the afternoon. What
a dream, what a dream. He was exhausted.

He moved, thinking of getting up to use the toilet.
Only then did he realize that he was not alone on the
bed, and it was not his bed. She stirred and nestled
against him, and he cried out in fear and anger.

It startled her awake. "What is it?" she asked.

"It was a dream," he insisted. "All a dream."

"Ah yes," she said, "it was. But last night, Sam, we
dreamed the same dream." She giggled. "All night
long."

In his sleep. It happened in his sleep. And it did not
fade like common dreams, the memory was clear,
pouring himself into her again and again, her fingers
gripping him, her breath against his cheek, whispering
the same thing, over and over. "Aceito, aceito-te,
aceito." Not love, no, not when he came with the land
controlling him, she did not love him, she merely
accepted the burden he placed within her. Before tonight she had been a virgin, and so had he. Now she
was even purer than before, Virgem America, but his

purity was hopelessly, irredeemably gone, wasted, poured out into this old woman who had haunted his dreams. "I hate you," he said. "What you stole from me."

He got up, looking for his clothing, ashamed that she was watching him.

"No one can blame you," she said. "The land married us, gave us to each other. There's no sin in that."

"Yeah," he said.

"One time. Now I am whole. Now I can begin."

And now I'm finished.

"I didn't mean to rob you," she said. "I didn't know you were dreaming."

"I thought I was dreaming," he said, "but I loved the dream. I dreamed I was fornicating and it made me glad." He spoke the words with all the poison in his heart. "Where are my clothes?"

"You arrived without them," she said. "It was my first hint that you wanted me."

There was a moon outside. Not yet dawn. "I did what you wanted," he said. "Now can I go home?"

"Do what you want," she said. "I didn't plan this."

"I know. I wasn't talking to you." And when he spoke of home, he didn't mean the shack where his father would be snoring and the air would stink of beer.

"When you woke me, I was dreaming," she said.

"I don't want to hear it."

"I have him now," she said, "a boy inside me. A lovely boy. But you will never see him in all your life, I think."

"Will you tell him? Who I am?"

She giggled. "Tell Quetzalcoatl that his father is a European? A man who blushes? A man who burns in the sun? No, I won't tell him. Unless someday he becomes cruel, and wants to punish the Europeans even after they are defeated. Then I will tell him that the first European he must punish is himself. Here, write your name. On this paper write your name, and give me your fingerprint, and write the date."

"I don't know what day it is."

"October twelfth," she said.

"It's August."

"Write October twelfth," she said. "I'm in the legend business now."

"August twenty-fourth," he murmured, but he wrote the date she asked for.

"The helicopter comes this morning," she said.

"Good-bye," he said. He started for the door.

Her hands caught at him, held his arm, pulled him back. She embraced him, this time not in a dream, cool bodies together in the doorway of the house. The geis was off him now, or else he was worn out; her body had no power over his anymore.

"I did love you," she murmured. "It was not just the god that brought you."

Suddenly he felt very young, even younger than fifteen, and he broke away from her and walked quickly away through the sleeping village. He did not try to retrace his wandering route through the jungle; he stayed on the moonlit path and soon was at his father's hut. The old bastard woke up as Sam came in.

"I knew it'd happen," Father said.

Sam rummaged for underwear and pulled it on.

"There's no man born who can keep his zipper up when a woman wants it." Father laughed. A laugh of malice and triumph. "You're no better than I am, boy."

Sam walked to where his father sat on the bed and imagined hitting him across the face. Once, twice, three times.

"Go ahead, boy, hit me. It won't make you a virgin again."

"I'm not like you," Sam whispered.

"No?" asked Father. "For you it's a sacrament or something? As my daddy used to say, it don't matter who squeezes the toothpaste, boy, it all squirts out the same."

"Then your daddy must have been as dumb a jackass as mine." Sam went back to the chest they shared, began packing his clothes and books into one big suitcase. "I'm going out with the chopper today. Mom will wire me the money to come home from Manaus."

"She doesn't have to. I'll give you a check."

"I don't want your money. I just want my passport."

"It's in the top drawer." Father laughed again. "At least I always wore my clothes home."

In a few minutes Sam had finished packing. He picked up the bag, started for the door.

"Son," said Father, and because his voice was quiet, not derisive, Sam stopped and listened. "Son," he said, "once is once. It doesn't mean you're evil, it doesn't even mean you're weak. It just means you're human." He was breathing deeply. Sam hadn't heard him so emotional in a long time. "You aren't a thing like me, son," he said. "That should make you glad."

Years later Sam would think of all kinds of things he should have said. Forgiveness. Apology. Affection. Something. But he said nothing, just left and went out to the clearing and waited for the helicopter. Father didn't come to try to say good-bye. The chopper pilot came, unloaded, left the chopper to talk to some people. He must have talked to Father because when he came back he handed Sam a check. Plenty to fly home, and stay in good places during the layovers, and buy some new clothes that didn't have jungle stains on them. The check was the last thing Sam had from his father. Before he came home from that rig, the Venezuelans bought a hardy and virulent strain of syphilis on the black market, one that could be passed by casual contact, and released it in Guyana. Sam's father was one of the first million to die, so fast that he didn't even write.

Page, Arizona

The state of Deseret had only sixteen helicopters, all desperately needed for surveying, spraying, and medical emergencies. So Governor Sam Monson rarely risked them on government business. This time, though, he had no choice. He was only fifty-five, and in good shape, so maybe he could have made the climb into Glen Canyon and back up the other side. But Carpen-

ter wouldn't have made it, not in a wheel-chair, and
Carpenter had a right to be here. He had a right to see
what the red-rock Navaho desert had become.

Deciduous forest, as far as the eye could see.

They stood on the bluff where the old town of Page
had once been, before the dam was blown up. The
Navahos hadn't tried to reforest here. It was their
standard practice. They left all the old European towns
unplanted, like pink scars in the green of the forest.
Still, the Navahos weren't stupid. They had come to
the last stronghold of European science, the University of Deseret at Zarahemla, to find out how to use
the heavy rainfalls to give them something better than
perpetual floods and erosion. It was Carpenter who
gave them the plan for these forests, just as it was
Carpenter whose program had turned the old Utah
deserts into the richest farmland in America. The
Navahos filled their forests with bison, deer, and bears.
The Mormons raised crops enough to feed five times
their population. That was the European mindset, still
in place: enough is never enough. Plant more, grow
more, you'll need it tomorrow.

"They say he has two hundred thousand soldiers,"
said Carpenter's computer voice. Carpenter *could* speak,
Sam had heard, but he never did. Preferred the syn-
thesized voice. "They could all be right down there,
and we'd never see them."

"They're much farther south and east. Strung out
from Phoenix to Santa Fe, so they aren't too much of
a burden on the Navahos."

"Do you think they'll buy supplies from us? Or send
an army in to take them?"

"Neither," said Sam. "We'll give our surplus grain
as a gift."

"He rules all of Latin America, and he needs *gifts*
from a little remnant of the U.S. in the Rockies?"

"We'll give it as a gift, and be grateful if he takes it
that way."

"How else might he take it?"

"As tribute. As taxes. As ransom. The land is his
now, not ours."

"We made the desert live, Sam. That makes it ours."

"There they are."

They watched in silence as four horses walked slowly from the edge of the woods, out onto the open ground of an ancient gas station. They bore a litter between them, and were led by two—not Indians—Americans. Sam had schooled himself long ago to use the word *American* to refer only to what had once been known as Indians, and to call himself and his own people Europeans. But in his heart he had never forgiven them for stealing his identity, even though he remembered very clearly where and when that change began.

It took fifteen minutes for the horses to bring the litter to him, but Sam made no move to meet them, no sign that he was in a hurry. That was also the American way now, to take time, never to hurry, never to rush. Let the Europeans wear their watches. Americans told time by the sun and stars.

Finally the litter stopped, and the men opened the litter door and helped her out. She was smaller than before, and her face was tightly wrinkled, her hair steel-white.

She gave no sign that she knew him, though he said his name. The Americans introduced her as Nuestra Señora. Our Lady. Never speaking her most sacred name: Virgem America.

The negotiations were delicate but simple. Sam had authority to speak for Deseret, and she obviously had authority to speak for her son. The grain was refused as a gift, but accepted as taxes from a federal state. Deseret would be allowed to keep its own government, and the borders negotiated between the Navahos and the Mormons eleven years before were allowed to stand.

Sam went further. He praised Quetzalcoatl for coming to pacify the chaotic lands that had been ruined by the Europeans. He gave her maps that his scouts had prepared, showing strongholds of the prairie raiders, decommissioned nuclear missiles, and the few places where stable governments had been formed. He offered and she accepted, a hundred experienced scouts to travel with Quetzalcoatl at Deseret's expense, and promised that when he chose the site of his North American capital, Deseret would provide architects and engineers and builders to teach his American workmen how to build the place themselves.

She was generous in return. She granted all citizens of Deseret conditional status as adopted Americans, and she promised that Quetzalcoatl's armies would stick to the roads through the northwest Texas panhandle, where the grasslands of the newest New Lands project were still so fragile that an army could destroy five years of labor just by marching through. Carpenter printed out two copies of the agreement in English and Spanish, and Sam and Virgem America signed both.

Only then, when their official work was done, did the old woman look up into Sam's eyes and smile. "Are you still a heretic, Sam?"

"No," he said. "I grew up. Are you still a virgin?"

She giggled, and even though it was an old lady's broken voice, he remembered the laughter he had heard so often in the village of Agualinda, and his heart ached for the boy he was then, and the girl she was. He remembered thinking then that forty-two was old.

"Yes, I'm still a virgin," she said. "God gave me my child. God sent me an angel, to put the child in my womb. I thought you would have heard the story by now."

"I heard it," he said.

She leaned closer to him, her voice a whisper. "Do you dream, these days?"

"Many dreams. But the only ones that come true are the ones I dream in daylight."

"Ah," she sighed. "My sleep is also silent."

She seemed distant, sad, distracted. Sam also; then, as if by conscious decision, he brightened, smiled, spoke cheerfully. "I have grandchildren now."

"And a wife you love," she said, reflecting his brightening mood. "I have grandchildren, too." Then she became wistful again. "But no husband. Just memories of an angel."

"Will I see Quetzalcoatl?"

"No," she said, very quickly. A decision she had long since made and would not reconsider. "It would not be good for you to meet face to face, or stand side by side. Quetzalcoatl also asks that in the next election, you refuse to be a candidate."

"Have I displeased him?" asked Sam.

"He asks this at my advice," she said. "It is better, now that his face will be seen in this land, that your face stay behind closed doors."

Sam nodded. "Tell me," he said. "Does he look like the angel?"

"He is as beautiful," she said. "But not as pure."

They embraced each other and wept. Only for a moment. Then her men lifted her back into her litter, and Sam returned with Carpenter to the helicopter. They never met again.

In retirement, I came to visit Sam, full of questions lingering from his meeting with Virgem America. "You knew each other," I insisted. "You had met before." He told me all this story then.

That was thirty years ago. She is dead now, he is dead, and I am old, my fingers slapping these keys with all the grace of wooden blocks. But I write this sitting in the shade of a tree on the brow of a hill, looking out across woodlands and orchards, fields and rivers and roads, where once the land was rock and grit and sagebrush. This is what America wanted, what it bent our lives to accomplish. Even if we took twisted roads and got lost or injured on the way, even if we came limping to this place, it is a good place, it is worth the journey, it is the promised, the promising land.

CRYING IN THE RAIN
By Tanith Lee

A moving story of a life in a world half-destroyed by military folly and the nuclear Sword of Damocles. The soaring talent of the author of The Birthgrave *and the Flat Earth novels is at its best in this short but very disturbing tale.*

There was a weather Warning that day, so to start with we were all indoors. The children were watching the pay-TV and I was feeding the hens on the shutyard. It was about 9 a.m. Suddenly my mother came out and stood at the edge of the yard. I remember how she looked at me: I had seen the look before, and although it was never explained, I knew what it meant. In the same way she appraised the hens, or checked the vegetables and salad in their grow-trays. Today there was a subtle difference, and I recognized the difference too. It seemed I was ready.

"Greena," she said. She strode across to the hen-run, glanced at the disappointing hens. There had only been three eggs all week, and one of those had registered too high. But in any case, she wasn't concerned with her poultry just now. "Greena, this morning we're going into the Center."

"What about the Warning, Mum?"

"Oh, that. Those idiots, they're often wrong. Anyway, nothing until noon, they said. All Clear till then. And we'll be in by then."

"But, Mum," I said, "there won't be any buses.

There never are when there's a Warning. We'll have to walk."

Her face, all hard and eaten back to the bone with life and living, snapped at me like a rat-trap: "So we'll *walk*. Don't go on and on, Greena. What do you think your legs are for?"

I tipped the last of the feed from the pan and started toward the stair door.

"And talking of legs," said my mother, "put on your stockings. And the things we bought last time."

There was always this palaver. It was normally because of the cameras, particularly those in the Entry washrooms. After you strip, all your clothes go through the cleaning machine, and out to meet you on the other end. But there are security staff on the cameras, and the doctors, and they might see, take an interest. You had to wear your smartest stuff in order not to be ashamed of it, things even a Center doctor could glimpse without repulsion. A stickler, my mother. I went into the shower and took one and shampooed my hair, and used powder bought in the Center with the smell of roses, so all of me would be gleaming clean when I went through the shower and shampooing at the Entry. Then I dressed in my special underclothes, and my white frock, put on my stockings and shoes, and remembered to drop the carton of rose powder in my bag.

My mother was ready and waiting by the time I came down to the street doors, but she didn't upbraid me. She had meant me to be thorough.

The children were yelling round the TV, all but Daisy, who was seven and had been left in charge. She watched us go with envious fear. My mother shouted her away inside before we opened up.

When we'd unsealed the doors and got out, a blast of heat scalded us. It was a very hot day, the sky so far clear as the finest blue perspex. But of course, as there had been a weather Warning, there were no buses, and next to no one on the streets. On Warning days, there was anyway really nowhere to go. All the shops were sealed fast, even our three area pubs. The local train station ceased operating when I was four, eleven years ago. Even the endless jumble of squats had their boards in place and their tarpaulins over.

The only people we passed on the burning dusty pavements were a couple of fatalistic tramps, in from the green belt, with bottles of cider or petromix; these they jauntily raised to us. (My mother tugged me on.) And once a police car appeared which naturally hove to at our side and activated its speaker.

"Is your journey really necessary, madam?"

My mother, her patience eternally tried, grated out furiously, "Yes it is."

"You're aware there's been a forecast of rain for these sections?"

"*Yes*," she rasped.

"And this is your daughter? It's not wise, madam, to risk a child—"

"My daughter and I are on our way to the Center. We have an appointment. Unless we're *delayed*," snarled my mother, visually skewering the pompous policeman, only doing his job, through the Sealtite window of the car, "we would be inside before any rain breaks."

The two policemen in their snug patrol vehicle exchanged looks.

There was a time we could have been arrested for behaving in this irresponsible fashion, my mother and I, but no one really bothers now. There was more than enough crime to go round. On our own heads it would be.

The policeman who'd spoken to us through the speaker smiled coldly and switched it off—speaker, and come to that, smile.

The four official eyes stayed on me a moment, however, before the car drove off. That at least gratified my mother. Although the policemen had called me a child for the white under-sixteen tag on my wristlet, plainly they'd noticed I looked much older and besides, rather good.

Without even a glance at the sky, my mother marched forward. (It's true there are a few public weather-shelters but vandals had wrecked most of them.) I admired my mother, but I'd never been able to love her, not even to like her much. She was phenomenally strong and had kept us together, even after my father canced, and the other man, the father of Jog, Daisy and Angel. She did it with slaps and harsh tirades, to show us what we could expect in life. But she must have had her fanciful side once: for instance, the silly name she gave me, for green trees and green pastures and waters green as bottle-glass that I've only seen inside the Center. The trees on the streets and in the abandoned gardens have always been bare, or else they have sparse foliage of quite a cheerful brown color. Sometimes they put out strange buds or fruits and then someone reports it and the trees are cut down. They were rather like my mother, I suppose, or she was like the trees. Hard-bitten to the bone, enduring, tough, holding on by her root-claws, not daring to flower.

Gallantly she showed only a little bit of nervousness when we began to see the glint of the dome in the sunshine coming down High Hill from the old cinema ruin. Then she started to hurry quite a lot and urged me to be quick. Still, she didn't look up once, for clouds.

In the end it was perfectly all right: the sky stayed empty and we got down to the concrete underpass. Once we were on the moving way I rested my tired feet by standing on one leg then the other like a stork I once saw in a TV program.

As soon as my mother noticed she told me to stop it. There are cameras watching, all along the underpass to the Entry. It was useless to try persuading her that it didn't matter. She had never brooked argument and though she probably wouldn't clout me before the cameras she might later on. I remember I was about six or seven when she first thrashed me. She used a plastic belt, but took off the buckle. She didn't want to scar me. Not to scar Greena was a part of survival, for even then she saw something might come of me. But the belt hurt and raised welts. She said to me as I lay

howling and she leaned panting on the bed, "I won't
have any back-answers. Not from you and not from
any of you, do you hear me? There isn't time for it.
You'll do as I say."

After we'd answered the usual questions, we joined
the queue for the washroom. It wasn't much of a
queue, because of the Warning. We glided through
the mechanical check, the woman operator even con-
gratulating us on our low levels. "That's section SEK,
isn't it?" she said chattily. "A very good area. My
brother lives out there. He's over thirty and has three
children." My mother congratulated the operator in
turn and proudly admitted our house was one of the
first in SEK fitted with Sealtite. "My kids have never
played outdoors," she assured the woman. "Even
Greena here scarcely went out till her eleventh birthday. We grow most of our own food." Then, feeling
she was giving away too much—you never knew who
might be listening, there was always trouble in the
suburbs with burglars and gangs—she clammed up
tighter than the Sealtite.

As we went into the washroom a terrific argument
broke out behind us. The mechanical had gone off
violently. Some woman was way over the acceptable
limit. She was screaming that she had to get in to the
Center to see her daughter, who was expecting a baby—
the oldest excuse, perhaps even true, though pregnancy is strictly regulated under a dome. One of the
medical guards was bearing down on the woman, asking if she had Insurance.

If she had, the Entry hospital would take her in and
see if anything could be done. But the woman had
never got Insurance, despite having a daughter in the
Center, and alarms were sounding and things were
coming to blows.

"Mum," I said, when we passed into the white
plastic-and-tile expanse with the black camera eyes
clicking overhead and the Niagara rush of showers,
"who are you taking me to see?"

She actually looked startled, as if she still thought

me so naïve that I couldn't guess she too, all this time, had been planning to have a daughter in the Center. She glared at me, then came out with the inevitable.

"Never you mind. Just you hope you're lucky. Did you bring your talc?"

"Yes, Mum."

"Here then, use these too. I'll meet you in the cafeteria."

When I opened the carton I found "Smoky" eye make-up, a cream lipstick that smelled of peaches, and a little spray of scent called *I Mean It*.

My stomach turned right over. But then I thought, So what. It would be frankly stupid of *me* to be thinking I was naïve. I'd known for years.

While we were finishing our hamburgers in the cafeteria, it did start to rain, outside. You could just *sense* it, miles away beyond the layers of protection and lead-glass. A sort of flickering of the sight. It wouldn't do us much harm in here, but people instinctively moved away from the outer suburb-side walls of the café even under the plastic palm-trees in tubs. My mother stayed put.

"Have you finished, Greena? Then go to the Ladies and brush your teeth, and we'll get on. And spray that scent again."

"It's finished, Mum. There was only enough for one go."

"Daylight robbery," grumbled my mother, "you can hardly smell it." She made me show her the empty spray and insisted on squeezing hissing air out of it into each of my ears.

Beyond the cafeteria, a tree-lined highway runs down into the Center. Real trees, green trees, and green grass on the verges. At the end of the slope, we waited for an electric bus painted a jolly bright color, with a rude driver. I used to feel that everyone in the Center must be cheery and contented, bursting with optimism and the juice of kindness. But I was always disappointed. They know you're from outside at once, if nothing else gives you away, skin-tone is different

from the pale underdome skin or chocolaty solarium
Center tan. Although you could never have got in here
if you hadn't checked out as acceptable, a lot of people draw away from you on the buses or underground
trains. Once or twice, when my mother and I had gone
to see a film in the Center no one would sit near us.
But not everybody had this attitude. Presumably, the
person my mother was taking me to see wouldn't
mind.

"Let me do the talking," she said as we got off the
bus. (The driver had started extra quickly, half shaking our contamination off his platform, nearly breaking our ankles.)

"Suppose he asks me something?"

"*He?*" But I wasn't going to give ground on it now.
"All right. In that case, answer, but be careful."

Parts of the Center contain very old historic buildings and monuments of the inner city which, since
they're inside, are looked after and kept up. We were
now under just that sort of building. From my TV
memories—my mother had made sure we had the
educational TV to grow up with, along with lesson
tapes and exercise ropes—the architecture looked late
eighteenth or very early nineteenth, white stone, with
toplids on the windows and pillared porticos up long
stairs flanked by black metal lions.

We went up the stairs and I was impressed and
rather frightened.

The glass doors behind the pillars were wide open.
There's no reason they shouldn't be, here. The cool-
warm, sweet-smelling breezes of the dome-conditioned
air blew in and out, and the real ferns in pots waved
gracefully. There was a tank of golden fish in the
foyer. I wanted to stay and look at them. Sometimes
on the Center streets you see well-off people walking
their clean, groomed dogs and foxes. Sometimes there
might be a silken cat high in a window. There were
birds in the Center parks, trained not to fly free anywhere else. When it became dusk above the dome,
you would hear them tweeting excitedly as they roosted.
And then all the lights of the city came on and moths

danced round them. You could get proper honey in the Center, from the bee-farms, and beef and milk from the cattle-grazings, and salmon, and leather and wine and roses.

But the fish in the tank were beautiful. And I suddenly thought, if I get to stay here—if I really *do*—but I didn't believe it. It was just something I had to try to get right for my mother, because I must never argue with her, ever.

The man in the lift took us to the sixth floor. He was impervious; we weren't there, he was simply working the lift for something to do.

A big old clock in the foyer had said 3 p.m. The corridor we came out in was deserted. All the rooms stood open like the corridor windows, plushy hollows with glass furniture: offices. The last office in the corridor had a door which was shut.

My mother halted. She was pale, her eyes and mouth three straight lines on the plain of bones. She raised her hand and it shook, but it knocked hard and loud against the door.

In a moment, the door opened by itself.

My mother went in first.

She stopped in front of me on a valley-floor of grass-green carpet, blocking my view.

"Good afternoon, Mr. Alexander. I hope we're not too early."

A man spoke.

"Not at all. Your daughter's with you? Good. Please do come in." He sounded quite young.

I walked behind my mother over the grass carpet, and chairs and a desk became visible, and then she let me step around her, and said to him, "This is my daughter, Mr. Alexander. Greena."

He was only about twenty-two, and that was certainly luck, because the ones born in the Center can live up until their fifties, their sixties even, though that's rare. (They quite often don't even cance in the domes, providing they were born there. My mother used to say it was the high life killed them off.)

He was tanned from a solarium and wore beautiful

clothes, a cotton shirt and trousers. His wristlet was silver—I had been right about his age: the tag was red. He looked so fit and hygienic, almost edible. I glanced quickly away from his eyes.

"Won't you sit down?" He gave my mother a crystal glass of Center gin, with ice-cubes and lemon slices. He asked me, smiling, if I'd like a milk-shake, yes with real milk and strawberry flavor. I was too nervous to want it or enjoy it, but it had to be had. You couldn't refuse such a thing.

When we were perched in chairs with our drinks (he didn't drink with us) he sat on the desk, swinging one foot, and took a cigarette from a box and lit and smoked it.

"Well, I must say," he remarked conversationally to my mother, "I appreciate your coming all this way—after a Warning, too. It was only a shower I gather."

"We were inside by then," said my mother quickly. She wanted to be definite—the flower hadn't been spoiled by rain.

"Yes, I know. I was in touch with the Entry."

He would have checked our levels, probably. He had every right to, after all. If he was going to buy me, he'd want me to last for a while.

"And, let me say at once, just from the little I've seen of your daughter, I'm sure she'll be entirely suitable for the work. So pretty, and such a charming manner."

It was normal to pretend there was an actual job involved. Perhaps there even would be, to begin with.

My mother must have been putting her advert out since last autumn. That was when she'd had my photograph taken at the Center. I'd just worn my nylon-lace panties for it; it was like the photos they take of you at the Medicheck every ten years. But there was always a photograph of this kind with such an advert. It was illegal, but nobody worried. There had been a boy in our street who got into the Center three years ago in this same way. He had placed the advert, done it all himself. He was handsome, though his hair, like mine, was very fine and perhaps he would lose it before he was eighteen. Apparently that hadn't mattered.

Had my mother received any other offers? Or only this tanned Mr. Alexander with the intense bright eyes?

I'd drunk my shake and not noticed.

Mr. Alexander asked me if I would read out what was written on a piece of rox he gave me. My mother and the TV lessons had seen to it I could read, or at least that I could read what was on the rox, which was a very simple paragraph directing a Mr. Cleveland to go to office 170B on the seventh floor and a Miss O'Beale to report to the basement. Possibly the job would require me to read such messages. But I had passed the test. Mr. Alexander was delighted. He came over without pretense and shook my hand and kissed me exploringly on the left cheek. His mouth was firm and wholesome and he had a marvelous smell, a smell of money and safety. My mother had labored cleverly on me. I recognized it instantly, and wanted it. Between announcements, they might let me feed the fish in the tank.

Mr. Alexander was extremely polite and gave my mother another big gin, and chatted sociably to her about the latest films in the Center, and the color that was in vogue, nothing tactless or nasty, such as the cost of food inside, and out, or the SEO riots the month before, in the suburbs, when the sounds of the fires and the police rifles had penetrated even our sealed-tight home in SEK. He didn't mention any current affairs, either, the death-rate on the continent, or the trade-war with the USA—he knew our TV channels get edited. Our information was too limited for an all-round discussion.

Finally he said, "Well, I'd better let you go. Thank you again. I think we can say we know where we stand, yes?" He laughed over the smoke of his fourth cigarette, and my mother managed her deaths-head grin, her remaining teeth washed with gin and lemons. "But naturally I'll be writing to you. I'll send you the

details Express. That should mean you'll get them—
oh, five days from today. Will that be all right?"

My mother said, "That will be lovely, Mr. Alexander. I can speak for Greena and tell you how very
thrilled she is. It will mean a lot to us. The only thing
is, Mr. Alexander, I do have a couple of other
gentlemen—I've put them off, of course. But I have to
let them know by the weekend."

He made a gesture of mock panic. "Good God, I
don't want to lose Greena. Let's say three and a half
days, shall we? I'll see if I can't rustle up a special
courier to get my letter to you extra fast."

We said good-bye, and he shook my hand again and
kissed both cheeks. A great pure warmth came from
him, and a sort of power. I felt I had been kissed by a
tiger, and wondered if I was in love.

At the Entry-exit, though it didn't rain again, my
mother and I had a long wait until the speakers broadcast the All Clear. By then the clarified sunset lay
shining and flaming in six shades of red and scarlet-
orange over the suburbs.

"Look, Mum," I said, because shut up indoors so
much, I didn't often get to see the naked sky, "isn't it
beautiful? It doesn't look like that through the dome."

But my mother had no sympathy with vistas. Only
the toxins in the air, anyway, make the colors of
sunset and dawn so wonderful. To enjoy them is therefore idiotic, perhaps unlawful.

My mother had, besides, been very odd ever since
we left Mr. Alexander's office. I didn't properly understand that this was due to the huge glasses of gin
he'd generously given her. At first she was fierce and
energetic, keyed up, heroic against the polished sights
of the Center, which she had begun to point out to me
like a guide. Though she didn't say so, she meant
Once you live here. But then, when we had to wait in
the exit lounge and have a lot of the rather bad coffee-
drink from the machine, she sank in on herself, brooding. Her eyes became so dark, so bleak, I didn't like
to meet them. She had stopped talking at me.

Though the rain-alert was over, it was now too late for buses. There was the added problem that gangs would be coming out on the streets, looking for trouble.

The gorgeous poisoned sunset died behind the charcoal sticks of trees and pyramids and oblongs of deserted buildings and rusty railings.

Fortunately, there were quite a few police-patrols about. My mother gave them short shrift when they stopped her. Generally they let us get on. We didn't look dangerous.

On SEK, the working street-lights were coming on and there were some ordinary people strolling or sitting on low broken walls, taking the less unhealthy air. They pop up like the rabbits used to, out of their burrows. We passed a couple of women we knew, outside the Sealtite house on the corner of our road. They asked where we'd come from. My mother said tersely we'd been at a friend's, and stopped in till the All Clear.

Although Sealtite, as the advert says, makes secure against anything but gelignite, my mother had by now got herself into an awful sort of rigid state. She ran up the concrete to our front door, unlocked it and dived us through. We threw our clothes into the wash-bin, though they hardly needed it as we'd been in the Center most of the day. The TV was still blaring. My mother, dragging on a skirt and nylon blouse, rushed through into the room where the children were. Immediately there was a row. During the day Jog had upset a complete giant can of powdered milk. Daisy had tried to clear it up and they had meant not to tell our mother as if she wouldn't notice one was missing. Daisy was only seven, and Jog was three, so it was blurted out presently. My mother hit all of them, even Angel. Daisy, who had been responsible for the house in our absence, she belted, not very much, but enough to fill our closed-in world with screaming and savage sobs.

After it was over, I made a pot of tea. We drank it black since we would have to economize on milk for the rest of the month.

The brooding phase had passed from my mother. She was all sharp jitters. She said we had to go up and look at the hens. The eggs were always registering too high lately. Could there be a leak in the sealing of the shut-yard?

So that was where we ended up, tramping through lanes of lettuce, waking the chickens who got agitated and clattered about. My mother wobbled on a ladder under the roofing with a torch. "I can't see anything," she kept saying.

Finally she descended. She leaned on the ladder with the torch dangling, still alight, wasting the battery. She was breathless.

"Mum . . . the torch is still on."

She switched it off, put it on a post of the hen-run, and suddenly came at me. She took me by the arms and glared into my face.

"Greena, do you understand about the Alexander man? Well, do you?"

"Yes, Mum."

She shook me angrily but not hard.

"You know why you have to?"

"Yes, Mum. I don't mind, Mum. He's really nice."

Then I saw her eyes had changed again, and I faltered. I felt the earth give way beneath me. Her eyes were full of burning water. They were soft and they were frantic.

"Listen, Greena. I was thirty last week."

"I know—"

"You shut up and listen to me. I had my medicheck. It's no good, Greena."

We stared at each other. It wasn't a surprise. This happened to everyone. She'd gone longer than most. Twenty-five was the regular innings, out here.

"I wasn't going to tell you, not yet. I don't have to report into the hospital for another three months. I'm getting a bit of pain, but there's the Insurance: I can buy that really good pain-killer, the new one."

"Mum."

"Will you be quiet? I want to ask you, you know

what you have to do? About the kids? They're your
sisters and your brother, you know that, don't you?"

"Yes. I'll take care of them."

"Get him to help you. He will. He really wants you.
He was dead unlucky, that Alexander. His legal
girlfriend canced. Born in the Center and everything
and she pegged out at eighteen. Still, that was good
for us. Putting you on the sterilization program when
you were little, thank God I did. You see, he can't
legally sleep with another girl with pregnancy at all
likely. Turns out he's a high-deformity risk. Doesn't
look it, does he?"

"Yes, Mum, I know about the pregnancy laws."

She didn't slap me or even shout at me for answering back. She seemed to accept I'd said it to reassure
her I truly grasped the facts. Alexander's predicament
had anyway been guessable. Why else would he want
a girl from outside?

"Now, Angel—" said my mother "—I want you to
see to her the same, sterilization next year when she's
five. She's got a chance too: she could turn out very
nice-looking. Daisy won't be any use to herself, and
the boy won't. But you see you get a decent woman in
here to take care of them. No homes. Do you hear?
Not for my kids." She sighed, and said again, "*He'll*
help you. If you play your cards right, he'll do anything you want. He'll cherish you, Greena." She let
me go and said, grinning, "We had ten applications. I
went and saw them all. He's the youngest and the
best."

"He's lovely," I said. "Thanks, Mum."

"Well, you just see you don't let me down."

"I won't. I promise. I promise, really."

She nodded, and drew up her face into its sure
habitual shape, and her eyes dry into their Sealtite of
defiance.

"Let's get down now. I'd better rub some anesjel
into those marks on Daisy."

We went down and I heard my mother passing from
child to child, soothing and reprimanding them as she
harshly pummeled the anaesthetic jelly into their hurts.

For a moment, listening on the landing, in the clamped house-dark, I felt I loved my mother.

Then that passed off. I began to think about Mr. Alexander and his clothes and the brilliance of his eyes in his tanned healthy face.

It was wonderful. He didn't send a courier. He came out himself. He was in a small sealed armored car like a TV alligator, but he just swung out of it and up the concrete into our house. (His bodyguard stayed negligently inside the car. He had a pistol and a mindless attentive lethal look.)

Mr. Alexander brought me half a dozen perfect tawny roses, and a crate of food for the house, toys and TV tapes for the children, and even some gin for my mother. He presumably didn't know yet she only had three months left, but he could probably work it out. He made a fuss of her, and when she'd spoken her agreements into the portable machine, he kissed me on the mouth and then produced a bottle of champagne. The wine was very frothy, and the glassful I had made me feel giddy. I didn't like it, but otherwise our celebration was a success.

I don't know how much money he paid for me. I'd never want to ask him. Or the legal fiddles he must have gone through. He was able to do it, and that was all we needed to know, my mother, me. (She always kept the Insurance going and now, considerably swelled, the benefits will pass on to the children.)

She must have told him eventually about the hospital. I do know he saw to it personally that she had a private room and the latest in pain relief, and no termination until she was ready. He didn't let me see her after she went in. She'd said she didn't want it, either. She had already started to lose weight and shrivel up, the way it happens.

The children cried terribly. I thought it could never get put right, but in the end the agency he found brought us a nineteen-year-old woman who'd lost her own baby and she seemed to take to the children at once. The safe house, of course, was a bonus no one sane would care to ignore. The agency will keep an eye on things, but her levels were low, she should have at least six years. The last time I went there they all seemed happy. He doesn't want me to go outside again.

Six months ago, he brought me officially into the Center.

All the trees were so *green* and the fish and swans sparkled in and on the water, and the birds sang, and he gave me a living bird, a real live tweeting yellow jumping bird in a spacious, glamorous cage; I love this bird and sometimes it sings. It may only live a year, he warned me, but then I can have another.

Sometimes I go to a cubicle in the foyer of one of the historic buildings, and read out announcements over the speaker. They pay me in Center credit discs, but I hardly need any money of my own.

The two rooms that are mine on Fairgrove Avenue are marvelous. The lights go on and off when you come in or go out, and the curtains draw themselves when it gets dark, or the blinds come down when it's too bright. The shower room always smells fresh, like a summer glade is supposed to, and perhaps once did. I see him four, five or six times every week, and we go to dinner and to films, and he's always bringing me real flowers and chocolates and fruit and honey. He even buys me books to read. Some days, I learn new words from the dictionary.

When he made love to me for the first time, it was a strange experience, but he was very gentle. It seemed to me I might come to like it very much, (and I was right), although in a way, it still seems rather an embarrassing thing to do.

That first night, after, he held me in his arms, and I enjoyed this. No one had ever held me caringly, protectingly, like that, ever before. He told me, too, about the girl who canced. He seemed deeply distressed, as if no one ever dies that way, but then, in Centers, under domes, death isn't ever certain.

All my mother tried to get was time, and when that ran out, control of pain and a secure exit. But my darling seems to think that his girl had wanted much, much more, and that I should want more too. And in a way that scares me, because I may not even live to be twenty, and then he'll break his heart again. But then again he'll probably find someone else. And maybe I'll be strong like my mother. I hope so. I want to keep my promise about the children. If I can get Angel settled, she can carry on after me. But I'll need ten or eleven years for that.

Something funny happened yesterday. He said, he would bring me a toy tomorrow—today. Yes, a toy, though I'm a woman, and his lover. I never had a toy. I love my bird best. I love him, too.

The most peculiar thing is, though, that I miss my mother. I keep on remembering what she said to me, her blows and injunctions. Going shopping with her, or to the cinema; how, when her teeth were always breaking, she got into such a rage.

I remember mistily when I was small, the endless days of weather Warnings when she, too, was trapped in the house, my fellow prisoner, and how the rain would start to pour down, horrible sinister torrents that frightened me, although then I didn't know why. All the poisons and the radioactivity that have accumulated and go on gathering on everything in an unseen glittering, and which the sky somehow collects and which the rain washes down from the sky in a deluge. The edited pay-TV seldom reports the accidents and oversights which continually cause this. Sometimes an announcement would come on and tell everyone just to get indoors off the streets, and no reason given, and no rain or wind even. The police cars would go about the roads sounding their sirens, and then they too would slink into holes to hide. But next day, usually there was the All Clear.

In the Center, TV isn't edited. I was curious to see how they talked about the leaks and pollutions, here. Actually they don't seem to mention them at all. It can't be very important, underdome.

But I do keep remembering one morning, that morning of a colossal rain, when I was six or seven. I was trying to look out at the forbidden world, with my nose pressed to the Sealtite. All I could see through the distorting material was a wavering leaden rush of liquid. And then I saw something so alien I let out a squeal.

"What is it?" my mother demanded. She had been washing the breakfast dishes in half the morning ration of domestic filtered water, clashing the plates bad-temperedly. "Come on, Greena, don't just make silly noises."

I pointed at the Sealtite. My mother came to see.

Together we looked through the fall of rain, to where a tiny girl, only about a year old, was standing—*out on the street*. Not knowing how she got there—strayed from some squat, most likely. She wore a pair of little blue shorts and nothing else, and she clutched a square of ancient blanket that was her doll. Even through the sealed pane and the rainfall you could see she was bawling and crying in terror.

"Jesus Christ and Mary the Mother," said my own mother on a breath. Her face was scoured white as our sink. But her eyes were blazing fires, hot enough to quench the rain.

And next second she was thrusting me into the TV room, locking me in, shouting, *Stay there don't you move or I'll murder you!*

Then I heard both our front doors being opened. Shut. When they opened again and shut again, I heard a high-pitched infantile roaring. The roar got louder and possessed the house. Then it fell quiet. I realized my mother had flown out into the weather and grabbed the lost child and brought her under shelter.

Of course, it was no use. When my mother carried her to the emergency unit next day, after the All Clear, the child was dying. She was so tiny. She held her blanket to the end and scorned my mother, the nurse, the kindly needle of oblivion. Only the blanket was her friend. Only the blanket had stayed and suffered with her in the rain.

When she was paying for the treatment and our own

decontam, the unit staff said horrible things to my mother, about her stupidity until I started to cry in humiliated fear. My mother ignored me and only faced them out like an untamed vixen, snarling with her cracked teeth.

All the way home I whined and railed at her. Why had she exposed us to those wicked people with their poking instruments and boiling showers, the hurt and rancor, the downpour of words? (I was jealous too, I realize now, of that intruding poisonous child. I'd been till then the only one in our house.)

Go up to bed! shouted my mother. I wouldn't.

At last she turned on me and thrashed me with the plastic belt. Violent, it felt as if she thrashed the whole world, till in the end she made herself stop.

But now I'm here with my darling, and my lovely bird singing. I can see a corner of a green park from both my windows. And it never, never rains.

It's funny how I miss her, my mother, so much.

THE SUN SPIDER
By Lucius Shepard

*Lucius Shepard does not always write about
near-future wars in backward lands. Here
is what may be his first interplanetary novel-
ette—in which he dares "to boldly go where
no man has ever gone before" (to quote
Star Trek) to the surface of the blazing
sun itself and the possibility of a life form
to which such an atomic furnace would be
home.*

". . . In Africa's Namib Desert, one of the
most hostile environments on the face of the
earth, lives a creature known as the sun spider.
Its body is furred pale gold, the exact color of
the sand beneath which it burrows in search of
its prey, disturbing scarcely a grain in its passage. It emerges from hiding only to snatch its
prey, and were you to look directly at it from
an inch away, you might never notice its presence. Nature is an efficient process, tending to
repeat elegant solutions to the problem of survival in such terrible places. Thus, if—as I posit—
particulate life exists upon the Sun, I would
not be startled to learn it has adopted a similar
form."

from *Alchemical Diaries*
by Reynolds Dulambre

1
Carolyn

My husband Reynolds and I arrived on Helios Station
following four years in the Namib, where he had delivered himself of the *Diaries,* including the controversial
Solar Equations, and where I had become adept in the
uses of boredom. We were met at the docking arm by
the administrator of the Physics Section, Dr. Davis
Brent, who escorted us to a reception given in Reynolds' honor, held in one of the pleasure domes that
blistered the skin of the station. Even had I been
unaware that Brent was one of Reynolds' chief detrac-
tors, I would have known the two of them for adver-
saries: in manner and physicality, they were total
opposites, like cobra and mongoose. Brent was pudgy,
of medium stature, with a receding hairline, and dressed
in a drab standard-issue jumpsuit. Reynolds—at thirty-
seven, only two years younger—might have been ten
years his junior. He was tall and lean, with chestnut
hair that fell to the shoulders of his cape, and possessed of that craggy nobility of feature one associates
with a Shakespearean lead. Both were on their best
behavior, but they could barely manage civility, and so
it was quite a relief when we reached the dome and
were swept away into a crowd of admiring techs and
scientists.

Helios Station orbited the south pole of the Sun, and
through the ports I had a view of a docking arm to
which several of the boxy ships that journeyed into the
coronosphere were moored. Leaving Reynolds to be
lionized, I lounged beside one of the ports and gazed
toward Earth, pretending I was celebrating Nation
Day in Abidjan rather than enduring this gathering of
particle pushers and inductive reasoners, most of whom
were gawking at Reynolds, perhaps hoping he would
live up to his reputation and perform a drugged col-
lapse or start a fight. I watched him and Brent talking.
Brent's body language was toadying, subservient, like
that of a dog trying to curry favor; he would clasp his
hands and tip his head to the side when making some

point, as if begging his master not to strike him. Reynolds stood motionless, arms folded across his chest.

At one point Brent said, "I can't see what purpose you hope to achieve in beaming protons into coronal holes," and Reynolds, in his most supercilious tone, responded by saying that he was merely poking about in the weeds with a long stick.

I was unable to hear the next exchange, but then I did hear Brent say, "That may be, but I don't think you understand the openness of our community. The barriers you've erected around your research go against the spirit, the . . ."

"All my goddamned life," Reynolds cut in, broadcasting in a stagey baritone, "I've been harassed by little men. Men who've carved out some cozy academic niche by footnoting my work and then decrying it. Mousey little bastards like you. And that's why I maintain my privacy . . . to keep the mice from nesting in my papers."

He strode off toward the refreshment table, leaving Brent smiling at everyone, trying to show that he had not been affected by the insult. A slim brunette attached herself to Reynolds, engaging him in conversation. He illustrated his points with florid gestures, leaning over her, looking as if he were about to enfold her in his cape, and not long afterward they made a discreet exit.

Compared to Reynolds' usual public behavior, this was a fairly restrained display, but sufficient to make the gathering forget my presence. I sipped a drink, listening to the chatter, feeling no sense of betrayal. I was used to Reynolds' infidelities, and, indeed, I had come to thrive on them. I was grateful he had found his brunette. Though our marriage was not devoid of the sensual, most of our encounters were ritual in nature, and after four years of isolation in the desert, I needed the emotional sustenance of a lover. Helios would, I believed, provide an ample supply.

Shortly after Reynolds had gone, Brent came over to the port, and to my amazement, he attempted to pick me up. It was one of the most inept seductions to which I have ever been subject. He contrived to touch me time and again as if by accident, and complimented me several times on the largeness of my eyes. I managed to turn the conversation into harmless channels, and he got off into politics, a topic on which he considered himself expert.

"My essential political philosophy," he said, "derives from a story by one of the masters of twentieth century speculative fiction. In the story, a man sends his mind into the future and finds himself in a utopian setting, a greensward surrounded by white buildings, with handsome men and beautiful women strolling everywhere . . ."

I cannot recall how long I listened to him, to what soon became apparent as a ludicrous Libertarian fantasy, before bursting into laughter. Brent looked confused by my reaction, but then masked confusion by joining in my laughter. "Ah, Carolyn," he said. "I had you going there, didn't I? You thought I was serious!"

I took pity on him. He was only a sad little man with an inflated self-opinion; and, too, I had been told that he was in danger of losing his administrative post. I spent the best part of an hour in making him feel important; then, scraping him off, I went in search of a more suitable companion.

My first lover on Helios Station, a young particle physicist named Thom, proved overweening in his affections. The sound of my name seemed to transport him; often he would lift his head and say, "Carolyn, Carolyn," as if by doing this he might capture my essence. I found him absurd, but I was starved for attention, and though I could not reciprocate in kind, I was delighted in being the object of his single-mindedness. We would meet each day in one of the pleasure domes, dance to drift, and drink paradisiacs—I developed quite a fondness for Amouristes—and then retire to a private chamber, there to make love and watch the sunships return from their fiery journeys. It was Thom's dream to be assigned someday to a sunship, and he would rhapsodize on the glories attendant upon swooping down through layers of burning gases. His fixation with the scientific adventure eventually caused me to break off the affair. Years of exposure to Reynolds' work had armored me against any good opinion of science, and further I did not want to be reminded of my proximity to the Sun: sometimes I imagined I could hear it hissing, roaring, and feel its flames tonguing the metal walls, preparing to do us to a crisp with a single lick.

By detailing my infidelity, I am not trying to characterize my marriage as loveless. I loved Reynolds, though my affections had waned somewhat. And he loved me in his own way. Prior to our wedding, he had announced that he intended our union to be "a marriage of souls." But this was no passionate outcry, rather a statement of scientific intent. He believed in souls, believed they were the absolute expression of a life, a quality that pervaded every particle of matter and gave rise to the lesser expressions of personality and physicality. His search for particulate life upon the Sun was essentially an attempt to isolate and communicate with the anima, and the "marriage of souls" was for him the logical goal of twenty-first century physics. It occurs to me now that this search may have been his sole means of voicing his deepest emotions, and it was our core problem that I thought he would someday love me in a way that would satisfy me, whereas he felt my satisfaction could be guaranteed by the application of scientific method.

To further define our relationship, I should mention that he once wrote me that the "impassive, vaguely oriental beauty" of my face reminded him of "those serene countenances used to depict the solar disc on ancient sailing charts." Again, this was not the imagery of passion: he considered this likeness a talisman, a lucky charm. He was a magical thinker, perceiving himself as more akin to the alchemists than to his peers, and like the alchemists, he gave credence to the power of similarities. Whenever he made love to me, he was therefore making love to the Sun. To the great detriment of our marriage, every beautiful woman became for him the Sun, and thus a potential tool for use in his rituals. Given his enormous ego, it would have been out of character for him to have been faithful, and had he not utilized sex as a concentrative ritual, I am certain he would have invented another excuse for infidelity. And, I suppose, I would have had to contrive some other justification for my own.

During those first months I was indiscriminate in my choice of lovers, entering into affairs with both techs and a number of Reynolds' colleagues. Reynolds himself was no more discriminating, and our lives took separate paths. Rarely did I spend a night in our apartment, and I paid no attention whatsoever to Reynolds' work. But then one afternoon as I lay with my latest lover in the private chamber of a pleasure dome, the door slid open and in walked Reynolds. My lover—a tech whose name eludes me—leaped up and began struggling into his clothes, apologizing all the while. I shouted at Reynolds, railed at him. What right did he have to humiliate me this way? I had never burst in on him and his whores, had I? Imperturbable, he stared at me, and after the tech had scurried out, he continued to stare, letting me exhaust my anger. At last, breathless, I sat glaring at him, still angry, yet also feeling a measure of guilt . . . not relating to my affair, but to the fact that I had become pregnant as a result of my last encounter with Reynolds. We had tried for years to have a child, and despite knowing how important a child would be to him, I had put off the announcement. I was no longer confident of his capacity for fatherhood.

"I'm sorry about this." He waved at the bed. "It was urgent I see you, and I didn't think."

The apology was uncharacteristic, and my surprise at it drained away the dregs of anger. "What is it?" I asked.

Contrary emotions played over his face. "I've got him," he said.

I knew what he was referring to: he always personified the object of his search, although before too long he began calling it "the Spider." I was happy for his success, but for some reason it had made me a little afraid, and I was at a loss for words.

"Do you want to see him?" He sat beside me. "He's imaged in one of the tanks."

I nodded.

I was sure he was going to embrace me. I could see in his face the desire to break down the barriers we had erected, and I imagined now his work was done, he would be as close as we had once hoped, that honesty and love would finally have their day. But the moment passed, and his face hardened. He stood and paced the length of the chamber. Then he whirled around, hammered a fist into his palm, and with all the passion he had been unable to direct toward me, he said, "I've got him!"

"I had been watching him for over a week without knowing it: a large low-temperature area shifting about in a coronal hole. It was only by chance that I recognized him; I inadvertantly nudged the color controls of a holo tank, and brought part of the low-temperature area into focus, revealing a many-armed ovoid of constantly changing primary hues, the arms attenuating and vanishing: I have observed some of these arms reach ten thousand miles in length, and I have no idea what limits apply to their size. He consists essentially of an inner complex of ultracold neutrons enclosed by an intense magnetic field. Lately it has occurred to me that certain of the coronal holes may be no more than the attitude of his movements. Aside from these few facts and guesses, he remains a mystery, and I have begun to suspect that no matter how many elements of his nature are disclosed, he will always remain so."

from *Collected Notes*
by Reynolds Dulambre

2
Reynolds

Brent's face faded in on the screen, his features composed into one of those fawning smiles. "Ah, Reynolds," he said. "Glad I caught you."

"I'm busy," I snapped, reaching for the off switch.

"Reynolds!"

His desperate tone caught my attention.

"I need to talk to you," he said. "A matter of some importance."

I gave an amused sniff. "I doubt that."

"Oh, but it is . . . to both of us."

An oily note had crept into his voice, and I lost patience, "I'm going to switch off, Brent. Do you want to say good-bye, or should I just cut you off in mid-sentence?"

"I'm warning you, Reynolds!"

"Warning me? I'm all aflutter, Brent. Are you planning to assault me?"

His face grew flushed. "I'm sick of your arrogance!" he shouted. "Who the hell are you to talk down to me? At least I'm productive . . . you haven't done any work for weeks!"

I started to ask how he knew that, but then realized he could have monitored my energy usage via the station computers.

"You think . . ." he began, but at that point I did cut him off and turned back to the image of the Spider floating in the holo tank, its arms weaving a slow dance. I had never believed he was more than dreams, vague magical images, the grandfather wizard trapped in flame, in golden light, in the heart of power. I'd hoped, I'd wanted to believe. But I hadn't been able to accept his reality until I came to Helios, and the dreams grew stronger. Even now I wondered if belief was merely an extension of madness. I have never doubted the efficacy of madness: it is my constant, my referent in chaos.

The first dream had come when I was . . . what? Eleven, twelve? No older. My father had been chasing me, and I had sought refuge in a cave of golden light, a mist of pulsing, shifting light that contained a voice I could not quite hear: it was too vast to hear. I was merely a word upon its tongue, and there had been other words aligned around me, words I needed to understand or else I would be cast out from the light. The Solar Equations—which seemed to have been visited upon me rather than a product of reason—embodied the shiftings, the mysterious principles I had sensed in the golden light, hinted at the arcane processes, the potential for union and dissolution that I had apprehended in every dream. Each time I looked at them, I felt tremors in my flesh, my spirit, as if signaling the onset of a profound change, and . . .

The beeper sounded again, doubtless another call from Brent, and I ignored it. I turned to the readout from the particle traps monitored by the station computers. When I had discovered that the proton bursts being emitted from the Spider's coronal hole were patterned—coded, I'm tempted to say—I had been elated, especially considering that a study of these bursts inspired me to create several addenda to the Equations. They had still been fragmentary, however, and I'd had the notion that I would have to get closer to the Spider in order to complete them . . . perhaps join one of the flights into the coronosphere. My next reaction had been fear. I had realized it was possible the Spider's control was such that these bursts were living artifacts, structural components that maintained a tenuous connection with the rest of his body. If so, then the computers, the entire station, might be under his scrutiny . . . if not his control. Efforts to prove the truth of this had proved inconclusive, but this inconclusiveness was in itself an affirmative answer; the computers were not capable of evasion, and it had been obvious that evasiveness was at work here.

The beeper broke off, and I began to ask myself questions. I had been laboring under the assumption that the Spider had in some way summoned me, but now an alternate scenario presented itself. Could I have stirred him to life? I had beamed protons into the

coronal holes, hadn't I? Could I have educated some
dumb thing . . . or perhaps brought him to life? Were
all my dreams a delusionary system of unparalleled
complexity and influence, or was I merely a madman
who happened to be right?

These considerations might have seemed irrelevant
to my colleagues, but when I related them to my urge
to approach the spider more closely, they took on
extreme personal importance. How could I trust such
an urge? I stared at the Spider, at its arms waving in
their thousand-mile-long dance, their slow changes in
configuration redolent of Kali's dance, of myths even
more obscure. There were no remedies left for my
fear. I had stopped work, drugged myself to prevent
dreams, and yet I could do nothing to remove my
chief concern: that the Spider would use its control
over the computers (if, indeed, it did control them) to
manipulate me.

I turned off the holo tank and headed out into the
corridor, thinking I would have a few drinks. I hadn't
gone fifty feet when Brent accosted me; I brushed past
him, but he fell into step beside me. He exuded a false
heartiness that was even more grating than his usual
obsequiousness.

"Production," he said. "That's our keynote here,
Reynolds."

I glowered at him.

"We can't afford to have dead wood lying around,"
he went on. "Now if you're having a problem, perhaps
you need a fresh eye. I'd be glad to take a look . . ."

I gave him a push, sending him wobbling, but it
didn't dent his mood.

"Even the best of us run up against stone walls,"
he said. "And in your case, well, how long has it been
since your last major work. Eight years? Ten? You
can only ride the wind of your youthful successes for
so . . ."

My anxiety flared into rage. I drove my fist into his
stomach, and he dropped, gasping like a fish out of
water. I was about to kick him, when I was grabbed
from behind by the black-clad arms of a security guard.

Two more guards intervened as I wrenched free, cursing at Brent. One of the guards helped Brent up and asked what should be done with me.

"Let him go," he said, rubbing his gut. "The man's not responsible."

I lunged at him, but was shoved back. "Bastard!" I shouted. "You smarmy little shit, I'll kill you if . . ."

A guard gave me another shove.

"Please, Reynolds," Brent said in a placating tone. "Don't worry . . . I'll make sure you receive due credit."

I had no idea what he meant, and was too angry to wonder at it. I launched more insults as the guards escorted him away.

No longer in the mood for a public place, I returned to the apartment and sat scribbling meaningless notes, gazing at an image of the Spider that played across one entire wall. I was so distracted that I didn't notice Carolyn had entered until she was standing close beside me. The Spider's colors flickered across her, making her into an incandescent silhouette.

"What are you doing?" she asked, sitting on the floor.

"Nothing." I tossed my notepad aside.

"Something's wrong."

"Not at all . . . I'm just tired."

She regarded me expressionlessly. "It's the Spider, isn't it?"

I told her that, Yes, the work was giving me trouble, but it wasn't serious. I'm not sure if I wanted her as much as it seemed I did, or if I was using sex to ward off more questions. Whatever the case, I lowered myself beside her, kissed her, touched her breasts, and soon we were in the heated secret place where—I thought—not even the Spider's eyes could pry. I told her I loved her in that rushed breathless way that is less an intimate disclosure than a form of gasping, of shaping breath to accommodate movement. That was the only way I have ever been able to tell her the best of my feeling, and it was because I was shamed by this that we did not make love more often.

Afterward I could see she wanted to say something

important: it was working in her face. But I didn't
want to hear it, to be trapped into some new level of
intimacy. I turned from her, marshaling words that
would signal my need for privacy, and my eyes fell on
the wall where the image of the Spider still danced
. . . danced in a way I had never before witnessed. His
colors were shifting through the spectrum of reds and
violets, and his arms writhed in a rhythm that brought
to mind the rhythms of sex, the slow beginning, the
furious rush to completion, as if he had been watching
us and was now mimicking the act.

Carolyn spoke my name, but I was transfixed by the
sight and could not answer. She drew in a sharp breath,
and seconds later I heard her cross the room and make
her exit. The Spider ceased his dance, lapsing into one
of his normal patterns. I scrambled up, went to the
controls and flicked the display switch off. But the
image did not fade. Instead, the spider's colors grew
brighter, washing from fiery red to gold and at last to
a white so brilliant, I had to shield my eyes. I could
almost feel his heat on my skin, hear the sibilant kiss
of his molten voice. I was certain he was in the room,
I knew I was going to burn, to be swallowed in that
singing heat, and I cried out for Carolyn, not wanting
to leave unsaid all those things I had withheld from
her. Then my fear reached such proportions that I
collapsed and sank into a dream, not a nightmare as
one might expect, but a dream of an immense city,
where I experienced a multitude of adventures and
met with a serene fate.

". . . To understand Dulambre, his relationship with his father must be examined closely.
Alex Dulambre was a musician and poet, regarded to be one of the progenitors of drift: a
popular dance form involving the use of impro-
vised lyrics. He was flamboyant, handsome,
amoral, and these qualities, allied with a talent
for seduction, led him on a twenty-five-year fling
through the boudoirs of the powerful, from the
corporate towers of Abidjan to the Gardens of

Novo Sibersk, and lastly to a beach on Mozambique, where at the age of forty-four he died horribly, a victim of a neural poison that purportedly had been designed for him by the noted chemist Virginia Holland. It was Virginia who was reputed to be Reynolds' mother, but no tests were ever conducted to substantiate the rumor. All we know for certain is that one morning Alex received a crate containing an artificial womb and the embryo of his son. An attached folder provided proof of his paternity and a note stating that the mother wanted no keepsake to remind her of an error in judgment.''

"Alex felt no responsibility for the child, but liked having a relative to add to his coterie. Thus it was that Reynolds spent his first fourteen years globe-trotting, sleeping on floors, breakfasting off the remains of the previous night's party, and generally being ignored, if not rejected. As a defense against both this rejection and his father's charisma, Reynolds learned to mimic Alex's flamboyance and developed similar verbal skills. By the age of eleven he was performing regularly with his father's band, creating a popular sequence of drifts that detailed the feats of an all-powerful wizard and the trials of those who warred against him. Alex took pride in these performances; he saw himself as less father than elder brother, and he insisted on teaching Reynolds a brother's portion of the world. To this end he had one of his lovers seduce the boy on his twelfth birthday, and from then on Reynolds also mimicked his father's omnivorous sexuality. They did, indeed, seem brothers, and to watch Alex drape an arm over the boy's shoulders, the casual observer might have supposed them to be even closer. But there was no strong bond between them, only a history of abuse. This is not to say that Reynolds was unaffected by his father's death, an event to which he was witness. The sight of Alex's agony left him severely trau-

matized and with a fear of death bordering on
the morbid. When we consider this fear in alli-
ance with his difficulty in expressing love—an
legacy of his father's rejections—we have gone
far in comprehending both his marital problems
and his obsession with immortality, with immortality in any form, even that of a child . . ."

> from *The Last Alchemist*
> by Russell E. Barrett

3
Carolyn

Six months after the implantation of Reynolds' daughter in an artificial womb, I ran into Davis Brent at a
pleasure dome where I had taken to spending my
afternoons, enjoying the music, writing a memoir of
my days with Reynolds, but refraining from infidelity.
The child and my concern for Reynolds' mental state
had acted to make me conservative: there were important decisions to be made, disturbing events afoot, and
I wanted no distractions.

This particular dome was quite small, its walls
Maxfield Parrish holographs—alabaster columns and
scrolled archways that opened onto rugged mountains
drenched in the colors of a pastel sunset; the patrons
sat at marble tables, their drab jumpsuits at odds with
the decadence of the decor. Sitting there, writing, I
felt like some sad and damaged lady of a forgotten
age, brought to the sorry pass of autobiography by a
disappointment at love.

Without announcing himself, Brent dropped onto
the bench opposite me and stared. A smile nicked the
corners of his mouth. I waited for him to speak, and
finally asked what he wanted.

"Merely to offer my congratulations," he said.

"On what occasion?" I asked.

"The occasion of your daughter."

The implantation had been done under a seal of

privacy, and I was outraged that he had discovered my secret.

Before I could speak, he favored me with an unctuous smile and said, "As administrator, little that goes on here escapes me." From the pocket of his jumpsuit he pulled a leather case of the sort used to carry holographs. "I have a daughter myself, a lovely child. I sent her back to Earth some months back." He opened the case, studied the contents, and continued, his words freighted with an odd tension. "I had the computer do a portrait of how she'll look in a few years. Care to see it?"

I took the case and was struck numb. The girl depicted was seven or eight, and was the spitting image of myself at her age.

"I never should have sent her back," said Brent. "It appears the womb has been misshipped, and I may not be able to find her. Even the records have been misplaced. And the tech who performed the implantation, he returned on the ship with the womb and has dropped out of sight."

I came to my feet, but he grabbed my arm and sat me back down. "Check on it if you wish," he said. "But it's the truth. If you want to help find her, you'd be best served by listening."

"Where is she?" A sick chill spread through me, and my heart felt as if it were not beating but trembling.

"Who knows? Sao Paolo, Paris. Perhaps one of the Urban Reserves."

"Please," I said, a catch in my voice. "Bring her back."

"If we work together, I'm certain we can find her."

"What do you want, what could you possibly want from me?"

He smiled again. "To begin with, I want copies of your husband's deep files. I need to know what he's working on."

I had no compunction against telling him; all my concern was for the child. "He's been investigating the possibility of life on the Sun."

The answer dismayed him. "That's ridiculous."

"It's true, he's found it!"

He gaped at me.

"He calls it the Sun Spider. It's huge . . . and made of some kind of plasma."

Brent smacked his forehead as to punish himself for an oversight. "Of course! That section in the *Diaries*." He shook his head in wonderment. "All that metaphysical gabble about particulate life . . . I can't believe that has any basis in fact."

"I'll help you," I said. "But please bring her back!"

He reached across the table and caressed my cheek. I stiffened but did not draw away. "The last thing I want to do is hurt you, Carolyn. Take my word, it's all under control."

Under control.

Now it seems to me that he was right, and that the controlling agency was no man or creature, but a coincidence of possibility and wish such as may have been responsible for the spark that first set fire to the stars.

Over the next two weeks I met several times with Brent, on each occasion delivering various of Reynolds' files; only one remained to be secured, and I assured Brent I would soon have it. How I hated him! And yet we were complicitors. Each time we met in his lab, a place of bare metal walls and computer banks, we would discuss means of distracting Reynolds in order to perform my thefts, and during one occasion I asked why he had chosen Reynolds' work to pirate, since he had never been an admirer.

"Oh, but I am an admirer," he said. "Naturally I despise his personal style, the passing off of drugs and satyrism as scientific method. But I've never doubted his genius. Why, I was the one who approved his residency grant."

Disbelief must have showed on my face, for he went on to say, "It's true. Many of the board were inclined to reject him, thinking he was no longer capable of important work. But when I saw the Solar Equations,

I knew he was still a force to reckon with. Have you looked at them?"

"I don't understand the mathematics."

"Fragmentary as they are, they're astounding, elegant. There's something almost mystical about their structure. You get the idea there's no need to study them, that if you keep staring at them they'll crawl into your brain and work some change." He made a church-and-steeple of his fingers. "I hoped he'd finish them here but . . . well, maybe that last file."

We went back to planning Reynolds' distraction. He rarely left the apartment anymore, and Brent and I decided that the time to act would be during his birthday party next week. He would doubtless be heavily drugged, and I would be able to slip into the back room and access his computer. The discussion concluded, Brent stepped to the door that led to his apartment, keyed it open and invited me for a drink. I declined, but he insisted and I preceded him inside.

The apartment was decorated in appallingly bad taste. His furniture was of a translucent material that glowed a sickly bluish-green, providing the only illumination. Matted under glass on one wall was a twentieth century poster of a poem entitled "Desiderata," whose verses were the height of mawkish romanticism. The other walls were hung with what appeared to be ancient tapestries, but which on close inspection proved to be pornographic counterfeits, depicting subjects such as women mating with stags. Considering these appointments, I found hypocritical Brent's condemnation of Reynolds' private life. He poured wine from a decanter and made banal small talk, touching me now and then as he had during our first meeting. I forced an occasional smile, and at last, thinking I had humored him long enough, I told him I had to leave.

"Oh, no," he said, encircling my waist with an arm. "We're not through."

I pried his arm loose: he was not very strong.

"Very well." He touched a wall control, and a door to the corridor slid open. "Go."

The harsh white light shining through the door transformed him into a shadowy figure and made his pronouncement seem a threat.

"Go on." He drained his wine. "I've got no hold on you."

God, he thought he was clever! And he was . . . more clever than I, perhaps more so than Reynolds. And though he was to learn that cleverness has its limits, particularly when confronted by the genius of fate, it was sufficient to the moment.

"I'll stay," I said.

". . . In the dance of the Spider, in his patterned changes in color, the rhythmic waving of his fiery arms, was a kind of language, the language that the Equations sought to clarify, the language of my dreams. I sat for hours watching him; I recorded several sequences on pocket holographs and carried them about in hopes that this propinquity would illuminate the missing portions of the Equations. I made some progress, but I had concluded that a journey sunwards was the sort of propinquity I needed—I doubted I had the courage to achieve it. However, legislating against my lack of courage was the beauty I had begun to perceive in the Spider's dance, the hypnotic grace: like that of a Balinese dancer, possessing a similar allure. I came to believe that those movements were signaling all knowledge, infinite possibility. My dreams began to be figured with creatures that I would have previously considered impossible—dragons, imps, men with glowing hands or whose entire forms were glowing, all a ghostly, grainy white; now these creatures came to seem not only possible but likely inhabitants of a world that was coming more and more into focus, a world to which I was greatly attracted. Sometimes I would lie in bed all day, hoping for more dreams of that world, of the wizard who controlled it. It may be that I was using the dreams to escape confronting a difficult and frightening choice. But in truth I have lately doubted that it is even mine to make."

from *Collected Notes*
by Reynolds Dulambre

4
Reynolds

I remember little of the party, mostly dazed glimpses of breasts and thighs, sweaty bodies, lidded eyes. I remember the drift, which was performed by a group of techs. They played Alex's music as an *hommage*, and I was taken back to my years with the old bastard-maker, to memories of beatings, of walking in on him and his lovers, of listening to him pontificate. And, of course, I recalled that night in Mozambique when I watched him claw at his eyes, his face. Spitting missiles of blood, unable to scream, having bitten off his tongue. Sobered, I got to my feet and staggered into the bedroom, where it was less crowded, but still too crowded for my mood. I grabbed a robe, belted it on and keyed my study door.

As I entered, Carolyn leaped up from my computer. On the screen was displayed what looked to be a page from my deep files. She tried to switch off the screen, but I caught her arm and checked the page: I had not been mistaken. "What are you doing?" I shouted, yanking her away from the computer.

"I was just curious." She tried to jerk free.

Then I spotted the microcube barnacled to the computer: she had been recording. "What's that?" I asked, forcing her to look at it. "What's that? Who the hell are you working for?"

She began to cry, but I wasn't moved. We had betrayed each other a thousand times, but never to this degree.

"Damn you!" I slapped her. "Who is it?"

She poured out the story of Brent's plan, his demands on her. "I'm sorry," she said, sobbing. "I'm sorry."

I felt so much then, I couldn't characterize it as fear or anger or any specific emotion. In my mind's eye I saw the child, that scrap of my soul, disappearing down some earthly sewer. I threw off my robe, stepped into a jumpsuit.

"Where are you going?" Carolyn asked, wiping away tears.

I zipped up the jumpsuit.

"Don't!" Carolyn tried to haul me back from the door. "You don't understand!"

I shoved her down, locked the door behind me, and went storming out through the party and into the corridor. Rage flooded me. I needed to hurt Brent. My reason was so obscured that when I reached his apartment, I saw nothing suspicious in the fact that the door was open . . . though I later realized he must have had a spy at the party to warn him of anything untoward. Inside, Brent was lounging in one of those ridiculous glowing chairs, a self-satisfied look on his face, and it was that look more than anything, more than the faint scraping at my rear, that alerted me to danger. I spun around to see a security guard bringing his laser to bear on me. I dove at him, feeling a discharge of heat next to my ear, and we went down together. He tried to gouge my eyes, but I twisted away, latched both hands in his hair and smashed his head against the wall. The third time his head impacted, it made a softer sound than it had the previous two, and I could feel the skull shifting beneath the skin like pieces of broken tile in a sack. I rolled off the guard, horrified, yet no less enraged. And when I saw that Brent's chair was empty, when I heard him shouting in the corridor, even though I knew his shouts would bring more guards, my anger grew so great that I cared nothing for myself, I only wanted him dead.

By the time I emerged from the apartment, he was sprinting around a curve in the corridor. My laser scored the metal wall behind him the instant before he went out of sight. I ran after him. Several of the doorways along the corridor slid open, heads popped out, and on seeing me, ducked back in. I rounded the curve, spotted Brent, and fired again . . . too high by inches. Before I could correct my aim, half-a-dozen guards boiled out of a side corridor and dragged him into cover. Their beams drew smoldering lines in the metal by my hip, at my feet, and I retreated, firing as I did, pounding on the doors, thinking that I would barricade myself in one of the rooms and try to debunk Brent's lies, to reveal his deceit over the intercom. But none of the doors opened, their occupants having apparently been frightened by my weapon.

Two guards poked their heads around the curve, fired, and one of the beams came so near that it torched the fabric of my jumpsuit at the knee. I beat out the flames and ran full tilt. Shouts behind me, beams of ruby light skewering the air above my head. Ahead, I made out a red door that led to a docking arm, and having no choice, I keyed it open and raced along the narrow passageway. The first three moorings were empty, but the fourth had a blue light glowing beside the entrance hatch, signaling the presence of a ship. I slipped inside, latched it, and moved along the tunnel into the airlock; I bolted that shut, then went quickly along the mesh-walled catwalk toward the control room, toward the radio. I was on the point of entering the room, when I felt a shudder go all through the ship and knew it had cast loose, that it was headed sunwards.

Panicked, I burst into the control room. The chairs fronting the instrument panel were empty, the panel itself aflicker with lights; the ship was being run by computer. I sat at the board, trying to override, but no tactic had any effect. Then Brent's voice came over the speakers. "You've bought yourself a little time, Reynolds," he said. "That's all. When the ship returns, we'll have you."

I laughed.

It had been my hope that he had initiated the ship's flight, but his comments made clear that I was now headed toward the confrontation I had for so long

sought to avoid, brought to this pass by a computer
under the control of the creature for whom I had
searched my entire life, a creature of fire and dreams,
the stuff of souls. I knew I would not survive it. But
though I had always dreaded the thought of death,
now that death was hard upon me, I was possessed of
a strange confidence and calm . . . calm enough to
send this transmission, to explore the confines of this
my coffin, even to read the manuals that explain its
operation. I had never attempted to understand the
workings of the sunships, and I was interested to read
of the principles that underlie each flight. As the ship
approaches the Sun, it will monitor the magnetic field
direction and determine if the Archimedean spiral of
the solar wind is oriented outward.

If all is as it should be, it will descend to within one
A.U. and will skip off the open-diverging magnetic
field of a coronal hole. It will be traveling at such a
tremendous speed, its actions will be rather like those
of a charged particle caught in a magnetic field, and as
the field opens out, it will be flung upward, back
toward Helios . . . that is, it will be flung up and out if
a creature who survives by stripping particles of their
charge does not inhabit the coronal hole in question.
But there is little chance of that.

I wonder how it will feel to have my charge stripped.
I would not care to suffer the agonies of my father.

The closer I come to the Sun, the more calm I
become. My mortal imperfections seem to be flaking
away. I feel clean and minimal, and I have the notion
that I will soon be even simpler, the essential splinter
of a man. I have so little desire left that only one
further thing occurs to me to say.

Carolyn, I . . .

      ". . . A man walking in a field of golden grass
   under a bright sky, walking steadfastly, though
   with no apparent destination, for the grasslands
   spread to the horizon, and his thoughts are crystal-
   clear, and his heart, too, is clear, for his past has

become an element of his present, and his future—visible as a sweep of golden grass carpeting the distant hills, beyond which lies a city sparkling like a glint of possibility—is as fluent and clear as his thought, and he knows his future will be shaped by his walking, by his thought and the power in his hands, especially by that power, and of all this he wishes now to speak to a woman whose love he denied, whose flesh had the purity of the clear bright sky and the golden grasses who was always the heart of his life even in the country of lies, and here in the heartland of the country of truth is truly loved at last . . ."

from *The Resolute Lover*
part of The White Dragon Cycle

5
Carolyn

After Reynolds had stolen the sunship—this, I was informed, had been the case—Brent confined me to my apartment and accused me of conspiring with Reynolds to kill him. I learned of Reynolds' death from the security guard who brought me supper that first night; he told me that a prominence (I pictured it to be a fiery fishing lure) had flung itself out from the Sun and incinerated the ship. I wept uncontrollably. Even after the computers began to translate the coded particle bursts emanating from the Spider's coronal hole, even when these proved to be the completed Solar Equations, embodied not only in mathematics but in forms comprehensible to a layman, still I wept. I was too overwhelmed by grief to realize what they might portend.

I was able to view the translations on Reynolds' computer, and when the stories of the White Dragon Cycle came into view, I understood that whoever or whatever had produced them had something in particular to say to me. It was *The Resolute Lover*, the first of the cycle, with its numerous references to a wronged

beautiful woman, that convinced me of this. I read the
story over and over, and in so doing I recalled Brent's
description of the feelings he had had while studying
the equations. I felt in the focus of some magical lens,
I felt a shimmering in my flesh, confusion in my thoughts
. . . not a confusion of motive but of thoughts running
in new patterns, colliding with each other like atoms
bred by a runaway reactor. I lost track of time, I lived
in a sweep of golden grasses, in an exotic city where
the concepts of unity and the divisible were not opposed, where villains and heroes and beasts enacted
ritual passions, where love was the ordering pulse of
existence.

One day Brent paid me a visit. He was plumped
with self-importance, with triumph. But though I hated
him, emotion seemed incidental to my goal—a goal his
visit helped to solidify—and I reacted to him mildly,
watching as he moved about the room, watching me
and smiling.

"You're calmer than I expected," he said.

I had no words for him, only calm. In my head the
Resolute Lover gazed into a crystal of Knowledge,
awaiting the advent of Power. I believe that I, too,
smiled.

"Well," he said. "Things don't always work out as
we plan. But I'm pleased with the result. The Spider
will be Reynolds' great victory . . . no way around
that. Still, I've managed to land the role of Sancho
Panza to his Don Quixote, the rationalist who guided
the madman on his course."

My smile was a razor, a knife, a flame.

"Quite sufficient," he went on, "to secure my post
. . . and perhaps even my immortality."

I spoke to him in an inaudible voice that said Death.

His manner grew more agitated; he twitched about
the room, touching things. "What will I do with you?"
he said. "I'd hate to send you to your judgment. Our
nights together . . . well, suffice it to say I would be
most happy if you'd stay with me. What do you think?
Shall I testify on your behalf, or would you prefer a
term on the Urban Reserves?"

Brent, Brent, Brent. His name was a kind of choice.

"Perhaps you'd like time to consider?" he said.

I wished my breath was poison.

He edged toward the door. "When you reach a decision, just tell the guard outside. You've two months 'til the next ship. I'm betting you'll choose survival."

My eyes sent him a black kiss.

"Really, Carolyn," he said. "You were never a faithful wife. Don't you think this pose of mourning somewhat out of character?"

Then he was gone, and I returned to my reading.

Love.

What part did it play in my desire for vengeance, my furious calm? Sorrow may have had more a part, but love was certainly a factor. Love as practiced by the Resolute Lover. This story communicated this rigorous emotion, and my heartsickness translated it to vengeful form. My sense of unreality, of tremulous being, increased day by day, and I barely touched my meals.

I am not sure when the Equations embodied by the story began to take hold, when the seeded knowledge became power. I believe it was nearly two weeks after Brent's visit. But though I felt my potential, my strength, I did not act immediately. In truth, I was not certain I could act or that action was to be my course. I was mad in the same way Reynolds had been: a madness of self-absorption, a concentration of such intensity that nothing less intense had the least relevance.

One night I left off reading, went into my bedroom and put on a sheer robe, then wrapped myself in a cowled cloak. I had no idea why I was doing this. The seductive rhythms of the story were coiling through my head and preventing thought. I walked into the front room and stood facing the door. Violent tremors shook my body. I felt frail, insubstantial, yet at the same time possessed of fantastic power: I knew that nothing could resist me . . . not steel or flesh or fire. Inspired by this confidence, I reached out my right hand to the door. The hand was glowing a pale white, its form flickering, the fingers lengthening and attenuating, appearing to ripple as in a graceful dance. I did not wonder at this. Everything was as it should be. And when my hand slid into the door, into the metal, neither did I consider that remarkable. I could feel the mechanisms of the lock, I—or rather my ghostly fingers—seemed to know the exact function of every metal bit, and after a moment the door hissed open.

The guard peered in, startled, and I hid the hand behind me. I backed away, letting the halves of my cloak fall apart. He stared, glanced left and right in the corridor, and entered. "How'd you do the lock?" he asked.

I said nothing.

He keyed the door, testing it, and slid it shut, leaving the two of us alone in the room. "Huh," he said. "Must have been a computer foul-up."

I came close beside him, my head tipped back as if to receive a kiss, and he smiled, he held me around the waist. His lips mashed against mine, and my right hand, seeming almost to be acting on its own, slipped into his side and touched something that beat wildly for a few seconds, and then spasmed. He pushed me away, clutching his chest, his face purpling, and fell to the floor. Emotionless, I stepped over him and went out into the corridor, walking at an unhurried pace, hiding my hand beneath the cloak.

On reaching Brent's apartment, I pressed the bell, and a moment later the door opened and he peered forth, looking sleepy and surprised. "Carolyn!" he said. "How did you get out?"

"I told the guard I planned to stay with you," I said, and as I had done with the guard, I parted the halves of my cloak.

His eyes dropped to my breasts. "Come in," he said, his voice blurred.

Once inside, I shed the cloak, concealing my hand behind me. I was so full of hate, my mind was heavy and blank like a stone. Brent poured some wine, but I refused the glass. My voice sounded dead, and he shot me a searching look and asked if I felt well. "I'm fine," I told him.

He set down the wine and came toward me, but I moved away.

"First," I said, "I want to know about my daughter."

That brought him up short. "You have no daughter," he said after a pause. "It was all a hoax."

"I don't believe you."

"I swear it's true," he said. "When you went for an exam, I had the tech inform you of a pregnancy. But you weren't pregnant. And when you came for the implantation procedure, he anesthetized you and simply stood by until you woke up."

It would have been in character, I realized, for him to have done this. Yet he also might have been clever enough to make up the story, and thus keep a hold on me, one he could inform me of should I prove recalcitrant.

"But you can have a child," he said, sidling toward me. "Our child, Carolyn. I'd like that, I'd like it very much." He seemed to be having some difficulty in getting the next words out, but finally they came: "I love you."

What twisted shape, I wondered, did love take in his brain?

"Do you?" I said.

"I know it must be hard to believe," he said. "You can't possibly understand the pressure I've been under, the demands that forced my actions. But I swear to you, Carolyn, I've always cared for you. I knew how oppressed you were by Reynolds. Don't you see? To an extent I was acting on your behalf. I wanted to free you."

He said all this in a whining tone, edging close, so close I could smell his bitter breath. He put a hand on my breast, lifted it . . . Perhaps he did love me in his way, for it seemed a treasuring touch. But mine was not. I laid my palely glowing hand on the back of his neck. He screamed, went rigid, and oh, how that scream made me feel! It was like music, his pain. He

stumbled backward, toppled over one of the luminous
chairs, and lay writhing, clawing his neck.

"Where is she?" I asked, kneeling beside him.

Spittle leaked between his gritted teeth. "I'll . . .
find her, bring her . . . oh!"

I saw I could never trust him. Desperate, he would
say anything. He might bring me someone else's child.
I touched his stomach, penetrating the flesh to the first
joint of my fingers, then wiggling them. Again he
screamed. Blood mapped the front of his jumpsuit.

"Where is she?" I no longer was thinking about the
child: she was lost, and I was only tormenting him.

His speech was incoherent, he tried to hump away. I
showed him my hand, how it glowed, and his eyes
bugged.

"Do you still love me?" I asked, touching his groin,
hooking my fingers and pulling at some fiber.

Agony bubbled in his throat, and he curled up around
his pain, clutching himself.

I could not stop touching him. I orchestrated his
screams, producing short ones, long ones, ones that
held a strained hoarse chord. My hatred was a distant
emotion. I felt no fury, no glee. I was merely a crafts-
man, working to prolong his death. Pink films oc-
cluded the whites of his eyes, his teeth were stained
to crimson, and at last he lay still.

I sat beside him for what seemed a long time. Then
I donned my cloak and walked back to my apartment.
After making sure no one was in the corridor, I dragged
the dead guard out of the front room and propped him
against the corridor wall. I reset the lock, stepped
inside, and the door slid shut behind me. I felt nothing. I took up *The Resolute Lover*, but even my interest in it had waned. I gazed at the walls, growing
thoughtless, remembering only that I had been somewhere, done some violence; I was perplexed by my
glowing hand. But soon I fell asleep, and when I was
waked by the guards unlocking the door, I found that
the hand had returned to normal.

"Did you hear anything outside?" asked one of the
guards.

"No," I said. "What happened?"

He told me the gory details, about the dead guard and Brent. Like everyone else on Helios Station, he seemed more confounded by these incomprehensible deaths than by the fantastic birth that had preceded them.

"The walls of the station have been plated with gold, the corridors are thronged with tourists, with students come to study the disciplines implicit in the Equations, disciplines that go far beyond the miraculous transformation of my hand. Souvenir shops sell holos of the Spider, recordings of The White Dragon Cycle (now used to acclimate children to the basics of the equations), and authorized histories of the sad events surrounding the Spider's emergence. The pleasure domes reverberated with Alex Dulambre's drifts, and in an auditorium constructed for this purpose, Reynolds' clone delivers daily lectures on the convulted circumstances of his death and triumph. The place is half amusement park, half shrine. Yet the greatest memorial to Reynolds' work is not here; it lies beyond the orbit of Pluto and consists of a vast shifting structure of golden light wherein dwell those students who have mastered the disciplines and overcome the bonds of corporeality. They are engaged, it is said, in an unfathomable work that may have taken its inspiration from Reynolds' metaphysical flights of fancy, or—and many hold to this opinion—may reflect the spider's design, his desire to rid himself of the human nuisance by setting us upon a new evolutionary course. After Brent's death I thought to join in this work. But my mind was not suited to the disciplines; I had displayed all the mastery of which I was capable in dispensing with Brent.

"I have determined to continue the search for my daughter. It may be—as Brent claimed—that she does not exist, but it is all that is left to me, and I have made my resolve accordingly. Still, I have not managed to leave the station, because I am drawn to Reynolds' clone. Again and again I find myself in the rear of the auditorium, where I watch him pace the dais, declaiming in his most excited manner. I yearn to approach him, to learn how like Reynolds he truly is. I am certain he has spotted me on several occasions, and I wonder what he is thinking, how it would be to speak to him, touch him. Perhaps this is perverse of me, but I cannot help wondering . . ."

from *Days In The Sun*
by Carolyn Dulambre

6
Carolyn/Reynolds

I had been wanting to talk with her since . . . well, since this peculiar life began. Why? I loved her, for one thing. But there seemed to be a far more compelling reason, one I could not verbalize. I suppressed the urge for a time, not wanting to hurt her; but seeing that she had begun to appear at the lectures, I finally decided to make an approach.

She had taken to frequenting a pleasure dome named Spider's. Its walls were holographic representations of the Spider, and these were strung together with golden webs that looked molten against the black backdrop, like seams of unearthly fire. In this golden dimness the faces of the patrons glowed like spirits, and the glow seemed to be accentuated by the violence of the music. It was not a place to my taste, nor—I suspect—to hers. Perhaps her patronage was a form of courage, of facing down the creature who had caused her so much pain.

I found her seated in a rear corner, drinking an Amouriste, and when I moved up beside her table, she paid me no mind. No one ever approached her; she was as much a memorial as the station itself, and though she was still a beautiful woman, she was treated like the wife of a saint. Doubtless she thought I was merely pausing by the table, looking for someone. But when I sat opposite her, she glanced up and her jaw dropped.

"Don't be afraid," I said.

"Why should I be afraid?"

"I thought my presence might . . . discomfort you."

She met my eyes unflinchingly. "I suppose I thought that, too."

"But. . . ?"

"It doesn't matter."

A silence built between us.

She wore a robe of golden silk, cut to expose the upper swells of her breasts, and her hair was pulled back from her face, laying bare the smooth serene lines of her beauty, a beauty that had once fired me, that did so even now.

"Look," I said. "For some reason I was drawn to talk to you, I feel I have . . ."

"I feel the same." She said this with a strong degree of urgency, but then tried to disguise the fact. "What shall we talk about?"

"I'm not sure."

She tapped a finger on her glass. "Why don't we walk?"

Everyone watched as we left, and several people followed us into the corridor, a circumstance that led me to suggest that we talk in my apartment. She hesitated, then signaled agreement with the briefest of nods. We moved quickly through the crowds, managing to elude our pursuers, and settled into a leisurely pace. Now and again I caught her staring at me, and asked if anything was wrong.

"Wrong?" She seemed to be tasting the word, trying it out. "No," she said. "No more than usual."

I had thought that when I did talk to him would find he was merely a counterfeit, that he would be nothing like Reynolds, except in the most superficial way. But this was not the case. Walking along the golden corridor, mixing with the revelers who poured between the shops and bars, I felt toward him as I had on the day we had met in the streets of Abidjan: powerfully attracted, vulnerable, and excited. And yet I did perceive a difference in him. Whereas Reynolds' presence had been commanding and intense, there had been a brittleness to that intensity, a sense that his diamond glitter might easily be fractured. With this Reynolds, however, there was no such inconstancy. His presence—while potent—was smooth, natural, and unflawed.

Everywhere we walked we encountered the fruits of the Equations: matter transmitters; rebirth parlors, where one could experience a transformation of both body and soul; and the omnipresent students, some of them half-gone into a transcorporeal state, cloaked to hide this fact, but their condition evident by their inward-looking eyes. With Reynolds beside me, all this seemed comprehensible, not—as before—a carnival of meaningless improbabilities. I asked what he felt on seeing the results of his work, and he said, "I'm really not concerned with it."

"What are you concerned with?"

"With you, Carolyn," he said.

The answer both pleased me and made me wary. "Surely you must have more pressing concerns," I said.

"Everything I've done was for you." A puzzled expression crossed his face.

"Don't pretend with me!" I snapped, growing angry. "This isn't a show, this isn't the auditorium."

He opened his mouth, but bit back whatever he had been intending to say, and we walked on.

"Forgive me," I said, realizing the confusion that must be his. "I . . ."

"No need for forgiveness," he said. "All our failures are behind us now."

I didn't know from where these words were coming. They were my words, yet they also seemed spoken from a place deep inside myself, one whose existence had been hidden until now, and it was all I could do to hold them back. We passed into the upper levels of the station, where the permanent staff was quartered, and as we rounded a curve, we nearly ran into a student standing motionless, gazing at the wall: a pale young man with black hair, a thin mouth, and a gray cape. His eyes were dead-looking, and his voice sepulchral. "It awaits," he said.

They are so lost in self-contemplation, these students, that they are likely to say anything. Some fancy them oracles, but not I: their words struck me as being random, sparks from a frayed wire.

"What awaits?" I asked, amused.

"Life . . . the city."

"Ah," I said. "And how do I get there?"

"You . . ." He lapsed into an open-mouthed stare.

Carolyn pulled at me, and we set off again. I started to make a joke about the encounter, but seeing her troubled expression, I restrained myself.

When we entered my apartment, she stopped in the center of the living room, transfixed by the walls. I had set them to display the environment of the beginning of *The Resolute Lover:* an endless sweep of golden grasses, with a sparkling on the horizon that might have been the winking of some bright tower.

"Does this bother you?" I asked, gesturing at the walls.

"No, they startled me, that's all." She strolled along, peering at the grasses, as if hoping to catch sight of someone. Then she turned, and I spoke again from that deep hidden place, a place that now—responding to the sight of her against those golden fields—was spreading all through me.

"Carolyn, I love you," I said . . . and this time I knew who it was that spoke.

He had removed his cloak, and his body was shimmering, embedded in that pale glow that once had made a weapon of my right hand. I backed away, terrified. Yet even in the midst of fear, it struck me that I was not as terrified as I should have been, that I was not at the point of screaming, of fleeing.

"It's me, Carolyn," he said.

"No," I said, backing further away.

"I don't know why you should believe me." He looked at his flickering hand. "I didn't understand it myself until now."

"Who are you?" I asked, gauging the distance to the door.

"You know," he said. "The Spider . . . he's all through the station. In the computer, the labs, even in the tanks from which my cells were grown. He's brought us together again."

He tried to touch me, and I darted to the side.

"I won't hurt you," he said.

"I've seen what a touch can do."

"Not my touch, Carolyn."

I doubted I could make it to the door, but readied myself for a try.

"Listen to me, Carolyn," he said. "Everything we wanted in the beginning, all the dreams and fictions of love, they can be ours."

"I never wanted that," I said. "You did! I only wanted normalcy, not some . . ."

"All lovers want the same thing," he said. "Disillusionment leads them to pretend they want less." He stretched out his hands to me. "Everything awaits us, everything is prepared. How this came to be, I can't explain. Except that it makes a funny kind of sense for the ultimate result of science to be an incomprehensible magic."

I was still afraid, but my fear was dwindling, lulled by the rhythms of his words, and though I perceived him to be death, I also saw clearly that he was Reynolds, Reynolds made whole.

"This was inevitable," he said. "We both knew something miraculous could happen . . . that's why we stayed together, despite everything. Don't be afraid. I could never hurt you more than I have."

"What's inevitable?" I asked. He was too close for

me to think of running, and I thought I could delay
him, put him off with questions.

"Can't you feel it?" He was so close now, I could
feel his heat. "I can't tell you what it is, Carolyn, only
that it is, that it's life . . . a new life."

"The Spider," I said. "I don't understand, I . . ."

"No more questions," he said, and slipped the robes
from my shoulders.

His touch was warmer than natural, making my
eyelids droop, but causing no pain. He pulled me
down to the floor, and in a moment he was inside me,
we were heart to heart, moving together, enveloped in
that pale flickering glow, and amidst the pleasure I felt,
there was pain, but so little it did not matter . . .

. . . and I, too, was afraid, afraid I was not who I
thought, that flames and nothingness would obliterate
us, but in having her once again, in the consummation
of my long wish, my doubts lessened . . .

. . . and I could no longer tell whether my eyes were
open or closed, because sometimes when I thought
them closed, I could see him, his face slack with pleasure, head flung back . . .

. . . and when I thought they were open I would
have a glimpse of another place wherein she stood
beside me, glimpses at first too brief for me to fix
them in mind . . .

. . . and everything was whirling, changing, my body,
my spirit, all in flux, and death—if this was death—
was a long decline, a sweep of golden radiance, and
behind me I could see the past reduced to a plain and
hills carpeted with golden grasses . . .

. . . and around me golden towers, shimmering, growing more stable and settling into form moment by
moment, and people shrouded in golden mist who
were also becoming more real, acquiring scars and
rags and fine robes, carrying baskets and sacks . . .

. . . and this was no heaven, no peaceful heaven, for as we moved beneath those crumbling towers of yellow stone, I saw soldiers with oddly shaped spears on the battlements, and the crowds around us were made up of hardbitten men and women wearing belted daggers, and old crones bent double under the weight of sacks of produce, and younger women with the look of ill-usage about them, who leaned from the doors and windows of smoke-darkened houses and cried out their price . . .

. . . and the sun overhead seemed to shift, putting forth prominences that rippled and undulated as in a dance, and shone down a ray of light to illuminate the tallest tower, the one we had sought for all these years, the one whose mystery we must unravel . . .

. . . and the opaque image of an old man in a yellow robe was floating above the crowd, his pupils appearing to shift, to put forth fiery threads as did the sun, and he was haranguing us, daring us all to penetrate his tower, to negotiate his webs and steal the secrets of time . . .

. . . and after wandering all day, we found a room in an inn not half a mile from the wizard's tower, a mean place with grimy walls and scuttlings in the corners and a straw mattress that crackled when we lay on it. But it was so much more than we'd had in a long, long time, we were delighted, and when night had fallen, with moonlight streaming in and the wizard's tower visible through a window against the deep blue of the sky, the room seemed palatial. We made love until well past midnight, love as we had never practiced it: trusting, unfettered by inhibition. And afterward, still joined, listening to the cries and music of the city, I suddenly remembered my life in that other world, the Spider, Helios Station, everything, and from the tense look on Carolyn's face, from her next words, I knew that she, too, had remembered.

"Back in Helios," she said, "we were making love,

lying exactly like this, and . . ." She broke off, a worry line creasing her brow. "What if this is all a dream, a moment between dying and death?"

"Why should you think that?"

"The Spider . . . I don't know. I just felt it was true."

"It's more reasonable to assume that everything is a form of transition between the apartment and this room. Besides, why would the Spider want you to die?"

"Why has he done any of this? We don't even know what he is . . . a demon, a god."

"Or something of mine," I said.

"Yes, that . . . or death."

I stroked her hair, and her eyelids fluttered down.

"I'm afraid to go to sleep," she said.

"Don't worry," I said. "I think there's more to this than death."

"How do you know?"

"Because of how we are."

"That's why I think it *is* death," she said. "Because it's too good to last."

"Even if it is death," I told her, "in this place death might last longer than our old lives."

Of course I was certain of very little myself, but I managed to soothe her, and soon she was asleep. Out the window, the wizard's tower—if, indeed, that's what it was—glowed and rippled, alive with power, menacing in its brilliance. But I was past being afraid. Even in the face of something as unfathomable as a creature who has appropriated the dream of a man who may have dreamed it into existence and fashioned thereof either a life or a death, even in a world of unanswerable questions, when love is certain—love, the only question that is its own answer—everything becomes quite simple, and, in the end, a matter of acceptance.

"We live in an old chaos of the sun."
Wallace Stevens

ANGEL

By Pat Cadigan

*I don't know whether the author would call
this a "cyberpunk" story or not, but in any
case, it is fascinating, unusual, and perhaps
even inspirational.*

Stand with me awhile, Angel, I said, and Angel said
he'd do that. Angel was good to me that way, good to
have with you on a cold night and nowhere to go. We
stood on the street corner together and watched the
cars going by and the people and all. The streets were
lit up like Christmas, streetlights, store lights, mar-
quees over the all-night movie houses and bookstores
blinking and flashing; shank of the evening in east
midtown. Angel was getting used to things here and
getting used to how I did, nights. Standing outside,
because what else are you going to do. He was *my*
Angel now, had been since that other cold night when
I'd been going home, because where are you going to
go, and I'd found him and took him with me. It's good
to have someone to take with you, someone to look
after. Angel knew that. He started looking after me, too.

Like now. We were standing there awhile and I was
looking around at nothing and everything, the cars
cruising past, some of them stopping now and again
for the hookers posing by the curb, and then I saw it,
out of the corner of my eye. Stuff coming out of the
Angel, shiny like sparks but flowing like liquid. Silver
fireworks. I turned and looked all the way at him and
it was gone. And he turned and gave a little grin like

he was embarrassed I'd seen. Nobody else saw it, though; not the short guy who paused next to the Angel before crossing the street against the light, not the skinny hype looking to sell the boom-box he was carrying on his shoulder, not the homeboy strutting past us with both his girlfriends on his arms, nobody but me.

The Angel said, Hungry?

Sure, I said. I'm hungry.

Angel looked past me. Okay, he said. I looked, too, and here they came, three leather boys, visor caps, belts, boots, keyrings. On the cruise together. Scary stuff, even though you know it's not looking for you.

I said, them? *Them?*

Angel didn't answer. One went by, then the second, and the Angel stopped the third by taking hold of his arm.

Hi.

The guy nodded. His head was shaved. I could see a little gray-black stubble under his cap. No eyebrows, disinterested eyes. The eyes were because of the Angel.

I could use a little money, the Angel said. My friend and I are hungry.

The guy put his hand in his pocket and wiggled out some bills, offering them to the Angel. The Angel selected a twenty and closed the guy's hand around the rest.

This will be enough, thank you.

The guy put his money away and waited.

I hope you have a good night, said the Angel.

The guy nodded and walked on, going across the street to where his two friends were waiting on the next corner. Nobody found anything weird about it.

Angel was grinning at me. Sometimes he was *the* Angel, when he was doing something, sometimes he was Angel, when he was just with me. Now he was Angel again. We went up the street to the luncheonette and got a seat by the front window so we could still watch the street while we ate.

Cheeseburger and fries, I said without bothering to

look at the plastic-covered menus lying on top of the napkin holder. The Angel nodded.

Thought so, he said. I'll have the same, then.

The waitress came over with a little tiny pad to take our order. I cleared my throat. It seemed like I hadn't used my voice in a hundred years. "Two cheeseburgers and two fries," I said, "and two cups of—" I looked up at her and froze. She had no face. Like, *nothing,* blank from hairline to chin, soft little dents where the eyes and nose and mouth would have been. Under the table, the Angel kicked me, but gentle.

"And two cups of coffee," I said.

She didn't say anything—how could she?—as she wrote down the order and then walked away again. All shaken up, I looked at the Angel, but he was calm like always.

She's a new arrival, Angel told me and leaned back in his chair. Not enough time to grow a face.

But how can she breathe? I said.

Through her pores. She doesn't need much air yet.

Yah, but what about—like, I mean, don't other people *notice* that she's got nothing there?

No. It's not such an extraordinary condition. The only reason you notice is because you're with me. Certain things have rubbed off on you. But no one else notices. When they look at her, they see whatever face they expect someone like her to have. And eventually, she'll have it.

But you have a face, I said. You've always had a face.

I'm different, said the Angel.

You sure are, I thought, looking at him. Angel had a beautiful face. That wasn't why I took him home that night, just because he had a beautiful face—I left all that behind a long time ago—but it was there, his beauty. The way you think of a man being beautiful, good clean lines, deep-set eyes, ageless. About the only way you could describe him—look away and you'd forget everything except that he was beautiful. But he did have a face. He *did.*

Angel shifted in the chair—these were like some-

body's old kitchen chairs, you couldn't get too comfortable in them—and shook his head, because he
knew I was thinking troubled thoughts. Sometimes
you could think something and it wouldn't be troubled
and later you'd think the same thing and it would be
troubled. The Angel didn't like me to be troubled
about him.

Do you have a cigarette? he asked.

I think so.

I patted my jacket and came up with most of a pack
that I handed over to him. The Angel lit up and
amused us both by having the smoke come out his ears
and trickle out of his eyes like ghostly tears. I felt my
own eyes watering for his; I wiped them and there was
that *stuff* again, but from me now. I was crying silver
fireworks. I flicked them on the table and watched
them puff out and vanish.

Does this mean I'm getting to *be* you, now? I asked.

Angel shook his head. Smoke wafted out of his hair.
Just things rubbing off on you. Because we've been
together and you're—susceptible. But they're different for you.

Then the waitress brought our food and we went on
to another sequence, as the Angel would say. She still
had no face but I guess she could see well enough
because she put all the plates down just where you'd
think they were supposed to go and left the tiny little
check in the middle of the table.

Is she—I mean, did you know her, from where
you—

Angel gave his head a brief little shake. No. She's
from somewhere else. Not one of my—people. He
pushed the cheeseburger and fries in front of him over
to my side of the table. That was the way it was done;
I did all the eating and somehow it worked out.

I picked up my cheeseburger and I was bringing it
up to my mouth when my eyes got all funny and I saw
it coming up like a whole *series* of cheeseburgers,
whoom-whoom-whoom, trick photography, only for
real. I closed my eyes and jammed the cheeseburger

into my mouth, holding it there, waiting for all the
other cheeseburgers to catch up with it.

You'll be okay, said the Angel. Steady, now.

I said with my mouth full, That was—that was *weird*.
Will I ever get used to this?

I doubt it. But I'll do what I can to help you.

Yah, well, the Angel *would* know. Stuff rubbing off
on me, he could feel it better than I could. He was the
one it was rubbing off *from*.

I had put away my cheeseburger and half of Angel's
and was working on the french fries for both of us
when I noticed he was looking out the window with
this hard, tight expression on his face.

Something? I asked him.

Keep eating, he said.

I kept eating, but I kept watching, too. The Angel
was staring at a big blue car parked at the curb right
outside the diner. It was silvery blue, one of those
lots-of-money models and there was a woman kind of
leaning across from the driver's side to look out the
passenger window. She was beautiful in that lots-of-
money way, tawny hair swept back from her face, and
even from here I could see she had turquoise eyes.
Really beautiful woman. I almost felt like crying. I
mean, jeez, how did people get that way and me too
harmless to live.

But the Angel wasn't one bit glad to see her. I knew
he didn't want me to say anything, but I couldn't help
it.

Who is she?

Keep eating, Angel said. We need the protein, what
little there is.

I ate and watched the woman and the Angel watch
each other and it was getting very—I don't know, very
something between them, even through the glass. Then
a cop car pulled up next to her and I knew they were
telling her to move it along. She moved it along.

Angel sagged against the back of his chair and lit
another cigarette, smoking it in the regular, unremark-
able way.

*   *   *

What are we going to do tonight? I asked the Angel as we left the restaurant.

Keep out of harm's way, Angel said, which was a new answer. Most nights we spent just kind of going around soaking everything up. The Angel soaked it up, mostly. I got some of it along with him, but not the same way he did. It was different for him. Sometimes he would use me like a kind of filter. Other times he took it direct. There'd been the big car accident one night, right at my usual corner, a big old Buick running a red light smack into somebody's nice Lincoln. The Angel had had to take it direct because I couldn't handle that kind of stuff. I didn't know how the Angel could take it, but he could. It carried him for days afterwards, too. I only had to eat for myself.

It's the intensity, little friend, he'd told me, as though that were supposed to explain it.

It's the intensity, not whether it's good or bad. The universe doesn't know good or bad, only less or more. Most of you have a bad time reconciling this. *You* have a bad time with it, little friend, but you get through better than other people. Maybe because of the way you are. You got squeezed out of a lot, you haven't had much of a chance at life. You're as much an exile as I am, only in your own land.

That may have been true, but at least I *belonged* here, so that part was easier for me. But I didn't say that to the Angel. I think he liked to think he could do as well or better than me at living—I mean, I couldn't just look at some leather boy and get him to cough up a twenty dollar bill. Cough up a fist in the face or worse, was more like it.

Tonight, though, he wasn't doing so good, and it was that woman in the car. She'd thrown him out of step, kind of.

Don't think about her, the Angel said, just out of nowhere. Don't think about her anymore.

Okay, I said, feeling creepy because it was creepy when the Angel got a glimpse of my head. And then, of course, I couldn't think about anything else hardly.

Do you want to go home? I asked him.

No. I can't stay in now. We'll do the best we can tonight, but I'll have to be very careful about the tricks. They take so much out of me, and if we're keeping out of harm's way, I might not be able to make up for a lot of it.

It's okay, I said. I ate. I don't need anything else tonight, you don't have to do anymore.

Angel got that look on his face, the one where I knew he wanted to give me things, like feelings I couldn't have any more. Generous, the Angel was. But I didn't need those feelings, not like other people seem to. For awhile, it was like the Angel didn't understand that, but he let me be.

Little friend, he said, and almost touched me. The Angel didn't touch a lot. I could touch him and that would be okay, but if *he* touched somebody, he couldn't help *doing* something to them, like the trade that had given us the money. That had been deliberate. If the trade had touched the Angel first, it would have been different, nothing would have happened unless the Angel touched him back. All touch meant something to the Angel that I didn't understand. There was touching without touching, too. Like things rubbing off on me. And sometimes, when I did touch the Angel, I'd get the feeling that it was maybe more his idea than mine, but I didn't mind that. How many people were going their whole lives never being able to touch an Angel?

We walked together and all around us the street was really coming to life. It was getting colder, too. I tried to make my jacket cover more. The Angel wasn't feeling it. Most of the time hot and cold didn't mean much to him. We saw the three rough trade guys again. The one Angel had gotten the money from was getting into a car. The other two watched it drive away and then walked on. I looked over at the Angel.

Because we took his twenty, I said.

Even if we hadn't, Angel said.

So we went along, the Angel and me, and I could feel how different it was tonight than it was all the other nights we'd walked or stood together. The Angel was kind of pulled back into himself and seemed to be keeping a check on me, pushing us closer together. I was getting more of those fireworks out of the corners of my eyes, but when I'd turn my head to look, they'd vanish. It reminded me of the night I'd found the Angel standing on my corner all by himself in pain. The Angel told me later that was real talent, knowing he was in pain. I never thought of myself as any too talented, but the way everyone else had been just ignoring him, I guess I must have had something to see him after all.

The Angel stopped us several feet down from an all-night bookstore. Don't look, he said. Watch the traffic or stare at your feet, but don't look or it won't happen.

There wasn't anything else to see right then, but I didn't look anyway. That was the way it was sometimes, the Angel telling me it made a difference whether I was watching something or not, something about the other people being conscious of me being conscious of them. I didn't understand, but I knew Angel was usually right. So I was watching traffic when the guy came out of the bookstore and got his head punched.

I could almost see it out of the corner of my eye. A lot of movement, arms and legs flying and grunty noises. Other people stopped to look but I kept my eyes on the traffic, some of which was slowing up so they could check out the fight. Next to me, the Angel was stiff all over. Taking it in, what he called the expenditure of emotional kinetic energy. No right, no wrong, little friend, he'd told me. Just energy, like the rest of the universe.

So he took it in and I *felt* him taking it in, and while I was feeling it, a kind of silver fog started creeping around my eyeballs and I was in two places at once. I was watching the traffic and I was in the Angel watching the fight and feeling him charge up like a big battery.

It felt like nothing I'd ever felt before. These two

guys slugging it out—well, one guy doing all the slugging and the other skittering around trying to get out from under the fists and having his head punched but good, and the Angel drinking it like he was sipping at an empty cup and somehow getting it to have something in it after all. Deep inside him, whatever made the Angel go was getting a little stronger.

I kind of swung back and forth between him and me, or swayed might be more like it was. I wondered about it, because the Angel wasn't touching me. I really was getting to *be* him, I thought; Angel picked that up and put the thought away to answer later. It was like I was traveling by the fog, being one of us and then the other, for a long time, it seemed, and then after awhile I was more me than him again, and some of the fog cleared away.

And there was that car, pointed the other way this time, and the woman was climbing out of it with this big weird smile on her face, as though she'd won something. She waved at the Angel to come to her.

Bang went the connection between us dead and the Angel shot past me, running away from the car. I went after him. I caught a glimpse of her jumping back into the car and yanking at the gear shift.

Angel wasn't much of a runner. Something funny about his knees. We'd gone maybe a hundred feet when he started wobbling and I could hear him pant. He cut across a Park & Lock that was dark and mostly empty. It was back-to-back with some kind of private parking lot and the fences for each one tried to mark off the same narrow strip of lumpy pavement. They were easy to climb but Angel was too panicked. He just *went* through them before he even thought about it; I knew that because if he'd been thinking, he'd have wanted to save what he'd just charged up with for when he really needed it bad enough.

I had to haul myself over the fences in the usual way, and when he heard me rattling on the saggy chainlink, he stopped and looked back.

Go, I told him. Don't wait on me!

He shook his head sadly. Little friend, I'm a fool. I could stand to learn from you a little more.

Don't stand, run! I got over the fences and caught up with him. Let's go! I yanked his sleeve as I slogged past and he followed at a clumsy trot.

Have to hide somewhere, he said, camouflage ourselves with people.

I shook my head, thinking we could just run maybe four more blocks and we'd be at the freeway overpass. Below it were the butt-ends of old roads closed off when the freeway had been built. You could hide there the rest of your life and no one would find you. But Angel made me turn right and go down a block to this rundown crack-in-the-wall called Stan's Jigger. I'd never been in there—I'd never made it a practice to go into bars—but the Angel was pushing too hard to argue.

Inside it was smelly and dark and not too happy. The Angel and I went down to the end of the bar and stood under a blood-red light while he searched his pockets for money.

Enough for one drink apiece, he said.

I don't want anything.

You can have soda or something.

The Angel ordered from the bartender, who was suspicious. This was a place for regulars and nobody else, and certainly nobody else like me or the Angel. The Angel knew that even stronger than I did but he just stood and pretended to sip his drink without looking at me. He was all pulled into himself and I was hovering around the edges. I knew he was still pretty panicked and trying to figure out what he could do next. As close as I was, if he had to get real far away, he was going to have a problem and so was I. He'd have to tow me along with him and that wasn't the most practical thing to do.

Maybe he was sorry now he'd let me take him home. But he'd been so weak then, and now with all the filtering and stuff I'd done for him he couldn't just cut me off without a lot of pain.

I was trying to figure out what I could do for him

now when the bartender came back and gave us a look
that meant order or get out, and he'd have liked it
better if we got out. So would everyone else there.
The few other people standing at the bar weren't
looking at us, but they knew right where we were, like
a sore spot. It wasn't hard to figure out what they
thought about us, either, maybe because of me or
because of the Angel's beautiful face.

We got to leave, I said to the Angel but he had it in
his head this was good camouflage. There wasn't enough
money for two more drinks so he smiled at the bartender and slid his hand across the bar and put it on
top of the bartender's. It was tricky doing it this way;
bartenders and waitresses took more persuading because it wasn't normal for them just to give you
something.

The bartender looked at the Angel with his eyes
half closed. He seemed to be thinking it over. But the
Angel had just blown a lot going through the fence
instead of climbing over it and the fear was scuttling
his concentration and I just knew that it wouldn't
work. And maybe my knowing that didn't help, either.

The bartender's free hand dipped down below the
bar and came up with a small club. "Faggot!" he
roared and caught Angel just over the ear. Angel
slammed into me and we both crashed to the floor.
Plenty of emotional kinetic energy in here, I thought
dimly as the guys standing at the bar fell on us, and
then I didn't think anything more as I curled up into a
ball under their fists and boots.

We were lucky they didn't much feel like killing
anyone. Angel went out the door first and they tossed
me out on top of him. As soon as I landed on him, I
knew we were both in trouble; something was broken
inside him. So much for keeping out of harm's way. I
rolled off him and lay on the pavement, staring at the
sky and trying to catch my breath. There was blood in
my mouth and my nose, and my back was on fire.

Angel? I said, after a bit.

He didn't answer. I felt my mind get kind of all
loose and runny, like my brains were leaking out my

ears. I thought about the trade we'd taken the money from and how I'd been scared of him and his friends and how silly that had been. But then, I was too harmless to live.

The stars were raining silver fireworks down on me. It didn't help.

Angel? I said again.

I rolled over onto my side to reach for him, and there she was. The car was parked at the curb and she had Angel under the armpits, dragging him toward the open passenger door. I couldn't tell if he was conscious or not and that scared me. I sat up.

She paused, still holding the Angel. We looked into each other's eyes, and I started to understand.

"Help me get him into the car," she said at last. Her voice sounded hard and flat and unnatural. "Then you can get in, too. In the *back* seat."

I was in no shape to take her out. It couldn't have been better for her if she'd set it up herself. I got up, the pain flaring in me so bad that I almost fell down again, and took the Angel's ankles. His ankles were so delicate, almost like a woman's, like *hers*. I didn't really help much, except to guide his feet in as she sat him on the seat and strapped him in with the shoulder harness. I got in the back as she ran around to the other side of the car, her steps real light and peppy, like she'd found a million dollars lying there on the sidewalk.

We were out on the freeway before the Angel stirred in the shoulder harness. His head lolled from side to side on the back of the seat. I reached up and touched his hair lightly, hoping she couldn't see me do it.

Where are you taking me, the Angel said.

"For a ride," said the woman. "For the moment."

Why does she talk out loud like that? I asked the Angel.

Because she knows it bothers me.

"You know I can focus my thoughts better if I say things out loud," she said. "I'm not like one of your little pushovers." She glanced at me in the rear view mirror. "Just *what* have you gotten yourself into since you left, darling? Is that a boy or a girl?"

I pretended I didn't care about what she said or that I was too harmless to live or any of that stuff, but the way she said it, she meant it to sting.

Friends can be either, Angel said. It doesn't matter which. Where are you taking us?

Now it was *us*. In spite of everything, I almost could have smiled.

"Us? You mean, you and me? Or are you really referring to your little pet back there?"

My friend and I are together. You and I are *not*.

The way the Angel said it made me think he meant more than not together; like he'd been with her once the way he was with me now. The Angel let me know I was right. Silver fireworks started flowing slowly off his head down the back of the seat and I knew there was something wrong about it. There was too much all at once.

"Why can't you talk out loud to me, darling?" the woman said with fakey-sounding petulance. "Just say a few words and make me happy. You have a lovely voice when you use it."

That was true, but the Angel never spoke out loud unless he couldn't get out of it, like when he'd ordered from the bartender. Which had probably helped the bartender decide about what he thought we were, but it was useless to think about that.

"All right," said Angel, and I knew the strain was awful for him. "I've said a few words. Are you happy?" He sagged in the shoulder harness.

"Ecstatic. But it won't make me let you go. I'll drop your pet at the nearest hospital and then we'll go home." She glanced at the Angel as she drove. "I've missed you so much. I can't *stand* it without you, without you making things happen. Doing your little miracles. You knew I'd get addicted to it, all the things you could do to people. And then you just took off, I didn't know what had happened to you. And it *hurt*." Her voice turned kind of pitiful, like a little kid's. "I was in real *pain*. You must have been, too. Weren't you? Well, *weren't you*?"

Yes, the Angel said. I was in pain, too.

I remembered him standing on my corner, where I'd hung out all that time by myself until he came. Standing there in pain. I didn't know why or from what then, I just took him home, and after a little while, the pain went away. When he decided we were together, I guess.

The silvery flow over the back of the car seat thickened. I cupped my hands under it and it was like my brain was lighting up with pictures. I saw the Angel before he was my Angel, in this really nice house, the woman's house, and how she'd taken him places, restaurants or stores or parties, thinking at him real hard so that he was all filled up with her and had to do what she wanted him to. Steal sometimes; other times, weird stuff, make people do silly things like suddenly start singing or taking their clothes off. That was mostly at the parties, though she made a waiter she didn't like burn himself with a pot of coffee. She'd get men, too, through the Angel, and they'd think it was the greatest idea in the world to go to bed with her. Then she'd make the Angel show her the others, the ones that had been sent here the way he had for crimes nobody could have understood, like the waitress with no face. She'd look at them, sometimes try to do things to them to make them uncomfortable or unhappy. But mostly she'd just stare.

It wasn't like that in the very beginning, the Angel said weakly and I knew he was ashamed.

It's okay, I told him. People can be nice at first, I know that. Then they find out about you.

The woman laughed. "You two are *so* sweet and pathetic. Like a couple of little children. I guess that's what you were looking for, wasn't it, darling? Except children can be cruel, too, can't they? So you got this—*creature* for yourself." She looked at me in the rear view mirror again as she slowed down a little, and for a moment I was afraid she'd seen what I was doing with the silvery stuff that was still pouring out of the

Angel. It was starting to slow now. There wasn't much
time left. I wanted to scream, but the Angel was
calming me for what was coming next. "What happened to you, anyway?"

Tell her, said the Angel. To stall for time, I knew,
keep her occupied.

I was born funny, I said. I had both sexes.

"A hermaphrodite!" she exclaimed with real delight.

She loves freaks, the Angel said, but she didn't pay
any attention.

There was an operation, but things went wrong.
They kept trying to fix it as I got older but my body
didn't have the right kind of chemistry or something.
My parents were ashamed. I left after awhile.

"You poor thing," she said, not meaning anything
like that. "You were *just* what darling, here, needed,
weren't you? Just a little nothing, no demands, no
desires. For anything." Her voice got all hard. "They
could probably fix you up now, you know."

I don't want it. I left all that behind a long time ago,
I don't need it.

"*Just* the sort of little pet that would be perfect for
you," she said to the Angel. "Sorry I have to tear you
away. But I can't get along without you now. Life is so
boring. And empty. And—" She sounded puzzled.
"And like there's nothing more to live for since you
left me."

That's not me, said the Angel. That's you.

"No, it's a lot of you, too, and you know it. You
know you're addictive to human beings, you knew that
when you came here—when they *sent* you here. Hey,
you, *pet,* do you know what his crime was, why they
sent him to this little backwater penal colony of a
planet?"

Yeah, I know, I said. I really didn't, but I wasn't
going to tell her that.

"What do you think about *that*, little pet neuter?"
she said gleefully, hitting the accelerator pedal and
speeding up. "What do you think of the crime of
refusing to mate?"

The Angel made a sort of an out-loud groan and

lunged at the steering wheel. The car swerved wildly and I fell backwards, the silvery stuff from the Angel going all over me. I tried to keep scooping it into my mouth the way I'd been doing, but it was flying all over the place now. I heard the crunch as the tires left the road and went onto the shoulder. Something struck the side of the car, probably the guard rail, and made it fishtail, throwing me down on the floor. Up front the woman was screaming and cursing and the Angel wasn't making a sound, but, in my head, I could hear him sort of keening. Whatever happened, this would be it. The Angel had told me all that time ago, after I'd taken him home, that they didn't last long after they got here, the exiles from his world and other worlds. Things tended to *happen* to them, even if they latched on to someone like me or the woman. They'd be in accidents or the people here would kill them. Like antibodies in a human body rejecting something or fighting a disease. At least I belonged here, but it looked like I was going to die in a car accident with the Angel and the woman both. I didn't care.

The car swerved back onto the highway for a few seconds and then pitched to the right again. Suddenly there was nothing under us and then we thumped down on something, not road but dirt or grass or something, bombing madly up and down. I pulled myself up on the back of the seat just in time to see the sign coming at us at an angle. The corner of it started to go through the windshield on the woman's side and then all I saw for a long time was the biggest display of silver fireworks ever.

It was hard to be gentle with him. Every move hurt but I didn't want to leave him sitting in the car next to her, even if she was dead. Being in the back seat had kept most of the glass from flying into me but I was still shaking some out of my hair and the impact hadn't done much for my back.

I laid the Angel out on the lumpy grass a little ways from the car and looked around. We were maybe a hundred yards from the highway, near a road that ran parallel to it. It was dark but I could still read the sign that had come through the windshield and split the woman's head in half. It said, *Construction Ahead, Reduce Speed.* Far off on the other road, I could see a flashing yellow light and at first I was afraid it was the police or something but it stayed where it was and I realized that must be the construction.

"Friend," whispered the Angel, startling me. He'd never spoken aloud to me, not directly.

Don't talk, I said, bending over him, trying to figure out some way I could touch him, just for comfort. There wasn't anything else I could do now.

"I have to," he said, still whispering. "It's almost all gone. Did you get it?"

Mostly, I said. Not all.

"I meant for you to have it."

I know.

"I don't know that it will really do you any good." His breath kind of bubbled in his throat. I could see something wet and shiny on his mouth but it wasn't silver fireworks. "But it's yours. You can do as you like with it. Live on it the way I did. Get what you need when you need it. But you can live as a human, too. Eat. Work. However, whatever."

I'm not human, I said. I'm not any more human than you, even if I do belong here.

"Yes, you are, little friend. I haven't made you any less human," he said, and coughed some. "I'm not sorry I wouldn't mate. I couldn't mate with my own. It was too . . . I don't know, too little of me, too much of them, something. I couldn't bond, it would have been nothing but emptiness. The Great Sin, to be unable to give, because the universe knows only less or more and I insisted that it would be good or bad. So they sent me here. But in the end, you know, they got their way, little friend." I felt his hand on me for a moment before it fell away. "I did it after all. Even if it wasn't with my own."

The bubbling in his throat stopped. I sat next to him for awhile in the dark. Finally I felt it, the Angel stuff. It was kind of fluttery-churny, like too much coffee on an empty stomach. I closed my eyes and lay down on the grass, shivering. Maybe some of it was shock but I don't think so. The silver fireworks started, in my head this time, and with them came a lot of pictures I couldn't understand. Stuff about the Angel and where he'd come from and the way they mated. It was a lot like how we'd been together, the Angel and me. They looked a lot like us but there were a lot of differences, too, things I couldn't make out. I couldn't make out how they'd sent him here, either—by *light,* in, like, little bundles or something. It didn't make any sense to me, but I guessed an Angel could be light. Silver fireworks.

I must have passed out, because when I opened my eyes, it felt like I'd been laying there a long time. It was still dark, though. I sat up and reached for the Angel, thinking I ought to hide his body.

He was gone. There was just a sort of wet sandy stuff where he'd been.

I looked at the car and her. All that was still there. Somebody was going to see it soon. I didn't want to be around for that.

Everything still hurt but I managed to get to the other road and start walking back toward the city. It was like I could *feel* it now, the way the Angel must have, as though it were vibrating like a drum or ringing like a bell with all kinds of stuff, people laughing and crying and loving and hating and being afraid and everything else that happens to people. The stuff that the Angel took in, energy, that I could take in now if I wanted.

And I knew that taking it in that way, it would be bigger than anything all those people had, bigger than anything I could have had if things hadn't gone wrong with me all those years ago.

I wasn't so sure I wanted it. Like the Angel, refusing to mate back where he'd come from. He wouldn't, there, and I couldn't, here. Except now I could do something else.

I wasn't so sure I wanted it. But I didn't think I'd be able to stop it, either, any more than I could stop my heart from beating. Maybe it wasn't really such a good thing or a right thing. But it was like the Angel said: the universe doesn't know good or bad, only less or more.

Yeah. I heard *that*.

I thought about the waitress with no face. I could find them all now, all the ones from the other places, other worlds that sent them away for some kind of alien crimes nobody would have understood. I could find them all. They threw away their outcasts, I'd tell them, but here, we *kept* ours. And here's how. Here's how you live in a universe that only knows less or more.

I kept walking toward the city.

FOREVER YOURS, ANNA
By Kate Wilhelm

An enigma of past, present and future, in which an authority on handwriting attempts to determine the nature of the author of the letters signed as the title of this story. There's a surprise in store at the end.

Anna entered his life on a spring afternoon, not invited, not even wanted. Gordon opened his office door that day to a client who was expected and found a second man also in the hallway. The second man brought him Anna, although Gordon did not yet know this. At the moment, he simply said, "Yes?"

"Gordon Sills? I don't have an appointment, but . . . may I wait?"

"Afraid I don't have a waiting room."

"Out here's fine."

He was about fifty, and he was prosperous. It showed in his charcoal-colored suit, a discreet blue-gray silk tie, a silk shirt. Gordon assumed the stone on his finger was a real emerald of at least three carats. Ostentatious touch, that.

"Sure," Gordon said, and ushered his client inside. They passed through a foyer into his office workroom. The office section was partitioned from the rest of the room by three rice-paper screens with beautiful Chinese calligraphy. In the office area was his desk and two chairs for visitors, his chair, and an overwhelmed bookcase, with books on the floor in front of it.

When his client left, the hall was empty. Gordon

177

shrugged and returned to his office; he pulled his
telephone across the desk and dialed his former wife's
apartment number, let it ring a dozen times, hung up.
He leaned back in his chair and rubbed his eyes ab-
sently. Late-afternoon sunlight streamed through the
slats in the venetian blinds, zebra light. *I should go
away for a few weeks,* he thought. Just close shop and
walk away from it all until he started getting overdraft
notices. Three weeks, he told himself; that was about
as long as it would take. *Too bad about the other guy,*
he thought without too much regret. He had a month's
worth of work lined up already, and he knew more
would trickle in when that was done.

Gordon Sills was thirty-five, a foremost expert in
graphology, and could have been rich, his former wife
had reminded him quite often. If you don't make it
before forty, she had also said—too often—you simply
won't make it, and he did not care, simply did not
care about money, security, the future, the children's
future . . .

Abruptly he pushed himself away from the desk and
left the office, going into his living room. Like the
office, it was messy, with several days' worth of
newspapers, half a dozen books, magazines scattered
haphazardly. To his eyes it was comfortable looking,
comfort giving; he distrusted neatness in homes. Two
fine Japanese landscapes were on the walls.

The buzzer sounded. When he opened the door, the
prosperous, uninvited client was there again. He was
carrying a brushed-suede briefcase.

Gordon opened the door wider and motioned him
on through the foyer into the office. The sunlight was
gone, eclipsed by the building across Amsterdam Avenue. He indicated a chair and took his own seat behind the desk.

"I apologize for not making an appointment," his
visitor said. He withdrew a wallet from his breast
pocket, took out a card, and slid it across the desk.

"I'm Avery Roda. On behalf of my company I
should like to consult with you regarding some corre-
spondence that we have in our possession."

"That's my business," Gordon said. "And what is your company, Mr. Roda?"

"Draper Fawcett."

Gordon nodded slowly. "And your position there?"

Roda looked unhappy. "I am vice president in charge of research and development, but right now I am in charge of an investigation we have undertaken. My first duty in connection with this was to find someone with your expertise. You come very highly recommended, Mr. Sills."

"Before we go on any further," Gordon said, "I should tell you that there are a number of areas where I'm not interested in working. I don't do paternity suits, for example. Or employer–employee pilferage cases."

Roda flushed.

"Or blackmail," Gordon finished equably. "That's why I'm not rich, but that's how it is."

"The matter I want to discuss is none of the above," Roda snapped. "Did you read about the explosion we had at our plant on Long Island two months ago?" He did not wait for Gordon's response. "We lost a very good scientist, one of the best in the country. And we cannot locate some of his paperwork, his notes. He was involved with a woman who may have them in her possession. We want to find her, recover them."

Gordon shook his head. "You need the police, then, private detectives, your own security force."

"Mr. Sills, don't underestimate our resolve or our resources. We have set all that in operation, and no one has been able to locate the woman. Last week we had a conference during which we decided to try this route. What we want from you is as complete an analysis of the woman as you can give us, based on her handwriting. That may prove fruitful." His tone said he doubted it very much.

"I assume the text has not helped."

"You assume correctly," Roda said with some bitterness. He opened his briefcase and withdrew a sheaf of papers and laid it on the desk.

From the other side Gordon could see that they

were not the originals but photocopies. He let his gaze roam over the upside-down letters and then shook his head. "I have to have the actual letters to work with."

"That's impossible. They are being kept under lock and key."

"Would you offer a wine taster colored water?" Gordon's voice was bland, but he could not stop his gaze. He reached across the desk and turned the top letter right side up to study the signature. ANNA. Beautifully written. Even in the heavy black copy it was delicate, as artful as any of the Chinese calligraphy on his screens. He looked up to find Roda watching him intently. "I can tell you a few things from just this, but I have to have the originals. Let me show you my security system."

He led the way to the other side of the room. Here he had a long worktable, an oversize light table, a copy camera, an enlarger, files. There was a computer and printer on a second desk. It was all fastidiously neat and clean.

"The files are fireproof," he said dryly. "and the safe is also. Mr. Roda, if you've investigated me, you know I've handled some priceless documents. And I've kept them right here in the shop. Leave the copies. I can start with them, but tomorrow I'll want the originals."

"Where's the safe?"

Gordon shrugged and went to the computer, keyed in his code, and then moved to the wall behind the worktable and pushed aside a panel to reveal a safe front. "I don't intend to open it for you. You can see enough without that."

"Computer security?"

"Yes."

"Very well. Tomorrow I'll send you the originals. You said you can already tell us something."

They returned to the office space. "First you," Gordon said, pointing to the top letter. "Who censored them?"

The letters had been cut off just above the greeting, and there were rectangles of white throughout.

"That's how they were when we found them," Roda said heavily. "Mercer must have done it himself. One of the detectives said the holes were cut with a razor blade."

Gordon nodded. "Curiouser and curiouser. Well, for what it's worth at this point, she's an artist more than likely. Painter would be my first guess."

"Are you sure?"

"Don't be a bloody fool. Of course I'm not sure— not with copies to work with. It's a guess. Everything I report will be a guess. Educated guesswork, Mr. Roda, that's all I can guarantee."

Roda sank down into his chair and expelled a long breath. "How long will it take?"

"How many letters?"

"Nine."

"Two, three weeks."

Very slowly Roda shook his head. "We are desperate, Mr. Sills. We will double your usual fee if you can give this your undivided attention."

"And how about your cooperation?"

"What do you mean?"

"His handwriting also. I want to see at least four pages of his writing."

Roda looked blank.

"It will help to know her if I know her correspondent."

"Very well."

"How old was he?"

"Thirty."

"Okay. Anything else you can tell me?"

Roda seemed deep in thought, his eyes narrowed, a stillness about him that suggested concentration. With a visible start he looked up, nodded. "What you said about her could be important already. She mentions a show in one of the letters. We assumed a showgirl, a dancer, something like that. I'll put someone on it immediately. An artist. That could be right."

"Mr. Roda, can you tell me anything else? How important are those papers? Are they salable? Would anyone outside your company have an idea of their value?"

"They are quite valuable," he said with such a lack of tone that Gordon's ears almost pricked to attention. "If we don't recover them in a relatively short time, we will have to bring in the FBI. National security may be at stake. We want to handle it ourselves, obviously."

He finished in the same monotone, "The Russians would pay millions for them, I'm certain. And we will pay whatever we have to. She has them. She says so in one of her letters. We have to find that woman."

For a moment Gordon considered turning down the job.

Trouble, he thought. *Real trouble.* He glanced at the topmost letter again, the signature "Anna," and he said, "Okay. I have a contract I use routinely. . . ."

After Roda left, he studied the one letter for several minutes, not reading it, in fact, examining it upside down again; and he said softly, "Hello, Anna."

Then he gathered up all the letters, put them in a file, and put it in his safe. He had no intention of starting until he had the originals. But it would comfort Roda to believe he was already at work.

Roda sent the originals and a few samples of Mercer's writing before noon the next day, and for three hours Gordon studied them all. He arranged hers on the worktable under the gooseneck lamp and turned them this way and that, not yet reading them, making notes now and then. As he had suspected, her script was fine, delicate, with beautiful shading. She used a real pen with real ink, not a felt-tip or a ballpoint. Each stroke was visually satisfying, artistic in itself. One letter was three pages long; four were two pages; the others were single sheets. None of them had a date, an address, a complete name. He cursed the person who had mutilated them. One by one he turned them over to examine the backs and jotted: PRESSURE— LIGHT TO MEDIUM. His other notes were equally brief: FLUID, RAPID, NOT CONVENTIONAL, PROPORTIONS ONE TO FIVE. That was European, and he did not think she was, but it would bear close examination. Each note was simply a direction marker, a first impression. He was whistling tunelessly as he worked and was startled when the telephone rang.

It was Karen, finally returning his many calls. The children would arrive by six, and he must return them by seven Sunday night. Her voice was cool, as if she were giving orders about laundry. He said okay and hung up, surprised at how little he felt about the matter. Before, it had given him a wrench each time they talked; he had asked questions: How was she? Was she working? Was the house all right? She had the house on Long Island, and that was fine with him; he had spent more and more time in town anyway over the past few years. But still, they had bought it together, he had repaired this and that, put up screens, taken them down, struggled with the plumbing.

That night he took the two children to a Greek restaurant. Buster, eight years old, said it was yucky; Dana, ten, called him a baby, and Gordon headed off the fight by saying he had bought a new Monopoly game. Dana said Buster was into winning. Dana looked very much like her mother, but Buster was her true genetic heir. Karen was into winning, too.

They went to The Cloisters and fantasized medieveal scenarios; they played Monopoly, and on Sunday he took them to a puppet show at the Met and then drove them home. He was exhausted. When he got back he looked about, deeply depressed. There were dirty dishes in the sink and on the table, in the living room. Buster had slept on the couch, and his bedclothes and covers were draped over it. Karen said they were getting too old to share a room any longer. Dana's bedroom was also a mess. She had left her pajamas and slippers.

Swiftly he gathered up the bedding from the living room and tossed it all onto the bed in Dana's room and closed the door. He overfilled the dishwasher and turned it on and finally went into his workroom and opened the safe.

"Hello, Anna," he said softly, and tension seeped from him; the ache that had settled in behind his eyes vanished; he forgot the traffic jams coming home from

Long Island, forgot the bickering his children seemed
unable to stop.

He took the letters to the living room and sat down
to read them through for the first time. Love letters,
passionate letters, humorous in places, perceptive, intelligent. Without dates it was hard to put them in
chronological order, but the story emerged. She had
met Mercer in the city; they had walked and talked,
and he had left. He had come back, and this time they
were together for a weekend and became lovers. She
sent her letters to a post office box; he did not write to
her, although he left pages of incomprehensible notes
in her care. She was married or lived with someone,
whose name had been cut out with a razor blade every
time she referred to him. Mercer knew him, visited
him apparently. They were even friends and had long,
serious talks. She was afraid; Mercer was involved in
work that was dangerous, and no one told her what it
was. She called Mercer her mystery man and specu-
lated about his secret life, his family, his insane wife or
tyrannical father, or his own lapses into lycanthropy.

Gordon smiled. Anna was not a whiner or a weeper;
but she was hopelessly in love with Mercer and did not
know where he lived, where he worked, what danger
threatened him, anything about him except that when
he was with her, she was alive and happy. And that
was enough. Her husband understood and wanted only
her happiness, and it was destroying her, knowing she
was hurting him so much, but she was helpless.

He pursed his lips and reread one. "My darling, I
can't stand it. I really can't stand it any longer. I
dream of you, see you in every stranger on the street,
hear your voice every time I answer the phone. My
palms become wet, and I tingle all over, thinking it's
your footsteps I hear. You are my dreams. So, I told
myself today, this is how it is? No way! Am I a silly
schoolgirl mooning over a television star? At twenty-
six! I gathered up all your papers and put them in a
box and addressed it, and as I wrote the number of the
box, I found myself giggling. You can't send a Dear
John to a post office box number. What if you failed

to pick it up and an inspector opened it finally? I should entertain such a person? They're all gray and dessicated, you know, those inspectors. Let them find their own entertainment! What if they deciphered your mysterious squiggles and discovered the secret of the universe? Do any of them deserve such enlightenment? No! I put everything back in [excised] safe—"

Mercer was not the mystery man, Gordon thought then; the mystery was the other man, the nameless one whose safe hid Mercer's papers. Who was he? He shook his head over the arrangement of two men and a woman and continued to read: "—and [excised] came in and let me cry on his shoulder. Then we went to dinner. I was starved."

Gordon laughed and put the letters down on the coffee table, leaned back with his hands behind his head, and contemplated the ceiling. It needed paint.

For the next two weeks he worked on the letters and the few pages of Mercer's handwriting. He photographed everything, made enlargements, and searched for signs of weakness, illness. He keystroked the letters into his computer and ran the program he had developed, looking for usages, foreign or regional combinations, anything unusual or revealing. Mercer, he decided, had been born in a test tube and never left school and the laboratory until the day he met Anna. She was from the Midwest, not a big city, somewhere around one of the Great Lakes. The name that had been consistently cut out had six letters. She had gone to an opening, and the artist's name had been cut out also. It had nine letters. Even without her testimony about the artist, it was apparent that she had been excited by his work. It showed in the writing. He measured the spaces between the words, the size of individual letters, the angle of her slant, the proportions of everything. Every movement she made was graceful, rhythmic. Her connections were garlands, open and trusting; that meant she was honest herself. Her threadlike connections that strung her words together indicated her speed in writing, her intuition, which she trusted.

As the work went on, he was making more complete notes, drawing conclusions more and more often. The picture of Anna was becoming real.

He paid less attention to Mercer's writing after making his initial assessment of him. A scientist, technologist, precise, angular, a genius, inhibited, excessively secretive, a loner. He was a familiar type.

When Roda returned, Gordon felt he could tell him more about those two people than their own mothers knew about them.

What he could not tell was what they looked like, or where Anna was now, or where the papers were that she had put in her husband's safe.

He watched Roda skim through his report on Anna. Today rain was falling in gray curtains of water; the air felt thick and clammy.

"That's all?" Roda demanded when he finished.

"That's it."

"We checked every art show in the state," Roda said, scowling at him. "We didn't find her. And we have proof that Mercer couldn't have spent as much time with her as she claimed in the letters. We've been set up. You've been set up. You say here that she's honest, ethical; and we say she's an agent or worse. She got her hooks in him and got those papers, and these letters are fakes, every one of them is a fake!"

Gordon shook his head. "There's not a lie in those letters."

"Then why didn't she come forward when he died? There was enough publicity. We made sure of that. I tell you, he wasn't with her. We found him in a talent hunt when he was a graduate student, and he stayed in that damn lab ever since, seven days a week for four years. He never had time to have a relationship of the sort she's talking about. It's a lie through and through. A fantasy." He slumped in his chair. His face was almost as gray as his very good suit. He looked years older than he had the last time he had been in the office. "They're going to win," he said in a low voice.

"The woman and her partner. They're probably out of the country already. Probably left the day after the accident, with the papers, the job done. Well-done. That stupid, besotted fool!" He stared at the floor for several more seconds, then straightened.

His voice was hard, clipped, when he spoke again. "I was against consulting you from the start. A waste of time and money. Voodoo crap, that's all this is. Well, we've done what we can. Send in your bill. Where are her letters?"

Silently Gordon slid a folder across the desk. Roda went through it carefully, then put it in his briefcase and stood up. "If I were you, I would not give our firm as reference in the future, Sills." He pushed Gordon's report away from him. "We can do without that. Good day."

It should have ended there, Gordon knew, but it did not end. *Where are you, Anna?* he thought at the world being swamped in cold rain. Why hadn't she come forward, attended the funeral, turned in the papers? He had no answers. He just knew that she was out there, painting, living with a man who loved her very much, enough to give her her freedom to fall in love with someone else. *Take good care of her,* he thought at that other man. *Be gentle with her; be patient while she heals. She's very precious, you know.*

He leaned his head against the window, let the coolness soothe him. He said aloud, "She's very precious."

"Gordon, are you all right?" Karen asked on the phone. It was his weekend for the children again.

"Sure. Why?"

"I just wondered. You sound strange. Do you have a girlfriend?"

"What do you want, Karen?"

The ice returned to her voice, and they made arrangements for the children's arrival, when he was to return them. *Library books,* he thought distantly. *Just like library books.*

When he hung up he looked at the apartment and

was dismayed by the dinginess, the disregard for the barest amenities. *Another lamp,* he thought. He needed a second lamp, at the very least. Maybe even two. Anna loved light. A girlfriend? He wanted to laugh, and to cry also. He had a signature, some love letters written to another man, a woman who came to his dreams and spoke to him in the phrases from her letters. A girlfriend! He closed his eyes and saw the name, Anna. The capital *A* was a flaring volcano, high up into the stratosphere, then the even, graceful *n*'s, the funny little final *a* that had trouble staying on the base line, that wanted to fly away. And a beautiful sweeping line that flew out from it, circled above the entire name, came down to cross the first letter, turn it into an *A*, and in doing so formed a perfect palette. A graphic representation of Anna, soaring into the heavens, painting, creating art with every breath, every motion. Forever yours, Anna. Forever yours.

He took a deep breath and tried to make plans for the children's weekend, for the rest of the month, the summer, the rest of his life.

The next day he bought a lamp and on his way home stopped in a florist's shop and bought a half a dozen flowering plants. She had written that the sunlight turned the flowers on the sill into jewels. He put them on the sill and raised the blind, and the sunlight turned the blooms into jewels. His hands were clenched; abruptly he turned away from the window.

He went back to work; spring became summer, hot and humid as only New York could be, and he found himself going from one art show to another. He mocked himself and cursed himself for it, but he attended openings, examined new artists' work, signatures, again and again and again. If the investigators trained in this couldn't find her, he told himself firmly, and the FBI couldn't find her, he was a fool to think he had even a remote chance. But he went to the shows. He was lonely, he told himself, and tried to become interested in other women, any other woman, and continued to attend openings.

In the fall he went to the opening of yet another

new artist, out of an art school, a teacher. And he cursed himself for not thinking of that before. She could be an art teacher. He made a list of schools and started down the list, perfecting a story as he worked down it one by one. He was collecting signatures of artists for an article he planned to write. It was a passable story. It got him nothing.

She might be ugly, he told himself. What kind of woman would have fallen in love with Mercer? He had been inhibited, constricted, without grace, brilliant, eccentric, and full of wonder. It was the wonder that she had sensed, he knew. She had been attracted to that in Mercer and had got through his many defenses, had found a boy-man who was truly appealing. And he had adored her. That was apparent from her letters; it had been mutual. Why had he lied to her? Why hadn't he simply told her who he was, what he was doing? The other man in her life had not been an obstacle; that had been made clear also. The two men had liked each other, and both loved her. Gordon brooded about her, about Mercer, the other man; and he haunted openings, became a recognized figure at the various studios and schools where he collected signatures. It was an obsession, he told himself, unhealthy, maybe even a sign of neurosis, or worse. It was insane to fall in love with someone's signature, love letters to another man.

And he could be wrong, he told himself. Maybe Roda had been right after all. The doubts were always short-lived.

The cold October rains had come. Karen was engaged to a wealthy man.

The children's visits had become easier because he no longer was trying to entertain them every minute; he had given in and bought a television and video games for them. He dropped by the Art Academy to meet Rick Henderson, who had become a friend over the past few months. Rick taught watercolors.

Gordon was in Rick's office waiting for him to finish with a class critique session when he saw the *A*, Anna's capital *A*.

He felt his arms prickle and sweat form on his hands and a tightening in the pit of his stomach as he stared at an envelope on Rick's desk.

Almost fearfully he turned it around to study the handwriting. The *A*'s in *Art Academy* were like volcanoes, reaching up into the stratosphere, crossed with a quirkly, insouciant line, like a sombrero at a rakish angle. Anna's *A*. it did not soar and make a palette, but it wouldn't, not in an address. That was her personal sign.

He let himself sink into Rick's chair and drew in a deep breath. He did not touch the envelope again. When Rick finally joined him, he nodded toward it.

"Would you mind telling me who wrote that?" His voice sounded hoarse, but Rick seemed not to notice. He opened the envelope and scanned a note, then handed it over. Her handwriting. Not exactly the same, but it was hers. He was certain it was hers, even with the changes. The way the writing was positioned on the page, the sweep of the letters, the fluid grace. . . . But it was not the same. The *A* in her name, Anna, was different. He felt bewildered by the differences and knew it was hers in spite of them. Finally he actually read the words. She would be out of class for a few days. It was dated four days ago.

"Just a kid," Rick said. "Fresh in from Ohio, thinks she has to be excused from class. I'm surprised it's not signed by her mother."

"Can I meet her?"

Now Rick looked interested. "Why?"

"I want her signature."

Rick laughed. "You're a real nut, you know. Sure. She's in the studio, making up for time off. Come on."

He stopped at the doorway and gazed at the young woman painting. She was no more than twenty, almost painfully thin, hungry looking. She wore scruffy sneakers, very old faded blue jeans, a man's plaid shirt. Not the Anna of the letters. Not yet.

Gordon felt dizzy and held onto the doorframe for a moment, and he knew what it was that Mercer had worked on, what he had discovered. He felt as if he had slipped out of time himself as his thoughts raced, explanations formed, his next few years shaped themselves in his mind. Understanding came the way a memory comes, a gestalt of the entire event or series of events, all accessible at once.

Mercer's notes had shown him to be brilliant, obsessional, obsessed with time, secretive. Roda had assumed Mercer failed, because he had blown himself up. Everyone must have assumed that. But he had not failed. He had gone forward five years, six at the most, to the time when Anna would be twenty-six. He had slipped out of time to the future. Gordon knew with certainty that it was his own name that had been excised from Anna's letters. Phrases from her letters tumbled through his mind. She had mentioned a Japanese bridge from his painting, the flowers on the sill, even the way the sun failed when it sank behind the building across the street.

He thought of Roda and the hordes of agents searching for the papers that were to be hidden, had been hidden in the safest place in the world—the future. The safe Anna would put the papers in would be his, Gordon's safe. He closed his eyes hard, already feeling the pain he knew would come when Mercer realized that he was to die, that he had died. For Mercer there could not be a love strong enough to make him abandon his work.

Gordon knew he would be with Anna, watch her mature, become the Anna of the letters, watch her soar into the stratosphere; and when Mercer walked through his time door, Gordon would still love her and wait for her, help her heal afterward.

Rick cleared his throat, and Gordon released his grasp of the doorframe, took the next step into the studio. Anna's concentration was broken; she looked up at him. Her eyes were dark blue.

Hello, Anna.

SECOND GOING
By James Tiptree, Jr.

James Tiptree, Jr. is now known to be the pen-name of Alice Sheldon, a woman of many talents who was connected with the CIA's photographic identification section. She took her own life early in 1987, having pondered the tragedy of her invalid husband. This story, dealing with the whole question of God and the gods of antiquity, was one of her last. It was written surely during the long period when she was contemplating her own death—and what came after—something that is noticeable in other short stories of hers in that time. In some ways there is a curiously light touch to her thoughts as shown in this tale—even though it deals with a basic problem which has disturbed people since earliest days of human existence.

I didn't mean to start like this. I wanted to make it a nice formal Appendix, or Addendum, to the official Archives. The account of man's first contact with aliens: what really happened.

But I can't find any bound copies of the White Book, not even in the President's office. Except one somebody got mustard all over and another piece the rats got at. What I suspect, what I think is, *they never finished it.* All I can find is some empty cover-boxes, so I'm going to put these discs in one of those so people will know it's important.

After all, I am the official Archivist—I typed the

192

promotion myself when Hattie went. I'm Theodora
Tanton, Chief NASA Archivist. And I'm seventy-six
years old, as of this morning. So is everybody, old—
everybody who can remember, that is. So who's going
to hear it, anyway? You with your six fingers or two
heads or whatever?

You'll be around, though. They promised us that,
that we wouldn't blow ourselves up. They said they
fixed it. And I believe them. Not because I *believe*
them exactly, but because I think they just might want
to come back someday and find more than ashes.

They didn't command us not to fire atomic weapons, by the way. I guess they knew by that time that
when a god commands Don't Eat Those Apples, or
Don't Open This Box—it's the first thing men'll do.
(And manage to blame it on a woman, too, if you'll
notice. But I digress.)

Nope, they just said, "We fixed that." Maybe the
Russians have found out what they did by this time.
Or the Israelis. What's left of the Pentagon is too
scared to try. So, Hello, Posterity.

This is about what really happened, to add to the
White Book, if you ever find one—ooops, that was a
rat. I have a Coleman lantern, and a hockey stick for
the rats.

Start with First Contact.

First Contact took place on Mars, with the men of
the First Mars Mission. The two who had landed, that
is. The command module pilot, Reverend Perry Danforth,
was just flying orbits, looking down and seeing peculiar things. Meeting them on Mars confused everybody
for a while. They were not Martians.

The best account of the meeting is from Mission
Control. I found a man who had been a boy there,
sort of a gofer. In that big room with all the terminals—
you've seen it a million times on TV if you watched
space stuff. So this first bit is dictated live by Kevin
(Red) Blake, now aged 99.5 years.

But before him I want to say a word about how
everything was. *So normal.* Nothing sinister or dra-
matic going on. Like in a ship that's slowly, very

slowly, listing to one side, only nobody's mentioning it. That's all underneath. But little things give it away, like this one Kevin told me before they landed.

It was a long trip, see, two years plus. They were all in the command module, called *Mars Eagle.* James Aruppa, commanding, and Todd Fiske, and the Reverend Perry, who wasn't going to get to land. (Personally, I'd have broken Todd's arm or something, if I'd been Perry, so I could get to land. Imagine getting so close—and then flying circles for a week while the others are on *Mars!* But he acted perfectly happy about it. He even made a joke about being "the most expensive valet parking service ever." Very cooperative and one-for-all, the Reverend. I never did find out exactly what he was the Reverend of; maybe it was only a nickname.)

Anyway about five or six months out, at a time when they were supposed to be fast asleep, they called Mission Control. "Are you all right back there?"

"Sure, everything's nominal here. What's with you?"

Well, it turned out that they'd seen this flash, some trick rock reflection or something that made a burst of light right where Earth was. And they thought it was missiles, see, World War III starting . . . anybody would've, in those days. That's what I mean by the feelings just underneath. But nobody ever said a gloomy word, on top.

There were other things underneath, of course, different for different people, all adding up to The End. But this is no place to talk about the old days; it's all changed now. So that's that, and now here comes Kevin:

"I can remember it like it was yesterday. All morning had been occupied with the Lander carrying Todd and Jim Aruppa coming down and finding a flat place. I nearly got thrown out of the control room for sticking my head in people's way to catch a glimpse of a screen while I was bringing stuff. The amount of coffee those NASA boys put away! And some of them ate—one man ate seven egg sandwiches—they were all keyed up like crazy. All right, I'll stick to the point. I know what you want to hear.

"So by then it was coming pitch dark on Mars, only the Lander's lights glaring on a pebbly plain with cracks in it. The computer colored it red, I guess it was. Mission Control wouldn't let them get out then. They were ordered to sleep until it got full light again. Ten hours . . . Imagine, *sleeping* your first night on Mars!

"The last thing was, Perry up in the command module reported a glow of light on the eastern horizon. It wasn't a moon rising—we'd already seen one of those. A little greenish crescent, going like crazy.

"So during the night Perry was supposed to check on what might be glowing toward the east—a volcano, maybe? But by the time he came around to where he could see the place again, the glow had faded to nearly nothing, and next trip there was nothing at all to see.

"At this time a relief crew was on the CRTs in Mission Control, but every so often one of the men who were supposed to be sleeping in their quarters next door would come in and just stare at the screens for a few minutes. All you could see was a faint, jagged horizon line, and then the stars began.

"First light was supposed to be at 5:50 A.M. our time (see, I even remember numbers!) and by that time the whole day crew was back in the room, everybody all mixed together, and all wanting coffee and Danishes.

"On the screens the sky was getting just a little lighter, so the horizon looked sharper and darker until suddenly a faint lightness came on the ground plain in front of the mountains. And then came a minute I'll never forget. Like the whole room was holding its breath, only whispering or rustling a little around their dark screens. And then Eggy Stone yelled out loud and clear:

" *'There's something there! It's big! Oh, man!'*

"That made it official, what the sharp-eyed ones thought they'd been picking up but couldn't believe, and everybody was jabbering at once. And the voices of the astronauts cutting through everything, with that four-and-a-half-minute lag, about how this Thing was sitting in front of them unlit, unmoving, no indication of how it had come there, whether it crawled or flew in or bored up out of the ground. Of course, they thought it was Martians.

"What it was was a great big, say fifty-meter-long, dumbbell shape lying there about a hundred meters in front of their main window. It was two huge spheroids, or hexasomethings, connected by one big fat center bar—really like a dumbbell. Only in the middle of the connection was a chamber, say three meters each way. We could see right in because its whole front side was folded back like a big gullwing door. It appeared to be padded inside. The computer called it light blue, with two rust-colored lumps like cushion seats back on the floor inside.

"And both of the big dumbbell chambers at the ends had like windows spaced all around them.

"And filling the window of the end nearest us, the window we could see into, was something moving or flickering slightly, something shiny and lighter blue. It took a second or two to recognize it, because of its size—it was over a meter long, almost round.

"It was an eye. A great, humongous, living eye, blue with a white rim. And looking at us.

"Like the creature it belonged to was so big it was all curled up inside its compartment, with its eye pressed to the glass. For some reason, right from the start we knew that the creature, or being, or whatever, had only one central eye.

"In addition to looking at us—that is, at the camera— most of the time, the eye was also swiveling to examine the Lander and everything around.

"Now all through the excitement Todd and Jim in the Lander were trying to tell us something. I wasn't in on this, but whenever I could get near Voice Contact I heard things like, 'We are not crazy! I tell you we are not crazy; it's talking in our heads. *Yes*, in English. We get two words very distinctly: *peace* and *welcome*. Over and over. And we are not out of our minds; if I could figure a way to get this on the caller you'd hear—'

"They sounded madder and madder. I guess Mission Control was giving them a hard time, especially General Streiter, who was sure it was a Soviet Commie trick of some kind. And of course there was no way for them to get a mental voice on the antennae. But then the aliens apparently solved that for themselves. Just as Jim was saying for the tenth time that he wasn't crazy or hadn't drunk too much coffee, all our communications went blooie for a minute and then this great big quiet voice drowned everything.

" 'PEACE . . .' it said. And then, 'WELL-COME!'

"Something about the voice, its tone, made Mission Control sound for a minute like a—well, like a cathedral. 'PEACE! . . . WELCOME! . . . PEACE . . . FRIENDS . . .' "

"And then it added, very gentle and majestic, 'COME . . . COME . . .'

"And Mission Control became aware that Todd and Jim were preparing to go out of the Lander.

"Pandemonium!

"Well, I'll skip all this bit where Mission Control was ordering them to stay inside, on no account to even put a hand out, to unsuit—Jim and Todd were calmly suiting up—and anything else they could think of and General Streiter ordering court-martials for everybody in sight, on Mars or Earth—it even went so far as getting the President out of bed to come and countermand them in person. I found out afterward that the poor man got so mixed up he thought they were *refusing* to go out onto Mars, and he was supposed to tell them to! And all with this four-and-a-half-minute lag, and this great hushy voice blanking everything out with 'PEACE . . . WELCOME . . .'

"Until finally it was obvious even to the general that nothing could be done, that forty-four million miles away two Earthmen were about to walk out onto Mars and confront The Alien."

(This is Theodora putting in a word here. See, everyone had been so convinced that there was no life

on Mars above something like lichen that absolutely
no instructions had been thought up for meeting large-
scale sentient life, let alone with telepathic communications.)

"Well, they evacuated the air, and as they went to
go down the ladder, Jim Aruppa grabbed Todd, and
we could hear him saying in his helmet, 'Remember,
you bastard! Count cadence *now!*'

"And nobody knew what that was until we found
out there'd been this private arrangement between the
two men. After all those months together, see, Jim
wasn't going to take all the glory for being the First
Man on Mars. As he put it to Todd, 'Who was the
second man to step onto the moon?' And Todd had to
guess twice, and nobody else knew either. And Jim
wasn't going to let that happen again. So he ordered
Todd to descend in sync with him and make an absolutely simultaneous first-foot-down. That was one of
the little squabbles that kept Mission Control lively all
those two years. Some kind of guy, Jim.

"So there they were counting cadence down the
ladder to Mars—to *Mars,* man!—with this alien Thing
a hundred yards away staring at them.

"And they walked over to it slowly and carefully,
looking at everything, the eye following them. And
there were no signs of how it had possibly moved
there except by some kind of very gentle flight. But no
machinery, nothing at all but these two big hexagonal
spheroids with windows. And the compartment between. The first word Jim sent back was, 'It seems to
be entirely non-metallic. Not plastic, either. More like
a—like a smooth shiny dry pod, with windows set in.
The frames are non-metallic too.'

"And then they got to where they could see the
windows on the farther-off spheroid—and there was
another eye looking out at them from it!

"It seemed exactly like the first eye, only slightly
larger and paler. The flesh around the eyes registered
blue too, by the way—and there was no sign of
eyelashes.

"And then both Jim and Todd claimed that this eye

winked at them and Mission Control went back to calling them crazy.

"When they got back in front, by the open compartment, they made signals as though they were hearing something. And then the voice we could hear via radio changed too. 'Come,' it said in sort of grand-friendly tones. 'Come . . . Please come in. Come with, say hello friends.'

"Well, that sent Mission Control into a new spasm of countercommands, in the midst of which the two men set the camera on its tripod outside, and walked into the open alien compartment, bouncing a little on the padded floor. Then they turned around to face us, and sat down on the seat-cushion-looking things. And at that the big overhead door slid smoothly forward and down and closed them in. It had a window in it—in fact it was mostly window. But before anybody could think of any reaction to *that*, it opened up again halfway, and Todd and Jim stepped out. Four and a half minutes later we heard, 'They say to bring food for one day.'

"And the man went back up into the Lander to collect supplies.

"Somehow the ordinariness, or what you might call considerateness of this just took the wind out of a lot of angry lungs.

" 'No water necessary, they say,' Jim Aruppa told us as they climbed back out of the Lander. 'But we brought some just in case. I never thought I'd be glad to see a can of Tab.' He grinned, holding up his little camp basin. 'But we can at least wash our hands in it.'

" 'Jeez, it's getting like a god-forsaken *picnic!*' Eggy Stone shouted over the general uproar.

"Well, the door snapped over and shut down again. We could see them through the window, waving. And then the thing simply lifted up quietly and flew like magic toward and over the camera, and over the Lander, and we couldn't pick it up again. And that was absolutely all for thirty-six long hours, until—

"—Say, Miz Tanton, haven't you got the tape of

what they said when they came back? I just can't talk one word more."

So here's a break. All this next part I put together from Jim and Todd's report-tapes of their trip, plus the officially cleaned-up version of it that was in the *Times*. I found a stack of archive tape dupes in the janitor's cubby.

But before that, I should say that the Reverend Perry had been busy, up in the Martian sky. Mission Control at least had one astronaut who would take orders, and they'd told him to try to check out where the Thing had come from during the night. So he got busy with his 'scopes and sensors, and about the time Jim and Todd were going back for their chow, he had a report. A Martian building, or structure, "like a big mound of bubbles," was located in the foothills of Mount Eleuthera to the east. But as a city it was strange—it had no suburbs, no streets, not much internal differentiation, and no roads leading to or away. (Of course not; we know now it was a ship.)

So when the flying dumbbell bearing the two humans went off NASA's cameras, Perry knew where to try to pick them up. And by the way, although Perry was obedient to orders, he too was acting strange. He didn't volunteer anything, but on direct questioning he admitted that he was hearing voices in his head—at first he said something about a "ringing in his ears" —and when the aliens' voices cut in on the radio wavelength, Perry pulled himself down to his knees and NASA could see enough to realize he was both trying to pray and weep. This didn't disturb them overmuch—considering what else was going on—because the Reverend was known to indulge in short prayers whenever some special marvel of space came up, and he was addicted to brief thanksgivings at any lucky break. He was quite unselfconscious about this, and it never interfered with his efficiency, so maybe NASA figured they were covering all bets by having him along. General Streiter asked him if he was all right.

"I shall say no more about this now, General," Perry replied. "I recognize it is inappropriate to this phase of our mission. But I sincerely believe we have contracted a . . . a Higher Power, and that some very great good may come of this if we prove worthy."

Streiter took this in silence; he knew Perry as a congenial fellow Commie-hater, and he had expected him to see Red skulduggery in the sudden materialization of the Thing. But Perry seemed to be taking another tack; the general respected him enough to let him be.

So back to Todd and Jim, who were being flown silently, magically, over the Martian landscape. They were at the big door-window. The lift-off was so gentle that Jim said he wouldn't have known they were moving if he hadn't been looking out. This reassured them about the absence of any straps or body-holds in the padded compartment they had entered.

They were of course looking for a city or town, or at least the openings of tunnels, and the "mound of bubbles" Perry was reporting took them by surprise. Near the top of the mound was an opening where a sphere or two seemed to be missing; as they came over it, they saw that their craft exactly fitted in. Forward motion ceased quietly, and with a soft, non-metallic brushing sound the modules that carried them dropped into the empty slots. Todd was inspired. "Hey, that's all one huge ship—and this is a dinghy!"

His mind had broadcast the right picture. "Yess!" the aliens chorused, "our ship!"

Before they could see anything of the interior, a side window in their compartment opened, and a light blue, leathery-looking trunk or tentacle about the size of a fire hose appeared. "Hello!" said the voice in their heads clearly.

"Hello," they said aloud.

The tentacle extended itself towards Jim's hand. Involuntarily he drew back. "Hello? Hello? Friends!" said the soundless voice. "Touch?"

Gingerly Jim extended his hand, and to his surprise, after a little confusion, the contact the alien wanted was achieved.

"It wants to shake hands!" Jim exclaimed to Todd.

"Yes! Friends! Shake!" And a similar window in the opposite wall opened, revealing the other alien. Its tentacle was larger, more wrinkled, and lighter blue. "Friends?"

A round of enthusiastic handshaking ensued. Then the second alien wanted something more. Its tentacle's tip pulled clumsily but gently at Todd's glove, and he got a confused message about taking it off and speaking.

When Todd got his glove off and took the alien's flesh barehanded, he gasped and seemed to stagger.

"What's wrong? Todd?"

"Okay—it's okay, very—. Try it."

Jim ungloved and grasped the tip of the alien limb. Then he too gasped—as contact occurred, there came with it a rush of communication, both verbal and pictorial, in which he could pick out bits or sequences of past events, present communication, speculations, images—including a vision of himself—plans, questions—he was all but *inside* an alien mind!

They were both laughing, delighted at this immense novelty to explore—and from the other sides of their padded walls came echoing chuckles. A pleasant fragrance like cinnamon was coming through their air filters, too. They were the first humans to smell the spicy odor emitted by these aliens when excited and interested.

"This is going to take practice," Jim gasped. He tried to convey the idea to the alien whose blue tentacle he was clasping, and received a strong feeling of assent. Delicately, it moved its tentacle within his grip, so that only certain surfaces were apposed, and the rush of mindflow quieted down.

Then it tapped his palm in a way that they soon came to recognize as meaning "I have something to tell/show you." And he found himself seeing a connected, coherent "movie" of the alien's bubble-craft approaching Earth sometime earlier, sampling the airborne communications—both radio and video—and selecting the large land mass of North America to linger near. "All same language," and the voice in his head. "Many pictures—teach much." And then a sample of what they had set themselves to learn—recognizable segments of "Dallas," "All My Children," "Sesame Street," newscasts—and ads, ads, ads unceasing. "Much do not understand."

Whew! Jim tried to interrupt, but the flow went on. From it he gathered that the aliens had evoked a few hostile reactions from U.S. Air Force installations. Also the aliens soon learned that great intergroup hostilities existed on Earth. They had actually been on the verge of leaving—"Go look better planet"—when they learned about the Mars mission. It seemed to them that this would be the ideal place and way to meet humanity. So here they were, and here were our two astronauts—deep in converse, without having seen the forms or faces of their new friends. (For from the start, there had seemed to both men no question that a *friendly* meeting was in progress, and friendship was growing between them every moment.)

"Now you want to say Hello others, so we talk more?"

"Yes indeed."

A picture sequence in their minds prepared them and then the whole back wall of their compartment irised open, giving onto a great, softly glowing space. When they went to it they saw that the "mound of bubbles" was actually a shell around an open core; all the "bubbles" gave onto a common open space, in which were a few structures whose use or meaning they couldn't guess. All around the walls, ceiling, floor were the openings of compartments similar to their own, some brightly lighted, some dim, some dark, so that the whole formed a kind of grand auditorium or meeting hall. At the mouths of nearly every individual compartment was an alien, or two or more, all with their great single eyes turned eagerly in their direction.

And here I have to pause, or put in asterisks or somehow prepare you before I describe what you notice I've omitted so far—the aliens' shapes.

The color of course you know—sky blue in the main, with here and there blues lighter or darker, from slate to peacock blue, from pale blue foam to deep marine. And the great eyes were quite human-shaped, though the size of footlockers. And the tentacles you have met—each had groups of sucker-discs which were apparently quiescent unless the owner wished to cling.

It is their general shape you don't yet know.

There is one, and only one, Earthly animal that they resembled, and they resembled it very closely. To put it bluntly, the aliens looked like gigantic cerulean octopuses.

Imagewise, of course, it was terrible.

In addition to being unspellable (octopusses, octopuses, octopoi, octopi, octopodes?), it conjured up every old horror cliché. And it was undeniable—they *were* in fact simply big, air-breathing octopuses; we all learned later that they had evolved in their planet's oceans, and slowly adapted to land as their oceans dried. Their mantles had lost the propulsive function, and four of their back tentacles had evolved to limbs suitable for walking on land, leaving the other four to take on hand-and-arm and telepathic transmission abilities.

Their heads were large and bald and shiny above the single eye, and their mantles began where a chin should be, concealing their noses and mouths, or beaks, or whatever. Also to be glimpsed beneath the mantle's rippling edges was a mass of darker blue furlike organs, among which seemed to be some very small, delicate tentacles of unknown use.

In all, had it not been for their truly lovely coloring and odor and the expressive friendliness of their large eyes, the first impression of the aliens to a human, would have to be revulsion bordering on terror.

The Earthly media of course went wild at first—GIANT BLUE OCTOPPUSES ON MARS! shrilled even the staidest. Octopus!—the name alone makes for the world's worst PR. That's why I've given you all this preliminary stuff, instead of just dictating from the newsclips.

The photos, when they came, made things a little better, because their postures were so versatile and graceful. And their basically radial bodies were obviously in transition to a bilaterally symmetrical form—the four "back" leg-tentacles were much larger and longer, to free the front four. In fact if—as happened later—a small one wore a long robe with a hood to conceal the shiny bald dome above the eye, it could pass for a large somewhat top-heavy human form. And they spent much of their time thus upright, looking rather like multiply armed Indian deities, and smelling delightful. So that, as soon as Earth saw more of them, the original "sci-fi" horror images were seen to be ludicrously inappropriate, and were forgotten.

While Todd and Jim were taking in the nature of their audience, and vice versa, their new friends were folding back the walls of their compartments and dragging the cushions to the edge of the front.

"We speak one-to-all like this. We show you." And they motioned Todd and Jim to take seats. "No fear fall off, everybody catch."

Then they stationed themselves on each side, laid their transmission-tentacles across Jim's and Todd's shoulders, and seemed to listen.

"No—clothes too thick. Can take off, please? Air good here." So the men first gingerly lifted off their helmets—getting a real blast of carnation scent—and then started peeling down. They felt a bit odd about it in front of all those eager eyes, but what the hell, their bodies were no more to the aliens than a wombat's to them. So they sat back down again, nude, and the tentacles came back. "Ahhh! Good!"

And with that the two big aliens stretched their other transmitter arms out to the aliens in the compartments next door, and these did the same to those around them, so that in a minute the whole great amphitheater was intricately laced together, with the men as foci.

While this was happening, Todd felt a plucking at his shins. He looked down, and there was this dark blue tentacle coming up at him from the compartment below. He heard, or sensed, what could only be a giggle, and next instant three big round bright eyes were staring up at him over the edge of his floor. A spicy fume of interest wafted up.

The alien next to him emitted a reproving sound, and batted at the eyes with a spare limb. "Young ones!" Peering down, Todd and Jim saw a cluster of smaller aliens in the chamber below, evidently trying to get in on the network by short circuit. "It's okay." He grinned. "No problem to us."

So their two big friends let the little fellows sneak tendrils in to touch the men's legs and feet.

"Okay . . . you go first?" said the one next to Jim. "Oh, wait. Us name Angli. An-gli," it repeated aloud. "You name?"

"Hello, Angli!" said Jim to them both. "Us name hu-mans. But"—he pointed at the other—"you have special personal name, for you only?"

Well, that was their introduction to the one great difficulty of mind-speech—asking questions. It took minutes for them to get sorted out as individuals, and even so they weren't sure they had it right. Jim said, "The customary thing here seems to be to call up a quick flash-image of the person, or his eye, or something special about him or her. I don't think verbal names are used much. But our friends seem to be something like Urizel and Azazel, for what it's worth. We'll try calling them that and see if it works." Then he put his arm around Todd. "We together, hu-mans," he said. "But *he* alone"—testuring—"is *Todd*. I—me, here—am *Jim*. Todd . . . Jim. Jim . . . Todd. Get it?"

"Me Jane, you Tarzan," muttered Todd.

"Shut up, you idiot, this is no time to clown. We'll have to be sure somehow that they know what a joke is. All right. Urizel, Azazel, and all the rest of you Angli—what do you want to know about us humans first?"

And so started the greatest show-and-tell anthropology class of their lives.

Surprisingly soon, it got itself organized with their two friends alternately passing questions to the men. Not surprisingly, in view of their TV fare, the first queries were mainly about economics. Todd had the pleasure of trying to answer, "What is 'money?' " He managed to form a picture of a medium of exchange passing from hand to hand in the human world. And luckily, the Angli seemed to have something to relate this to; Jim got a visual image of furry brown creatures carrying on their tails stacks of big square things with holes in them that had to be clumsy coins.

"Gosh, what does a really rich one do?" Todd didn't expect an answer, but the Angli had picked up the drift of his query, and he got a clear mental picture of a pompous-looking brown alien followed by a formal train of specialized coin-bearers, their long tails erect and loaded to the tips with big discs.

Both humans and Angli laughed.

"What do you do with money?" Azazel asked. Jim gulped and tried to visualize a bank teller, vaults, checkbooks.

"I fear I'm not doing justice to the international banking system," he said to Todd. "But, dammit, ours has to make more sense than carrying your money around on your tail!"

"I'm beginning to wonder," Todd muttered. "No, no," he said to Azazel, "Not important."

It was now very apparent that the humans were by no means the first new race the Angli had met. Fleeting images of many other aliens, worlds, cities, ships, crossed their perceptions from various Angli minds. These aliens seemed to have spent years jaunting about the galaxy, meeting people and things.

As to the Angli's own home world—the notion that they were Martians was disposed of very early—they were shown an image of a planet not unlike Earth, but greener, near a GO-type sun. A view of the nearby constellations enabled the men to guess that it was near the nebula in Orion's sword. A close-up view showed a lush, attractive landscape with a bubble-dome town.

And the Angli were not alone! Another intelligent race lived there—no, wait, *had* lived there once—"many times ago." The blurred image of a porpoiselike creature with legs seemed to have passed through many minds. "They go"—but whether they had left or died off was never clear; these Angli perhaps didn't know. The Angli were alone there now.

One last fact that came out was sensational: the "bubbles" the men were in wasn't their only ship. They had maybe half a dozen ships and stuff parked on Luna, on the back side of our moon, where we couldn't see them. One or more contained a lot more Angli, who wanted simply to sleep until a really promising planet was found. ("Wake us when we get someplace!") Very young Angli were also asleep there. Another one—or more—contained members of another race, whose planet had been in trouble, so the Angli volunteered to find them a new one. (In their experience, the galaxy seemed to be full of all kinds of planets just waiting to be found.) This particular race needed an aquatic environment, it seemed.

Another ship seemed to contain assorted seeds and supplies; despite their casual behavior, the Angli really had great practical sense about essentials. And at least two were empty—one had contained a race the Angli had successfully relocated. And a final one contained a spectacular cargo we on Earth were soon to get a view of.

(Of course, on learning that other ships existed, the general and others promptly began to suspect that the Angli also had battleships or other military capabilities parked up there, and many covert plans were laid to sneak around Luna and peek. But they all came to nothing, and nothing hostile ever showed up.)

Each query raised a dozen others; the hours passed like minutes. Finally, a growing emptiness in their middles forced the men to call a halt.

"We eat now?"

The Angli too, it seemed, were tired and hungry, although so fascinated that they seemed ready to go on indefinitely. But at Jim's question a cheer broke out among the young ones below. In no time they had produced great baskets of what looked like hardtack, and were carrying them around the auditorium, passing a container out to each row. Each Angli in turn helped him- or herself to a piece, and tucked it neatly under a mantle fold in their central bodies, where the men had surmised their mouths, or beaks, might be.

"We've got to get this gender business straightened out," Todd said with his mouth full. "Oh, cripes. How do we do *that*, Tarzan?"

"Maybe we don't, until we can produce a real Jane." And so it turned out. He seemed to evoke a response to his first tries at describing human sexes—"Humans like Jim and me here"—he indicated his genitalia—"we call 'men.' Other humans have lumps *here* but not *here*—we call them 'women.' And it takes the two kinds together to make young ones." Todd continued. "How do you make young?"

But here all impression of understanding faded, and an Angli question, "What you call Mathlon?" stumped everybody. Mind-visions of an Angli picking things out of a puddle didn't help.

Theodora Tanton here again. I just excerpted all that above from Jim's long report, to give the atmosphere and show some of the problems; I guess that some parts belong in the after-lunch session. And don't shoot me, sisters, about the gender part and the "lumps" —that's just what the man said. I put most dialogue as if it were ordinary speech instead of explaining whether it was telepathy or audible speech each time. Men and Angli were developing a sort of half-speech/ half-thought lingo that worked well.

The afternoon, or what was left of it, went as fast as the morning, and soon the sunlight that filtered through into the great central dome was visibly reddening into a typical Martian sunset.

"We go back now, please," the men said. "Our people have much fear."

"Ohh-kayee!" said Urizel, and they all laughed. One thing the men couldn't get over was how human their laughter was—and they thought ours was incredibly Anglian.

So they closed up the doors, the humans suited up, the module lifted away silently from its slot, and the trip repeated itself in reverse. They tried again—it had come up all day—to understand the source of its power, but always the same answer baffled them. "We do with bodies. Like so—" and the speaker would loft himself a few meters, apparently effortlessly, and descend again. "You no do, eh? We find many races no do; only one we find can do." And a picture came in their minds of a large, raylike being, sailing and flapping above an alien landscape. The Angli tapped his head regretfully. "Fly pretty, but not have much brain. Come later, maybe."

Now on their return trip they could see their friends loading in, and it was obvious that they propelled their craft by simply *pushing* it up from inside, as a man under a table might lift it with his back—but with no need to press down on anything. Nor did it seem tiring.

"Antigravity is the best guess we can make," Jim told Earth later.

One more item they were shown: in both the end compartments was a window in the floor, beside which was a bank of what turned out to be outside lights, including infrared. They were powered by small batteries.

"Use up fast," Azazel said, frowning. And they didn't turn the lights on again until they were over the Earth Lander. This contraption was the first construction of metal or wires the men had seen. It looked handmade. "We get from special people," Azazel said, and transmitted a brief shot of some sort of aliens in an apparent workshop. "Not on our home."

"We make light too," Uriel said, and from under his (or her) mantle suddenly came a soft blue glow, which brightened to a point, then turned off. "Is work," the big Angli said expressively. Light was evidently strictly for emergency use. They seemed to have fantastically good night vision; the men suspected that their use of the floodlights as they neared the Lander was more for the Earthmen's sake than their own. "You no see so good in dark."

"Maybe they were surprised when we didn't seem to see their approach last night," Jim said.

And then it was time to say good-bye and get back in their own little craft. And report to Mission Control.

"I bet they don't let us off the hook for hours and hours and hours," Todd said. And he was proved right. Kevin remembers vividly the shout that rang through Mission Control when the camera picked up their approaching lights. And then it took half the night to relay and record what I've put down here, plus a lot of repeats and mix-ups I've cut out.

Oh—I've forgotten one big thing. Just as they were leaving the dome a senior-looking Angli sent them a message through Azazel.

"He say, why not we take you home to Earth? Go quick, like maybe thirty-forty your days. We get human now up in sky, leave your ships here, you come back and get some other time. And you help us say Hello and make friendship with Earth?"

What an offer!" And with a soft landing at the end," crooned Todd ecstatically.

"Tell him yes, most happy," replied Jim. "Say—is he your leader?"

Now that brings up another subject I've been postponing—their government. As far as we ever found out, they virtually had none. The older Angli formed a loose set of council that anybody who wanted to could be in. Any question, like where to go next, or what to do about a specific problem, was apparently solved by informal mind-melding. People would put up ideas, and they'd be mulled over until a consensus evolved. What happened in the event of a serious disagreement? But there doesn't seem to have been any. "Oh, we take turns," said Azazel negligently.

Anyway, thus it was that the great homecoming of our successful Mars mission was in an alien ship in no way under the control of NASA, although they politely accepted all our communications. And they seemed surprised at the close supervision expected from and by Mission Control. On their home world, apparently, people just wandered hither and yon, off to a moon, or whatever.

One of the rites of growing up, it seemed, was making your own vehicle (they were indeed gigantic dried seed pods) and fitting it out for long trips. With their long-range mind-speech capability, there were no problems about getting lost, and their world seemed to have had few dangers. About the only mishap that seemed likely to occur to young ones jaunting about was when their presence or chatter annoyed some elder citizen who would complain to the council and have them grounded for a week or two. Like youngers everywhere, they prized mobility and were always putting in work improving their craft, which virtually served as alternate homes. The climate, one gathered, was very benign.

It sounded idyllic; I wasn't the only one to start to wonder why, really, they had left. . . .

The day of their arrival on Earth has been so amply covered in schoolbooks that I have only small pieces to add, like about the riot. What went on at first was all standard—this great beige bubble-nest wafting down toward a cleared-off area in a sea of people, escorted for the last miles by practically everything the Air Force could put in the air. It sat down resiliently and before it had finished heaving. Angli all over the top began opening doors and looking out. A group escorting the three astronauts got out together and flew them down to where a cordoned and carpeted way to the receiving stand was marked off.

There were Urizel and Azazel, and a pair of aged senior councillors the men had persuaded to come along. Their progress was highly informal; people could see that the men were trying to report back to their Commander-in-Chief in a stylish, military way, but the Angli were hard to keep in line. They began thought-broadcasting to the crowd in general, right over the heads of the officials. And then they hooked into the PA system with "Hello! Peace! Friends!" And the press corps broke the lines by the ship and began infiltrating everywhere. Kevin was with the NASA

Press contingent; he passed me a few tidbits. And the aged councillors, to whom one Earthman was much like another, began greeting the police and Secret Service men who were standing, arms linked, with their backs to the ship, trying to contain the swaying crowd. And during the official party's slow progress to the stand, Angli began coming out of the ship and making short flights over the heads of the crowd.

The stage was set for trouble, and it happened—five or six dark blue young Angli came out together with their arms full of something and flew over the crowd to the right, looking for a place to land and calling out "Friends!" and laughing that human laugh. What they had was blooms from the ship's hydroponics—big, fragrant stalks that unfortunately looked a bit like hand grenades. The crowd was too thick below them, so they began dropping the flowers onto people's heads. At that, the humans below started to mill, some people backing away in alarm while others pressed forward curiously. And the youngsters circled overhead, laughing and pelting people with flowers.

Suddenly someone took real fright, and a small local stampede away from the Angli started. Others, seeing people running and feeling themselves pushed, began to run and push aimlessly too. Shouting broke out. The pushing intensified fast—and a woman screamed and went down.

All this showed only as a confused place on the edge of the TV screens, while the astronauts and the Angli were still straggling up the cordoned pathway to the stand where the presidential party was waiting. As the sound of shouting rose from off-screen, the United States Marine Band broke into a louder march piece, which amplified the confusion over an outbreak of real screaming and yells.

Urizel, sensing what was happening, dropped Todd's arm and flew over the tangle with the idea of shooing the youngsters back to the ship. But the arrival of this monster of much greater size frightened more people. The fallen woman was trampled and began to shriek. Urizel, spotting her, dived to the spot and sent his long tentacles down to extricate her, really scaring the people nearby

About then, police sirens started up, an ambulance got its warbler going and began pressing into the scene. This excited more people outside the immediate nucleus. Some tried to gather their families and run, while others ran toward the uproar. The yelling developed a panicky, ominous beat. Meanwhile, those on the red carpet were still making their slow way to the President on the stand.

Now, every telepathic race is well aware of the terrible danger of contagious panic, the threat of a mind-storm. Both inside the ship and out, the Angli became aware of what was going on, and about to get much worse. Their response was automatic.

In perfect synchrony, they all stopped whatever they were doing, and sent out a united, top-power mental command: "*Quiet! Be calm! Sleep!* . . . QUIET! BE CALM! SLEEP!" It blasted the field.

So powerful was this thought-command that by the first repetition the yells and shouts died in people's throats. The uproar tapered down to a strange silence, in which the band raggedly played on for a few bars before they too were overwhelmed. Running people slowed to a walk, to a standstill; their heads drooped, and they saw the ground looking invitingly comfortable, attracting them to relax down. And suddenly, all in the moments that the great command silently went out, what had been a wildly agitated mob became a field of peaceful sleepers. Some slept sitting with their heads on their knees, others sprawled full length, their heads on any neighboring body.

The police and Secret Service men were of course affected too, and after a moment's heroic resistance, they went down in waves atop their sleeping charges.

The band and the PA system were silent, and on the receiving stand the dignitaries retained presence of mind only to locate a convenient chair before collapsing into sleep. The President was already dozing; he opened his mouth and emitted a few snorts indicative of deeper slumbers, while his lady slept decorously beside him. A stray seagull alighted on the Secretary of State, and went to sleep on one leg.

Close overhead, at what had been the center of the disturbance, floated Urizel, the woman he had rescued sleeping in his grasp. He spotted the stalled ambulance, which emanated images of physical aid.

"Wake up," he said to the crew. "Here is human hurt." They snapped back to conciousness rubbing their eyes, and jumped to man the stretcher.

"Put her here."

A press photographer beside them also woke, reaching by reflex for his camera, and got the banner headline shots of his life—Urizel stooping low with the unconscious woman draped photogenically across his tentacles, his great eye luminous with compassion and concern. "ALIEN RESCUES WOMAN FROM CROWD! ALIEN CARRYING GIRL HE SAVED TO AMBULANCE!"

(I found out from Kevin, who had been there too and waked first, that the photographer had luckily missed an even more sensational shot. Urizel, noting that this human he carried seemed to differ from the astronauts, had seized the opportunity to check out the locations and nature of those "lumps" Todd had told him of—in the process rearranging quite a lot of her clothes.)

The woman turned out to be a Mrs. C. P. Boynton. She was only slightly bruised, and her statements to the press were ecstatic.

"I was so scared, I knew that hundreds of people would trample on me and I'd be killed. I just prayed to God. 'Help me!' And suddenly there was this great blue being flying over me like an angel, and he just reached down and pulled me out from under all those terrible feet! And oh, he smells so lovely!"

What I want to convey is that the Angli would be getting a very good press, right from Day One.

Back at the stand, the official greetings to and by the President finally came off. Perry tactfully roused the great man by murmuring, "Sir, I believe you were about to say a few words," and he automatically rose up into his speech—just in time to divert the aged councillors from returning to their ship. And the band began to play, rather disjointedly—but it isn't true that they then or ever played "Nearer My God to Thee." And the reception rolled off.

When it came time for Todd, Jim, and Perry to part company from their alien friends, with whom they'd spent over a month of intimate travel, things got pretty emotional. During the voyage home, the Rev. Perry had been observed to attach himself to Azazel in particular. Now, up on the receiving stand, the great blue forms of the Angli were turning away, to go back to their ship and leave the humans to their own. They were up on their back tentacles, their heads towering above everything as they bade polite farewells to the President, his lady, and the Secretary of State, now minus his seagull. Perry quietly moved closer. Suddenly he dropped to his knees and flung his long arms around the tentacles Azazel was standing on. (Perry was a huge man.) After a moment of confusion, it became clear that he was simply hugging the alien, his face laid against Azazel's side, and weeping. He was also mumbling something that sounded so private that no one listened, except Kevin. And no one knew what thought-speech he was sending to his big alien friend, or receiving back from him.

The strange tableau lasted only an instant. Then Perry got up with great dignity and stepped back into line with Todd and Jim. And the moment was swamped by the hand-tentacle shaking going on all around.

Kevin, who had been just outside the stand, told me afterward that at the end Perry had said clearly, "*Non Angli sed angeli*"—and if you don't place the quotation at first, listen on.

Now to sum up the impression the aliens were making, I'll give you a letter I received in response to my first appeal for eyewitnesses. It was written by one Cora Lee Boomer, aged eighty-nine, like this:

"Of course I only saw it on TV you know. Maybe I saw it better that way. The Army cleared off this big sandy place, Dry Lake Something. And they had guards all over. But the people just filled it up. And about eleven A.M., I remember because it was time to feed the baby, Donald, we saw it coming down in the sky. It was like a big bunch of grapes only no stems.

"And it kept coming down, real slow, I guess not to hurt anything, and pretty soon a helicopter was going around it, taking pictures. It was kind of tan-colored, with antennae sticking out. All these round things pressed together like something I used to see—honeycombs. When they sent pictures from close up you could see all these blue eyes inside looking out. So beautiful. Excuse me, I can't say it right.

"Mostly I try not to think about it; even today I can just see it. But that man I had then, he thought he was so smart. And I was a young fool, I did whatever he wanted. He said that it was all no good. Stay away from Whitey junk, he said. Excuse me. I was so young.

"But when they landed and got out with the three men and I saw their eyes close up, I had a feeling he was wrong. They looked so beautiful. Like caring and understanding. And smiling too. I should have believed my own eyes.

"So I only saw things start. He came in and saw me looking at it and turned the set off—it was on all the channels, see—and said, 'Get my lunch,' so I never saw much of them after that. And of course I never got to go.

"I think now he was wrong, he was crazy. They were good, good. But I was so young and the baby kept me pretty busy, and with my job. Now I'm old I know there's more to life I wonder what it be like. George, he's long gone.

"I just remember that big loving eye. Sometimes I cry a lot.

"I hope this is what you said you wanted. Sincerely, Cora Lee Boomer."

This is Theodora Tanton again, saying, well, that was the way the Earth's first meeting with the Angli went. I know the White Book doesn't tell about the riot, and the little points Kevin saw. But they're important, to show how people were starting to *feel* a certain way about the aliens, to explain part of what happened later.

People could have been disappointed, see, or bored. The aliens brought no hardware. And all the films and fiction we used to see kind of assumed that our first contact with ALIENS was going to result in a lot of new fancy technology, or at least a cure for the common cold. Goodies. But as Urizel said, these people brought us only peace and friendship—at least on the surface people could see. Their own goodies, like anti-gravity and telepathy, were just in their bodies—they could no more explain them or transmit them than we could hand over our sense of smell.

And then more things happened to excite the press. To everyone's surprise, the big ship simply broke up next day, with Angli flying pieces of it all over. soon there was nothing left in NASA's guard ring but some struts and potted plants.

"ALIENS WANT TO SEE WORLD! ALIENS TO VISIT CATHEDRALS! ALIENS STUDY WORLD RELIGIONS! CALL FOR LANGUAGE-SPEAKERS! ALIENS DO NOT READ OR WRITE! ALIENS WANT TO MEET EVERYBODY ON EARTH!" (That would be some of the youngsters chatting up the press. People had trouble sorting out the kids' stuff, at first.)

So Angli started turning up in little groups, or even alone, all over, at any time of day or night. Of course that gave the security forces of all the big nations total fits.

It turned out they needn't have worried too much about the Angli's safety. (Their own security was another matter.) But it's hard to assassinate a telepath—hostile thoughts blasted out signals to them long before the thinker could act. I don't know if this is in the White Book or not, but just to show you:

One afternoon some Angli were in Libya, chatting with people at a market by a highway where cars were whizzing by like mad amongst the livestock and all. Suddenly every Angli grabbed a nearby human or two and shot straight up in the air, maybe twenty meters.

At the same time, two more Angli grabbed a certain car, and flying with it, simply flipped it tail over into the empty space they'd made. Next second there was an explosion as a bomb went off inside the car, and a few people got cuts. The would-be bombers were dead.

It all happened so fast people were totally bewildered; they had to piece together afterward that some crazies had been going to blow the Angli up. And the Angli had taken defensive steps both for themselves and nearby people. That part of it was what stuck in people's minds when it was all over—that Angli automatically rescued you.

Then there was another big episode that may be in the White Book. It was when an Angli named Gavril was being taken on a scenic drive down the great road called the Corniche, in France, Gavril got tired of looking at the dirty Mediterranean—I guess he could hear the thoughts of dying fish and seabirds—and started casting about.

Next thing, he had flashed up onto the air from the open convertible, paced the car briefly, and then come to rest on a railway overpass. A rail line ran below the road. By the time his hosts got back to him, he was standing with closed eye, so evidently deep in concentration that they just waited.

Then train hootings began in the distance and Gavril opened his eye.

"Is o-kayee now," he said. "People see people." And he lofted back into the car, offering no explanation. Of course his hosts began questioning, especially as there seemed to be some excitement starting, down by the railroad.

What had happened, it transpired, is that Gavril had picked up the thoughts of two trainloads of people approaching each other at terrific speed in the tunnels below. Happening to notice that the line was single track, he became concerned and hopped off to check.

Yes, he realized. They were heading for a frightful crash. Gavril shot strong mental blasts at the trains' engineers—it was hard work among simultaneously at targets speeding opposite ways—"*Danger!* STOP!" As

I said, it was difficult. When he finally brought them to a stop, the headlight of each train was just visible to the other.

Well, when his hosts realized what he'd done, they called in the press, and hundreds of grateful passengers besieged the scene. A photo of Gavril hovering over a locomotive, captioned, "ANGE DE MERCI," appeared in all the big French papers that night. Apparently about six hundred people would have died without his intervention; somebody, presumably terrorists, had buggered the automatic switch and alarm systems.

Well, of course there was no holding the media after that, and scads of episodes, true and concocted, were headlined. There grew up a feeling that Angli were symbols of benevolence or good fortune and that it was lucky to be in the presence of one. People actually began plucking at them, hoping to tear off a little scrap of "armor" to carry with them like rabbit's feet, I guess. But of course they weren't wearing armor; they were in their skins. The situation would have been dangerous and painful had it not been for their telepathic warnings. As it was, a couple of youngsters got scratched, and they all took to wearing flowing scarves they could cut up and pass out. "Is a little cra-zee, people your world," Todd said Urizel told him. Of course profuse apologies were extended by all authorities, but there is no controlling mobs. And the Angli began drawing *mobs*, crowds of every emotionally wrought-up people, quite different from merely curious or sensation-seekers.

During this period, there were things going on that I should know and tell you, because for sure they're not in the White Book, but you know, I never completed my research—never began it really. To do so I've have had to go to what's left of a dozen countries, and get into the U.S.S.R. and even find certain hospitals. For the Angli were visiting places and talking to people they never saw fit to mention to NASA or anybody here, even to Todd, Jim, and Perry who had become their more or less official escorts.

Well, you may ask, what kind of inside story do I

have, if I never did the research? Oh, the research was just an ornament I envisioned to the real tale that fell into my hands. Wait!

And that aside about the hospitals is a guess, by the way. It could have been university labs, or even private industry facilities. The gist of it is that somehow some Angli found the means to do a spot of sophisticated scientific research into human physiology. And they seemed to have an instinct for places where the press was strictly controlled, but that only came out later.

What came out then were two things of overpowering interest.

First was their plan to leave.

To leave? To *leave*? To just go jaunting off somewhere out in the galaxy—and maybe never come back?

This was a jolt. Maybe some higher-ups somewhere had done some serious thinking about how all this would end, but it hadn't reached the public. In fiction and films there was always some sort of permanence after the great Earth/Alien meeting; either the aliens were trying to take over, or Earthmen had beaten a path to their planetary doorstep, or *something* implied that there would be more contact, or at least some permanent effects. Not just this "Hello, nice-to-meet-you, bye-bye" business the aliens seemed to have in mind. A *visit*. Was that all this was?

The answer seemed to be Yes.

Why? Not that anyone had thought seriously of their staying around forever, but, well, why leave so *soon?*

Answer: They had things to attend to. There were all those beavers, or crodociles, or whatever, sleeping up on the moon, waiting for the Angli to find them a water-world. And there were—God, there were all those *other* Angli up there, waiting to wake up when they found a real planet! And of course Earth wouldn't do. Here the Angli tried to be tactful, but it soon came out—Earth was to them a sort of planetary slum, too dirty and polluted and used up and overcrowded to live in. "An interesting place to *visit*, but—"

Not, of course, that any government had actually extended them an offer of real estate. (Some private citizens, especially those from Texas and Australia who seemed to own extraordinary amounts of the Earth's surface, did make some offers to "interested Angli families.")

What would be really nice, people thought, would be if the Angli were to settle on the Moon, or someplace relatively close. What about Venus or Mars? Couldn't they remake one, with some magical planet-shaping devices? And stay around?

Answer: Too bad, but we really haven't any magical planet-shaping tools, and everything else in your particular solar system is quite, quite uninhabitable. Sorry again.

As all this went on at an accelerating tempo, various people extended to the Angli some truly remarkable job offers, or suggested ways that they could make a living on Earth. Even the Mafia turned out to be very interested in their possibilities as security guards, with that telepathic alarm system. Strange Arabs called upon them at night. Several large churches even offered them substantial sums to stay and lead services. And a great many national intelligence or security agencies tendered offers.

All of these the Angli listened to with good-humored mystification. One evening when Earthly economics were being discussed, an Angli pulled out a coconut-sized pod filled with what appeared to be five- to ten-carat diamonds of exquisite color. "Like these good?" he asked. "We pick up, over there"— waving a tentacle in the general direction of the Alpha Centauri. "Get get quick." By the time the matter was explained the bottom had fallen out of the diamond market from Pretoria to Zurich. And it was intimated that they had resources of gold, or anything you cared to name, cached about.

What they really liked personally, was flowers. Particularly dandelions of large size. Private applications to the Angli took on a distinctly different tone after this.

But it did not affect the public's emotional view of them as simply benevolent miracle workers, angels of mercy—or, now that we are getting nearer to the point, simply angels. Clearly a great outcry of mourning, a great weeping, lay ahead. The day they would leave would be so black. People couldn't think about it.

And then came the second event, or shock.

The Angli seemed to be completing their study of our cultures and especially our religions—if "study" isn't too formal a term for what they did, which was simply to ask questions. They were very interested in anything we were doing, whether it was running a paint factory or conducting a service in Notre-Dame. But they always asked people about their beliefs, or rather, about their god or gods. And one question which never failed to come up was, "Where is your god?"

After they had received an inventory of descriptions of, say, the Hindu pantheon, they always wound things up by asking, "Where are they? Where are they *now?*"

They got strange answers, of course. People pointed to the sky, or Westminster Abbey, or the Golden Pavilion; one man took them to the Grand Canyon. But when it came to *seeing* a given god or gods—well, we had to struggle with terms like "immaterial" or "transcendent" or "immanent." And they seemed . . . not exactly disappointed, but very serious.

Finally one day Todd turned the tables on them. "Do you have a god?" he asked.

"Oh yes. Many."

"And where are your gods?"

They were talking on a balcony overlooking the moonlit Great Pagoda of Moulmein. Azazel waved a tentacle moonward. "Up there."

"Your gods are up there with your ships? In spirit, you mean?"

"No. Gods—there! Many. Most medium, some very old, one new big one, the greatest now. In ship."

Well, everybody figured they were sculptures, or images, or sacred relics of some sort. But the Angli assured us they were alive, very much alive. Only sleeping, like the other Angli.

Well, uh, er . . . could they be seen? Could we go there and see some?

But they were asleep, Azazel repeated. Then he and Urizel conferred.

"Maybe is good they wake up one time," Urizel concluded. "Travel sleep long. You want me bring them here, show you?"

Did we!

Three reporters were present.

"ANGLI HAVE REAL GODS ASLEEP ON MOON."
"ANGLI GODS TO VISIT EARTH!"

And so an Angli delegation took off for Luna, to prepare their gods. And U.S. officialdom prepared to receive a supernatural visitation. Of course they didn't believe, then, that they'd be getting anything supernatural; their thinking ran to imagining Angli dressed up in costumes.

But the Angli seemed to be taking this very seriously. They returned from all over Earth, and their original ship reconstituted itself. Seeing this, the reception committee decided they had best take it more seriously too, and a committee of Earth's religious heads were convened to be in the reception stand. The Pope at that time was a great traveler, and very with-it; he insisted on being present. Of course, this threw official ecclesiastical circles into turmoil, as sanctioning a pagan religion. But he said, "Nonsense. All of us better come, to see what they've got." And the Patriarch of the Greek Orthodox faith for once agreed. The two British Archbishops were naturally eager. And the Protestant denominations joined in. So, seeing this unprecedently ecumenical gathering of Christians, the heads of other faiths were stimulated to attend, and what had started as a simple showing of alien idols, or something of the sort, grew into the full scale worldwide summit meeting of every religious affiliation that we all saw on TV. It all required a special super-committee, and the protocol was a nightmare.

What it was really like, by the end of a few days,

was a sort of confrontation of all Earth's religions with their alien counterparts. But it was a confrontation we'd lost from the start: while we had human officials in all kinds of fancy garb and ceremonial ways, they had—gods.

As we soon saw, when, that night a week or so later—it took place at night—another great bubble-ship came drifting moth-quiet into the searchlights' glare and settled into its cleared landing spot. (The officials had learned from the first fiasco; there was a carpeted path to the reception committee, but the whole area alongside the ship where informal Angli excursions might take place was cleared too. And the crowd was held well back, behind some temporary banks of seats to which admission was charged. Great video screens hung over the field, so all who came could see.)

And they came! The stands were soon overfull, with people crammed in everywhere.

As the ship settled, it could be seen that this was a larger craft, with bigger "bubbles," and a huge central bubble or dome. All the Angli were now present, lined up in a cordon around the perimeter in an unusually orderly fashion. And with them were a troop of Earth children, their arms full of flowers to present to the visiting divinities.

An outer door opened, and out shambled a huge, somewhat decrepit Angli figure, his great eye watering and blinking in the glare. He was festooned all over with what appeared to be animal remains, especially fish heads and tails, and his head bore the gigantic mask of some unknown beast.

"An—er—animist totem of early days," said the announcer's voice. "Surprisingly long-lived." Angli attendants handed the tribal godlet a dripping morsel to eat, and led it to a roped-off area of resting couches. It sprawled on tentacles rather than walking upright, being evidently from a time when the Angli were still semi-aquatic.

Next to emerge was a swathed barrel shape, obese and possibly somewhat senile. Its eye rolled in what appeared to be malevolent confusion, as it was led away waddling, leaving a wet, slimy trail.

"An early fertility deity," the announcer—a hastily summoned anthropologist—explained. "The next to appear will be avatars of this early form. You will note the increasing cultural complexity."

(The more alert members of the press, seeing the trend of events, were sending out emergency calls for anthropologists, ethnologists, and anyone who might interpret matters.)

"This," said one of these, as the file of ever-taller and more impressive Angli divinities made their various ways down the red carpet, "would represent about the Earthly level of Astarte or Ishtar."

The Angli goddess, a veiled form undulating past him, turned her huge eye and sent him a look that made him drop his notepad.

By this time it was evident, from the height and demeanor of the newcomers, that they were not ordinary Angli dressed in costumes, let alone statuary or mobile idols. No; this was another order of beings, coming into view before them in the night, and the crowd grew strangely silent. Even today, we don't know what they were. We only know we saw gods.

The last in this group struck even Earthly eyes as a radiant figure, and she alone appeared conscious of the dignitaries' stand. The dazzling lights, her sparkling, shimmering form and veils, made her—for it was to all Earthly eyes a "she"—at one moment a bizarrely seductive alien, at the next a surpassing Earthly beauty. As she paced gracefully down the carpet, she flung up one cerulean limb, and out of the dark overhead a nighthawk dropped to it and perched there. From somewhere strange music played.

With a slight air of disdain she let her attendants turn her into the roped-off waiting area, and as she turned, her painted eye shot straight at the Papal Eminence an unmistakable wink. Then she stooped to accept an armful of flowers from a bedazzled child, proceeded into the reserved area, and stretched out upon an oversized, scroll-ended divan.

It needed no commentator to tell the viewers that great Aphrodite had passed by.

Behind her came a vast grizzled figure who limped, as had the Earthly Vulcan. And after a little space, a towering, commanding figure who glittered with menace as he strode contemptuously down the way, alien weapons held high. Yet his eye seemed clear and boyish, though all else spoke of war and wrath; even so had Mars appeared to his mother.

Then came troops and bevies of bewilderingly decked and jeweled figures, some carrying emblematic instruments—minor deities, as they might be Muses, or Nereids, Oreads, Dryads of the Greek pantheon, or Peris and Algerits and Indus of others. These danced along under rainbows, piping or singing, to herald the advent of a grand, hoary elder figure, the inevitable old male of unlimited power and authority, whether Zeus, Jove, Wotan, of Jehovah. Although the night was perfectly clear, the rumble of far-off thunder accompanied them.

Singing had broken out among the Angli as they all passed by; it was the first time humans had heard the Angli sing, and they found the chants both strange and pleasing.

And on and on they came, deities resembling nothing familiar to Western eyes but more familiar to Persian, Indian, or Chinese: some in weird built-out costumes and serpentine decorations, great curled and feathered headpieces representing frowning grins, or elongations of the eye to dreamlike proportions. In hieratic poses, they made their ways to the appointed spot, and attendant heraldic animals came with them. Also in the air were random sparks, or flames, that looked sometimes like flowers, sometimes like snowflakes, but seemed to have a life of their own, as they danced and clustered here and there.

Finally in the midst of what appeared to be a throng of patriarchal tribal or national divinities, there stood out one of seemingly great power, draped in long white robes. He was oddly attended by what looked at first like small mechanical toys in the shapes of alien children, with sweet luminous eyes. But they were alive.

"A culminant patristic deity," the announcer explained. "He repeatedly reincarnated himself in his own son. Evidently he still has a few believers left. And now—" He went into a huddle with his Angli consultants.

In the pause that followed, all could see that one of the small son-figures had slowed to a stop, and seemed disoriented or ill. But a nearby Angli stooped and patted it solicitously, and it soon revived and ran on.

The somewhat shaken commentator was asking the Angli, "Why do you carry with you these—uh—apparently living gods of old dead religions? I'd think that your one real god or gods would be enough."

"Ah," said the Angli (some of whom could now speak several Earth languages quite well), "but you see, the minds and spirits of those who worshiped those gods are still in us, under the surface of civilization. And civilization can fail. When we notice that one of those old divinities is growing in vigor, in vitality, yes?—it gives us warning. Too many among us are unknowingly worshiping those qualities again. So"—he made stamping motions—"like small fires, we put out quick. You see? But now—"

The singing had fallen silent, and for a few breaths no one moved; there was a feeling of something impending.

Into the silence there stepped, or materialized, a tall robed and veiled figure twice the height of any that had gone before. It was indefinably female. As she came down the way, her face turned toward the dignitaries' stand, she gave no sign, but there was a concerted indrawing of breaths, almost a gasp. Across her single eye was a domino mask; in the depths of its opening could be seen a deep spark of smoldering red-gold. But where the rest of her face and head should be was only black emptiness under the hood. Her garments moved as though covering a gaunt figure, but no feet or hands revealed themselves. Where she passed, children hid their faces in their flowers.

And the line of Angli bowed like willows in a silent wind.

Beside her paced an alien animal that she seemed to be restraining on a choke-chain; one of her long sleeves descended to its head, but no hand could be seen. Below the creature's eye was a tangle of tusks and cruel fangs; its limbs were coarsely padded and savagely spurred, and its expression was a blend of coldness and hate. Once, as she moved, her beast lifted its head and gave out a long-drawn baying sound, and the distant thunder growled.

As this apparition neared the stand, it was seen that a great single regal seat was placed for her apart from the others. In this she seated herself impassively. The surrounding Angli had dropped to what would have been a kneeling position in humans, and the nearby humans involuntarily turned their eyes away, and dropped their heads low.

"This is she whom we now worship," the Angli by the announcer said. "She has many names but only one essence. Here you might call her the Law of Cause and Effect."

"What is the . . . the animal?"

"That is her instrument of vengeance on all who violate her commandments. Either knowingly or unknowingly. Listen!"

From all around the horizon came the echo of a baying sound.

"Alas, my poor friends on your Earth—you do not worship her, but I fear your race has done violence to her Law. It may be that some terrible punishment is readying itself for your innocent ones."

Bravely, the human commentator asked, "You mean, like meddling with the atom?"

"No. That is just what I do not mean. That might have fretted only one of our tribal gods. The Law of Cause and Effect has no objection to inquiry, and she will always answer. Her vengeance is reserved for those who activate a Cause without desiring its Effect. Like the failure to anticipate the result of accelerated multiplication upon a finite surface.

"But—"

"Hush." To the crowds, who had heard little of this complex interchange and were becoming restless, he spoke out: "Please do not rise now. There is one more to pass."

But nothing visible came from the great ship. Only those nearest to it suddenly shivered, as though a cold wind had passed, though nothing stirred. It reached the stairs to the reception stand, and apparently flowed upward; several dignitaries were seen to hug their elbows to their sides and shudder.

Far away, lightning flashed, once. Then all was over.

"That was the shadow of the God to Come," the announcer said clearly. "Though what it will be we know no more than you . . ."

Did you see the Pope cross himself?

Well, the rest you must have seen; they took the ropes down and invited everyone who wanted to to mingle with the gods. (Luckily the security forces had been prepared for some such Angli-type informality, and got things organized in time.)

"In their present incarnate form, our gods are quite harmless," the announcer said. "But they do have a habit, when bored or restless, of dematerializing into pure energy—if I grasp your language correctly—and in that form they can be very dangerous indeed."

Even as he spoke, there came a high tinkling crash like expensive crystal breaking, from the direction of Aphrodite's couch, and it was seen that the goddess had vanished, leaving only a cloud of white particles like doves or long-finned white fishes, who danced in Brownian motion before dispersing.

A moment later the original old tribal animist deity also took himself out, with a minor boom, and the dancing of a few unidentifiable particles in the air where he had been.

But all this you have seen, and even also the preparation of the Angli for immediate departure, after they took their refreshed gods back to Luna in the morning.

Their preparations also were highly informal, consisting merely of getting into their bubbles and reconstituting their ship with what souvenirs they had picked up. (They were partial to postcards of cathedrals and bathing beaches, and dried flowers.)

Aghast at the suddenness of all this, Earth prepared to mourn the departure of those wonderful visitors. And then the great announcement came. That you must remember. A senior Angli simply asked, "Anybody want come with us? We find good place."

Yes, they meant it. Would humans care to come a-roving with them? Not to be parted, but instead to find, with their dear new friends, a pristine Earth of clear sky and blue waters? A whole fresh start, with guardian angels?

Would they? WOULD THEY?

They would!—In such numbers that the Angli had to announce a limit of a million, to be accommodated asleep in their empty bubble-ships. There would be, by the way, no aging or death while in cold-sleep.

Their selection process, like everything else, was simple and informal. In the United States, Angli simply asked for room in parking lots (every shopping mall owner in the land offered one) and stationed themselves in any convenient place, holding a football-size pod that had an open end. Applicants were invited to hold one hand in the pod for a minute or two, while the Angli stared at it. The pod felt empty inside. Applicants could wiggle their fingers, hold still, or feel the sides; it seemed to make no difference, and the pod did not appear to change. After an instant or so the Angli simply said Yes or No, and that was that. Those accepted were told to go out to the ship with three kilos—6.6 pounds—of whatever they wanted. Suggested wear—this got printed on a slip—was one comfortable exercise suit, work-gloves, sun visor, and sneakers.

What basis were they chosen on, for this momentous voyage?

"They take the ones they like," Waefyel told me.

"But what does the pod do?"

"That way no arguments." I remembered these people were telepaths. An Angli could investigate a mind in depth while its owner was holding his hand in a pod.

But who is Waefyel?

Well, I forgot to tell you about meeting my own special Angli friend. Most of the rest of this comes from him. I met him, like so much else, through Kevin. Waefyel was acting as gofer for one of the aged councillors, who turned out to enjoy meeting humans at those big receptions. The aged councillor would run out of water, or that hard-tack stuff, which was all they ate, and Waefyel would get it for him. He met Kevin bringing coffee to a human counterpart.

Technically, Waefyel was a young adult, male (question mark—we *never* got that straightened out) and as nice as an Angli could be, which was very sweet indeed. But nice as he was, he couldn't get me accepted to go after I flunked the pod test. I tried again—they had no objection—and again and again, but it was always No—and then they were over their million.

"What's the matter with me, Waefyel?"

He shrugged, an impressive gesture in an octopus.

"Maybe know too much."

"*Me?* But don't you people like one to be smart?"

"No, *we* like. Only some kinds smart get killed by other humans."

"Oh." But I knew what he meant.

However, the Anglis didn't take a million boneheads, or a million anything. The group, what I saw of it when I went out to the ship, was as close to a random sample as you could come. (One selector *had* a weakness for redheads.) However, they did appear to eliminate obvious no-goods, junkies, the badly crippled—I tell you, *everybody* tried, before it was over!—and a lot of people I personally didn't like the looks of either.

The ones who got to go had a stamper pressed to their foreheads. It didn't leave any detectable mark, and they were told they could wash the place, or whatever. (That had to be printed too; the Angli got tired of answering.) At the ship, an Angli just glanced at the spot.

I asked Waefyel if it was a thought-imprint, and he laughed. "No need." I kicked myself mentally—of course, if a telepath looked there, the person's thoughts would automatically tell whether he'd been stamped or not.

Oh—one more thing about the selectees: At the ship, the men got misted with an aerosol and were given an injection.

"What's that for?"

Waefyel giggled.

"For fertility. You make too many young ones, no can educate."

"You mean they'll all be infertile? Won't they die out?"

"For twenty of your years only. Then another twenty. Then another." The concept in his mind was *cycle*. "Yes—that way no spoil everything, until learn better."

"How do they do it?"

And here's where I learned about the sophisticated research. Apparently some Angli who liked fussing with bioscience had found an opportunity to gene-splice a bacterium that would cause a human male's immune system to destroy, or rather inactivate, his own sperm. The antibodies, or whatever, wore out after about twenty years, thus allowing the man a couple of fertile ejaculations; but the system was self-renewing, and it kicked back in and the infertility closed down for another two decades. And so on. It was also dominant-inheritable.

Neat, no?

It seems there was an argument about the twenty years. Some Angli opted for forty, but they were persuaded that they were overreacting from revulsion at the state of our affairs.

And of course you know all about the rest.

I remarked to Waefyel, a pity they couldn't do it to all Earth. But the men's objections would be violent. He giggled again.

"You no see sunsets? Pretty green lights, no?"

"Well, yes, but they've been explaining that—"

"We do it already," he said. "Coming down in air

now. Trouble, whew! To make so much. Good your
bacteria breed fast too."

"What?"

Well, as I say, you know all about that. I was just
the first to happen to know. Lord, I remember all the
to-do, the fertility clinics besieged—of course it was
blamed on women first. But finally it became too clear
to ignore, especially as it affected a few related pri-
mates in a partial way. And the men had symptoms,
too—they got sore and puffy when a large number of
active sperm were getting killed.

But you know all that: how we have an oldest generation of mixed ages, like me and older, and after
that one generation all aged about forty, and then
another about twenty. And then nobody, but some
women are just getting pregnant now. ("MOTHER-
HOOD AGAIN!" "HUMAN BIRTHS RESUME!"
"WILL IT LAST THIS TIME?" It won't, I promise
you.)

This was their going-away present to us, see.

"We do good thing you," as Waefyel put it. "Now
maybe bad trouble coming not so bad."

And it hasn't, has it? We did just tiptoe by the worst
of the war scares, but everyone worldwide was so
preoccupied with trying to make babies that things
quieted down fast. Of course it was hell on economies
that were based on the asinine idea of endless growth,
but that's a lot better than being exterminated. People
who really go for the idea of a planet with fifty billion
people standing on top of each other were disappointed.
But all the ecological stuff, the poisoning and wastage
and sewage and erosion, all became soluble, once the
steady thunder of newborn humans cascading from
ever-fertile bellies eased to a sprinkle every twenty
years.

People would have had to face the idea of a static
economy sooner or later; it was the Angli's gift to let
us do it while there were still living oceans left.

But that's all beside the point.

When I got over the trauma of not being selected to
go—no, I only *sound* like I'm crying—I was still wor-

rying that little old question: Why, really, did the
Angli leave that paradise planet they came from? *Why?*

"We want go see new places," Waefyel said. "We
bored."

But he didn't say it right. Maybe telepaths transmit
whether they want to or not.

"Waefyel—what *really* happened to those other people who were living on your planet?"

"They go away, maybe, or they die. I think they
die."

That sounded sincere.

"Your people didn't kill them off, by any chance?"

"Oh no! *No!*"

You can't fake shock like that—I think.

"So you just left, bringing your gods with you. What
about the Angli that are still there? What'll they do
with no gods?"

"No Angli stay, is all here. Up on moon."

"Hmm. Small race, aren't you?"

"Three, four million. Is enough."

"And your gods. Hey, those gods were really *alive,*
weren't they?"

We were lying on a little beach on one of the Virgin
Islands, where Waefyel had flown us. (If only I could
live on hardtack, what journeys we could have made! I
did try the stuff, but it tasted like dried galoshes.)

"Of course they live," he said. "They do things for
people. All gods do."

"Ours don't," I said lazily. "Hey, do other peoples
have live gods?"

"Yes." His big eye looked sad. "Except you. You
first we find. No live gods here."

"Hey, you mean it. I thought gods were just an
idea."

"Oh no, is real. Look out, you getting too hot."

"Yeah, thanks. Why did your gods want to leave
that lovely planet?"

"Go with us."

"You mean a god has to go where its people go?
Hey, what happened to the other people's gods, the

ones that died off? What happens to gods when their
people die?"

"Usually—new word, see? Usually, gods go too.
Lost in air, finish. Sometimes . . . not." His big eye
was looking somber again. Not sad, just very serious.
"We don't know why."

"Dead people's gods just evaporate. How sad. Hmm.
But sometimes not, eh? What happens to a bunch of
gods who live on with no people?"

"I don't know." He sat up. "Look, is too hot for
you here. I listen your skin burning."

"Sorry. I didn't mean to fry audibly." But I picked
it up. What? Just something. Time to change the subject, for Waefyel. Well, maybe it bored him. But I
didn't think it was that. In my bones, I felt I was
poking into something hidden. Something the Angli
wanted hidden.

"I hope your gods will like the new planet you find.
You'll be there, with the humans, won't you?"

"Oh yes!" He smiled. "We find nice big one, lots of
room. Lots of flowers." He touched a neck chain of
dandelion flowers I had twisted for him. (Yes, they
have dandelions and crabgrass even on the Virgin
Islands.)

"I bet our people will go back to the stone age," I
said idly. (I didn't care if they went back to the
Paleocene, if only I could have gone with them.) "Hey,
maybe they'll start worshiping that old totem-animal
of yours."

"Maybe." As though involuntarily, his eye took on
a dreamy smile.

"And then when they get more advanced, they can
worship that Old Fertility Symbol. I guess they'll be in
the mood. And work up to the lovelies. You know,
that's neat! Here we don't have any gods of our own,
and you provide us with a complete set, ready-to-go,
carry-out gods! Why do you suppose we don't have
gods of our own, Waefyel? Is something wrong with
us? People *make* their gods, really, don't they?"

"I think so. Yes. What is wrong by you? We don't
know. Maybe you have poison, maybe you kill gods!"

He laughed and fussed at my hair—I had pretty hair then—with his tentacle tip. "But I don't think so. Some of the wise ones think you made a bad pattern of gods, some kind missing, see, so they couldn't go on and make more. A 'defective series,' that's right?"

"That's wrong, apparently. I wonder what we left out. Do you know?"

"No . . . but I think you got too many war gods. Not enough ones who take care."

"That sounds right." I was about falling asleep there in the beauty with the lapping little waves on the pink sand, and this lovely friend beside me. . . .

"I think we go inside now. Look Tee-Vee. I carry you."

"Oh, Waefyel." (Don't expect me to tell you about it, but we had something physical going between us. Especially then. It's not what you'd guess, either.)

Now there was a man staying at the hotel there. A serious older man, a sort of student. That evening we all got chatting, out on the terrace looking at the sunset. It *did* show the most lovely weird green light. Beautiful infertility, drifting down. The uproar about that hadn't started yet. Anyway, this older man started talking about angels. Rather pointedly, too. Funny topic, I thought.

"Did you know that angels were the lowest order of divine beings?" he asked me. "If there was something to be done, a flaming sword to be brandished, somebody to be admonished, or a message delivered—particularly a message—they called in an angel. They were the workhorses and message-bearers."

"Yes," said Waefyel unguardedly. I wondered what interest ancient myths about angels could possibly have for him. Probably he just enjoyed practicing his English; he did love that.

"Like gofers," I said. "The gofers of the gods."

So of course I had to explain gofers. (He *was* an older man.) Waefyel was delighted too. His first English pun, if that's what it is.

"How did angels get born?" I asked. "What about

those little ones, cherubs, cherubim? Were they little
angels?"

"No," said the man. "The connection of cherubs
with infants is a late degradation. As to how angels got
born, I wonder. I've never herd of an angel's mother
or father."

"From the energy in the air," said Waefyel unex-
pectedly. "Elementals."

"Is there energy in the air?" I asked.

"You saw it. When gods dematerialize, a lot of it is
around. Elementals," he repeated. And then suddenly
frowned as if he were mad at himself, and shut up.

Next day we had to fly back. It was the twenty-third
of August. The day after was the twenty-fourth. And
even you must know what happened then:

They left.

Don't expect me to tell you a word about *that*,
either.

Me just standing there, looking up at a vanishing
point that reflected sunlight for one last instant. Me
and a couple of million, no more than that—just standing there with eyes streaming our hearts out, looking
up at a sky that would be empty forever. . . .

But at least I know, for all the good it does me,
what had held me in its arms. Waefyel let out just
enough so it had to be true. You get the picture, don't
you? Or do I have to explain it?

I put it to Waefyel once, at the end.

"You're not an animal, like me, are you? You're
something created out of energy, out of the minds of
that race that died. You Angli are just pretending to
be people."

"Smart little one."

"Like parasites. Oh, Waefyel!"

"No. Symbiotes—I know word. You good for us,
we good for you."

"But you've trapped a million humans to go with
you and keep you alive!"

"They need us. They happy."

Surely you see. There they were, when that other
race who had made them died off—a whole complete

pantheon-of-pantheons, all those gods from earliest to last, from highest to the lowest "workhorses." As good as dead, doomed to live forever on an empty planet with no living energy to need them or support them.

So what did they do? I mean, what did the higher-ups, the really big gods, do? This whole evolution of orphaned, unemployed gods, doomed with no people?

Why, they ordered their faithful workhorses, their lowest order of functionaries, their *angeli* (the sound of that name was just one of those cosmic coincidences, by the way; it meant nothing to them)—well, they ordered their angeli to build ships and *take* them somewhere. To find a race that needed gods and take them there!

And eventually they got here and found a people with no gods. . . .

And now some of our people will have gods again. And the gods will have people. Let them; I'm not jealous. All I want is one of the gofers back.

My gofer of the gods.

DINOSAURS

By Walter Jon Williams

*Let us not deceive you—this is not a tale
of the prehistoric and there are no dinosaurs
as such in it. This is a tale of a very far
future and of a highly evolved and changed
human being. It is also, in its own subtle
way, a tale that lives up to its deceptive
title.*

The Shars seethed in the dim light of their ruddy sun.
Pointed faces raised to the sky, they sniffed the faint
wind for sign of the stranger and scented only hydro-
carbons, far-off vegetations, damp fur, the sweat of
excitement and fear. Weak eyes peered upward, glis-
tened with hope, anxiety, apprehension, and saw only
the faint pattern of stars. Short, excited barking sounds
broke out here and there, but mostly the Shars crooned,
a low ululation that told of sudden onslaught, destruction, war in distant reaches, and now the hope of
peace.
 The crowds surged left, then right. Individuals
bounced high on their third legs, seeking a view, seeing
only the wide sea of heads, the ears and muzzles
pointed to the stars.
 Suddenly, a screaming. High-pitched howls, a bright
chorus of barks. The crowds surged again.
 Something was crossing the field of stars.
 The human ship was huge, vaster than anything
they'd seen, a moonlet descending. Shars closed their
eyes and shuddered in terror. The screaming turned to
moans. Individuals leaped high, baring their teeth,

barking in defiance of their fear. The air smelled of terror, incipient panic, anger.

War! cried some. *Peace!* cried others.

The crooning went on. *We mourn, we mourn,* it said, *we mourn our dead billions.*

We fear, said others.

Soundlessly, the human ship neared them, casting its vast shadow. Shars spilled outward from the spot beneath, bounding high on their third legs.

The human ship came to a silent rest. Dully, it reflected the dim red sun.

The Shars crooned their fear, their sorrow. And waited for the humans to emerge.

These! Yes. These. Drill, the human ambassador, gazed through his video walls at the sea of Shars, the moaning, leaping thousands that surrounded him. Through the mass a group was moving with purpose, heading for the airlock as per his instructions. His new Memory crawled restlessly in the armored hollow atop his skull. *Stand by,* he broadcast.

His knees made painful crackling noises as he walked toward the airlock, the silver ball of his translator rolling along the ceiling ahead of him. The walls mutated as he passed, showing him violet sky, far-off polygonal buildings; cold distant green . . . and here, nearby, a vast, dim plain covered with a golden tissue of Shars.

He reached the airlock and it began to open. Drill snuffed wetly at the alien smells—heat, dust, the musky scent of the Shars themselves.

Drill's heart thumped in his chest. His dreams were coming true. He had waited all his life for this.

Mash, whimpered Lowbrain. Drill told it to be silent. Lowbrain protested vaguely, then obeyed.

Drill told Lowbrain to move. Cool, alien air brushed his skin. The Shars cried out sharply, moaned, fell back. They seemed a wild, sibilant ocean of pointed ears and dark, questing eyes. The group heading for the airlock vanished in the general retrograde movement, a stone washed by a pale tide. Beneath Drill's feet was soft vegetation. His translator floated in the air before him. His mind flamed with wonder, but Lowbrain kept him moving.

The Shars fell back, moaning.

Drill stood eighteen feet tall on his two pillarlike legs, each with a splayed foot that displayed a horny underside and vestigial nails. His skin was ebony and was draped in folds over his vast naked body. His pendulous maleness swung loosely as he walked. As he stepped across the open space he was conscious of the fact that he was the ultimate product of nine million years of human evolution, all leading to the expansion, diversification, and perfection that was now humanity's manifest existence.

He looked down at the little Shars, their white skin and golden fur, their strange, stiff tripod legs, the muzzles raised to him as if in awe. *If your species survives,* he thought benignly, *you can look like me in another few million years.*

The group of Shars that had been forging through the crowd were suddenly exposed when the crowd fell back from around them. On the perimeter were several Shars holding staffs—weapons, perhaps—in their clever little hands. In the center of these were a group of Shars wearing decorative ribbon to which metal plates had been attached. *Badges of rank,* Memory said. *Ignore.* The shadow of the translator bobbed toward them as Drill approached. Metallic geometrics rose from the group and hovered over them.

Recorders, Memory said. *Artifical similarities to myself. Or possibly security devices. Disregard.*

Drill was getting closer to the party, speeding up his instructions to Lowbrain, eventually entering Zen Synch. It would make Lowbrain hungrier but lessen the chance of any accidents.

The Shars carrying the staffs fell back. A wailing went up from the crowd as one of the Shars stepped toward Drill. The ribbons draped over her sloping shoulders failed to disguise four mammalian breasts. Clear plastic bubbles covered her weak eyes. In Zen

Synch with Memory and Lowbrain, Drill ambled up to her and raised his hands in friendly greeting. The Shar flinched at the expanse of the gesture.

"I am Ambassador Drill," he said. "I am a human."

The Shar gazed up at him. Her nose wrinkled as she listened to the booming voice of the translator. Her answer was a succession of sharp sounds, made high in the throat, somewhat unpleasant. Drill listened to the voice of his translator.

"I am President Gram of the InterSharian Sociability of Nations and Planets." That's how it came through in translation, anyway. Memory began feeding Drill referents for the word "nation."

"I welcome you to our planet, Ambassador Drill."

"Thank you, President Gram," Drill said. "Shall we negotiate peace now?"

President Gram's ears pricked forward, then back. There was a pause, and then from the vast circle of Shars came a mad torrent of hooting noises. The awesome sound lapped over Drill like the waves of a lunatic sea.

They approve your sentiment, said Memory.

I thought that's what it meant, Drill said. *Do you think we'll get along?*

Memory didn't answer, but instead shifted to a more comfortable position in the saddle of Drill's skull. Its job was to provide facts, not draw conclusions.

"If you could come into my Ship," Drill said, "we could get started."

"Will we then meet the other members of your delegation?"

Drill gazed down at the Shar. The fur on her shoulders was rising in odd tufts. She seemed to be making a concerted effort to calm it.

"There are no other members," Drill said. "Just myself."

His knees were paining him. He watched as the other members of the Shar party cast quick glances at each other.

"No secretaries? No assistants?" the President was saying.

"No," Drill said. "Not at all. I'm the only conscious mind on Ship. Shall we get started?"

Eat! Eat! said Lowbrain. Drill ordered it to be silent. His stomach grumbled.

"Perhaps," said President Gram, gazing at the vastness of the human ship, "it would be best should we begin in a few hours. I should probably speak to the crowd. Would you care to listen?"

No need. Memory said. *I will monitor.*

"Thank you, no," Drill said. "I shall return to Ship for food and sex. Please signal me when you are ready. Please bring any furniture you may need for your comfort. I do not believe my furniture would fit you, although we might be able to clone some later."

The Shars' ears all pricked forward. Drill entered Zen Synch, turned his huge body, and began accelerating toward the airlock. The sound of the crowd behind him was the murmuring of wind through a stand of trees.

Peace, he thought later, as he stood by the mash bins and fed his complaining stomach. *It's a simple thing. How long can it take to arrange?*

Long, said Memory. *Very long.*

The thought disturbed him. He thought the first meeting had gone well.

After his meal, when he had sex, it wasn't very good.

Memory had been monitoring the events outside Ship, and after Drill had completed sex, Memory showed him the outside events. *They have been broadcast to the entire population,* Memory said.

President Gram had moved to a local elevation and had spoken for some time. Drill found her speech interesting—it was rhythmic and incantorial, rising and falling in tone and volume, depending heavily on repetition and melody. The crowd participated, issuing forth with excited barks or low moans in response to her statements or questions, sometimes babbling in confusion when she posed them a conundrum. Memory only gave the highlights of the speech. "Unknown

. . . attackers . . . billions dead . . . preparations advanced . . . ready to defend ourselves . . . offer of peace . . . hope in the darkness . . . unknown . . . willing to take the chance . . . peace . . . peace . . . hopeful smell . . . peace." At the end the other Shars were all singing "Peace! Peace!" in chorus while President Gram bounced up and down on her sturdy rear leg.

It sounds pretty, Drill thought. *But why does she go on like that?*

Memory's reply was swift.

Remember that the Shars are a generalized and social species, it said. *President Gram's power, and her ability to negotiate, derives from the degree of her popular support. In measures of this significance she must explain herself and her actions to the population in order to maintain their enthusiasm for her policies.*

Primitive, Drill thought.

That is correct.

Why don't they let her get on with her work? Drill asked.

There was no reply.

After an exchange of signals the Shar party assembled at the airlock. Several Shars had been mobilized to carry tables and stools. Drill sent a Frog to escort the Shars from the airlock to where he waited. The Frog met them inside the airlock, turned, and hopped on ahead through Ship's airy, winding corridors. It had been trained to repeat "Follow me, follow me" in the Shars' own language.

Drill waited in a semi-inclined position on a Slab. The Slab was an organic sub-species used as furniture, with an idiot brain capable of responding to human commands. The Shars entered cautiously, their weak eyes twitching in the bright light. "Welcome, Honorable President," Drill said. "Up, Slab." Slab began to adjust itself to place Drill on his feet. The Shars were moving tables and stools into the vast room.

Frog was hopping in circles, making a wet noise at each landing. "Follow me, follow me," it said.

The members of the Shar delegation who bore badges of rank stood in a body while the furniture-carriers bustled around them. Drill noticed, as Slab put him on his feet, that they were wrinkling their noses. He wondered what it meant.

His knees crackled as he came fully upright. "Please make yourselves comfortable," he said. "Frog will show your laborers to the airlock."

"Does your Excellency object to a mechanical recording of the proceedings?" President Gram asked. She was shading her eyes with her hand.

"Not at all." As a number of devices rose into the air above the party, Drill wondered if it were possible to give the Shars detachable Memories. Perhaps human bioengineers could adapt the Memories to the Shar physiology. He asked Memory to make a note of the question so that he could bring it up later.

"Follow me, follow me," Frog said. The workers who had carried the furniture began to follow the hopping Frog out of the room.

"Your Excellency," President Gram said, "may I have the honor of presenting to you the other members of my delegation?"

There were six in all, with titles like Secretary of Syncopated Speech and Special Executive for External Coherence. There was also a Minister for the Dissemination of Convincing Lies, whose title Drill suspected was somehow mistranslated, and an Opposite Secretary-General for the Genocidal Eradication of Alien Aggressors, at whom Drill looked with more than a little interest. The Opposite Secretary-General was named Vang, and was small even for a Shar. He seemed to wrinkle his nose more than the others. The Special Executive for External Coherence, whose name was Cup, seemed a bit piebald, patches of white skin showing through the golden fur covering his shoulders, arms, and head.

He is elderly, said Memory.

That's what I thought.

"Down, Slab," Drill said. He leaned back against

the creature and began to move to a more relaxed position.

He looked at the Shars and smiled. Fur ruffled on shoulders and necks. "Shall we make peace now?" he asked.

"We would like to clarify something you said earlier," President Gram said. "You said that you were the only, ah, conscious entity on the ship. That you were the only member of the human delegation. Was that translated correctly?"

"Why, yes," Drill said. "Why would more than one diplomat be necessary?"

The Shars looked at each other. The Special Executive for External Coherence spoke cautiously.

"You will not be needing to consult with your superiors? You have full authority from your government?"

Drill beamed at them. "We humans do not have a government, of course," he said. "But I am a diplomat with the appropriate Memory and training. There is no problem that I can foresee."

"Please let me understand, your Excellency," Cup said. He was leaning forward, his small eyes watering. "I am elderly and may be slow in comprehending the situation. But if you have no government, who accredited you with this mission?"

"I am a diplomat. It is my specialty. No accreditation is necessary. The human race will accept my judgment on any matter of negotiation, as they would accept the judgment of any specialist in his area of expertise."

"But why *you*. As an individual?"

Drill shrugged massively. "I was part of the nearest diplomatic enclave, and the individual without any other tasks at the moment." He looked at each of the delegation in turn. "I am incredibly happy to have this chance, honorable delegates," he said. "The vast majority of human diplomats never have the chance to speak to another species. Usually we mediate only in conflicts of interest between the various groups of human specialties."

"But the human species will abide by your decisions?"

"Of course," Drill was surprised at the Shar's persistence. "Why wouldn't they?"

Cup settled back in his chair. His ears were down. There was a short silence.

"We have an opening statement prepared," President Gram said. "I would like to enter it into our record, if I may. Or would your Excellency prefer to go first?"

"I have no opening statement," Drill said. "Please go ahead."

Cup and the President exchanged glances. President Gram took a deep breath and began.

Long. Memory said. *Very long*.

The opening statement seemed very much like the address President Gram had been delivering to the crowd, the same hypnotic rhythms, more or less the same content. The rest of the delegation made muted responses. Drill drowsed through it, enjoying it as music.

"Thank you, Honorable President," he said afterwards. "That was very nice."

"We would like to propose an agenda for the conference," Gram said. "First, to resolve the matter of the cease-fire and its provisions for an ending to hostilities. Second, the establishment of a secure border between our two species, guaranteeing both species room for expression. Third, the establishment of trade and visitation agreements. Fourth, the matter of reparations, payments, and return of lost territory."

Drill nodded. "I believe," he said, "that resolution of the second through fourth points will come about as a result of an understanding reached on the first. That is, once the cease-fire is settled, that resolution will imply a settlement of the rest of the situation."

"You accept the agenda?"

"If you like. It doesn't matter."

Ears pricked forward, then back. "So you accept that our initial discussions will consist of formalizing the disengagement of our forces?"

"Certainly. Of course I have no way of knowing

what forces you have committed. We humans have committed none."

The Shars were still for a long time. "Your species attacked our planets, Ambassador. Without warning, without making yourselves known to us." Gram's tone was unusually flat. Perhaps, Drill thought, she was attempting to conceal great emotion.

"Yes," Drill said. "But those were not our military formations. Your species were contacted only by our terraforming Ships. They did not attack your people, as such—they were only peripherally aware of your existence. Their function was merely to seed the planets with lifeforms favorable to human existence. Unfortunately for your people, part of the function of these lifeforms is to destroy the native life of the planet."

The Shars conferred with one another. The Opposite Secretary-General seemed particularly vehement. Then President Gram turned to Drill.

"We cannot accept your statement, your Excellency," she said. "Our people were attacked. They defended themselves, but were overcome."

"Our terraforming Ships are very good at what they do," Drill said. "They are specialists. Our Shrikes, our Shrews, our Sharks—each is a master of its element. But they lack intelligence. They are not conscious entities, such as ourselves. They weren't aware of your civilization at all. They only saw you as food."

"You're claiming that you *didn't notice us?*" demanded Secretary-General Vang. *"They didn't notice us as they were killing us?"* He was shouting. President Gram's ears went back.

"Not as such, no," Drill said.

President Gram stood up. "I am afraid, your Excellency, your explanations are insufficient," she said. "This conference must be postponed until we can reach a united conclusion concerning your remarkable attitude."

Drill was bewildered. "What did I say?" he asked.

The other Shars stood. President Gram turned and

walked briskly on her three legs toward the exit. The others followed.

"Wait," Drill said. "Don't go. Let me send for Frog. Up, Slab, up!"

The Shars were gone by the time Slab had got Drill to his feet. The Ship told him they had found their own way to the airlock. Drill could think of nothing to do but order the airlock to let them out.

"Why would I lie?" he asked. "Why would I lie to them?" Things were so very simple, really.

He shifted his vast weight from one foot to the other and back again. Drill could not decide whether he had done anything wrong. He asked Memory what to do next, but Memory held no information to comfort him, only dry recitations of past negotiations. Annoyed at the lifeless monologue, Drill told Memory to be silent and began to walk restlessly through the corridors of his Ship. He could not decide where things had gone bad.

Sensing his agitation, Lowbrain began to echo his distress. *Mash,* Lowbrain thought weakly. *Food, Sex.*

Be silent, Drill commanded.

Sex, sex, Lowbrain thought.

Drill realized that Lowbrain was beginning to give him an erection. Acceding to the inevitable, he began moving toward Surrogate's quarters.

Surrogate lived in a dim, quiet room filled with the murmuring sound of its own heartbeat. It was a human subspecies, about the intelligence of Lowbrain, designed to comfort voyagers on long journeys through space, when carnal access to their own subspecies might necessarily be limited. Surrogate had a variety of sexual equipment designed for the accommodation of the various human subspecies and their sexes. It also had large mammaries that gave nutritious milk, and a rudimentary head capable of voicing simple thoughts.

Tiny Mice, that kept Surrogate and the ship clean, scattered as Drill entered the room. Surrogate's little head turned to him.

"It's good to see you again," Surrogate said.

"I am Drill."

"It's good to see you again, Drill," said Surrogate. "It's good to see you again."

Drill began to nuzzle its breasts. One of Surrogate's male parts began to erect. "I'm confused, Surrogate," he said. "I don't know what to do."

"Why are you confused, Drill?" asked Surrogate. It raised one of its arms and began to stroke Drill's head. It wasn't really having a conversation: Surrogate had only been programmed to make simple statements, or to analyze its partners' speech and ask questions.

"Things are going wrong," Drill said. He began to suckle. The warm milk flowed down his throat. Surrogate's male part had an orgasm. Mice jumped from hiding to clean up the mess.

"Why are things going wrong?" asked Surrogate. "I'm sure everything will be all right."

Lowbrain had an orgasm, perceived by Drill as scattered, faraway bits of pleasure. Drill continued to suckle, feeling a heavy comfort beginning to radiate from Surrogate, from the gentle sound of its heartbeat, its huge, wholesome, brainless body.

Everything will be all right, Drill decided.

"Nice to see you again, Drill," Surrogate said. "Drill, it's *nice* to see you again."

The vast crowds of Shars did not leave when night fell. Instead they stood beneath floating globes dispersing a cold reddish light that reflected eerily from pointed ears and muzzles. Some of them donned capes or skirts to help them keep warm. Drill, watching them on the video walls of the command center, was reminded of crowds standing in awe before some vast cataclysm.

The Shars were not quiet. They stood in murmuring groups, but sometimes they began the crooning chants they had raised earlier, or suddenly broke out in a series of shrill yipping cries.

President Gram spoke to them after she had left Ship. "The human has admitted his species' attacks," she said, "but has disclaimed responsibility. We shall urge him to adopt a more realistic position."

"Adopt a position," Drill repeated, not understanding. "It is not a position. It is the truth. Why don't they understand?"

Opposite Minister-General Vang was more vehement. "We now have a far more complete idea of the humans' attitude," he said. "It is opposed to ours in every way. We shall not allow the murderous atrocities which the humans have committed upon five of our planets to be forgotten, or understood to be the result of some explicable lack of attention on the part of our species' enemies."

"That one is obviously deranged," thought Drill.

He went to his sleeping quarters and ordered the Slab there to play him some relaxing music. Even with Slab's murmurs and comforting hums, it took Drill some time before his agitation subsided.

Diplomacy, he thought as slumber overtook him, was certainly a strange business.

In the morning the Shars were still there, chanting and crying, moving in their strange crowded patterns. Drill watched them on his video walls as he ate breakfast at the mash bins. "There is a communication from President Gram," Memory announced. "She wishes to speak with you by radio."

"Certainly."

"Ambassador Drill." She was using the first tones again. A pity she was subject to such stress.

"Good morning, President Gram," Drill said. "I hope you spent a pleasant night."

"I must give you the results of our decision. We regret that we can see no way to continue the negotiations unless you, as a representative of your species, agree to admit responsibility for your peoples' attacks on our planets."

"Admit responsibility?" Drill said. "Of course. Why wouldn't I?"

Drill heard some odd, indistinct barking sounds that his translator declined to interpret for him. It sounded as if someone other than President Gram were on the other end of the radio link.

"You admit responsibility?" President Gram's amazement was clear even in translation."

"Certainly. Does it make a difference?"

President Gram declined to answer that question. Instead she proposed another meeting for that afternoon.

"I will be ready at any time."

Memory recorded President Gram's speech to her people, and Drill studied it before meeting the Shar party at the airlock. She made a great deal out of the fact that Drill had admitted humanity's responsibility for the war. Her people leaped, yipped, chanted their responses as if possessed. Drill wondered why they were so excited.

Drill met the party at the airlock this time, linked with Memory and Lowbrain in Zen Synch so as not to accidentally step on the President or one of her party. He smiled and greeted each by name and led them toward the conference room.

"I believe," said Cup, "we may avoid future misunderstandings, if your Excellency would consent to inform us about your species. We have suffered some confusion in regard to your distinction between 'conscious' and 'unconscious' entities. Could you please explain the difference, as you understand it?"

"A pleasure, your Excellency," Drill said. "Our species, unlike yours, is highly specialized. Once, eight million years ago, we were like you—a small, non-specialized species type is very useful at a certain stage of evolution. But once a species reaches a certain complexity in its social and technological evolution, the need for specialists becomes too acute. Through both deliberate genetic manipulations and natural evolution, humanity turned away from a generalist species, toward highly specialized forms adapted to particular functions and environments. We understand this to be a natural function of species evolution.

"In the course of our explorations into manipulating our species, we discovered that the most efficient way of coding large amounts of information was in our own cell structure—our DNA. For tasks requiring both large and small amounts of data, we arranged that, as much as possible, these would be performed by organic entities, human subspecies. Since many of these tasks were boring and repetitive, we reasoned that advanced consciousness, such as that which we both share, was not necessary. You have met several unconscious entities. Frog, for example, and the Slab on which I lie. Many parts of my Ship are also alive, though not conscious."

"That would explain the smell," one of the delegation murmured.

"The terraforming Ships," Drill went on, "which attacked your planets—these were also designed so as not to require a conscious operator."

The Shars squinted up at Drill with their little eyes. "But why?" Cup asked.

"Terraforming is a dull process. It takes many years. No conscious mind could possibly enjoy it."

"But your species would find itself at war without knowing it. If your explanation for the cause of this war is correct, you already have."

Drill shrugged massively. "This happens from time to time. Sometimes other species which have reached our stage of development have attacked us in the same way. When it does, we arrange a peace."

"You consider these attacks normal?" Opposite Minister-General Vang was the one who spoke.

"These occasional encounters seem to be a natural result of species evolution," Drill said.

Vang turned to one of the Shars near him and spoke in several sharp barks. Drill heard a few words: "Billions lost . . . five planets . . . atrocities . . . *natural result!*"

"I believe," said President Gram, "that we are straying from the agenda.

Vang looked at her. "Yes, honorable President. Please forgive me."

"The matter of withdrawal," said President Gram, "to recognized truce lines."

Species at this stage of their development tend to be territorial, Memory reminded Drill. *Their political mentality is based around the concept of borders. The idea of a borderless community of species may be perceived as a threat.*

I'll try and go easy on them, Drill said.

"The Memories on our terraforming Ships will be adjusted to account for your species," Drill said. "After the adjustment, your people will no longer be in danger."

"In our case, it will take the disengage order several months to reach all our forces." President Gram said. "How long will the order take to reach your own Ships?"

"A century or so." The Shars stared. "Memories at our exploration basis in this area will be adjusted first, of course, and these will adjust the Memories of terraforming Ships as they come in for maintenance and supplies."

"We'll be subject to attack for *another hundred years?*" Vang's tone mixed incredulity and scorn.

"Our terraforming Ships move more or less at random, and only come into base when they run out of supplies. We don't know where they've been till they report back. Though they're bound to encounter a few more of your planets, your species will still survive, enough to continue your species evolution. And during that time you'll be searching for and occupying new planets on your own. You'll probably come out of this with a net gain."

"Have you no respect for life?" Vang demanded. Drill considered his answer.

"All individuals die, Opposite Minister-General," he said. "That is a fact of nature which no species has been able to alter. Only species can survive. Individuals are easily replaceable. Though you will lose some planets and a large number of individuals, your species as a whole will survive and may even prosper. What more could a species or its delegated representatives desire?"

Opposite Minister-General Vang was glaring at Drill, his ears pricked forward, lips drawn back from his teeth. He said nothing.

"We desire a cease-fire that is a true cease-fire,"

President Gram said. Her hands were clasping and
unclasping rhythmically on the edge of her chair. "Not
a slow, authorized extermination of our species. Your
position has an unwholesome smell. I am afraid we
must end these discussions until you alter it."

"Position? This is not a position, honorable President. It is truth."

"We have nothing further to say."

Unhappily, Drill followed the Shar delegation to the
airlock. "I do not lie, honorable President," he said,
but Gram only turned away and silently left the human Ship. The Shars in their pale thousands received
her.

The Shar broadcasts were not heartening. Opposite
Minister-General Vang was particularly vehement. Drill
collected the highlights of the speeches as he speeded
through Memory's detailed remembrance. "Callous disregard . . . no common ground for communication
. . . casual attitude toward atrocity . . . displays of
obvious savagery . . . no respect for the individual . . .
defend ourselves . . . this stinks in the nose."

The Shars leaped and barked in response. There
were strange bubbling high-pitched laughing sounds
that Drill found unsettling.

"We hope to find a formula for peace," President
Gram said. "We will confer with all the ministers in
session." That was all.

That night, the Shars surrounding Ship moaned,
moving slowly in a giant circle, their arms linked. The
laughing sounds that followed Vang's speech did not
cease entirely. He did not understand why they did
not all go home and sleep.

Long, long, Memory said. No comfort there.

Early in the morning, before dawn, there was a
communication from President Gram. "I would like to
meet with you privately. Away from the recorders,
the coalition partners."

"I would like nothing better," Drill said. He felt a
small current of optimism begin to trickle into him.

"Can I use an airlock other than the one we've been using up till now?"

Drill gave President Gram instructions and met her in the other airlock. She was wearing a night cape with a hood. The Shars, circling and moaning, had paid her no attention.

"Thank you for seeing me under these conditions," she said, peering up at him from beneath the hood. Drill smiled. She shuddered.

"I am pleased to be able to cooperate," he said.

Mash! Lowbrain demanded. It had been silent until Drill entered Zan Synch. Drill told it to be silent with a snarling vehemence that silenced it for the present.

"This way, honorable President," Drill said. He took her to his sleeping chamber—a small room, only fifty feet square. "Shall I send a Frog for one of your chairs?" he asked.

"I will stand. Three legs seem to be more comfortable than two for standing."

"Yes."

"Is it possible, Ambassador Drill, that you could lower the intensity of the light here? I find it oppressive."

Drill felt foolish, knowing he should have thought of this himself. "I'm sorry," he said. "I will give the orders at once. I wish you had told me earlier." He smiled nervously as he dimmed the lights and arranged himself on his Slab.

"Honorable ambassador." President Gram's words seemed hesitant. "I wonder if it is possible . . . can you tell me the meaning of that facial gesture of yours, showing me your teeth?"

"It is called a smile. It is intended as a gesture of benevolent reassurance."

"Showing of the teeth is considered a threat here, honorable Ambassador. Some of us have considered this a sign that you wish to eat us."

Drill was astonished. "My goodness!" he said. "I don't even eat meat! Just a kind of vegetable mash."

"I pointed out that your teeth seemed unsuitable for eating meat, but still it makes us uneasy. I was wondering . . ."

"I will try to suppress the smile, yes. Eating meat! What an idea. Some of our military specialists, yes, and of course the Sharks and Shrikes and so on . . ." He told his Memory to enforce a strict ban against smiling in the presence of a Shar.

Gram leaned back on her sturdy rear leg. Her cape parted, revealing her ribbons and badges of office, her four furry dugs. "I wanted to inform you of certain difficulties here, Ambassador Drill," she said. "I am having difficulty holding together my coalition. Minister-General Vang's faction is gaining strength. He is attempting to create a perception in the minds of Shars that you are untrustworthy and violent. Whether he believes this, or whether he is using this notion as a means of destabilizing the coalition, is hardly relevant—considering your species' unprovoked attacks, it is not a difficult perception to reinforce. He is also trying to tell our people that the military is capable of dealing with your species."

Drill's brain swam with Memory's information on concepts such as "faction" and "coalition." The meaning of the last sentence, however, was clear.

"That is a foolish perception, honorable President," he said.

"His assurances on that score lack conviction." Gram's eyes were shiny. Her tone grew earnest. "You must give me something, ambassador. Something I can use to soothe the public mind. A way out of this dilemma. I tell you that it is impossible to expect us to sit idly by and accept the loss of an undefined number of planets over the next hundred years. I plead with you, ambassador. Give me something. Some way we can avoid attack. Otherwise . . ." She left the sentence incomplete.

Mash, Lowbrain wailed. Drill ignored it. He moved into Zen Synch with Memory, racing through possible solutions. Sweat gathered on his forehead, pouring down his vast shoulders.

"Yes," he said. "Yes, there is a possibility. If you could provide us with the location of all your occupied planets, we could dispatch a Ship to each with the appropriate Memories as cargo. If any of our terraforming Ships arrived, the Memories could be transferred at once, and your planets would be safe."

President Gram considered this. "Memories," she said. "You've been using the term, but I'm not sure I understand."

"Stored information is vast, and even though human bodies are large we cannot always have all the information we need to function efficiently even in our specialized tasks," Drill said. "Our human brains have been separated as to function. I have a Lowbrain, which is on my spinal cord above my pelvis. Lowbrain handles motor control of my lower body, routine monitoring of my body's condition, eating, excretion, and sex. My perceptual centers, short-term memory, personality, and reasoning functions are handled by the brain in my skull—the classical brain, if you like. Long-term and specialized memory is the function of the large knob you see moving on my head, my Memory. My Memory records all that happens in great details, and can recapitulate it at any point. It has also been supplied with information concerning the human species' contacts with other nonhuman groups. It attaches itself easily to my nervous system and draws nourishment from my body. Specific memories can be communicated from one living Memory to another, or if it proves necessary I can simply give my Memory to another human, a complete transfer. I have another Memory aboard that I'm not using at the moment, a pilot Memory that can navigate and handle Ship, and I wore this Memory while in transit. I also have spare Memories in case my primary Memories fall ill. So you see, our specialization does not rule out adaptability—any piece of information needed by any of us can easily be transferred, and in far greater detail than by any mechanical medium."

"So you could return to your base and send our pilot Memories to your planets," Gram said. "Memories that could halt your terraforming ships."

"That is correct." Just in time, Memory managed to stop the twitch in Drill's cheeks from becoming a smile. Happiness bubbled up in him. He was going to arrange this peace after all!"

"I am afraid that would not be acceptable, your Excellency," President Gram said. Drill's hopes fell.

"Whyever not?"

"I'm afraid the Minister-General would consider it a naïve attempt of yours to find out the location of our populated planets. So that your species could attack them, ambassador."

"I'm trying very hard, President Gram," Drill said.

"I'm sure you are."

Drill frowned and went into Zen Synch again, ignoring Lowbrain's plantive cries for mash and sex, sex and mash. Concepts crackled through his mind. He began to develop an erection, but Memory was drawing off most of the available blood and the erection failed. The smell of Drill's sweat filled the room. President Gram wrinkled her nose and leaned back far onto her rear leg.

"Ah," Drill said. "A solution. Yes. I can have my Pilot memory provide the locations to an equivalent number of our own planets. We will have one another's planets as hostage."

"Bravo, ambassador," President Gram said quietly. "I think we may have a solution. But—forgive me—it may be said that we cannot trust your information. We will have to send ships to verify the location of your planets."

"If your ships go to my planet first," Drill said, "I can provide your people with one of my spare Memories that will inform my species what your people are doing, and instruct the humans to cooperate. We will have to construct some kind of link between your radio and my Memory . . . maybe I can have my Ship grow one."

President Gram came forward off her third leg and began to pace forward, moving in her strange, fast, hobbling way. "I can present it to the council this way, yes," she said. "There is hope here." She stopped her movement, peering up at Drill with her ears pricked forward. "Is it possible that you could allow me to present this to the council as my own idea?" she asked. "It may meet with less suspicion that way."

"Whatever way is best," said Drill. President Gram gazed into the darkened recesses of the room.

"This smells good," she said. Drill succeeded in suppressing his smile.

"It's nice to see you again."

"I am Drill."

"It's nice to see you again, Drill."

"I think we can make the peace work."

"Everything will be all right, Drill. Drill, I'm sure everything will be all right."

"I'm so glad I had this chance. This is the chance of a lifetime."

"Drill, it's *nice* to see you again."

The next day President Gram called and asked to present a new plan. Drill said he would be pleased to hear it. He met the party at the airlock, having already dimmed the lights. He was very rigid in his attempts not to smile.

They sat in the dimmed room while President Gram presented the plan. Drill pretended to think it over, then acceded. Details were worked out. First the location of one human planet would be given and verified—this planet, the Shar capital, would count as the first revealed Shar planet. After verification, each side would reveal the location of two planets, verify those, then reveal four, and so on. Even counting the months it would take to verify the location of planets, the treaty should be completed within less than five years.

That night the Shars went mad. At President Gram's urging, they built fires, danced, screamed, sang. Drill watched on his Ship's video walls. Their rhythms beat at his head.

He smiled. For hours.

The Ship obligingly grew a communicator and coupled it to one of Drill's spare Memories. The two were put aboard a Shar ship and sent in the direction of

Drill's home. Drill remained in his ship, watching entertainment videos Ship received from the Shars' channels. He didn't understand the dramas very well, but the comedies were delightful. The Shars could do the most intricate, clever things with their flexible bodies and odd tripod legs—it was delightful to watch them.

Maybe I could take some home with me, he thought. *They can be very entertaining*.

The thousands of Shars waiting outside Ship began to drift away. Within a month only a few hundred were left. Their singing was quiet, triumphant, assured. Sometimes Drill had it piped into his sleeping chamber. It helped him relax.

President Gram visited informally every ten days or so. Drill showed her around Ship, showing her the pilot Memory, the Frog quarters, the giant stardrive engines with their human subspecies' implanted connections, Surrogate in its shadowed, pleasant room. The sight of Surrogate seemed to agitate the President.

"You do not use sex for procreation?" she asked. "As an expression of affection?"

"Indeed we do. I have scads of offspring. There are never enough diplomats, so we have a great many couplings among our subspecies. As for affection . . . I think I can say that I have enjoyed the company of each of my partners."

She looked up at him with solemn eyes. "You travel to the stars, Drill," she said. "Your species expands randomly in all directions, encountering other species, sometimes annihilating them. Do you have a reason for any of this?"

"A reason?" Drill mused. "It is natural to us. Natural to all intelligent species, so far as we know."

"I meant a conscious reason. Is it anything other than what you do in an automatic way?"

"I can't think of why we would need any such reasons."

"So you have no philosophy of constant expansion? No ideology?"

"I do not know what those words mean," Drill said.

Gram closed her eyes and lowered her head. "I am sorry," she said.

"No need. We have no conflicts in our ideas about ourselves, about our lives. We are happy with what we are."

"Yes. You couldn't be unhappy if you tried, could you?"

"No," Drill said cheerfully. "I see that you understand."

"Yes," Gram said. "I scent that I do."

"In a few million years," Drill said, "these things will become clear to you."

The first Shar ship returned from Drill's home, reporting a transfer of the Memory. The field around Ship filled again with thousands of Shars, crying their happiness to the skies. Other Memories were now taking instructions to all terraforming bases. The locations of two new planets were released. Ships carrying spare Memories leaped into the skies.

It's working, Drill told Memory.

Long, Memory said. *Very long.*

But Memory could not lower Drill's joy. This was what he had lived his life for, and he knew he was good at it. Memories of the future would take this solution as a model for negotiations with other species. Things were working out.

One night the Shars outside Ship altered their behavior. Their singing became once again a moaning, mixed with cries. Drill was disturbed.

A communication came from the President. "Cup is dead," she said.

"I understand," Drill said. "Who is his replacement?"

Drill could no read Gram's expression. "That is not yet known. Cup was a strong person, and did not like other strong people around him. Already the successors are fighting for the leadership, but they may not be able to hold his faction together." Her ears flickered. "I may be weakened by this."

"I regret things tend that way."

"Yes," she said. "So do I."

The second set of ships returned. More Memories embarked on their journeys. The treaty was holding.

There was a meeting aboard Ship to formalize the agreement. Cup's successor was Brook, a tall, elderly Shar whose golden fur was darkened by age. A compromise candidate, President Gram said, his election determined after weeks of fighting for the successorship. He was not respected. Already pieces of Cup's old faction were breaking away.

"I wonder, your Excellency," Brook said, after the formal business was over, "if you could arrange for our people to learn your language. You must have powerful translation modules aboard your ship in order to learn our language so quickly. You were broadcasting your message of peace within a few hours of entering real space."

"I have no such equipment aboard Ship," Drill said. "Our knowledge of your language was acquired from Shar prisoners."

"Prisoners?" Shar ears pricked forward. "We were not aware of this," Brook said.

"After our base Memories recognized discrepancies," Drill said, "we sent some Ships out searching for you. We seized one of your ships and took it to my home world. The prisoners were asked about their language and the location of your capital planet. Otherwise it would have taken me months to find your world here, and learn to communicate with you."

"May we ask to arrange for the return of the prisoners?"

"Oh." Drill said. "That won't be possible. After we learned what we needed to know, we terminated their lives. They were being kept in an area reserved for a garden. The landscapers wanted to get to work." Drill bobbed his head reassuringly. "I am pleased to inform you that they proved excellent fertilizer for the gardens. The result was quite lovely."

"I think," said President Gram carefully, "that it

would be best that this information not go beyond those of us in this room. I think it would disturb the process."

Minister-General Vang's ears went back. So did others'. But they acceded.

"I think we should take our leave," said President Gram.

"Have a pleasant afternoon," said Drill.

"It's important." It was not yet dawn. Ship had awakened Drill for a call from the President. "One of your ships has attacked another of our planets."

Alarm drove the sleep from Drill's brain. "Please come to the airlock," he said.

"The information will reach the population within the hour."

"Come quickly," said Drill.

The President arrived with a pair of assistants, who stayed inside the airlock. They carried staves. "My people will be upset," Gram said. "Things may not be entirely safe."

"Which planet was it?" Drill asked.

Gram rubbed her ears. "It was one of those whose location went out on the last peace shuttle."

"The new Memory must not have arrived in time."

"That is what we will tell the people. That it couldn't have been prevented. I will try to speed up the process by which the planets receive new Memories. Double the quota."

"That is a good idea."

"I will have to dismiss Brook. Opposite Minister-General Vang will have to take his job. If I can give Vang more power, he may remain in the coalition and not cause a split."

"As you think best."

President Gram looked up at Drill, her head rising reluctantly, as if held back by a great weight. "My son," she said. "He was on the planet when it happened."

"You have other offspring," Drill said.

Gram looked at him, the pain burning deep in her eyes. "Yes," she said. "I do."

The fields around Ship filled once again. Cries and howls rent the air, and dirges pulsed against Ship's uncaring walls. The Shar broadcasts in the next weeks seemed confused to Drill. Coalitions split and fragmented. Vang spoke frequently of readiness. President Gram succeeded in doubling the quota of planets. The decision was a near one.

Then, days later, another message. "One of our commanders," said President Gram, "was based on the vicinity of the attacked planet. He is one of Vang's creatures. On his own initiative he ordered our military forces to engage. Your terraforming Ship was attacked."

"Was it destroyed?" Drill asked. His tone was urgent. There is still hope, he reminded himself.

"Don't be anxious for your fellow humans," Gram said. "The Ship was damaged, but escaped."

"The loss of a few hundred billion unconscious organisms is no cause for anxiety," Drill said. "An escaped terraforming Ship is. The Ship will alert our military forces. It will be a real war."

President Gram licked her lips. "What does that mean?"

"You know of our Shrikes and so on. Our military people are worse. They are fully conscious and highly specialized in different modes of warfare. They are destructive, carnivorous, capable of taking enormous damage without impairing function. Their minds concentrate only on tactics, on destruction. Normally they are kept on planetoids away from the rest of humanity. Even other humans find their proximity too . . . disturbing." Drill put all the urgency in his speech that he could. "Honorable President, you must give me the locations of the remaining planets. If I can get Memories to each off them with news of the peace, we may yet save them."

"I will try. But the coalition . . ." She turned away from the transmitter. "Vang will claim a victory."

"It is the worst possible catastrophe," Drill said.

Gram's tone was grave. "I believe you," she said.

Drill listened to the broadcasts with growing anxiety. The Shars who spoke on the broadcasts were making angry comments about the execution of prisoners, about flower gardens and values Drill didn't understand. Someone had let the secret loose. President Gram went from group to group outside Ship, talking of the necessity of her plan. The Shars' responses were muted. Drill sensed they were waiting. It was announced that Vang had left the coalition. A chorus of triumphant yips rose from scattered members of the crowd. Others only moaned.

Vang, now simply General Vang, arrived at the field. His followers danced intoxicated circles around him as he spoke, howling their responses to his words. "Triumph! United will!" they cried. "The humans can be beaten! Treachery avenged! Dictate the peace from a position of strength! We smell the location of their planets!"

The Shars' weird cackling laughter followed him from point to point. The laughing and crying went on well into the night. In the morning the announcement came that the coalition had fallen. Vang was now President-General.

In his sleeping chamber, surrounded by his video walls, Drill began to weep.

"I have been asked to bear Vang's message to you," Gram said. She seemed smaller than before, standing unsteadily even on her tripod legs. "It is his . . . humor."

"What is the message?" Drill said. His whole body seemed in pain. Even Lowbrain was silent, wrapped in misery.

"I had hoped," Gram said, "that he was using this simply as an issue on which to gain power. That once he had the Presidency, he would continue the diplomatic effort. It appears he really means what he's been saying. Perhaps he's no longer in control of his own people."

"It is war," Drill said.

"Yes."

You have failed, said Memory. Drill winced in pain.

"You will lose," he said.

"Vang says we are cleverer than you are."

"That may be the case. But cleverness cannot compete with experience. Humans have fought hundreds of these little wars, and never failed to wipe out the enemy. Our Memories of these conflict are intact. Your people can't fight millions of years of specialized evolution."

"Vang's message doesn't end there. You have till nightfall to remove your Ship from the planet. Six days to get out of real space."

"I am to be allowed to live?" Drill was surprised.

"Yes. It is our . . . our custom."

Drill scratched himself. "I regret our efforts did not succeed."

"No more than I." She was silent for a while. "Is there any way we can stop this?"

"If Vang attacks any human planets after the Memories of the peace arrangement have arrived," Drill said, "the military will be unleashed to wipe you out. There is no stopping them after that point."

"How long," she asked, "do you think we have?"

"A few years. Ten at the most."

"Our species will be dead."

"Yes. Our military are very good at their jobs."

"You will have killed us," Gram said, "destroyed the culture that we have built for thousands of years, and you won't even give it any thought. Your species doesn't think about what it does any more. It just acts, like a single-celled animal, engulfing everything it can reach. You say that you are a conscious species, but that isn't true. Your every action is . . . instinct. Or reflex."

"I don't understand," said Drill.

Gram's body trembled. "That is the tragedy of it," she said.

*   *   *

An hour later Ship rose from the field. Shars laughed their defiance from below, dancing in crazed abandon.

I have failed, Drill told Memory.

You knew the odds were long, Memory said. *You knew that in negotiations with species this backward there have only been a handful of successes, and hundreds of failures.*

Yes, Drill acknowledged. *It's a shame, though. To have spent all these months away from home.*

Eat! Eat! said Lowbrain.

Far away, in their forty-mile-long Ships, the human soldiers were already on their way.

ALL FALL DOWN
By Don Sakers

*Age is not always a bringer of intelligence—
at least where flesh and blood is concerned.
But what of the kind of life that is not flesh
and blood? There is such life all around us
and in greater quantity than we may ordi-
narily consider in our work. In fact, is this—
and possibly all other habitable planets—the
property of its walking, talking, constructing
inhabitants or of that other omnipresent form
of being?*

In the quiet night of this eternal wood, I lift my soul to
the stars in the waves of the Inner Voice. I sing, as the
Hlutr have sung since the beginnings of life. My roots
are deep in the lush soil of this world that now, after
the fashion of the Humans, we call Amny. My limbs
rise high into the flesh, clear air, reaching for the dim
radiance of the distant stars in lieu of the vanished
sun. And I sing.

Answering voices come from the sky and beyond: a
chorus of my brethren on a million worlds. Most of them
are Hlutr, for we alone of all the races have mastered
the mystery of the Inner Voice. In this way, as in our
physical stature, we stand above all over creatures; in
this way, we do our duty to the Universal Song. For how
could there be a Song, without the Hlutr to sing. . . ?

I sing, and this should be pleasure. I seek the communion of my race, the oneness that comes through

the Inner Voice and lifts us all far beyond the various
worlds we inhabit. The animal races, however mobile,
are bound by their very nature, bound in space to one
particular location; only the plants, seemingly sessile,
have truly transcended all boundaries. This night, I
sing, and in my song I seek to become one with the
Universal Song.

This should be a pleasure. Yet too soon, before I
am even begun, a discord intrudes. It begins faintly, a
mere hint of the song gone wrong, and I turn my soul
away from it in my attempt to fly the night. Yet the
discord is still there, on the worlds of the Hlutr and in
the empty spaces where only our dormant spores drift;
in the oceans and the clouds, spoiling their wet happy
melodies; in the soil and the turf, poisoning their deep
restful peace.

It is the Humans.

I know, my brothers, that many of you do not agree
with me. Many of you, I know, do not see them as I
do, these sons and daughters of Terra with their machines and their Thrones and their ever-continuing
raucous jabber. Most of you do not concern yourselves with the Humans. Many of you feel that they
are not truly sapient, that they do not have enough
sense of the Inner Voice to *cause* any discord in its
melodies. You are wrong. I live in their midst, not a
dozen Hlutr-lengths from one of their cities, not eight
hundred parsecs from one of their most populated
worlds, and I know: this dissonance I feel comes from
them.

Still more of you, my siblings, feel that the Humans
are sapient and feel a special compassion for them,
silly and weak as they are. You may remember our
dealings with them, and our strange brother who left
Amny and went to the world where the Humans live. I
think of him always as "The Traveler," for he went
places where Hlutr seldom go.

The last remnants of his carcass stand yet, in the
clearing only a Hlut-length or so from me. He had
been specially-bred for his mission, and he burned out

his stunted life in a very short time. But his memory
lives on, in all of us. It comes through our roots from
the wet ground, it descends on us in the summer
winds, and it echoes yet in the waves of the Inner
Voice. We will never forget the Traveler . . . and I
least of all. I was his Teacher; I bear some of the
responsibility for his mission, for making him what he
was. Sometimes, when I contemplate the grand sweep
of time, I feel that he is near, and I can almost hear
his whisper. It is a sad whisper, a lost sound as he
entreats us on behalf of those strange folk he came to
love—as if a Hlut *could* truly love any of the Little
Ones.

You remember our decision, in that time of judgment and the appeal of the Traveler. We spared Man,
when we could have eliminated him from the Universal Song like the violent blight he sometimes seems.
This was the will of the Hlutr, and this was my will
too—and yet at times I wonder.

What did we know of Humans, then? Few enough
of us had paid any attention to them. We had a few
flashes of Inner Voice, the knowledge we gained from
the poor children of Nephestal, and the ravings of our
misshapen brother.

It is so different now. We have lived with Humans
on ten thousand worlds, for twice a thousand of their
years. There is still little exchange between our folk,
but some of us Elders have watched Man carefully,
have listened to the song of his soul. And while we
have found beauty, ever have we also found discord.

And now the Humans disturb Hlutr meditation.

I live more slowly, allowing night to blossom into
day, day to fade to night, and the planet to move
forward in its orbit. Usually this helps, for Humans
are ephemeral and their disturbance does not last long.
They cannot live slower than their accustomed rate.

Now, though, I find no peace in living slowly. The
Human cacophony builds rather than subsides, and
with each swift-passing day it grows worse. Soon all
space cries with their boiling thoughts, their imperti-
nent distress, their anguish. Soon the noise overwhelms

the communion of the Hlutr, it stirs eddies in the waves of the Inner Voice, it brings violence to our quiet galaxy. Humans are screaming, Humans are dying, Humans are afraid—and worst of all, their little ones are crying.

I hear you wonder, my brothers and sisters: what is happening? You cast your thoughts outward, appealing . . . you who live on the worlds of Man open your senses, drinking in the sights and sounds of their tiny lives. Are they killing each other in yet another of their wars? Are they staining the stars with their blood, in a mad series of pogroms?

The answer comes, voiced by one of us who trembles at the magnitude of his news. A disease is taking Mankind, a disease that Human medical ability cannot reverse. It two short Human years, it has become a plague that engulfs half the galaxy and brings certain death to all it touches. Human lives are threatened, Human civilization totters, Human agony disturbs even the song of the Hlutr.

Is it any wonder that they cry?

And now the question comes, as I knew it would— whispered anonymously on the waves of the Inner Voice, spoken secretly to the winds of Amny, welling up from the soil with the memories of the Traveler: what should the Hlutr do?

I ask you, my brethren—why should the Hlutr do a thing?

Compassion, says the memory of the Traveler, the one who came to love these Humans.

In the name of compassion, then, should we turn away from Hlutr tradition? When have we ever stirred ourselves to prevent the deaths of any ephemerals? But a few seasons ago as the Hlutr count time, the great lizards roamed Amny; when the swamps dried up and the ice came, when diseases took them by their millions . . . did we interfere then? When the subtle, beautiful fishes died, leaving the oceans to the coarser beasts who succeeded them . . . did we put forth our power to save them?

Not just on Amny, but on a million worlds in all the

long history of the Hlutr race—how often have we
stood between ephemerals and their fates? And how
often have our attempts met with defeat? The vanished Coruma, the lost children of Lavarren, the lovely
singing trees of the Mehbis Cluster: all gone, forever.

You remember better than I, my brothers, my Elders.
The Hlutr have watched many races die, watched with
compassion; but we have not interfered. It is not our
way. Should we do so now?

We have pled for interference before, you say. In
ones and twos, some of you have asked for this or that
race to be spared. Some of you have tried, in defiance
of the will of the Hlutr—and all have failed.

Why should we try now?

There is among us here on Amny a youngster, barely
a sapling; she stands near the old Human settlement,
at the place where they still bring their disturbed children, their adults with defective brains. *This* we do for
the Humans . . . we care for their insane and their
defectives, we comfort them with soothing projections
of the Inner Voice.

The sapling calls for us now. Her message comes
through the First Language, on waves of color racing
through the Hlutr grove; it comes in the gentle sough-
ing of the Second Language, a muted sound like the
distant sea. "Elders," she tells us, "A Human calls for
you."

"For us?"

"He uses the old equipment, and speaks to me in
pidgin First Language on luminous screens. He asks to
address our Elders."

I tremble in the wind. Is there no end to Human
audacity? First they shatter the peace of Hlutr meditation; now one of them demands an audience?

Compassion, Brother, the memory of the Traveler
tells me.

Sooner or later I must deal with the Humans; I
decide it will be now. "Send him," I tell the sapling.

Before the man arrives, he is heralded by the other
Hlutr. Broad waves of contrasting color move through
their leaves and across their trunks, and when he

enters my glade he is accompanied by the swishing of a million Hlutr leaves.

He is a small creature, even for a Human; his sparse fur is ashen and his artificial hide a dirty white. He stops before my trunk, then raises equipment designed to generate lights that mock the First Language.

The memories of the Traveler have prepared me; I bend my lower limbs to the ground, and I vibrate their leaves in controlled patterns, far faster than usual. The technique is difficult even for an Elder like myself, with full control over my body. We use it to communicate with the lesser orders in their own familiar languages. I do not intend to set the Human at ease; rather, I wish to show him the abilities of the Hlutr from the very beginning.

"Who are you, Human?"

He bows. "I am Doctor Alex Saburo, of the Credixian Imperial Navy."

This tells me little. His name is a sound, nothing else. His title indicates one who is accorded knowledge and wisdom, as Humans know it. As for his affiliation, not even the Ancients of Nephestal are able to keep track of everchanging Human political systems.

"Why do you come before me?"

"To ask for help."

Up close, it is easy to read these creatures through the Inner Voice. The tenor of his emotions matches his voice: firmly controlled, yet aware that he stands in the presence of a vastly superior being.

Emotions, but their minds are not coherent enough to project thoughts. "Ask, then," I say

"The Death," he said, spreading his upper limbs. "We can do nothing to stop it. It's infected half the Galaxy, and it's entered the Imperium. In another year it'll have spread to every Human world." His control wavers, and I glimpse emotional storms beneath the surface of this man's mind.

"So you come to the Hlutr for help. Why?"

"Where else would I turn. Your Greatness?"

"You may address me as 'Teacher.' "

"Our medical science cannot cope with the plague. Teacher. I know that the Hlutr have the ability to modify the very genetic code itself; I know that your Elders have the intelligence to analyze the Plaque and perhaps stop it."

So the Universal Song mocks me, my brethren. I cannot evade the question that is whispered in the night: Should Hlutr help Humans?

I appeal to my own Elders for a decision, and they are strangely silent. It is I who began this thing, two millennia ago when I prepared the Traveler to judge Humanity, when I came before the Elders to say that we needed to know more of the children of Earth. Now it is *I* who must decide whether we will spare Mankind in this time of crisis.

Although the Traveler's memories beat strongly within me, how can I say yes? How can I throw off geological ages of Hlutr tradition, all for the sake of a brutish creature who thinks himself grand because he can disturb our meditations? How can I justify saving *this* people, when we have allowed so many others to perish?

The man is waiting for an answer; and suddenly, I have one for him. "You ask much of me, Doctor Alex Saburo. Perhaps too much." I tell him of our traditions. I tell him of the Coruma, the Lavarren, the Mehbis folk. I tell him that all living creatures—yes, even the Hlutr—meet death, that it is part of the Universal Song. In the end, my twigs ache from making such precise vibrations for so long.

"Teacher, I have heard that the Hlutr value life. Old tales tell of their compassion for all Little Ones. For the sake of that compassion, won't you help us?"

"We are compassionate . . . but you do not know what you ask. You Humans occupy over twelve thousand worlds; within one year, all will be stricken with your Death. You ask that we create a defense, then that we sacrifice ourselves to spread that defense on all your planets. . . ?"

"The sacrifice would be great—but without it, my civilization, perhaps my entire race, will die."

"The sacrifice is greater than you think." I groped in the vast collective Hlutr memory for the Human words I needed. "You think we Hlutr can synthesize genetic material without effort. Know then, Doctor Alex Saburo, that when a Hlutr makes new DNA and RNA, that Hlut dies—violently, in a bursting that spreads the new material on all the winds. Even if we *can* save your people, to do so means that many times twelve thousand Hlutr must perish in agony."

A brief torrent of anger, quickly suppressed, flashes forth in the Inner Voice. "I had not thought," he says, "That the Hlutr were so selfish."

"'We have our duty to the Universal Song. If that melody declares that Humans just pass away, we cannot gainsay it."

He is an odd creature, in whom passion and reason can coexist, each as forceful as the other. Now he touches my trunk, and the warmth of his hand surprises me and moves me in a way his words have not. "If you wish, Doctor Alex Saburo, the Hlutr can offer your people counsel. We can help you prepare for the Death, can make it easier for you to meet your end. We have done this for others."

"No." His denial is strong. "I thank you then. Elder, and I beg your permission to leave. There is little time."

That should be the end of it—yet it is not. "What will you do, Human?"

"I'll seek an answer. Somewhere, someone must have the knowledge that will help me to end the Death. As long as I can, I'll keep searching." He turns, and begins the slow walk away from my grove.

There is an outcry from some of my brethren, a gentle protest that falls from the stars like cold Autumn rain. From within me, where the memory of the Traveler lives, there is a stronger objection.

Brothers and sisters, how can I yield to you? How can I deny our traditions? You are but a few—and when the Hlutr act, they must act in agreement.

How, you ask me, can I ignore the pain?

"Wait, Alex Saburo."

If for nothing more than the sake of the Traveler, whose spirit gnaws at me. I make the Human an offer. "I will go with you."

"B-but how? I will travel beyond this world, to planets where the Death has hit."

I do not know, my brethren, why I agree to do a thing that the Hlutr seldom do. Perhaps I, too, am overly fond of these Humans. Perhaps I want to find something in them that would be worth the death of a hundred thousand Hlutr. Perhaps I am simply reluctant to waste all the time I have spent studying them. "The Human children on yonder hill are mentally defective, yet they are strongly sensitive to the Hlutr Inner Voice. One of them shall become my operative—it shall accompany you, and I will see what it sees, hear what it hears, and communicate with you through its mouth. I will also sing with my brethren and my Elders, and perhaps . . . perhaps we will find a way to help you."

He is flabbergasted; both the power and the mercy of the Hlutr are beyond him. "Go back to the sanitarium," I tell him. "My operative will greet you there."

"I . . . thank you, Teacher."

His words are echoed by the voice of the Traveler within: *Thank you.*

The body is awkward, soft, confining. Through its limited senses, I perceive a truncated world; vision spans merely one octave, and the threshold of hearing is far above the quiet susurrus of the Hlutr Second Language. The Human chemical senses show more promise, yet the body does not know how to properly interpret them.

There is no mind, no awareness of identity. If such ever existed, it is buried too deeply for even the Hlutr to find. Although it wears an animal body, the creature's soul is more like the lesser plants. It has life, it responds to its environment, but it has no volition. Until I animate it.

Motion, that is the most difficult thing. The Hlutr move slowly—swaying with the wind, making tiny ovals in sympathy with the yearly movement of the sun, pulsing our rhythms of growth and life with the music of the Inner Voice. We are not accustomed to the rush of animal motion, and it takes me a time to become comfortable as the new body walks.

I have not animated a body for Human millennia . . . not since I attended conferences of the Free Peoples of the Scattered Worlds in borrowed Avethellan form. Slowly, the process comes back to me, and I am more confident. The raucous Human voices do not sound so harsh, the claustrophobic Human rooms begin to seem less close.

While I am adjusting to the change, Alex Saburo leads me to a transport capsule, and in minutes I am in the Human city. Confusion and disharmony fill my senses, and I simply withdrew my attention from the body. I sing with the winds, I feel the happy touch of flying beasts upon my limbs, I dig my roots in the cool earth and inhale nutrients from the brisk air. In time, Saburo and my operative reach the spaceport; after a few moments of disorientation they have left the surface of Amny and are speeding out into the dark, peaceful gulfs of space.

Now at last I can return to the body, can begin to bring my Human operative completely under control. I concentrate, matching my time sense to the fast, inflexible Human metabolism. The world of my experience narrows in concentric circles, until I bid temporary farewell to grove, earth and winds and open my eyes on a small spacecraft lounge. I am upon a divan before a wall that mimics the sight of naked space; Saburo sits next to me, watching instruments in his lap. When I stir, he looks up.

"Teacher?" He asks.

"I am here, Saburo." my voice . . . my *Human* voice . . . sounds hollow in Human ears.

"We'll be shifting into tachyon phase in a moment," he says. "We've been under way for just under two hours; it's almost ten hours since we left your grove."

I shake my head. The animal attitude toward time is very hard for Hlutr to grasp. Everything is impatience,

everything is motion. We who count time by the movement of stars and the seasons of slow Hlutr life, we
have difficulty binding ourselves to rigid Human concept of interval. "I have the Human body under control now," I assure him. "I long to experience your
tachyon drive. It is a thing that Hlutr seldom endure:
to travel nearly as fast as the waves of the Inner Voice
can move."

"Will you be able to maintain communication with
. . . your host?"

"I feel confident that I can do so. Our minds are
much more flexible than you believe." Indeed, the
change comes even as we talk; the Human ship twists
in a direction totally unknown to Hlutr, but I do not
lose contact with my operative. My awareness has
taken root in the alien animal brain cells, and it will
not be dislodged easily.

"What is our destination?"

Saburo sighs. "First, to Taglierre, to stop in at the
Credixian Medical Association convention. I don't ex-
pect them to have any more leads than they did when
I was there last week." He spreads his hands. "After
that, I guess it's on to Eironea to consult with the
Grand Library."

"I do not know these places."

"We're flying to Galactic West; from Amny, roughly
in the direction of the constellation called Aurick's
Tower." He touches a few keys on a panel, and the
wall shows Amny's night sky. He points toward a
particular grouping of stars. "Here."

Nodding comes almost as easily to me as the azure
hue by which the Hlutr signal assent. We move in the
direction of sad, bright Dorasc. Even now I hear the
song of my brothers and sisters on Dorasc's starbright
plains, and I sing with them. The song is distorted: in
part because of the tremendous speed at which the
vehicle moves, but in part also because of the wails of
a billion Human voices. And somewhere, between
here and distant Dorasc, the cry of a single Human
child cuts across the harmony of the Inner Voice like
thunder across a peaceful Summer afternoon.

*   *   *

Ere I have begun to probe the nature of that dreadful cry, the ship twists again, returning to normal space. Before my Human eye is the cool, white globe of Taglierre.

Scarce two sevens of Galactic Revolutions have passed since Hlutr seeds first came to Taglierre. In that time, the planet has grown steadily more inhospitable, slowly getting colder as it leaks its atmosphere to space. Human terraformers have arrested the process, and for now Taglierre has an air blanket two-thirds as dense as Amny's and temperatures no worse than the deepest winter of my home. Yet Humans will not stay forever. Seventy times seventy Hlutr remain, proud and lonely in the tropics; within their lifetimes Taglierre will become a frozen ghost of a world.

As we jockey for an approach pattern, I greet these lofty brothers and sisters, who have the honor of presiding over the death of a world. They work their works well, as the generations progress . . . urging the Little Ones along, nudging them now and again when their normal evolution does not keep pace with Taglierre's dissipation. When their efforts are successful, life will survive on this globe; yet the struggle is a hard one. They sing me ritual greeting, but pay me little attention otherwise; the doings of Humans are their least concern.

Still, from their song and the eddies of the Inner Voice that lap the shores of this planet's waterless seas, I glimpse loneliness and despair in the once-teeming Human cities, and I know that the Hlutr are not the *only* ones waiting for a world to die.

"Many of your people have left Taglierre," I say to Saburo.

Discarded memories in my host's brain tell me that Saburo's wrinkled face is sad. "The Death will be here soon—within weeks, probably. Everyone who can leave, has. Only military ships can land safely; the poor fools will stampede themselves trying to steal anything else."

"Why do they not prohibit travel, thus containing the disease?"

"On Taglierre? They depend on trade for food and repair parts. That world can't support a half-billion people on its own." He runs a hand through his white hair. "We've done what we can. The Imperator ordered the boundaries closed a year ago—so the Imperium escaped for a while." The ship cuts through air, leaving a brief flash like the trail of a meteorite visible to Hlutr below. "But we can't stop interstellar trade. The Death has entered the Imperium now, it's only a matter of weeks until . . ." He does not finish.

We settle to a desolate landing field, while cold sand blows across the empty plain.

These are Human Elders and wise ones? I came to Taglierre, my brothers and sisters, convinced that I would witness something like a council of Hlutr, all joined in the swaying and the song as they contemplate mysteries and seek for answers. Instead, I have fallen into a madhouse!

Listen to them, my fellows:

"The Death is a prion-based disease; my simulations make an analogy with the treatment of Gerstman-Straussler syndrome," says one of them, a tall and slender woman with hair the color of the Springtime sky. "Thus, your attempt to modify DNA-based antiviritics shall fail no matter what starting point you use."

"*My* computers," says another from a communications screen, "assure me that there are no effective prophylactic measures. We can only treat the disease after it is manifest—and that treatment relies on massive doses of general-series antiviritics."

"You are wrong," shouts a third, ludicrously holding up his computer display for all to see. "The analogy must be two classic toxic reactions. The only way to stop this scourge is to spread organisms capable of breaking down the toxin. I suggest that we allow our linked medicomps to write a simulation involving a gengineered variant of current antidote-antibodies."

The meeting hall, although large, is mostly empty. The doctors—the Human Elders—sit or stand near the center, each of them without exception behind a computer terminal. Saburo and I sit with a few quiet visitors on one side of the chamber. On the other are the members of the press: frightened or confident, they do not understand what the doctors say, yet they feel that these idiots will find an answer. Billions of Humans watch the proceedings through their eyes and their instruments, billions who see the doctors as wise seekers of knowledge. Am I the only one who recognizes them as fools?

No. For Saburo rises to speak.

"My God, you've been here for two months and you're still having the same arguments. Still linking your medicomps to your diagnostitrons and running simulation after simulation. I don't believe it."

The tall woman looks down her nose. "If it isn't Doctor Saburo. Or should I say, *Lieutenant* Saburo?"

"Brevet Colonel for the duration, Doctor Melus. I've never tried to hide my connection with the Navy."

"No." She smiles. "You just couldn't find any school or reputable hospital that would put up with you. So you think we're wasting our time?"

"I do. Simulations and computer analyses aren't going to stop the Death—"

"Oh, and I suppose you will? How? Your habit of playing about with corpses hasn't yielded any results, nor have your excursions into vivisection. . . ."

"Legitimate experimentation, if you please."

"Have it your own way. I don't see any cure from your latest brainstorm of appealing to aliens, Lieutenant."

Saburo clenches his fists, but says nothing.

The woman dismisses him with a wave. "Here we have gathered in one room, the greatest expert databases in the Imperium and beyond. The Universities of Skapton, Prakis and Credix itself are tied into our network. We have the wisdom of the ancients, in the form of the programs they left us. This convention has

brought together the greatest resources of medicine in
recorded history—"

"And you'll still be running your simulations and
consulting the ancients when the last of you drops
dead from the Plague!" Saburo takes the arm of my
operative, draws her toward the door. "Come on, I
should have known better than to stop here."

As the door slams shut behind us, the Human doctor begin again their comparison of the results of mindless computer programs.

No wonder they are dying.

On the way to Eironea, we pass warships—Saburo
tries to explain to me why Humans have been killing
one another, but I cannot comprehend. We Hlutr are
all one tribe, since the time of the Great Schisms more
than a billion years ago . . . we do not fight among
ourselves for territory, nor do we seek vain power.
The Hlutr are united in the songs we sing and the
Universal Song of which all are part; even when we
disagree (as some of you, my brothers and sisters,
disagree with me about helping the Humans), we do
so without rancor, malice or violence.

And what need have the Hlutr to fight with the
other orders? When they menace us, they are dealt
with; otherwise, the Hlutr conquer as they have always conquered, in the slow yet inexorable fashion of
the plant kingdom. Why should we fight?

"Your warships sit idle, Saburo. Why do they not
fight?" For though ships from both sides challenge us
as we pass, there is no hostility along a border that
stretches for a kiloparsec in every direction.

He manipulates his keyboard, stares into a small
screen, then shrugs. "The Death. They've declared a
truce for the duration."

"Yours are a strange folk, Saburo."

Now he does a thing which convinces me that none
of the Wise will *ever* understand Humans, a thing that
makes me withdraw for a time to my quiet grove and
the fresh dew of a misty Amny dawn.

He laughs.

In due time we come to Eironea, and reluctantly I return from Amny. Your attention is on me now, brothers and sisters, and on this strange journey which has become my mission. Some of you sing of our obligation to save the Humans; others sing that we must maintain the precious Hlutr detachment that has served us since the far-off days of the Pylistroph, when Life was but a dream in the Scattered Worlds.

And others . . . others breathe a different opinion, born of smothering hatred and cold revenge. *These* Hlutr rejoice at the Death, and would have us hurry it along so that Humans can be wiped out once and for all.

Have you forgotten, brethren, that once the Hlutr swore to aid Mankind in his quest for maturity, his fulfillment of his potential? Saburo may succeed, despite us—Humanity may survive the Death without Hlutr aid. Will you then have us slay the survivors, cast this people out from the Universal Song? Would you have the Hlutr forsworn before the stars and the sacred melodies?

What the Hlutr do, we shall do in full agreement. Nay, my brothers and sisters: for now, Man will make his own destiny, and the Hlutr . . . the Hlutr will watch.

Our ship enters normal space, and we drop toward verdant Eironea. The Hlutr of this world, who live mainly in rich, wet tropical forests, sing me welcome and concern in the Inner Voice. Theirs is a song tinged with despair; the Death has come to Eironea, and Humans have died: seventy times itself four times and more of them. Ten times that many are near death, and their despondency shakes the planet. These Hlutr are fond of their Humans; they cry sadness to the unfeeling stars at the passing of their Little Ones.

We land on an untenanted field near one of their great cities, as the sun climbs slowly toward zenith and shadows pool beneath buildings. A drawn Human face appears on the wall: the commander of our ship.

"We're down, sir. If it's all the same to you . . . er . . . the crew has voted to remain shipboard. Your cabin connects directly to the main airlock; we'd appreciate it if you'd . . ."

Saburo raises a quivering hand. "I understand, Commander. Rest assured that we'll remain in our sealed area of the ship."

"Very good, sir." The face disappears.

With a heavy sigh, Saburo stands. "Come with me," he says.

"What is our destination?"

"The Library." His tread is heavy, his body stooped like a tree that has seen too many harsh winters.

I can do nothing but follow.

There in the empty streets of the city Shiau Shi on the planet Eironea, Saburo tells me what the Humans have done. Let me share this with you, brethren, for it is a marvelous thing.

Like the Daamin, the Kreen and the happy children of grand Avethell, Humans gathered together in one place all their knowledge of the Universal Song. This was in the days of their great Empire, fifteen hundred years ago. Once, every Human world, settlement or starship in the Galaxy could access this knowledge; today, only a few outposts remain in contact with the central Library. Eironea is one of them. Here, in the care of a devoted priesthood, the machinery is available to all who need it. Through the political upheavals of nearly seventy Human generations, Eironea has remained free, unconquered and neutral, guarding its precious treasure.

The network of transit capsules is not working, and no auto-taxis answer Saburo's summons, so our ship gives birth to a small vehicle and we travel in this metal shell. Human watch us as we pass, hidden in their buildings or behind directional signs and structural members; the few whom we catch in the open scurry for cover as soon as they see us.

The Temple of Knowledge soars above us as we disembark; Saburo makes his way to a row of waiting computer terminals; their screens remain dark.

I sense another Human presence behind us, and turn to see a pale, emaciated woman dressed in a tattered frock. Her long hair is the black of space, and her eyes hold Springtime green.

"If you're here to consult the Grand Library," she says in a thin voice, "I'm sorry, but you won't have any success."

"The machinery doesn't work?" Saburo asks.

"It works fine. There's no one at the other end to answer." She spreads her arms, a sapling opening to the sun. "The Library staff was hit hard by the Death; we last heard from them months ago." Her lips form a weak smile. "Come on to my quarters, I'll give you some tea. We might as well be comfortable." She introduces herself as we follow. "I am Yee Bair. And you?"

"Doctor Alex Saburo. My companion is the Teacher. Do . . . did you work here?"

"At the Temple? Goodness, no. I was a frequent customer." She pauses to cough. "After the Death hit and the priests either died or moved away, I figured, why not move in? It's a lot nicer than my two-room flat, and I have plenty of time for my work."

Something sings in her, just the briefest flash of an incomplete melody in the Inner Voice. "Your work?" I ask.

"I'm an artist." She pauses before a closed door, presses her palm against it and it slides open. "Here, look."

Yee Bair makes pictures with light—raw, vibrant pictures that distort reality as soon through Human eyes. Some of her works are tame, gentle scenes of towers, spaceports and lounging Human beings. Others feature scenes of the Death, and they breathe with the fear, anguish and defiance that radiate from Human worlds in these terrible times.

"You're a genius," Saburo says.

In spite of myself, I nod. "You give form and definition to a bit of the Universal Song. Your work ranks with the greatest of your people."

"These were early attempts," she says, pointing out the tame visions. "Before . . ." she does not finish, but busies herself with the tea.

This is the mystery, brothers and sisters, that we have faced before and will face again in a thousand different races. We, whose only artform is the substance of the Universal Song itself—we cannot capture its essence in the way that these Little Ones, these animals, can. We who are masters of creation are also its prisoners; we cannot step beyond it to create things that cannot be, to see things that cannot exist. We who never know the fullness of despair that these creatures feel, will also never know the urge that pushes them beyond despair's limits. The ecstasy and the pain of a Hlutr in the final death-blast, imposing the will of our folk on the malleable genetics of reality— this is the closest we poor Hlutr can approach the emotion that Yee Bair feels whenever she picks up her light-wand.

Should the Hlutr cry then for Humans, as they face the terror of the Death—or should Humans cry for us?

Human pain rips across the Universal Song, and for a moment my Human brain aches with that plaintive cry. Somewhere, nearer than ever, a Human child is crying as none has ever cried before. Soon, no Hlutr will be able to ignore that cry.

Saburo gives a noiseless whistle of awe, and my attention is drawn to Yee Bair's current work.

She has given form to this child's cry that echoes from star to star.

It is a scene almost as the Hlutr might see it, a million colors overlaid one atop the other, a jagged slice of vision that oozes with raw pain. Human eyes and brain must study the picture to see what it represents, but I *know* even as I glance at it. A Human boy-child wails, surrounded by the dead bodies of seven times seventy Human adults. Behind him, dimly seen, are the figures of other races who watch the Human tragedy: the wise Daamin, the sad sons of Metrin, the compassionate Iaranori who even now struggle to bring relief where they can . . . and the Hlutr, proud and tall in our distant sympathy. And beyond us, even the cold unfeeling stars rain tears of light on the child. The picture brings tears to my borrowed Human eyes, as the cry it represents could not.

The stars . . .

I touch Yee Bair's arm. "These are the stars of Eironea's sky, no?"

"Yes." Of course they are. How could one who is so attuned to the waves of the Inner Voice, avoid hearing that call of agonized loneliness? And hearing it, how could she not know from whence it came?

"Show me . . . show Saburo . . . where those star-groupings lie."

Why am I doing this thing? Brothers, sisters, what is the fate of one Human child to me? Some of you ask me that question, and I cannot but wonder with you. Yet others—the voice of the dead Traveler among them, he who knew Humans better than any of us—others sing to me that a Little One is in pain, and the Hlutr must answer. If only to still the pain with a merciful stroke. This is our way, our purpose, our duty since the first Hlutr raised itself above the soil of forgotten Paka Tel.

Yee Bair describes the area of the sky, and Saburo relates it to galactic charts in his computer terminal. When he is done, he looks at me, his face filled with questions.

"Take us there, Saburo."

"Why?"

I ask myself the same thing, brethren, and receive no answer save that which I know already: a Little One is crying. "It is in the Universal Song," I tell Saburo, hoping that will content him. And it does.

We share tea with Yee Bair, then return to the ship. Saburo must be desperate, his last chance flown away in the empty halls of the Temple; he gives orders quickly, and soon we are climbing from green Eironea into the black of endless space.

On the way, Saburo coughs a few times, then turns away from me.

* * *

"Tell me of the Death. How does it come upon your people, and what do they feel when it strikes?"

Eironea is far behind, the crying Human child still lost in the star ahead of us. Saburo looks up from his computer and frowns.

"Sometimes it comes quickly, and death follows in a few days. In other cases it can take months to develop. The symptoms vary: coughing, headaches, difficult breathing, swelling in the joints—then pneumonia, vitamin deficiency, nerve disfunction—if the patient lives long enough, total disruption of the immune system and advanced malnutrition."

"None escape?"

"Some who caught it nearly two years ago, at the beginning, are still alive . . . but still infected and still showing symptoms. We've never had a case of someone exposed to the disease who didn't catch it, or anyone who recovered from it once infected."

"And your science cannot prevent the spread?"

"That fool Melus was right about one thing—it's a prion-based disease. No DNA. We haven't even been able to isolate the infectious agent, much less counter it." His hands twist hopelessly in his lap. "As long as our doctors continue to play with computer programs left over from the ancients, we'll never make any progress."

I look out at the swiftly-moving stars, and I listen to the eddies of the Inner Voice as it moves between the worlds. And I wonder. Where did this plague come from?

Some say that it is natural outgrowth of evolutionary systems that contain Humans. A variant of diseases known to Mankind even before he ventured off his home planet. This is indeed possible; Life's ingenuity knows no bounds, and other such diseases have developed in the long course of Galactic history.

Others say that the Death was artificially engineered as a weapon against these people—either by Humans themselves, or by one of the malevolent races of the Galactic Core. This theory, too, has its antecedents; this will not be the first time a promising race has died in biological suicide . . . or been victim of the Gathered Worlds.

Some even say—although not in words—that the Death was started by the Hlutr. I have sung the question in the Inner Voice, casting suspicions out into the starry night, but I have received no answer. No one admits, and yet . . .

One cannot but have suspicions. The Death is said to have started on Laxus, a planet not too far from the very Earth upon which these Humans sprang. The very Earth on which the last descendants of their own Hlutr choked to death on Human poisons. Often I have contemplated the infinitely sad story of the Redwoods, often I have wondered at their stunted lives: only a shadow of what they could be, what their distant ancestors had been; blind, dumb, all but deaf; hearing only the barest echoes of the Inner Voice, while all around them ranged the awesome and beautiful symphony of the Hlutr singing each to the others. The Redwoods were not Hlutr, at best they were only a kind of degenerate Hlutr kin, leftovers from a damaged line that had never been able to sing the Inner Voice. Their minds, what minds they had, must have been twisted beyond all recognition; their pitiful short lives must have been an agony.

And the Traveler within me whispers at these times: although they did not know it, did Humans do a merciful thing when they allowed the Redwoods to die?

And we Hlutr—what is the course of mercy for *us?* To allow death, or to deny it? Even if it is a death that some of us might have caused. . . ?

The ship shudders, and comes out of tachyon phase in the shadow of a huge banded gas giant.

"What now?" Saburo says.

The Commander answers, his face appearing ghostly over the magnificent view. "Refueling stop, sir. Settlement called Kef. Hope you don't mind—it's the only place on our charts that has a treaty with the Imperium."

"Carry on." Saburo turns to me. "I hope you don't mind."

"No." I reach out, calling for Hlutr—there are none in their planetary system, none for sevens of parsecs. We move, and a shrunken sun rises over the orange limb of the gas giant; light glitters briefly from a narrow ring of ice particles.

No brothers, no sisters—only the pulse of nearby Human life, a distant echo that might be some form of developing plant life on a rocky worldlet close to the sun . . . and the slow, incomprehensible hum that comes from the crystalline Talebba, a race whose existence Humans do not even suspect. The Talebba go their own way, living out their geological lifespans in planetary rings, asteroid belts and the clouds of primordial stuff that hide from stellar heat out where space is nearly flat and their own sun but another bright star. Now and again one of them dies, flaming, as it topples toward the inner system; occasionally one of these survives long enough to impact on a planet, and possibly create a new race of rocklike intelligences to succeed it.

I do not greet the Talebba of this system. To do so, I would have to live nearly as slowly as they do, and to them Galactic Years are like the days and nights to other creatures.

Saburo is consulting his computer; he grins. "Kef is a settlement in orbit around this gas giant, and something of a leader in local trade. I'm hoping they'll have charts that might help you locate whatever you're on the track of."

"I do not know." The Inner Voice is, for the moment, undisturbed. The song of the Hlutr sounds in lonely splendor, untouched by the cry of Humanity. The child is sleeping . . . or dead.

"There," he points, and Kef swings into view.

It is an untidy thing, a construct of glass, metal and light that resembles a bird's nest as much as it does a spaceship or Human city. Around the whole assembly is a ring of violent red, so bright that it hurts my Human eyes. Suddenly a loud klaxon rings, making both Saburo and me start.

"What is it?" Saburo says.

The Commander replies, "We're getting a transmission on the emergency band. I'll put it on your screen."

The Human face that greets us is gaunt and wild-eyed. "Turn back," the man croaks through dry lips. "Docking permission is denied."

"We are a ship of the Credixian Navy, on a refueling stop—"

"For your own sake, keep away. Do not pass our circle of quarantine. Don't you understand? *We've all caught the Death.*"

Saburo shakes his head. "We've already been exposed. We just need fuel, and a look at your charts."

"No." The face is sad, but hard with unbending determination as strong as Hlutr bark. "There's hydrogen enough in the atmosphere of the gas giant— you're a military ship, you can refuel with ramscoops. You can tie your navicomp into our central computer if you think our charts will be of any use to you. Just stay away."

"I don't understand. If you're already infected, how do you think we can make it worse?"

The man shakes his head. "By carrying this thing elsewhere. We all took a vow, destroyed our ships, set up the circle to warn others off." His eyes plead with Saburo as his hollow voice cannot. "We're ready to die . . . but we're not going to take the rest of the Galaxy with us. Go away, please—before you tempt us too far."

Saburo nods, touches the intercom. "Take us into a dive, Commander. We'll skim the atmosphere and then get on our way." He turns back to the man from Kef. "I understand. We're leaving. G-gods be with you."

"Gods be with us all." The image fades, and red-ringed Kef falls behind us until it is lost in the stars.

"The poor fools," the Commander says.

Tight-lipped, Saburo shakes his head, but says nothing. Soon we are in tachyon phase again.

Certain of my brethren sing the courage of Kef in the Inner Voice, determined that such heroism should not be lost to the Universal Song. And who am I to deny them? More and more Hlutr join this song, more and more regard me and the progress of my journey; not just saplings and adults, but Elders as well. And now, for the first time, I feel the chill touch of the attention of the Eldest of all, from her vast island in the Secluded Realm. As yet, she pays only the slightest heed, just a hint of scrutiny.

This matter is becoming far more important, my brothers and sisters, than I ever intended.

Now, as if aware of the presence of so many Hlutr minds, the Human child shrieks again, splintering the mass concentration of the Inner Voice. For all that this cry tears at my soul, I welcome it: I am not too late to help.

If I can help at all . . .

In the end, I enlist the aid of the Hlutr of Telorbat and a dozen other worlds within a kiloparsec. That the Human child is somewhere within this volume of space there can be no doubt; no Hlut can mistake its anguished wail. At my direction, the Hlutr listen closely, then each tells me the direction from which the cry comes. I mark these on Saburo's master charts; we wait for a few hours, then we try again.

This is exactly the sort of work at which animal intelligences excel: the splitting of time and space into tiny bits, the measurement of direction and duration. With computers to do his calculation and Kef's star charts as a basis, Saburo manages to pinpoint the source to within a few billion cubic kilometers. The size of a planetary system, and in an empty volume far from any planet! Are we mad to think we can locate the child?

No.

The emotion is unmistakable as the echo on a radar screen, and in Human hours we have located the center of the disturbance that called me from Amny seven thousand parsecs away. A lone Human starship floats powerless in starry space. Saburo is taken by a coughing fit, then gains control of himself. "Commander, take us in. Dock with that ship."

"They don't answer our challenges, sir. I think it's a ghost ship."

I shake my head. *Something* is alive aboard that dark hulk.

"Just follow my orders," Saburo says evenly. The commander shrugs, and turns to his control board.

Soon the ships are mated together, and Saburo and I stand before a closed hatch that leads to the mystery vessel. I do not know what to expect; seventy thousand times seventy Hlutr, and more, watch with me as the door slides back.

The sight, the smell, the sound we experience is something that no living being should ever face. Saburo, retching, falls back; even some of the Elders turn away from that terrible scene.

The ship—a cargo vessel—is crammed with dead, decaying Human bodies. Most of them show the ravages of the Death: flat, empty stomachs, the agony of death, the trace of fluids on faces and chests. It is indeed a ghost ship, one inhibited by victims of the Death. Or so we think. Only when we blast into the sealed control room, only when we inspect the destroyed panels and recover the damaged log, do we find the truth. And when we find that horrible truth, it is *my* cry that echoes in the heavens and disturbs the Hlutr at their meditation.

We may never know the home planet of that charnel ship, for all references were carefully edited out of the log. Only the record of their deeds remained, as if they were actually proud of what they had done.

Over seventy times seventy times seventy Humans were put aboard the ship: more than four hundred thousand bodies. And more than half of them were still alive. The unknown rulers of that unknown world herded all the victims of the Death, along with their families and friends, along with the doctors who tried to treat them, along with the ministers who tried to comfort them—herded all into that vast cargo hold, then sealed them off and set them on a journey to nowhere. The controls were set to destroy themselves after a certain time in tachyon phase; after which, the ship dropped back into normal space and floated aimlessly, a macabre prison that offered no hope of escape.

There the tragedy did not end . . . for somewhere in this ship, a Human child still cries.

It is Saburo who finds him, huddled in a curve of the hull with corpses pressed tight around him. The boy is naked, filthy and starved; he draws back with a scream when Saburo reaches for him.

"Let me." I step forward, and call on all the Hlutr to help me. All Human children are sensitive to the Inner Voice, this one more than most: we join in a song of reassurance, of peace, and the boy falls silent. I lift him, and Saburo leads the way back to our own ship.

His name is Ved, and he does not know where he comes from. As I probe his mind, I sense a good deal of damage; he builds walls against the terror he has experienced, and I am loath to disturb those walls. Later, in the care of Hlutr specialists on Amny, perhaps Ved can be brought back to full mental health; for now I am content to let him fall asleep to the Hlutr lullaby.

When I am sure that the boy will not wake, I face Saburo. For once, I feel something akin to animal rage . . . and I know that you, my brothers and sisters, feel this anger with me.

"You dare?" I challenge him. "You dare to crawl to the Hlutr and ask us to spare your race? To spare *that?!*" With one gesture, I indicate the charnel ship, the world that launched it, the people who committed this atrocity and all their brothers, sisters and cousin throughout the Galaxy. "Beg rather that we do not increase the virulence of the Death seventy-times-seventy-fold, to give your people the agony they deserve."

Saburo coughs, falls into his chair, then raises defiant eyes. "Is this Hlutr compassion?"

"The Hlutr do not waste compassion on beasts who have proven unworthy of it. We do not grant compassion to creatures who are incapable of showing it."

"Do you think *I'm* not sickened by what I saw today? Do you think I don't want revenge on those who did it? By what right do you condemn all of us on the basis of some who commit atrocity?" He turns to the intercom. "Take us to Telorbat. I need a planet with medical facilities."

"Our right comes from our nature. Our place in the Universal Song. The power that we alone possess." He bends over Ved's sleeping form, and I catch his arm. "What are you doing?"

"In dwelling on his tragedy, you obviously haven't noticed the most important thing about this child. The fact that he's alive."

"He lives—which is the core of his tragedy."

"You still don't get it. Look at him. *He hasn't caught the Death.*"

My Human body shivers. "After days . . . weeks . . . of exposure . . ."

Saburo nods. "He's immune. And if I can figure out why, we might have a chance to end the Death yet."

And if you do, Saburo . . . will the Hlutr permit it?

In confusion, I withdraw to Amny and the song of the Hlutr, while our ship races toward Telorbat.

I think too much like a Human; my sojourn with them has affected me. For Galactic Revolutions have I stood faithfully in my grove, while the patterns of stars and the very face of Amny changed around me, and I have sung the will of the Universal Song. I have earned the title of Elder and the name of Teacher. I have sung in the councils of the Hlutr, and have even advised the Eldest of all. Yet these Humans make of me but a newborn seeding, a foolish sapling facing his first Winter snows.

My brothers and sisters, tell me what I should do.

You sing, and I listen.

You will counsel me, you will give me reasons and opinions . . . but you will not decide for me. Some of you think the Humans should be saved, others believe they should perish—and still more of you think that we ought to ignore these children of Terra. Brethren, what am I to do?

Saburo, Ved and my operative arrive on Telorbat, and I am drawn to them once again.

It is the season of cold in the higher latitudes where the major Human city sits. You are there already, my fellows, rising snow-clad only a few kilometers from the city—for Ciudad Telorba rises like a vast pyramid from the midst of a great forest, and since Humans arrived on this world you have kept watch on them. I wonder, have you ever seen events like today's?

Saburo coughs, and even my operative is not spared the curse of the Death; my borrowed body is wracked with a choking fit, and when it is over I still find it hard to breathe. I begin to ease my awareness out of that fleshy prison, leaving the body to manage itself. I want nothing more than to return to Amny and be done with this sordid matter . . . yet I must see it through to a conclusion.

We are met by a robot on whose shoulders floats the image of a woman's head. She nods. "I am Gingiber Maur, undersecretary of state. We received your message, Doctor Saburo, and our foremost medical laboratory is yours. You will forgive me for not meeting you in person. . . ?" She seems a little embarrassed, yet Saburo pays her no mind.

"Yes, yes," he says, suppressing a cough. "Show me to the lab. I must examine the boy with proper instruments."

"We have few visitors from space," she tells us as we board an empty train and are whisked forth. "Have you come from afar?"

"From the Credixian Imperium, ultimately. Immediately, from a ship a few parsecs out from your sun."

She glances at Ved and my operative. "Tell me, you are escaping from the Death? This ship, was it infected?"

Ved quivers at this talk of the Death, and I broaden my awareness to sing him calm melodies of the Inner Voice. He is not yet sure who I am, but he responds to the song of the Hlutr.

Saburo nods, foaming with impatience. "We rescued the boy from a charnel ship—he was the only survivor. The sooner I get to your medical equipment, the sooner I'll be able to start figuring out why he lived."

"To be sure." The train slows, and the robot shows us through the door into a narrow corridor. As soon as we are through, the door slides shut. The robot stands before it, pointing toward the opposite end. "This way, if you please."

Saburo's eyes narrow. "This isn't a hospital. Where are we?"

The robot advances, and we have no choice but to fall back before it. Gingiber Maur's smile fades. "I am sorry, Doctor. Telorbat is under strict quarantine. We have no choice but to isolate those who have had contact with the Death." We are halfway down the corridor, now, and the far door begins to open. "As a medical man, I am sure you understand. You will be cared for; our prisons have a complete range of services."

"Prison?" Saburo echoed. Then the robot shoves us forward, and we tumble through the door.

Ved clings to my operative's hand, and I wrap an arm about him, all the while singing to quiet him. For we have surely walked into his worst nightmares.

A room the size of a spacecraft hangar is crowded with coughing, weeping Humans. Some are dead already, others are motionless upon mats and have only hours of life left. Some of the healthier ones are ministering to the others.

"Keep Ved back," Saburo tells me, and I am only too glad to comply. We stand in the middle of an open space, and I turn the boy's face to the wall while at the same time I hiss, "Saburo, what are we to do?"

"Don't worry. These people are paranoid, but they're stupid." He glances at an instrument clasped about his wrist. "My ship will be here in five minutes, and in another five we'll be blasted out of here."

"Unless they have ships to destroy yours."

"You won't find a working starship *on* this planet. Everyone who could leave, did. That's why the city's so empty. The ones who got left behind decided to set up this quarantine, but it won't help them." He bared his teeth in haughty animal aggression. "How's Ved?"

"Upset. We sing to calm him, and it seems to help."

"Good. Keep it up."

When Saburo's ship arrives, there is no doubt: a bright flash and a noise like thunder, then half a wall collapses in upon itself. Through smoke and dust, I see a moving wall of dark metal—the ship.

Saburo points and slaps my operative on the back. "Run!" he shouts.

By the time we reach the ship's hatch, twice seventy others have arrived as well. Some are too sick to move, yet they push themselves forward only to fall into the path of others. Their minds beat with terror and panic.

Saburo pushes through them roughly, then grabs Ved and my operative in firm hands and pulls us toward the ship as if through crashing surf. Human bodies press up against me, choking and vomiting, and I feel Ved's mind shake in counterpoint to his nervous body. The quiet melody of the Inner Voice pauses, then fragments as the boy's mental walls break and the full horror of his last few weeks comes smashing down on him.

He screams in an agony that paralyzes Hlutr on all nearby worlds. And I—who stand as close to that cry as I am to the soil of Amny—I stagger back, nearly driven from my perch in my Human operative's brain.

In that brain, in the confusion of the Inner Voice and Ved's pain, a miracle happens.

A personality submerged for a lifetime—the original identity of my operative—hears Ved's cry through the endless distance that she has driven between herself and reality. I feel her stir in that Human brain, and I am shocked to silence. Even the Hlutr could not reach her! Yet she comes forth, responding to a pain greater than her own.

Her name is Irisa, this Human whose body I have borrowed. She is almost as sensitive to the Inner Voice as is Ved, and she knows only that she must help him.

Limbs move of their own volition, and Irisa lifts Ved, hugs him to herself. The ship's solid wall parts, and she carries him across the threshold to safety, followed by Saburo. The hatch closes, and the ship lifts off, soaring high above city and forest.

Rejoice with me, brothers and sisters of Telorbat. Give me your Inner Voices in song: for Irisa was lost, and has come back. For Ved, whose cry brought even the Hlutr out of their age-old reveries, is delivered from his hell, Irisa, moved to mercy by his need, has saved him.

Riding high above that world, rooted unregarded in Irisa's brain, I sigh. When a poor creature such as this, so frightened of mere existence that she turns her back on it and chooses the cool depths of madness . . . when this poor beast can feel such mercy, dare a Teacher of the Hlutr feel less? These Humans are wild and terrible, yet there is within them a core of true beauty. An age ago as they count time, we Hlutr agreed to help them as we could, to find and develop that beauty. To guide them when they faltered on their road to truth. To aid the honest ones among them as they sought maturity. And now, as I watch the dawning of a consciousness even I had thought lost forever, I reaffirm that vow.

Behind me, I feel my own Elders, and *their*, perhaps up to Eldest herself, I feel them sway in agreement. *You have learned, Little One,* they seem to say.

Irisa knows what I require, and gladly she gives me the use of her body one last time. "Very well, Saburo," I say, "Bring Ved to me on Amny. We will find your cure to the Death. And the Hlutr shall administer it, though it cost the lives of many times twelve thousand of us."

Saburo nods, and the ship turns back toward home.

Ved and Irisa stand before me, in the peaceful night of Amny, and the gentle breeze brings me their alien scents. Saburo is weak, and must be carried on a litter; they settle him next to my trunk, where I can feel the fevered warmth of his body.

Help me, brothers and sisters. Sing with me, Elders. Time is short, and the problem very complex. You who know Humans, and you who are experts in animal biochemistry: sing with me.

The Hlutr sing in the Inner Voice, for now we are decided and there can be no hesitation. Those of us who study the problem, must live more quickly than is our wont—for the Death would require many seasons of Human study to yield its secrets. We Hlutr do not have their machines, their computers, their vast laboratories; we have far better, the massed minds of Hlutr themselves. This is our work, the work we are meant for, and as we unlock the mysteries of the Death, I feel the orange-red flush of deepest happiness creep over my body.

Now we live still faster, and seasons of time to us are but minutes to the watching Humans. The song builds upon itself, reaching toward a shattering crescendo— then there is the taste of victory, the rush of joy, and . . . silence.

I slow my rate of living, until once again I am in the time-frame of Humans. Exhilarated, I have complete control over my entire body; my answer comes in a song that fills the whole glade.

"Saburo, it is done. We can make a counter-virus for the Death. Hlutr will manufacture it, then spread it on all your twelve thousand worlds. In weeks, the Death will be over."

"Thank you, Teacher," he croaks, "W-when will you begin?"

Before I can even frame the question in the Inner Voice, my Elders answer it. *When you wish, Brother Hlutr.*

"We will commence the cure at once." On all those twelve thousand worlds, many times twelve thousand Hlutr stand ready to give their lives in the final detonation that will assure survival for Mankind. The night is alive with their song, a mixed song of triumph and a twinge of regret.

One of us must be first.

To the memory of the Traveler within me, I say, "Are you happy with me, little brother?"

"I am happy with you," he seems to say. "Come, Teacher . . . join me and be remembered forever."

"Stand back," I tell the waiting Humans. The dissolution is catastrophic, as it spreads Hlutr-substance on the winds and streams—but most of the force is directed upward. They need not withdraw too far. And I want Saburo near enough to catch full benefit of the cure.

Now I feel it build within me, as my Elders guide me in this final, most difficult task. The change comes like a building glow from the very center of my being, a welcome swell of warmth that lifts me toward the cool, eternal stars.

Hlutr have done their job well. The cure, I know, will work. There is a last surge in the song of Hlutr . . . my brothers and sisters, saluting me and this thing I do. Two faltering Human voices join this song; I look down and see Irisa and Ved standing hand-in-hand over Saburo. And ultimate peace rises from the soil to engulf me.

Content, I fly upward to meet the stars and at last to take my place in the Universal Song.

DAW

Don't Miss These Exciting DAW Anthologies